Celebrate the sunshine w...

Summer
Loving

Forget the stresses and strains of every day and
escape to a paradise with these sultry stories –
perfect for the summer time!

Every Woman's Fantasy
by Vicki Lewis Thompson

'...an outstanding read...funny
yet sizzling...'
—*Romantic Times*

The Future Widow's Club
by Rhonda Nelson

'Quirky, irreverent and laugh-out-
loud hilarious.'
—*New York Times* bestselling author
Vicki Lewis Thompson

Award-winning author **Vicki Lewis Thompson** hangs her hat in Arizona, where the sun's hot and the chili peppers are even hotter. Her more than fifty sizzling romances fit right into the landscape. With more than fifteen million books in print worldwide, Vicki's earned international recognition. She lives with her husband, to whom she's been married for an astonishing number of years, and a very spoiled tuxedo cat. Because desert living requires that she spend a great deal of time in the pool, she's waiting for someone to invent a waterproof laptop.

Rhonda Nelson can't remember when she hasn't had her nose buried in a book, and most likely, her husband can't, either. Though she took several creative writing courses in college, she never considered a career in writing until her mother pointed out—as mothers are everlastingly wont to do—that she should give it a try. Rhonda married her very own hero many moons ago, and she and her family make their home in a small town in northern Alabama. If you like a little giggle amid the sizzle, then her books are for you.

Summer Loving

Vicki Lewis Thompson
Rhonda Nelson

MILLS & BOON®

*MILLS & BOON and MILLS & BOON with the Rose Device
are registered trademarks of the publisher.*

*First published in Great Britain 2005
Harlequin Mills & Boon Limited,
Eton House, 18-24 Paradise Road, Richmond, Surrey, TW9 1SR*

SUMMER LOVING © Harlequin Enterprises II B.V., 2005

The publisher acknowledges the copyright holders of the
individual works as follows:

Every Woman's Fantasy © Vicki Lewis Thompson 2001
The Future Widow's Club © Rhonda Nelson 2005

ISBN 0 263 84539 7

049-0605

*Printed and bound in Spain
by Litografia Rosés S.A., Barcelona*

CONTENTS

Every Woman's Fantasy

by Vicki Lewis Thompson

PROLOGUE

"I CAN'T BELIEVE you did it again."

Mark O'Grady glanced across the table littered with peanut shells and a couple of half-empty beer bottles. His very pissed-off best man Sam Cavanaugh, who'd uttered those words of disgust, sat across from him, still dressed in his tux. So was Mark. Going back to his apartment to change had seemed too risky.

Fortunately he and Sam were the only ones of their crowd who patronized this little bar in downtown Houston. Their friends considered it too shabby, which was fine with Sam and Mark, who had designated it their special hidey-hole ever since they'd been old enough to drink legally. And Mark needed a place to hide…again.

He tried to come up with something to say to Sam, but he couldn't think of a damned thing. He was slime. Somebody should just shoot him.

"Ten minutes before the processional! Ten friggin' *minutes*. How could you *do* that?"

"It was her cell phone," Mark said.

"What do you mean, her *cell phone?* I fail to see how anything about a cell phone could cause you to back out of your wedding ten minutes before the ceremony. If Deborah hadn't smashed her wedding bouquet in your face, I would have done it for her!"

Mark gazed at his long-suffering friend. "You're right. It was horrible, and I should have figured it out sooner. We'd had some big arguments about how much she used that phone. She took it everywhere, and I mean *everywhere,* and it's not like the calls were critical or anything. Most of them sounded like a lot of gossip to me. But I kept thinking it was a small issue. I could deal."

"It *is* a small issue. The woman has friends. She likes to talk to them on the phone. If you love somebody, you put up with a few things that aren't perfect about them." Sam gave him another disgusted look before taking a swallow of his beer and setting it on the table with a clunk. "God knows you're a long way from being perfect."

"You've got that right." Mark turned his beer bottle around and around in his hands. "And I told myself all that. I thought I was fine with her cell phone habit. Then, remember how we were going up to the altar to take our places, and we passed by that room where Deb and her bridesmaids were waiting, and the door was open?"

"Yeah, I most certainly do. Because that's when you lost it and called the whole thing off."

"There she was, in her wedding dress, looking gorgeous, and she had that damned cell phone to her ear, jabbering away to somebody. I couldn't even imagine who she'd find to talk to! Every person she knew was sitting in the church!"

"That is kind of amazing, when you think about it," Sam conceded. "Maybe she was talking to somebody who was in the church, someone who also had their cell phone turned on."

"No doubt! And I don't want any part of that! I saw our whole married life dominated by that thing. The wedding night, the honeymoon, the delivery room when we had a kid, the family vacations, the visits to the folks. I mean, if she had to talk on the phone ten minutes before we were about to say our vows, then nothing was sacred."

Sam blew out a breath. "Okay, I can see your point. I wouldn't like that prospect myself, but I sure as hell wish you'd figured all this out sooner."

"So do I."

Leaning both arms on the table, Sam trained his no-nonsense look, the one he used to intimidate juries, on Mark. "In case you've lost count, this is the fifth time this has happened. None of your friends except yours truly will show up anymore. Even your mother refuses the invitations. Is it possible you don't want to get married?"

Mark had given that considerable thought himself. He'd been raised by a single mother who'd divorced his father when Mark was two. She'd never remarried, and when he was old enough to ask about that, she'd told him she found marriage too confining and time-consuming.

Because she was all he had, he'd tried to see things her way. But he couldn't help envying kids like Sam, who had a cozy family with two parents and a bunch of noisy siblings. Finally he'd decided he couldn't agree with his mother. Although the single life might suit her, he wanted to find a woman to share his life and be the mother of their kids.

He met Sam's gaze. "I do want to get married. It's divorce I want to avoid."

"At this rate you'll never have to worry about divorce, old buddy. Now if you'll excuse me, I'm going to the can. You can sort through your options while I'm gone."

Mark watched his friend leave. Sam appeared to be in no rush to get married, and yet the guy was extremely eligible. With his dark blond mustache and lean good looks, he was often mistaken for Alan Jackson. Plus he was a successful lawyer and drove a beautifully restored red '57 Chevy that always drew attention. Yet he'd only been engaged once, and that hadn't lasted more than two months before they'd both decided they weren't right for each other.

Obviously Sam wasn't desperate to create a family for himself because he'd had that growing up. Mark had hungered for that kind of stability ever since he could remember. But he wasn't any closer to getting it than he had been seven years ago, when he'd proposed to Hannah, his first fiancée. Something had to change, but he didn't know what.

The waitress came by and he ordered another round. Then he called her back. "Add a shooter to the beer," he said. "No, wait. *Five* shooters." It seemed like a fitting number.

The waitress blinked. "Five? All at once?"

"Yep." Mark held up his hand, fingers spread. "And you might as well bring five for my buddy, too." When the waitress continued to stare at him, he added, "We'll both be taking cabs home, so don't worry."

With a nod, the waitress left.

Mark decided if he couldn't figure out how to fix his sorry situation, he might as well get drunk with Sam. He could bail his Lexus out of the parking garage in the morning.

An extra few hours of parking expense was nothing compared to the bills he had run up with these five canceled weddings. In each case, he'd let his fiancées keep the rings and even go on the honeymoon if they could find somebody else to go along. Three had taken that option, and two had said they'd rather rot in hell. Deb had been one of those.

On top of that, Mark had covered the cost of the reception and other incidentals. He hadn't wanted his fiancées or their families to suffer financially, considering they'd be suffering emotionally. If he hadn't brokered his talent for playing the stock market into a lucrative career, he'd really be in the poorhouse. As it was, the weddings had eaten up any financial gains he'd made.

With that depressing thought, he started on the shooters the waitress had brought.

Sam took quite a while returning, and when he finally did, he eyed the shot glasses lined up on the table. "I take it the number is significant?"

Mark had already polished off three of his. "You betcha. Pull up a seat and get started. You're behind. What took you so long?"

"The waitress stopped me to ask if we were in here for the same reason as the last couple of times. I had to offer her ten bucks to keep her from coming over here and pouring a pitcher of beer on your head."

"Thanks." The shooters were starting to kick in, slowly taking the tension out of his body. Ah, this was much better.

Sam sat down and threw a magazine on the table.

"I found some interesting reading material in the john," he said. "I think this might be the answer."

Mark tossed down the fourth shooter and picked up the magazine. *"Texas Men?"* He leafed through the ads for eligible bachelors, then glanced over at Sam and grinned. He was getting *very* relaxed, relaxed enough to find Sam's gesture hilarious. "Sorry to dis'ppoint you, but I'm stickin' with girls."

"You are so dense. No wonder you're such a mess. I'm suggesting we put *you* in that magazine."

"Why?" Mark was beginning to feel really goofy. "So I can rack up more broken engagements? Get in the *Guinness Book of World Records?*"

"No, the exact opposite. I'm trying to prevent another broken engagement. Here's what we'll—"

"Hey. I'll be a monk. Should've thought of that before. Where's the nearest monastery? I'll turn myself in." He picked up the last shooter. "Come on, Sammeeee. Get blitzed with me."

"Shut up and listen. I've thought about this, and the reason you get engaged to the wrong women is that they're beautiful, and so naturally you have sex with them."

"Nat-u-ral-ly." Mark spoke carefully so he wouldn't slur. "Sex's good."

"Except underneath that swinging bachelor exterior of yours, you have old-fashioned ideas. You think because you had sex, you should get married."

"True-de-doo-doo. And I'm grateful." He smiled at Sam. "Sooo grateful. Women are wunnerful, Sam. They smell so good, and they feel terrific, and...I love 'em, Sam. I want to marry one of them. I really, really do."

"You are stewed to the gills, aren't you?"

"Yep."

"Maybe that's just as well. You're more likely to agree to my plan if you're pickled. Here it is—we put an ad for you in this magazine, and then we sort through the prospects and find somebody perfectly suited to you. After that you write letters for a long time. A very, very long time. And during that correspondence, you find out if they're addicted to cell phones, or hate camping, or any of the other stupid reasons you've backed out."

"Not shtupid."

"Okay, they're not stupid. But with this woman, you're getting that all settled way in advance. Every possible glitch that would be a sticking point will be discussed, and analyzed, and dissected, *ad nauseum.*"

Mark frowned. "Don't like writin' letters."

"I don't care. I don't frigging care!" Sam jabbed a finger at him. "This is tough-love time. You are going to write those letters, and you'll get to know this person before you meet her, before you even *think* of going to bed with her. Because I know you, and once you do the nasty, you'll propose. Do you understand what I'm saying?"

"Yeah." Mark nodded slowly, so the room wouldn't start spinning. "I'm gonna have a pen pal." He paused to think. "And I'm not gettin' any for a long, lo-o-o-ng time."

CHAPTER ONE

Six months later

"ASHLEY, I'M SCARED." Charlie McPherson watched her older sister close out the cash register for the day. Ashley had worked her butt off in retail for five years and now owned Glam Girl, home to some of Austin's trendiest fashions.

Ashley glanced up. "About what?"

"Mark wants to meet me." Charlie wasn't into fashion, which was why she desperately needed advice and moral support from her big sis.

"Hey, you'll be fine." Ashley smiled. "Perfectly fine. He's a lucky guy."

"You're my sister. You're supposed to say that."

Ashley gazed at her. "I don't blame you for being nervous," she said gently. "Let me finish up here and we'll go get a couple of big old margaritas and talk about it."

"That would be good." Margaritas would definitely help give her the courage to explain her problem.

If she looked more like Ashley, she might not be so scared. Her sister could just as well be modeling fashions as selling them. Charlie envied three things about Ashley. She was nearly five-eight, which allowed her to wear every outfit in the store without hemming it. Secondly, her rich brown hair was wavy, not curly like Charlie's, so she could wear it long. Last of all, their parents had given Ashley a terrific name which required no fiddling to make it sound right.

Charlie had to hem up almost everything she bought, and if she didn't keep her blond hair short, she looked like Medusa. As for her name, she was still ticked off at her folks for saddling her with Charlene. Nobody these days was named Charlene.

She'd shortened it to Charlie, which sounded more twenty-first century and suited her outdoor lifestyle, but it wasn't half as distinctive as Ashley. Of course, Charlie had to admit she didn't *look* like an Ashley. Ashley belonged to someone elegant, like her sister. Nobody had ever accused Charlie of being elegant. Cute, bouncy, full of energy, yes. Never elegant. Making Charlie elegant would take a miracle.

Twenty minutes later, as Charlie sat across from Ashley at their favorite Tex-Mex restaurant, she was hoping her big sister would help her pull off that miracle.

"Here's to a great first date with Mark

O'Grady." Ashley lifted her frosty glass and touched it to Charlie's.

"Amen." Charlie took a sip of her drink and set it on the square cocktail napkin. Then she looked over at her sister. "The thing is, when Mark suggested we write to each other for several weeks so we could really learn about each other before we met, I got this idea."

Ashley put down her drink, too. "Which was?"

"I decided to change my image."

She had Ashley's total concentration now. "To what?" she asked carefully.

"Well, you know how most guys treat me like the girl next door. They see me as wholesome, low-maintenance, stuff like that."

"Charlie, that's because you are those things. They're all pluses, in my book."

"Whatever. The point is that in my whole life, I have never made a guy drool."

"Oh." Ashley gazed at her and the wheels were obviously going around. "So what kind of image does Mark have of you?"

"I didn't lie or anything," Charlie said quickly. "I mean, he knows I work for an outdoor adventure company, and he's seen my picture so he knows what I look like. But I made him think that underneath that girl-next-door persona I'm also this…well, this really hot babe. I, um, wrote some pretty racy stuff, things I probably would never have the nerve to say in person."

Ashley looked taken aback, but gradually her green eyes warmed. "Ah, I get it. You're afraid that when you two meet, he'll expect to jump into bed right away, and you're not ready for that."

"But I am ready for that."

Ashley blinked. "You are? Oh, Charlie, I don't think that's a very good idea. You need to—"

"I need to experience unbridled passion for once in my life! With every other guy I've dated, there's no mystery, no tension, no *lust*. But now I have that. We've had three months of postal foreplay. We are *so* loaded with tension. I just don't want to mess up and diffuse it."

Ashley stared at her. Then she took a quick drink of her margarita and cleared her throat. "Okay, let me get my bearings here. I can understand wanting to make a guy lust after you. But I can't go along with the hopping-into-bed part. I realize you've exchanged a lot of letters with Mark, but that's not the same as face-to-face contact. You need to give it more time before you get into a physical—"

Charlie let out a gusty sigh. "You sound so 'older sister.' Haven't you ever gone to bed with a guy on the first date?"

Ashley blushed. "We're not talking about me."

"What? We should live by different rules?"

Her sister looked disconcerted. "Well, I—"

"Exactly. We shouldn't. Now I'm not saying I *will* go to bed with him right away, but I might, if I don't mess it up and come on like a camp counselor on the first date. I want you to help me look like a sex goddess."

Ashley's eyes widened. "If Mom and Dad could hear this conversation, they'd have a hissy-fit. I'm supposed to look out for you, not help you get into trouble."

"Oh, so that's it. Look, when I moved to Austin I was twenty-two. Maybe I needed some looking after. But hel-*lo,* I'm five years older now! I'm even older than you were when I got here. And, damn it, I want to feel sexy and glamorous for once in my life. Will you help me or not?"

Ashley studied her for a long moment. "I don't know. This feels sort of weird. Do you have any idea where he'll take you on this first date?"

"Not yet."

"Well, once you know that, I'll…I'll at least help you find something great to wear."

"Great as in nice, or great as in hot?"

"Oh, God." Ashley looked at her and shook her head. "Unbridled lust? Are you sure that's what you want?"

"Yep."

Ashley rolled her eyes. "Mom and Dad would have a cow."

"CHARLIE'S PERFECT. My dream girl. My soul mate. My happily-ever-after." Mark brushed peanut shells from the table and wiped away a ring of moisture left by his empty beer bottle before laying a dog-eared picture on the table in front of Sam. "Look at that face and tell me she's not perfect."

"I've seen her face. In case you've forgotten, I'm the one who picked her out of the stack and told you she had promise."

"And you were right!"

"It remains to be seen whether I was right," Sam said. "All the information isn't in yet."

"Most of it. And her letters are so…friendly. I think she looks exactly the way her letters sound, don't you?"

Sam picked up the picture and studied it. Then he handed it back to Mark. "Okay, so she's a good prospect on paper, but with your record, I don't think you should rush into—"

"Sam, I'm ready to meet her. I'm *so* ready to meet her." He tucked Charlie's picture in his shirt pocket, right next to his heart.

Sam gave him the evil eye. "You said that with a little too much relish, good buddy. Just exactly what do you mean by *meet?*"

Mark threw up both hands. "I mean just meet! Like drive to Austin for the weekend, and—"

"Slow down, lover-boy! Are we talking an overnight here?"

"Well, yeah. If I take her out for a nice dinner somewhere, with wine, and candlelight, and…and stuff, then I don't want to drive all the way back to Houston that same night."

Sam leaned forward. "Dinner's fine, candlelight and wine is terrific. But it's the *and stuff* part that's got me worried. I'm coming with you."

"No way! Nobody's chaperoned my dates since I was fourteen, and I'm not about to reactivate the custom now."

Sam gazed at him for a long time, as if he was turning something over in his mind. Finally he settled back against the worn cushion of the booth with a sigh. "I hate to do this, because you're like a brother to me and I've tried to stick by you through everything, but here's the way it has to be. If you mosey on up to Austin and everything goes the way it always does with you, and you come back engaged after one romp in the sack, you'll have to find yourself another best man this time."

A cold chill washed over Mark. He'd known Sam all his life, and when he set his jaw like that, he was deadly serious. Apparently he'd had enough. To be honest, Mark couldn't blame him.

"I ran into Deborah at the grocery store last night," Sam said casually. "You know, it's a wonder she didn't sue you for breach of promise."

"You're right. She had grounds." He glanced nervously at Sam. "Is she still upset?" He was hoping that six months had soothed her feelings.

"I would say she's still upset. She asked if you'd contracted any deadly diseases yet. I think she's sticking pins in a voodoo doll or something."

"So she's not over it."

"Doesn't look like it." Sam signaled to the waitress and glanced at Mark. "Want another beer?"

"I think I'm gonna need one if we're discussing Deb." He waited until Sam had put in their order for two more long-necks. "So what else did she say about me?"

"Oh, the usual. That you're a pimple on the backside of humanity, a virus on the Internet of life. That kind of thing. From the look in her eyes, she was thinking even worse insults than that, but I think she held back because she knows I'm your best friend and we were in a public place."

"I really was hoping she'd be over it by now." He was a rat, no doubt about it. Whenever he thought of how he'd left her high and dry, he used similar expressions to describe himself.

"Well, she's not over it, but she's trying to be. In fact, she's linked up with your four other victims."

"I wish you wouldn't use that word."

"I didn't. She did. She said they've formed a support group. Either they'll help each other to heal or they'll figure out a really hideous form of revenge, whichever comes first."

Mark gazed at Sam uneasily. "A support group? You mean with meetings and everything?"

"Why not? There's five of them, so that makes a group."

"I don't know what to think about this." Mark grabbed the bottle the waitress had just set in front of him and took a generous swig. "I mean, that's kind of scary, Sam. Five women plotting against me."

"You should be scared. Scared straight. They've even given themselves a name."

Mark gazed across the table at his buddy. "Do I want to know what it is?"

"Probably not. But I'm going to tell you anyway. They call their group DOA."

Mark choked on his beer. *"Dead On Arrival?"* He coughed and sputtered as he tried to assimilate the information. "Good God, Sam, what are they planning?"

"They just have a sick sense of humor. The letters actually stand for Damn O'Grady's Ass."

"Oh." Mark was relieved, but not a lot.

"I wouldn't ignore the implication of those three letters if I were you. I'm sure they didn't choose them at random. I think Deborah mentioned something about having T-shirts printed up." Sam took a long swallow of his beer.

Mark followed suit. This subject was giving him the willies. He'd felt like a heel each time he'd called off an impending wedding, and he'd certainly wanted his prospective brides to seek comfort in whatever way they could. But he'd never imagined that they'd band together against him.

"I don't think you can afford to screw up again, buddy," Sam said. "It wouldn't be good for your health."

"Well, I'm not going to screw up. Your idea about using *Texas Men* to find a woman who's really suited to me, and me to her, was a damned good one. Charlie and I have been writing back and forth for—what, three months now?"

"About that."

Mark patted his shirt pocket. "I know her better than I ever knew any of the others—until it was too late, that is. I know she's a morning person like me, but she needs her coffee. She's not anal but she likes to keep her place picked up. She loved *Survivor*, hated *Big Brother*. Even her job is perfect for me— an outdoor adventure guide."

"That is one of her good points, I agree. I've said that from the beginning. You kept dating these financial types you met at the office."

"Right. I wasn't working a big enough area. The

magazine changed that, and now I have Charlie, who's the exact right mix, sensible on the outside, but black lace and naughty thoughts underneath."

"Hold it. How do you know about the black lace and naughty thoughts?"

Mark had a feeling he'd just revealed too much. In the past few weeks, the correspondence had heated up considerably. "Just a guess. Come to think of it, I probably read too much into her comments."

"Like hell. Come on, Mark. What did she say?"

Time to backpedal, and fast. "Not much, really. I think she's shy, actually. Probably would be slow to warm up." He didn't think that for a minute. From the tone of her most recent letters, she had an instant on switch. He could hardly wait to trip it.

"Uh-huh." Sam's expression was grim. "I get the picture. No wonder you're so ready to meet her. Mr. Happy wants to meet her, too. That's your other problem. You're a washout at celibacy."

He was, but he didn't want to admit that he'd been dreaming about making love to Charlie McPherson for weeks. That would only confirm Sam's opinion that he couldn't go to Austin alone. "This isn't only about sex. We like the same things. Not a single one of my fiancées wanted to go camping with me. Charlie would love to go camping." And he could hardly wait to get her alone in a cozy tent.

"What's this about camping? I thought you were going to ask her to dinner first."

"Well, dinner, or…I don't know. Camping would be nice."

"It would be a disaster! I know you, and you would not stay in your own little pup tent. No. Camping is out. O-U-T, out." Sam took a quick drink of his beer and glared at him.

Mark shrugged. "It was just an idea."

"A bad idea. Some guys can handle getting physical early in the relationship without losing their perspective on the situation. Take me, for instance. I've *never* proposed to a woman after making love to her the first time. With you, it's like an orgasm kills off half your brain cells. One night of nooky and you're headed for the altar. It's the damnedest thing I've ever seen."

"I admit I've made that mistake a few times."

"No kidding."

Mark sighed. "I've always moved too quick on this proposing business. I can see that now."

"Good. Glad to hear it. Then you'll let me go with you to Austin and make sure you don't screw this one up."

The very thought of dragging Sam along made Mark cringe. "Now, Sam, how's that gonna look? No telling what she'll think if I have to bring my best friend along when I go to meet her for the first time.

She'll think I don't trust my own judgment, or I'm lacking in confidence. It's the wrong way to start out."

Sam shrugged. "Then do it your way. I'm sure Jack will agree to be your best man. Maybe I'll tell him to bite the bullet and buy a tux. I'd be money ahead if I'd done that instead of renting one each time. And he can forget about writing a wedding toast. Talk about a waste. On the other hand, he should remember to bring a big box of tissues to the ceremony. No, make that two big boxes. One wasn't enough for this last disaster, by the time I'd passed them out to Deborah, her four bridesmaids, her mother, her—"

"Okay, okay! So you're going with me to-Austin." But how he'd manage to make a good impression on Charlie under such circumstances was beyond him. It would be a damned awkward visit.

Perhaps he could come up with a good cover story…

Sam smiled. "That's more like it. You know, I could go for a hamburger. Want a hamburger?"

"Sure, why not?"

"I'll go find our waitress."

"Okay." While he was gone Mark started brainstorming. He'd pulled a few excellent stunts in his college days. Like the time he and Sam had both wanted to date the same girl their senior year. Mark had gone in drag to the cafeteria and confided in this girl that Mark O'Grady had spent two years in China learning lovemaking secrets from the geishas. Sam never had a chance after that.

Hey, wait a minute. What if Sam needed a blind date when he went down to Austin? What if he was afraid to ask anybody out, because…because the woman he'd been dating had turned out to be a man. Perfect. So then Mark could ask Charlie to come up with a date for Sam, to get him back on track. While Sam was kept busy with her, Mark could get busy with Charlie. Brilliant.

Sam returned and slid into the booth. "I'm glad you came to your senses about taking me along to Austin."

Mark smiled, feeling much better about the situation now. "I can't have a wedding without you being my best man." That was certainly true. If Sam wasn't standing up at the altar with him, it wouldn't seem like he was really getting married. Of course, he never really *had* gotten married. But this time would be different. He could feel it.

"You sure look perky all of a sudden," Sam said.

"Why wouldn't I? I'm going to meet the woman of my dreams."

Gazing at him over the top of his beer bottle, Sam cleared his throat. "Mark, old buddy, one of your more endearing traits is your eternal optimism. But I want you to entertain the possibility that Charlie is not the one."

"But she is."

"I hope so, but the truth is we might have to put another ad in *Texas Men* and troll for more prospects. Because I'm not—I repeat, *not*—going through this again until I'm convinced that you won't back out at the last minute."

"I'm telling you, I won't back out. Charlie's the real deal."

"That remains to be seen. Go ahead and set up the weekend, but remember that there will be no getting horizontal with your darling Charlie if I have anything to say about it. You need to get to know her really well before that happens."

"But I do know her!"

"Only what she tells you in the letters, pal." Sam sipped his beer. "Only what she tells you in the letters."

CHAPTER TWO

A WEEK LATER, Charlie tried not to hyperventilate as she stood in front of the three-way mirror in Ashley's shop. The plunging neckline of the red dress nearly reached her belly button. If she had the nerve to buy this dress, it would go perfectly with some red high-heeled sandals she'd seen in a store window down the street.

She'd never owned anything like this dress in her life, but it fit the image she was trying to project for Saturday night's date with Mark. The longer she wore the dress, the more she believed in her seductive powers.

"Way too daring," Ashley said.

"No, I think this might be the one." Charlie turned this way and that to see if she looked sufficiently sexy. "But I wish it had a slit up the side."

"It used to." Ashley pulled a blue dress off the rack. "When I saw you eyeing that one the other day, I stitched it up. There's such a thing as over-exposed. Even so, that dress is cut way lower than I thought. Try this one instead." She held out the blue dress.

Charlie glanced at it. "Nope. It has sleeves."

"Try it." Ashley shoved the dress closer. "It matches your eyes."

"Who cares? All my life I've been wearing blue because it matches my eyes. And you know what that dress is? *Boring.* I will never get Mark to drool if I wear that. I'll look like Alice in Wonderland. I might as well tie a blue bow in my hair."

"You wear that red number and he'll drool, all right. I'm worried about what will happen after the drooling part."

Charlie turned to face her sister. "Okay, let's get to the bottom of this. Why are you so paranoid about the possibility that Mark and I will have sex on the first date?"

Ashley avoided her gaze and hung the blue dress on the circular rack. "Because I'm your older sister, and older sisters are supposed to keep their little sisters away from the Big Bad Wolf. At least on the first date."

"That's weak and you know it. What's the deal here?"

Ashley rummaged through the rack some more, but finally she turned, her cheeks rosy. "Remember Jason Danville?"

Charlie searched her memory. "Was he the guy who drove the Jaguar?"

Ashley nodded. "When he asked me out, I was the

envy of every girl in my sorority. He was older, sophisticated, rich."

"And you went to bed with him on the first date," Charlie guessed.

"On the first and only date." She sighed. "It was so humiliating that I never told anybody. Of course *he* probably told the world. It was so classic. We drank martinis and he convinced me that I was the girl he'd been waiting for all his life. Of course afterward he laughed and called me naive for believing that old line."

"Oh, Ashley." Charlie walked over and gave her sister a hug. "But Mark's not like that," she said. "He would never—"

"Maybe not." Ashley held her by the shoulders. "But don't forget I was there when Kevin Jasper turned you down for the Sadie Hawkins dance back in high school. The way you talk about Mark reminds me of the way you used to talk about Kevin. Come to think of it, you haven't been this excited about a guy since Kevin."

Charlie had to admit that was true. Maybe she hadn't liked being treated like a buddy by the men she'd gone out with, but she hadn't cared enough to try and change the dynamics, either.

"I know you, Charlie," Ashley said. "When your dreams are smashed, you don't recover so well. If Mark turned out to be a rat like Jason, I'd never forgive myself if I let you get hurt."

Charlie appreciated her sister's concern, but she knew it wasn't needed in this instance. Mark wasn't going to hurt her. Still, she wasn't above using an opening when it presented itself. "Okay, then like I asked you before, come with me Saturday night. You'll be able to make a judgment about Mark, help protect me and meet a new guy, all at the same time."

Ashley smiled. "You can stop pushing for the double date. You don't need protection if you drive yourself to the restaurant and drive yourself home, like we talked about, and don't take any side trips in between."

"Maybe he'll slip something in my drink."

"You don't believe that any more than I do. He's a stockbroker at the firm he claimed to be associated with—his letters of reference checked out. He won't do anything weird. But that red dress sends a definite signal, and we don't really know what this guy's agenda is. This three months of letter writing could be a technique to get you in bed."

If Ashley wanted to believe that, Charlie didn't care. It suited her purposes. "And you can keep me from getting carried away by the moment."

Ashley groaned. "Come on, Charlie. Wear a different dress and we don't have to worry. Sure, I feel sorry for this Sam person, but I don't think it's my job to toddle along on your date with you and try to rehabilitate Mark's friend."

"But, Ashley, can you imagine how traumatized he must be? Here he thought he was going out with a perfectly nice woman, and she turned out to be a man."

"I grant you that it might be difficult getting back into dating after something like that, but I—"

"And he didn't discover it until he started making love to her—I mean, *him*," Charlie said. "What a shock! And now the poor guy won't so much as go to dinner with a woman, let alone get sexually involved with someone. Doesn't that pull at your heartstrings?"

Ashley turned back to the rack and began sorting through it. "Well, sure. But he probably needs counseling, not a date with me."

"Mark said he won't go to counseling, but he said if I could just find Sam a nice girl so that we could have a double date, then maybe he will start to trust again. You're the perfect person to go with us Saturday night. Sherry and Dawn are both involved with someone, and I think Ellie's too aggressive for something this delicate. Besides, I want you to go. I'd like you to meet Mark."

"And I will." Ashley paused to look at a black dress, then rejected it and kept scooting dresses around the circular chrome bar. "But this double-date thing seems so contrived."

"Maybe, but Mark says it's the only thing he can figure out. I think it's sweet that he cares so much for his friend, don't you?"

"I suppose. Here, how about this one?" She took a white dress off the rack and held it up.

"*White?* You want him to think I'm virginal?"

"White can be very effective on blondes. I wish I could wear it."

Charlie rolled her eyes. "I don't even want to hear about it, Miss Everybody-Thinks-I'm-a-Model. Every single outfit in this store looks good on you. So white isn't your best color. Big deal. You'd still look glamorous, even in unflattering white. As for me, this red dress is the first thing I've ever tried on that didn't make me look cute. I'm tired of guys wanting to pat me on the head."

"So you're an ingenue type. There's nothing wrong with that."

"But I want them to pat me somewhere else for a change!"

"You can think about that on your second date." Ashley returned the white dress to the rack and found a pink one. "In the meantime, this will—"

"Ick! *Pink.* Barf-o-rama. Pink is exactly what I'm trying to get away from. Just once in my life, I want to knock a guy for a loop the first time he sees me. I don't want him to think, *Hey, I'll bet she plays a good game of tennis.* I want him to go, *Hey, I want a little one-on-one with that hot babe.*"

Ashley folded the pink dress over her arm and gazed at Charlie. "Then that's the dress."

"I thought so."

"But as your big sister, I can't in good conscience let you go to a restaurant alone to meet some guy you've only written letters to. If something awful happened I'd feel responsible because I was the one who dolled you up like that."

"So you'll go along and be Sam's date?"

"I will, but I'm only going to keep an eye on you in that dress. If my being there tricks Sam into finally having a 'date,' then I suppose I can live with that. Just so you and Mark don't expect this foursome to be a regular thing."

"Oh, Ashley, you're terrific! I knew I could count on you." Charlie threw both arms around her sister in an enthusiastic hug.

"I'm a sucker, that's what." Ashley's resigned expression changed to a frown as she stepped back and looked at Charlie. "Rule Number One. No hugging in that dress."

"Why not?"

"Take a look."

Charlie glanced down, and sure enough, one of her breasts had nearly sprung free of the plunging neckline. She grinned as she glanced at Ashley. "This is *such* a sexy dress."

Ashley gave her a stern look. "See that you keep it on."

AS MARK HANDED HIS CAR KEYS to the valet at the restaurant Saturday night, he was still trying to figure out how to tell Sam that Charlie's sister, Ashley, would be coming as Sam's date. He didn't think it was necessary to go into the transvestite story he'd cooked up, first of all because Sam might fail to see the humor in it, and secondly because he couldn't imagine either Charlie or Ashley would bring up the subject. They'd just be extra nice to Sam, which wouldn't hurt a thing.

He didn't like telling untrue stories about Sam, but this meeting with Charlie was so important. If she started thinking he needed a handler to keep him on a tight leash, as if he were some sort of lust-crazed maniac, that could give a bad impression. Likewise, he'd need to think of something to tell Sam that would explain why Charlie's sister was coming to dinner with them.

They'd left Houston in plenty of time to check into a hotel not far from the restaurant and then made it to the restaurant several minutes early. He'd clue Sam in before the women showed up. He just needed to figure out what to say. A beer would help both of them, but that wouldn't look so good, to be starting on the drinks before the women even arrived.

"Seems like a nice place," Sam commented as they walked toward a carpeted entryway covered with a green canopy. Flowers spilled out of stone planters and classical-looking nude statues stood sentry on either side of the glass doors. "But trust you to find the restaurant with naked women standing outside it."

"I had no idea," Mark said.

"Right."

"No, really. I got a recommendation from somebody at work." Mark thanked the doorman as they walked into the restaurant.

"In any case, Italian's usually a safe choice for a first date," Sam said. "Most people can find something to eat, even if they're picky."

"Charlie's not picky," Mark headed for the tuxedo-clad maître d'. "But I wanted something romantic. They're supposed to have a couple of strolling violinists and a flower girl who hands out long-stemmed roses to the women."

"That's a nice touch." Sam brushed a piece of lint from the lapel of his sport coat. "But I should warn you that just because a woman says she's not picky doesn't mean she's not. I've heard that line a million times, and then you take them out for sushi and they refuse to eat it."

"Well, when Charlie says she's not picky, I believe her." Mark glanced through the arched doorway into the dining room and was satisfied with what he saw. High, narrow windows looked out on a garden setting with twinkling white lights strung on the greenery. Inside, candles flickered on linen-draped tables and the chairs were upholstered in a soft green material that looked like velvet.

"And you told her I was coming, right?" Sam asked.

"Sure did." Mark listened for the violinists and, sure enough, he could hear them, but they were very soft. Good. Soft was better.

"Did you tell her why I was coming?"

Mark paused just short of the maître d's station. Time for his fast shuffle routine. "What do you mean?"

"I'm assuming that in all this letter writing you two have been doing, that you've mentioned your little problem with the five previous engagements."

"We haven't gotten into that, specifically, but—"

"You haven't?" Sam's jaw dropped. "Why wouldn't you? Any woman who gets involved with you should know about that small matter, don't you think?"

Mark glanced around nervously. "Keep your voice down, okay? Let's just get seated, and then we'll talk about it."

"Oh, we'll talk about it, all right. I have plenty to say on the subject."

Moments later they were ushered to a table for four in a secluded corner of the room.

Mark chose a chair facing the doorway so he'd know the minute Charlie arrived. "I think you should sit across from me."

"I don't. I think I should sit next to you so I can give you a swift kick under the table whenever necessary." He started to take the chair on Mark's right.

Mark grabbed his arm. "No, you need to sit across from me. Charlie's bringing her sister."

Sam looked at him in astonishment. "She's doing *what?*"

"Bringing her sister. The poor woman. She has this terrible problem. Whenever she's attracted to a guy, she breaks out in a rash. But she seems to be getting better, and Charlie thought it was time to test her recovery. She thought it would be better if Ashley, that's her name, started with a blind date."

Sam's jaw tensed, but he moved to the seat opposite Mark. "I'm not here to be Charlie's sister's blind date."

"I realize that, but when Charlie heard you were coming, she naturally thought about Ashley and her problem."

Sam pulled his chair in and leaned his elbows on the table. "Okay, let's get back to the original question. If Charlie doesn't know I'm here to ride herd on you, why does she think I'm coming?"

Mark shrugged. "As a friend, to meet the woman I've been raving about."

"Hmm." Sam smoothed his mustache. He didn't look particularly convinced. "There's something fishy about all of this, O'Grady. And you can be sure I'll find out what it is eventually."

Mark knew he wouldn't be able to fool Sam for long, but he only needed to have his cooperation for the next few hours. "All right, maybe I thought it would be kind of cool if you and Charlie's sister hit it off. One big happy family, right?"

Sam continued to look skeptical. "But according to you, if Ashley and I hit it off, then she'll break out in a rash."

"Maybe not. Maybe the hypnosis sessions are working. But don't bring up the subject, okay? She's very sensitive about it."

"Hmm," Sam said again, his gaze speculative.

"What?"

"I'm thinking about some of the stunts you pulled in college. This dinner setup has the same feel to it. And I—" He paused as a waiter arrived to fill their water goblets. "And I still want to know why you haven't told Charlie about all your prior engagements," he said after the waiter left.

"I'll tell her. I promise I'll tell her soon." Mark kept glancing toward the door. Charlie had mentioned she'd be wearing red, and that the dress was cut low in the front, just for him. He loved knowing that. "I wanted to get this first meeting out of the way, so that she'd understand how sincere I am. If she found out about my five engagements before meeting me, it might color everything."

"It damn well should color everything. Then she'd

know to take things slow and not go jumping into bed with you. You can't handle it."

"But, Sam, we've been taking it slow. We've been writing letters for three months. That's why this was such a great idea, the magazine thing and then the long correspondence. Now we know each other well enough to take our relationship to the next level."

Sam scowled across the table at him. "You're not changing levels on my watch. This will be a zipless weekend, buddy."

Mark sighed.

"It's for your own good. And hers."

"You're right. I know you're right." No matter how confident he felt this time, his record in such matters was lousy. And he didn't want to hurt Charlie. She already meant so much to him. Of course, if she meant so much to him, then there was no way he'd hurt her, because he'd go through with the ceremony.

"Come on, pal. What's one night compared to a whole lifetime?"

"Good point. Okay, I will not make love to Charlie this weekend. Maybe just a kiss or two. That wouldn't cause a problem. Just—" His breath caught. *There she was.* Oh, damn, she was gorgeous. And so hot. The red dress hugged her curves and swooped down in front to show off the sweetest cleavage he'd ever been privileged to ogle. Damn. He couldn't imagine how he'd keep his hands to himself, his zipper zipped. But he had to. He would. He *would*.

Their waiter was ready to escort her and a stunning brunette to the table, but Charlie spoke to him and the waiter paused.

Smart girl, Mark thought. She wanted to check out her date before the maître d' brought her over. If Mark turned out to be the Hunchback of Notre Dame or The Wolfman, then she could still leave. His Charlie was no dummy.

He stood and started toward her.

She scanned the room and when her gaze settled on him, her smile nearly caused his heart to stop beating. Adrenaline made him shaky as he approached. Seeing her picture hadn't prepared him for her megawatt smile or eyes that sparkled like the waters of the Gulf on a sunny day.

He glanced quickly at the waiter. "I'll escort them over," he said.

"As you wish, sir." The waiter nodded and walked away.

Mark's gaze settled on Charlie again and he couldn't stop grinning. Even her ears were sexy. Before Charlie, he hadn't been a fan of short hair, but with ears that cute, he could see the advantage. He wanted to nibble each diamond-studded lobe while he whispered sweet nothings to his Charlie.

"Hello, Mark." Her voice trembled just enough to tell him how excited she was.

"Hello, Charlie." He wasn't sure what to do next. He wanted to bury his fingers in her blond, wavy hair, tilt her head back and kiss that plump mouth covered in tomato-red lipstick to match her dress. But that probably wasn't a good idea right here in the middle of the restaurant. Besides, if a kiss or two was all he was allowed tonight, he needed to pace himself. "You're…beautiful," he said. "So beautiful."

"Thank you." Her cheeks grew pink. "You're quite the treat, yourself." Then she extended her hand. "Nice to meet you at last, Mark."

He took her warm, soft hand in both of his and held it as if he'd never let go. She was unbelievable. And that dress… His mouth grew moist and his groin tightened. "I'm sorry we waited three months," he said.

"We were trying to be sensible, I guess."

"That was stupid."

"Maybe." She gazed into his eyes for a moment longer before slowly easing her hand from his and shifting her attention to the brunette standing next to her. "Mark, I'd like you to meet my sister, Ashley McPherson."

He'd been so absorbed in Charlie that he'd practically forgotten about Ashley. Now that he took a good look at Charlie's sister, he wanted to laugh with pleasure. Sam was going to thank him for this day.

Ashley was tall, at least five-eight, but Sam was six-two, so no problem there. Her hair reminded him of a Cherry Coke—rich brown with red highlights—and she had green eyes. Green eyes were a particular weakness of Sam's. He wasn't averse to a dynamite figure, either. Yep, he would bless the day his good buddy Mark had set him up with Charlie's sister.

Well, he might not be thrilled about the stories Mark had concocted. But once he realized how necessary it had been in order to start Mark off on the right foot with Charlie, then old Sam would come around.

Ashley held out her hand. "Glad to meet you, Mark."

Mark shook her hand enthusiastically. "Ashley, it means so much to me that you agreed to come tonight. And I'm sure it will mean the world to Sam, too. Let's head over to the table and I'll introduce you."

"All right, but first I want to set my ground rules. I'm doing this as a special favor to Charlie, but please don't expect that we'll become a regular foursome."

"Absolutely. I completely understand." He gestured toward the table in the corner. "We're right over here."

As the women threaded their way through the tables with Mark following behind, Sam rose from his chair. Mark wondered if Ashley might be rethinking her comment about ending the foursome tonight. Sam usually attracted women like a magnet.

Of course Ashley also thought Sam had a serious phobia about women who turned out to be men, but that would be cleared up before too long. The more Mark thought about the idea of Sam and Ashley getting together, the more he liked it. He and Sam were like brothers, so how perfect if they ended up with sisters.

They reached the table, and Mark cleared his throat. "Sam Cavanaugh, I'd like you to meet Charlie and Ashley McPherson. Ladies, this is my best man—uh, I mean my best friend, Sam."

Sam shook hands with Charlie first. "It's a pleasure, Charlie." Then his gaze flicked over her shoulder to lock with Mark's. The message was clear. *Danger. Don't touch.*

Mark gave his buddy a short nod of understanding, which doubled as a pledge to be careful. Charlie's perfume, something spicy and exotic, wafted up to him. Oh, God, it was as if she'd set out to sabotage all his good intentions. Well, he'd have to be strong.

Then Sam shook hands with Ashley. This time he didn't bother to glance at Mark. Nope. All his concentration was fixed on the lovely Ashley in her elegant little black dress. "It's good to meet you," he said.

Mark recognized that tone of voice. Sam never

used it unless he was interested in a woman. Hot damn. This was going great. Sam would become mesmerized by Ashley, which would leave Mark free to…well, to do *something* special with Charlie. Not go to bed with her, of course. He cherished her too much to risk jeopardizing their future. But he would love to kiss her…a lot.

"Shall we sit down?" Ashley asked.

Mark snapped to attention. He'd been so busy dreaming and scheming that he'd left them all standing there by the table. His only consolation was that Sam must have been a little dazed by his first glimpse of Ashley, too, since he hadn't started pulling out chairs for the women, either.

"Yes," Mark said. "By all means." He hurried around to a chair and pulled it away from the table. "Charlie?"

"Thank you." She gave him another one of those dynamite smiles as she walked toward the chair. First she hooked the little red purse she was carrying over the chair by its long rhinestone-studded strap. Then she did that thing that always got Mark hot when he watched women seat themselves. She smoothed the skirt of her dress down over her bottom before she sat down, so she wouldn't wrinkle the material.

Mark loved it when women did that. And to watch Charlie slide both hands over that shiny red material was almost more than he could stand. After her wonderful behind was tucked in securely against the velvet seat, he gripped the back of her chair and scooted her in. That's when he chanced to look down over her shoulder. Oh, Lord. The neckline of her dress was like a curtain drawn back just enough to tease him with the possibilities lurking behind it.

Her breasts, rounded and perky, nestled just barely inside the sweep of red material. He could almost visualize how they'd look, but not quite. Very little material barred him from the view he was after, though. A man wouldn't have to work very hard to coax those treasures out of hiding.

But he'd vowed to limit himself to a couple of kisses. Still, he hadn't decided exactly where those kisses might be placed…. No. He couldn't chance kissing her anywhere but on the mouth. And he'd have to make sure his hands didn't wander, either, no matter how tempting the neckline of that dress was. And it was certainly very tempting….

"Mark?" Sam asked. "Will you be joining us this evening?"

CHAPTER THREE

ALL HER ADULT LIFE Charlie had dreamed of having a man transfixed by the sight of her cleavage. Yet until tonight, she hadn't had the nerve to dress to attract that kind of attention.

She hadn't even had the nerve to ask a guy to take her to fancy restaurants where plunging necklines would be appropriate. She'd been afraid they'd laugh. Her reputation as a tomboy had preceded her, partly because she met men on the hiking trail, for the most part. Because she was so obviously in her element there, they'd all assumed she preferred pizza parlors to five-star dining.

In general, she did, but she'd always longed for this—to appear in the doorway of an elegant room, to make heads turn as she walked to her table, and to be helped into her place by a fabulous-looking man who couldn't stop looking at her.

Ashley had been very perceptive to bring up Kevin Jasper. Kevin had chosen to go to that dance with someone more glamorous than Charlie, and from that moment on she'd decided her fate was cast. She wasn't the type of girl who could compete in a sophisticated arena.

Yet this time, she'd worked up the courage to try. Because she'd been able to control Mark's perception of her through the letters, she'd been able to indulge her secret longing to become a man's sexual fantasy.

And she'd been able to stage his first impression of her. Instead of meeting him in khaki shorts, T-shirt, hiking boots and backpack, with sweat beading her forehead and no makeup, she could show him this other side of her personality, one that no one understood.

She'd bet her comments about romantic candlelight dinners had prompted him to choose this restaurant. Everything about it thrilled her, from the soft lighting to the strolling violinists. Mark didn't seem to be paying much attention to the restaurant, though. She'd never made a man forget his surroundings before.

And what a man. His shoulders were broader, his rich brown hair thicker and his smile more devastating than she'd ever imagined by looking at his picture. She could write an entire essay on the cute dimple that appeared whenever he smiled, and the way his eyes crinkled at the corners.

And what fascinating eyes. That deep brown turned her knees to jelly, and when she caught the gleam of appreciation and knew it was all for her, she was ready to drag Mark off to the nearest secluded spot and get it on. The dress made her feel almost daring enough to do it, too.

From his reaction to her, he felt the same. His face was even a little red with embarrassment as he took his seat at the table, because he'd been caught ogling.

She flashed him a smile to let him know he hadn't offended her in the least with his preoccupation with her breasts. The attention was new and exciting to her. He could be preoccupied with any part of her he wanted, for as long as he liked.

He grinned back and nudged her knee gently under the table.

She nudged back. Wow, this was cool, playing a little footsie under the table. No guy had ever been moved to play footsie with her. Touch football, but never footsie. And every time he looked at her, she could tell he was thinking the same thing she was—that they needed to ditch their chaperones and get naked.

She'd achieved her goal. He was definitely, positively drooling. At last she had a man buggy-eyed over her, and it felt great. She was enjoying every second of this triumph.

Ashley, on the other hand, apparently wasn't so enthusiastic about it. Charlie could tell that immediately from the worried sound of her voice.

"Charlie, I seem to have something in my eye," she said. "If you two will excuse us for a minute, I'd like Charlie to come with me to the ladies' room and see if she can find anything."

"Of course." Mark leaped to his feet and grasped Charlie's chair once again.

"No problem." Sam followed suit and helped Ashley out of her chair.

Charlie figured Mark would be more careful not to stare at her chest this time, but at least she could use the opportunity to slide out of her chair in such a way that she brushed up against him. "Thank you," she murmured, turning to give him a subtle wink. "We'll be right back."

"Hope so." He gazed at her with pure relish.

She unhooked her purse from the back of the chair and positioned it over her bare shoulder before following Ashley toward the ladies' room. She had no doubt that Mark would watch her leave. That was a new and exhilarating feeling, too. She believed he had lust in his heart. Mission accomplished.

What a beautiful evening, she thought as she followed Ashley toward the tasteful sign marking the ladies' room. Even the bathroom was gorgeous. The door opened onto a sitting room, and the bathroom lay beyond that. A mural of the Italian countryside ran along the walls, and two green velvet love seats were grouped beneath the mural.

Ashley didn't seem inclined to sit on either one. The minute they were inside the door, she turned to Charlie. "You are scaring me to death!"

"Don't be scared. I'm a big girl."

"That's what I'm afraid of." Ashley reached over and tried to pull the neckline of Charlie's dress together more. "I should never have agreed to let you wear this dress."

"Ashley, if you hadn't been willing to sell me this dress, I would have gone to another dress shop and bought the closest thing to it. I wanted to knock his socks off, and by God, I'm doing it."

"I'm afraid more than his socks are due to come off if you parade around much longer in that dress." She snapped open her small evening purse and began to rummage through it. "I wonder if I brought any safety pins. Maybe we could—"

"I'm not going back out there with my dress pinned together, if that's what you're planning. Please relax. Mark is not like that Jason guy who was so cruel to you. He's the sort of person who cares about people. He cares about Sam, for instance."

Ashley stopped rummaging through her purse looking for safety pins. "Did you hear how he introduced Sam, by the way? At first he called him his best *man.* Then he corrected himself and said he was his best *friend.* What's up with that?"

Charlie smiled. "I'd say he's a guy with marriage

on his mind, that's what I'd say. That can't be bad, can it?"

Ashley seemed to be turning that over in her mind. "I guess not." She gazed at Charlie. "I would love it if he turned out to be the guy for you. I really would. But I still don't like the idea of you two rushing into a physical relationship."

"That's not very likely, is it, with our two chaperones in attendance?"

"Good point. Now that you mention that, I'm glad Sam and I are here."

Charlie had been mesmerized by Mark, but she hadn't been totally oblivious to the instant attraction between her sister and Sam. Still she wanted to play it close to the vest. "What do you think of Sam, by the way?"

"Well, he's very good-looking, if that's what you mean. But I can tell he's nervous in this situation."

"I'm not surprised. He doesn't know whether you used to be my brother Adam who turned into my sister Ashley. But eventually he'll probably relax."

"Doesn't really matter." Ashley glanced in an oval mirror hanging over an antique cherry vanity and fluffed her hair. "I doubt I'll see him again."

"Really? Why not?"

"He's got this whole psychological hang-up going on." Ashley pursed her lips, then opened her purse again and took out a tube of lipstick. "I'm really not interested in dealing with that."

Charlie couldn't resist. "Then why are you bothering to redo your lipstick?"

Ashley finished gliding the mocha lipstick over her mouth and twisted it back into its tube. "Habit," she said, dropping the tube back into her purse.

"If you say so."

"And even if I did find him attractive, I wouldn't get so involved that I'd forget why I'm here." Ashley fixed Charlie with a determined gaze. "Now promise me that you won't let that man get you alone tonight. I've been watching him, and his tongue is dragging on the floor. If you give him an opening, he's going to take it."

Charlie thought that sounded pretty darned thrilling.

"It's that gleam in your eye that has me so worried!" Ashley said. "Now please tell me you'll exercise some caution."

"Okay, I'll exercise some caution." She wondered if the condoms in her purse counted. "But you're the one who mentioned his slip of the tongue. If you ask me, Mark and I are practically engaged."

"Oh, then I guess that was a big diamond ring I saw in his pocket."

Charlie laughed. "Ashley, you don't know how long I've waited to get this reaction from a man. No man has ever had an erection just looking at me fully dressed, unless you count Donny Smoggles back in tenth grade, which I don't, considering every girl in school made Donny's little circus tent go up."

Ashley's stern expression dissolved into laughter. "I do remember Donny."

"Is it so wrong to want to make a man totally lose his mind?" She sent her sister a pleading glance.

Ashley studied her for a long moment. "No, I guess not." She sighed. "It's not his mind that concerns me."

"I know," Charlie said with a grin.

"And besides the obvious, I don't want him to break your heart, either."

"He won't. I know he won't."

"I hope you're right. Here. Let me adjust that neckline again."

ONCE THE WOMEN were out of earshot, Sam leaned across the table. "It's a damned good thing I came along, buddy boy, or you would be toast. Now, here's the plan. Under no circumstances are you to continue looking at her cleavage. Otherwise you are so dead."

Mark laughed in disbelief. "Not look? Are you insane? Why not tell me to do a few gymnastics while hanging from the chandelier? That would be a hell of a lot easier."

Sam blew out a breath and leaned back in his chair. "I get your point, but we've got to neutralize the effect of that dress."

"Unless you plan to make her wear your sport coat and put it on backward, I don't know how you're gonna neutralize anything. I think we'll just have to live with the situation." Mark wasn't particularly upset with that prospect. He thought it would be a crime to cover Charlie, sort of like throwing a blanket over one of those nude statues outside the door.

"Man, I never expected an outdoor adventure guide to show up in an outfit like that."

Mark decided not to tell Sam that he'd known about the dress all along. He also knew the color of her panties. Charlie's last letter to him had been filled with spicy little details like that. They'd been taunting each other with increasingly erotic messages. No, he'd better not tell Sam about that.

He decided to ease around to a different topic. "Don't forget that she is an outdoor adventure guide. Don't forget all the reasons why you advised me to write to her. She's everything I hoped for, and then some. To find out how beautiful and sexy she is in person is icing on the cake, because I was already convinced she was perfect for me."

"I do have a good feeling about this one," Sam admitted. "Still, I'd feel a hell of a lot better if you put off the proposal for as long as possible."

The waiter arrived with leather-bound menus, but Mark left his closed. He didn't really care about the food, anyway. "Tell you what. I'll do my best to ignore her cleavage," he said by way of trying to pacify Sam.

"Like you said, easier said than done." Sam opened his menu.

"I'll do my best. So, what did you think of Ashley?"

Immediately Sam glanced up from his perusal of the menu. Then he tried to look casual and nonchalant, the way he always did when he was intensely interested in a woman. "She's okay." He looked down at the menu again.

"Okay? Just okay? I don't think there's a woman you've dated in the past five years that compares to her. And how about those eyes? Are those the greenest eyes you've ever seen, or what?"

Sam shrugged and continued to examine the menu. "I guess. But what difference does it make? She's not breaking out in a rash, so she must not find me attractive."

Mark thought fast. Sam had a very tender ego, and whenever he thought a woman wasn't returning his interest, he bailed. If a woman played hard to get, then Sam didn't pursue her. He hoped Ashley wasn't into those kinds of games. "Um, I think Charlie said the rash appears on her...cheeks," he said.

"There was no rash on her cheeks."

"Her other cheeks."

Sam looked up. "Oh." He gazed at Mark for a

couple of seconds. "That's kind of weird, don't you think?"

"Stress affects everybody differently. She might have dragged Charlie into the ladies' room because her rash was starting to bother her."

Sam closed the menu and laid it beside his plate. "No, she dragged Charlie into the ladies' room because you were starting to bother her. She's protective of her little sister, and I don't blame her."

"There, see? That's a point scored by Ashley right off the bat. She's protective of her family members. You're protective of your family members. I remember when that kid tried to beat up your little brother and you got all over—"

"Let's get back to the subject at hand—which is her rash problem. You told me this rash of hers is a social embarrassment. If it only shows up on her backside, I don't understand how that would be an embarrassment, because nobody except her would even know about it."

"Of course it would be a problem." It was a good thing he was used to dealing with Sam's lawyerly logic. "If she's attracted to someone, that means that eventually she'd want to get physical with them, and yet she couldn't allow that to happen, because then the guy would see her rash."

"Oh." Sam frowned. "I still think there's something fishy about all of this. But in some stupid way, it makes sense. I can't imagine any other reason why a woman who looks like Ashley would agree to a blind date. She should have guys coming out of the woodwork."

"Aha! So you do think she's gorgeous."

"From what I can see. Of course I'm picturing this rash, and that's not exactly a turn-on, if you get my drift."

Mark was working hard not to laugh. He thought this whole thing was hilarious, and he hoped someday Sam would enjoy the joke as much as Mark did right now. "Maybe she's got the rash situation under control," he said. "Maybe she's very attracted to you, and yet she's not breaking out. If that's the case, you would want to continue to help her along with her recovery, wouldn't you?"

Sam rubbed his chin. "You're up to something, O'Grady. I figure it's based on fixing me up with Ashley so you can sneak off with Charlie and do the nasty."

"Not the nasty." Mark held up both hands when Sam lifted his eyebrows as if he didn't believe a word. "Really. I'm not going to do the nasty. But I'd like to kiss her, at least, which could be difficult if you and Ashley are watching us every damned minute. I wouldn't mind having the two of you talk among yourselves sometime during the evening."

"You plan to start making out with Charlie right here at the table?"

"Of course not! I thought later we might go dancing."

"Dancing? With her in that dress? Or sort of in that dress? I don't think so, Mark, old boy. You would—"

"Whoops, here they come. Now if you want to know if Ashley's attracted to you or not, look at her lipstick. If she globbed some more on while she was in the bathroom, then that means she wants you."

"You've said that before when we were out with women, and I think you're making it up. Women put on lipstick for no reason. They put on lipstick to go to the grocery store, for crying out loud. I never understood that."

"Because they might meet a hot prospect at the grocery store, that's why," Mark said. "Lipstick is part of that whole mating thing. Remember, we saw that on the Discovery Channel. Look at the lipstick."

"How do I know if she put it on for me? Maybe she wants the waiter really bad. Or the maître d', although personally I think he's a little old for—"

"Oh, for God's sake, Sam. I swear you'd make a sow's ear out of a silk purse." Then he got out of his chair so he could help his fabulous Lady in Red into her seat. And his vow not to look at her cleavage didn't last even for a second. But he rationalized that she'd worn the dress on purpose to make him notice, so if he didn't, she'd be disappointed.

He didn't want to disappoint this woman. Not

ever. And that was why he would be a good boy tonight and just enjoy the view from a distance.

"Did you get whatever it was out of your eye?" Sam asked Ashley, peering intently at her face.

Mark looked, too, and saw the fresh shine of new lipstick. Way to go, Ashley. Then he glanced over at Charlie and was gratified to see that she'd added more of that tomato-red color to her mouth. He'd ten times rather spend the next hour kissing that plump little mouth than eating pasta.

"My eye's fine," Ashley said. "Probably an eyelash or something."

"I can see how that would happen. Your eyelashes are pretty long," Sam said.

Good, Mark thought. Sam liked long eyelashes. Charlie's eyelashes were long, too, and she had mascara on them. Blondes usually used the stuff, he knew, because without mascara their eyelashes didn't stand out so much.

He'd like to see Charlie without her mascara, though. No doubt she'd look perfectly fine. He'd like to see her without her clothes, too. She'd look more than perfectly fine without her clothes.

But he wouldn't be doing that this weekend. No sir. So he'd content himself with simply sitting and watching Charlie. Somehow he managed to order his meal and make a wine decision, but he couldn't remember his choices thirty seconds after he'd made them.

Charlie totally absorbed his attention. He made small talk. So did she. But the conversation was unimportant. All that mattered was being here together, his knee touching hers, his hand resting on the tablecloth where he could accidentally brush her little finger with his.

Now she was picking up her water goblet. Now she was putting it up to those red lips. Now she was taking a sip. Now she was giving him that coy look that made his pulse hammer. He was vaguely aware that Ashley and Sam were talking to each other, but he wasn't aware of anything they said.

Charlie-watching was becoming his favorite activity. The only problem was that the more he watched, the more aroused he became. Well, too bad. Tonight he would be strong. For her sake.

CHAPTER FOUR

CHARLIE BARELY TASTED HER DINNER. Somehow she had to come up with a way to get her sister and Sam out of the picture so she could be alone with Mark. He was everything she'd hoped and she could hardly wait to get her hands on him.

After all the sexy things they'd said to each other in their letters recently, she was ready for more than heated glances and knees touching under the table. The single rose looked lovely resting beside her plate, and the strolling violinists were romantic, but by the end of the meal she needed more than that.

She wanted to be held, to be kissed, to be caressed. In the process, she'd find out what it was like to touch the dimple on Mark's cheek and feel the texture of his hair beneath her fingers. She might even find out what he looked like without his sport coat, without his tie, or even without…everything. Her body throbbed just thinking about that possibility.

But he'd brought Sam along, and that was the fly in the ointment.

She couldn't really blame him. It had been a decent and kind thing to do, and Sam seemed like a terrific guy, but it sure did make for an awkward situation having him and Ashley hanging around. The meal was drawing to a close and she didn't know what to suggest that would allow her an intimate encounter with Mark.

By the time they were standing outside the restaurant waiting for the valet to bring the cars, she still hadn't thought of a good solution for extending the evening. Inviting them all back to her apartment wasn't a very romantic thought, and they were overdressed for the movies.

Dancing would work, but she wasn't up on the dancing scene in Austin, even though she was a decent dancer. Her other dates hadn't thought she'd be into that, so she hadn't spent much time nightclubbing.

She glanced at Mark in silent appeal. The evening couldn't end now. It just couldn't.

He met her gaze and his eyes were filled with the same longing. Then he looked over at Sam. "I hate to call it a night so soon, don't you? Our hotel has a lounge with a live band and a small dance floor, so we could—"

"Great idea," Charlie said. At last a man had pictured her as an inviting dance partner. And she'd get to put her arms around him, at least while the music played. That was a beginning. "Isn't it a great idea, Ashley?"

"No!" said Ashley and Sam together.

Charlie seized the moment. "Then I have the perfect solution. We have two cars here. Mark and I can take one of them and go dancing, and Sam and Ashley can take the other one and do…whatever they want."

"On the other hand, dancing might be a good idea," Ashley said quickly.

"Sure," Sam added. "I could tag along for some dancing for a little while. Then Mark and I should probably turn in. Big day tomorrow."

"On Sunday?" Charlie asked.

"Oh, yeah. We're both behind at work, right, buddy?"

"Uh, right, Sam."

"Right." Sam sent a meaningful glance in Mark's direction. "So you and I can lead and the women can follow us over."

"Oh, for God's sake." Mark faced his friend. "This is getting ridiculous. I don't care how we divvy up the car situation, except that I plan to ride over with Charlie."

Charlie wanted to punch the air in victory.

"We only have a little time together," Mark continued, "and I don't want to waste it going in separate cars."

Sam considered that for a minute. "Okay, Ashley and I will take your Lexus."

"Fine." He started toward Charlie's little red Miata and paused. "How come?"

Ashley gestured to the two cars lined up in front of the restaurant. "Even I know why. Here we have your car, a luxury sedan, a make-out car if I ever saw one, with plush seats in front *and back*. Over here we have Charlie's car, a two-seater sports car. Try to make out in that and you'd need a chiropractor." She glanced at Sam. "Nice to know we're both on the same page."

Sam grinned at her. "Yeah, isn't it?"

"You guys are worse than parents!" Charlie said, hardly able to believe they were having this conversation. "Listen, Ashley, I have to agree with Mark on this one. The heavy-duty chaperone routine is getting ridiculous. Mark and I are adults. We don't have to be protected from each other, right, Mark?"

To her surprise, instead of backing her up, Mark hesitated. Then his face reddened. "Uh—of course not, but I'm sure Sam and Ashley have good intentions."

"I'm sure they do, too. Just misguided."

Sam looked amused. "Well, Ashley, let's take our misguided intentions and drive to the hotel in Mark's Lexus. You can keep an eye on the rearview mirror." He opened the passenger door for her.

"You're a man after my own heart." She smiled and got into the car.

"Whatever." Charlie threw up her hands and

looked at Mark. He was still gorgeous, but she was a little put out with him. He hadn't supported her bid to be alone. "Shall I drive or do you want to?"

"Let him drive," Sam called out before he climbed into the Lexus. "It'll keep his hands busy."

Mark gave her a sheepish grin. "You know, he's probably right. That dress really is tempting."

Charlie thought about that and was somewhat mollified. In a way, she liked knowing that Mark was worried about controlling himself with her, even on the short drive to the hotel. She'd never caused a man to be that wild and crazy. That everyone was so concerned about his ability to restrain himself was a boost to her ego, come to think of it.

She headed for the passenger side of her little Miata. "Okay," she said. "You can drive." When Mark helped her in, she gave his hand a squeeze and gazed up at him. His attention was firmly fastened on her breasts. "Thanks," she murmured.

He glanced at her and swallowed. "You're welcome."

Excitement curled in her tummy. She wanted to kiss him so much she could barely stand it. "We could always ditch our watchdogs."

"I—no, we'd better not. Sam would get worried and call the police. We'll just…go dancing."

She decided to settle for that, but she hoped he meant slow dancing. Very slow.

Mark rounded the car and climbed in, although his knees nearly hit the dashboard of the small car. "Tight fit."

"The seat moves back a little."

"Good." He adjusted the seat, and even so he looked a little cramped in her tiny car.

Personally Charlie liked the close quarters. Mark was within easy reach. She gazed at his profile and could barely believe that he was here. The scent of his aftershave teased her with possibilities.

"I guess you think Sam's concern is a little over the top," he said as he pulled out and followed the Lexus down the road. "But he means well."

Charlie sighed. "So does Ashley. She said writing to each other for three months isn't the same as dating for three months."

"Sam said the same thing."

Wow, this was cozy. Charlie wished the drive would take a while, but she knew they weren't far away from the hotel. "Is there any chance Sam is letting his own little problem get in the way of your dating life?"

"Problem?"

"You know. Maybe he thinks I'll suddenly turn out to be a man, too." She focused on Mark's lips. They were *so* tempting. No doubt he was a good kisser. You could tell those things by the look of a man's mouth.

"Oh, *that* problem. No, I don't think he believes that

about you or Ashley. In fact, from the way he's acting with Ashley, I think he's getting over his phobia."

"Good. Then maybe he'll leave us alone." *So I can start kissing you.*

Mark laughed. "Don't count on it. But I can't get too upset with him. He's always been there for me."

"Yeah, exactly." Charlie grinned. "And that's where he is right now. *There.*" She loved watching Mark's hands on the steering wheel and imagining them elsewhere….

"He doesn't want either of us to get hurt, that's all. And he's invested in making this work out for us. I've been through a few…experiences with women who were all wrong for me. He's the one who first suggested the *Texas Men* thing."

"Is he?" Charlie was feeling more mellow toward Sam already, knowing that. Now if only he'd go away. "Then I'll have to thank him."

"I've thanked him on a regular basis ever since you and I started writing to each other. I really do owe the guy, and it's true that he's worried that I'll move too fast with you. I've sort of promised him that I won't…I mean, that this first night, you and I won't…"

She reached over and slid her hand down his thigh. Her heart hammered as she felt the muscles tighten. "That we won't make love?"

He groaned. "Yep, and I'm in big trouble already.

I thought I could manage just a dinner and maybe some dancing, maybe even a nightcap, and then let you go home. But I'm about to combust."

"I'm glad." She squeezed his thigh and took her hand away. "That was my intention."

"Seriously?"

"Seriously." And now was as good a time as any to state her case. She took a deep breath. "You never asked why I wrote to you in the first place—why I decided to answer an ad in *Texas Men*."

"No, I guess I never did." He glanced at her. "So tell me."

"All my other relationships with men have been so...predictable. We'd meet on the trail or through friends, have a coffee date, have a lunch date, go on a few hikes, maybe, or play tennis once or twice. Then we'd do dinner a few times. Then finally we'd consider the matter of spending the night together. Often by that time I'd be so bored out of my tree I'd say to heck with the whole business."

His voice was husky. "I'm glad to hear it. I'm overjoyed to hear it. I don't like to think of you with anybody else."

"Mark, don't get me wrong. I'm not a virgin."

"That's okay. I just don't want anybody else to count."

She took satisfaction in the tense set of his jaw. He was already getting possessive about her. She liked that. "They don't count. Because there was no real excitement. I thought, by teasing you a bit in the letters, that when we finally met it would be dynamite."

"Well, that sure worked, especially with that dress to cap it off."

"But don't you see?" She had to make him understand. "If we do the dancing thing, and the nightcap thing, and then you go up to your hotel room and I go back to my apartment, it'll be like somebody threw water on the fuse!"

"No, it won't," he said with feeling. "I don't know about your fuse, but mine isn't about to go out. I think my fuse is permanently lit."

"Mark, listen to me. I want wild. I want reckless. I want unrestrained. Just once in my life."

"Couldn't you have all that next weekend? We could go camping, and then—"

She groaned. No way could she be a *femme fatale* when they went camping. "If we wait until next weekend, this will be like my other experiences with men."

"I beg to differ!"

"Well, it would feel like it, anyway. Sensible. Cautious. *Boring.*" She slid her hand over his thigh again. "You don't want us to be boring, do you, Mark?"

His breathing rasped in the confines of the small car. "Oh, Lord. Oh, Lord, Lord, Lord."

"Just go with the flow."

"Charlie, it's kind of like a point of honor with

me." He sounded desperate. "I've been known to rush into a physical relationship."

"I don't call this rushing, do you?"

"Well, maybe not, but I still think it would be good for me to get through this first date without—"

"Just relax." She stroked his thigh again and knew he was anything but relaxed. "Everything will work out."

"It has to."

"It will." She looked up ahead to where the Lexus was turning in to the entry of the hotel. "Well, here we are. Dancing will be nice."

Mark sounded short of breath. "Dancing will be torture."

She smiled. They were going dancing at a hotel. Hotels had lots of rooms and lots of beds. She had a feeling that she and Mark would get wild and crazy, just the way she'd hoped, before the night was over. He might be gun-shy because he'd made love with other women too quickly and been burned, but he hadn't been writing to other women for three months. He would be fine with her.

The Lexus came to a stop at the hotel entrance where lights from the portico illuminated its shiny black paint job, along with some white smudges on the back window.

"What's that on the back window of your car?" she asked.

Mark coughed. "What do you mean?"

"It looks like white paint, as if something was lettered on it."

"Uh, yeah, some guys painted a message on there, for a joke. They were smashed at the time and got the wrong kind of paint. I haven't been able to clean it all off yet. I need to buy some special solvent."

"The first letter looks like a *J*. What does that stand for?"

"Believe me, you don't want to know."

Charlie tried to think of an obscene word that started with a J. Nothing came to mind. "Oh, well. I'll bet you'll be glad when you finally get it all cleaned off, huh?"

"Yep. I most certainly will."

"SO, DID YOU TELL HER YET?" Sam asked as he and Mark stood at the bar waiting for the drinks they'd ordered for the four of them. The women were ensconced at a table near the minuscule dance floor. Both Sam's and Mark's jackets hung on the backs of the two empty chairs and their ties had been stuffed into the pockets in preparation for some serious dancing.

But the band had taken a break the moment they'd arrived, and none of the customers had chosen to dance to the recorded music flowing through the lounge's sound system. Consequently the cocktail waitress was very busy and Mark had suggested getting their own drinks while they waited for the band to come back.

"Well, did you?" Sam prompted.

Mark didn't have to ask what he meant. "I need some peace and quiet alone with her to explain that," he said. "But, for the record, as we drove up she noticed that somebody had painted something on the back window of my car."

"Now, see? That was the perfect time to tell her."

"Oh, yeah, sure. We were about to get out of the car and join you guys. How could I throw something like that at her without having time to explain?"

"I still say it was the perfect opening. You could have signaled to me that you needed time to talk with her. I would have picked up on that."

Mark rubbed the back of his neck. "It's not the kind of thing you can explain in five minutes. Think about it. People don't paint *Just Married* on the back window of your car until right before the wedding. I'd have to start the whole crummy story by giving her the worst scenario first. I want to lead up to the Deborah disaster. And I'd really like Charlie to be totally in love with me before I tell her about Deb. I think she'd take it better."

"I'm not sure I agree with you."

"Look, Sam, I gotta do this part my way. Not making love tonight—I'm willing to go along on that. It won't be easy holding off, but I'm committed to it.

As for telling her about those five broken engagements, that's something I have to do in my own time, when I feel it's right."

Sam glanced over at the table and then back at Mark. "Okay. But you'd better keep her out of Houston until you spill the beans. You'd be amazed how word's gotten around."

"Compliments of the DOA Support Group?"

"I'll admit they've been busy."

Mark scowled at him. "Did they buy you a T-shirt?"

"They did, but I told them that out of friendship for you I couldn't wear it." He grinned. "At least not yet. So try and stay on my good side, okay?"

"Hey, I introduced you to Ashley and bought you dinner." Mark paid the bartender before handing Sam one of the beers and Ashley's glass of Chardonnay, each with a cocktail napkin underneath. "Now I'm even buying you this drink. What more do you want from me?"

"A wedding that actually takes place."

"I'm working on that." Mark picked up his own beer and Charlie's glass of Merlot. "How's it going with Ashley?"

"We had sort of a strange conversation on the way over."

Mark held his breath. Now was not the time he wanted his little subterfuge to be revealed. He forced himself to relax. "Really? About what?"

"Transvestites, of all things. She wanted me to know that she doesn't approve of them pretending to be women and trying to pick up straight guys. I told her I wasn't big on that, either, but it was kind of weird that she'd choose that topic."

Mark tried to look casual. "Maybe she read something about it in one of those women's magazines. They're putting all kinds of things in those magazines these days. It's way beyond makeup and clothes."

"Could be. Anyway, she's not fond of lawyers in general, but she seems to be willing to make an exception in my case. I'll bet that's partly because she knows I'm trying to keep you and Charlie from getting horizontal."

Mark panicked. "You didn't tell her why, did you?"

"No. That's your job, not mine."

Mark let out his breath. "So how do you feel about Ashley?"

"I could stand to see her again," Sam said with studied nonchalance.

Mark laughed. "From the master of understatement, I'll take that to mean that you're hooked."

"I have to admit this is turning out better than I expected. But I don't think she's developing a rash. She's not squirming around or anything."

"I'm sure the rash problem is cured, because she does seem to be into you."

"You think so?" Sam looked pleased.

"I think so. Now, come on. The band's ready to play again, and I want to dance with my girl."

As they approached the table, the band launched into a fast number. Mark had been picturing something slow that allowed him to hold Charlie close, so he considered suggesting they sit this one out.

Charlie preempted him by leaving her chair as he deposited their drinks on the table. "Let's dance," she said.

"Sure." He wasn't about to refuse her if that's what she wanted. And maybe some rapid movement would work the tension out of his system.

He hadn't considered Charlie's rapid movement, which only added tension in his system. Her breasts quivered seductively. He was amazed that they stayed tucked inside the dress, but somehow, either by her efforts or the wonders of modern fashion, they did. And then he had to deal with the rhythm of her hips, and the look in her eyes, which had gone all smoky blue and mysterious. She was definitely taunting him.

As she danced, her lips parted and a tiny drop of moisture gathered in the hollow of her throat. He wanted to lick it off. He could almost taste the salt on his tongue. After he'd lapped up that single glistening drop, he'd run his tongue along the swooping neckline of her dress, over the inviting swell of her breast, and then…

"Mark, you're not dancing!" she said with a laugh.

He looked down at his feet, the way he used to when he was thirteen and just learning. And sure enough, his feet had stopped moving. He glanced back up and shrugged. "Batteries must be low." Then he grinned and started dancing again.

This had to be love. It had to be what he'd waited a lifetime to find. He'd never been out on the floor with a woman and totally forgotten to dance. Charlie was powerful medicine, all right.

By concentrating very hard on what he was doing, he managed to keep himself moving for the rest of the number. Between remembering to dance and trying to discipline his thoughts so he wouldn't get an erection, he was a busy man.

Eventually the music stopped, and he led Charlie back to their table in a state of semi-arousal that had threatened to become chronic. Ashley and Sam had also returned from the floor, both of them laughing and breathing hard. Mark hadn't even noticed they were out there, and it wasn't a large area. As he sat down he glanced around and noticed two couples remained standing, waiting for the next number, while another pair had returned to their seats. That dance floor must have been crowded, and he'd felt as if he and Charlie were all alone.

Yep, he had it bad.

Charlie picked up her glass of wine. "Here's to us," she murmured.

He touched his beer mug to her glass. "Here's to the U.S. Mail."

"I'd rather drink a toast to one particular U.S. male." She eyed him over the rim of her goblet and smiled. "And I'll bet you deliver." Holding his gaze, she sipped the red wine. Then she lowered the glass. A drop of ruby liquid trembled on her lower lip, and she licked it away with a slow swipe of her pink tongue.

Mark's chest grew tight and the erection he'd been trying to control all night threatened to make itself obvious.

"Hey, you guys want some pretzels?" Sam asked, shoving a bowl in Mark's direction.

"No, thanks." Mark realized that his voice sounded like a bullfrog's. He cleared his throat. "Charlie? Want some pretzels?"

The band moved into a slower song.

"I'd rather dance," she said.

"Sure." Anything. Anything she wanted. Well, except making love. But he had a feeling that was the single most important thing she wanted right now.

CHAPTER FIVE

CHARLIE THOUGHT she should be able to work this one out. She'd always been a leader. She'd led whole groups of people through rapids, up steep trails, into dark caves. She should be able to lead one sexually aroused man to bed. But apparently Sam had convinced him it wasn't a good idea.

That in itself was a fascinating concept. From her understanding of men, guys usually encouraged their friends to go for it. She had several male friends who thought of her as a buddy more than a prospective date, and maybe because of that they'd never edited their comments when she was around. From their conversations, she'd gathered that the sooner they could have sex with a woman who turned them on, the better.

She knew she turned Mark on. The trick was to convince him to do something about it. As she moved into the circle of Mark's arms, she hoped a long, slow, exchange of body heat on the dance floor might be all the convincing he would need.

His muffled groan as he pulled her close sounded encouraging.

He smelled so damned good. She breathed in his aftershave and buried her fingertips in his silky hair as she nestled her cheek against his. Her three-inch heels created the perfect alignment for brushing her pelvis across the ridge pushing at the material of his slacks. "This is nice."

"This is hell," he murmured against her ear. "I keep thinking of those black lace panties you told me you'd wear tonight. Did you?"

"Uh-huh."

"Oh, Lord."

"That black lace is quite damp, now," she whispered. "Very damp."

"You're killing me. I hope you know that."

"No, I'm seducing you."

"And you're doing a first-class job." He wrapped both arms around her. "Do you realize I haven't even kissed you yet?"

She leaned back to look into his eyes, and the desire she saw there raised her pulse rate another few notches. "Want to kiss me now?"

"Yes. But I'm afraid I'll lose it if I do."

"Chicken."

His gaze drifted to her mouth. "The thing is, once I start kissing you, I might not stop."

"I'll help you. We'll control it." She ran a fingertip over his lower lip and her breath caught. His mouth reminded her of the full-lipped ones on carved statues, only his were so warm and soft. She dented in his lower lip with her finger. "I want to kiss you, Mark, even if it's not for long, even if we have to be careful and not get carried away."

He closed his eyes as she traced the outline of his mouth.

"Could we?" she asked, lifting her finger away.

He opened his eyes again. "I guess…" He swallowed. "I guess we could count off seconds in our heads."

"You mean like when we were kids playing hide-and-seek?" She smiled.

"Yeah, like that." His gaze became heavy-lidded and filled with dark passions.

"So how did you do it you were a kid?"

"Not very well until I was about fourteen, and then I got better. I discovered what to do with my tongue."

Oh, boy. "I meant, how did you count?" Her breathing quickened at the delicious prospect ahead. "Did you say Mississippi-One, Mississippi-Two? Or One-Hundred-One, One-Hundred-Two?"

"We did the Mississippi thing." He drew her closer. "How about you?"

"We used Mississippi." She closed her eyes as his breath touched her mouth. "How many should we do it for?"

"Three," he murmured.

"Four."

"Five," he said. "Start counting."

Velvet lips settled over hers. *Mississippi-One.* Her heart went crazy. This was so good. He tasted like hot sex. *Mississippi-Two.* She pulled him closer, opened her mouth. *Mississippi-Three.* The warm stroke of his tongue made her whimper. *Mississippi....* She lost track as he took command. *Mississi—oh, yes. Like that. Exactly like—*

He pulled away, gasping. Then he cupped her head and cradled it against his chest as he swayed to the music. His chest continued to heave as he bowed his head over hers. "That was…a close call."

She nodded, dazed by the sexual pull of their kiss. Her whole body hummed, and tension settled between her thighs with such fierce determination that she sucked in a breath. Closing her eyes, she nestled her head against the soft silk of his dress shirt while she struggled with her urges. His heart beat wildly under her ear. Finally she cleared the huskiness from her throat. "I forgot to count."

His chest began to shake, and she finally realized he was laughing in between gasps.

His voice rasped in her ear. "No kidding."

Still shocked by the power of that brief kiss, she raised her head and looked into his eyes. She'd thought it would be exciting to make love to him tonight. She hadn't expected it to become a matter of such extreme urgency that she couldn't deal with not having him. Her voice trembled. "I suppose…I suppose you usually get that kind of charge from kissing."

He shook his head. "No."

"I thought I was in the space shuttle or something."

"We sure had ignition."

"Mark, this is serious stuff here." She clutched the back of his neck in both hands. "It's like sitting on a keg of dynamite."

His dark gaze held hers. "Or a nuclear bomb."

"Yeah." She cleared her throat again. "Here's the deal." She paused and took another breath. "I have to be honest with you. If you go back to Houston without making love to me, I'll be a basket case until you come back and finish what you just started."

He looked genuinely troubled. "It can't be until next weekend."

"Next *weekend?* Really? Oh, Mark."

"I know, but next week's packed for me."

"For me, too," she said with a soft groan. "I have two hiking trips, back-to-back." Her pulse was still racing. All thoughts of cleverly seducing him were gone. She spoke straight from the heart. "If you leave me this frustrated, I'm afraid I'll be a danger to myself and others out there in the wilderness."

He blinked. "God, I didn't even consider that. If I spent next week all tied up in knots because I wanted you so much, I could screw up somebody's whole portfolio. I could destroy their retirement account and trash their life's savings."

"And what about driving? We could have a wreck."

"We could step out in front of a bus."

"Well, you could. There won't be any buses on the trail. But I could fall over a cliff."

His arms tightened around her. "That's not going to happen."

"It's not?"

"No."

Her heart beat crazily. "You'll take care of this?"

"Yes." His gaze burned into hers.

She could barely breathe. "What about Ashley and Sam?"

He gazed across the dance floor. "I don't think we'll have a problem there. Take a look."

She followed the direction of his gaze and saw Sam and Ashley plastered together on the dance floor. "Wow. I guess that turned out okay."

"They wouldn't notice if we left."

She looked into his eyes and began to quiver with anticipation. "Shall we go now?"

His grip on her tightened. "Tell you what. You head on over to the elevators and I'll meet you there."

She hated to let him out of her sight. "Why aren't you going with me?"

"First I'm going to bribe the band to play another slow number right on the heels of this one, so Sam and Ashley will stay occupied and not miss us. Then I'm going to the desk and get another room. One Sam doesn't have a key for."

THE MANEUVER in the lounge was easier than Mark expected. The band cooperated beautifully. Two other couples besides Sam and Ashley stayed locked together on the floor, so Mark decided he'd done everybody a good turn.

Then, heart pounding, he headed for the front desk of the hotel and spoke to the young woman behind the polished wooden counter. "I'd like a room, please."

"Do you have a reservation?" she asked.

"No. I mean, yes. I already have a room here, but I'd like another room."

"The room you have isn't acceptable?"

"The room I have is fine, but I'd like a second room." This was starting to sound like a Three Stooges routine.

The clerk looked confused, but she obediently turned to her computer. "I'll see what I can do. Name, please?"

"Mark O'Grady."

"All right, Mr. O'Grady. I see your reservation here for a double for tonight only. Do you want the other room to be for one night only, as well?"

"Yes." This was taking longer than he'd planned. He didn't like the idea of Charlie loitering beside the elevator in that dress. Somebody could get the wrong idea.

The clerk typed some more, frowned, and typed in something else. "Ah. Good. I have a room that adjoins yours. If you like, I can put it on the same bill as the—"

"No!" He paused and cleared his throat. "I really don't want an adjoining room. That is, I'd actually like a room on a different floor."

The clerk glanced at him. "You want two rooms, on different floors."

"That's right."

She typed something into her computer. "All right, Mr. O'Grady. I can accommodate that request. Another double?"

Mark felt the color rising to his face. "Actually, no. I'd like this to be a king. No, wait. What's the best room you have in the hotel?"

"The Presidential Suite, but that's quite a bit more ex—"

"I'll take it. If you have it available, that is."

"Well, yes, I do." She seemed to be trying to hide her astonishment. "Would you like that on the same credit card as the double room?"

"Yes."

"And you're sure you don't want to know what the rate is?"

"I don't care what it is." *Condoms. He didn't have any. He'd deliberately not brought them, to help keep him honest.*

"How many keys will you be needing?"

"Two," he said. Then he glanced over at the gift shop. Closed. There might be a dispenser in the men's room, but to get there he'd have to go past the lounge, and that was dangerous. He could only think of one option, and he didn't like it.

"Here you go, sir." The clerk pushed a key folder toward him. "Take the elevator all the way to the top floor. It's the door on your right as you exit the elevator. Enjoy your stay."

"Thank you. Uh, I noticed the gift shop is closed."

"Yes, sir, it closes at ten."

He wondered how in the world to ask her for what he needed. He wasn't even sure if she could provide them. "The thing is, something unexpected has come up." He gulped. Wrong choice of words. "I mean, I didn't anticipate that I would be… I was wondering…that is, I…"

She gazed at him, stone-faced. Then her expression softened and she gave him a little smile. "Just a minute, sir. I think I can help you. I'll be right back." She turned and walked into the office right behind the reservation desk.

He had no idea if she knew what he was after, although from the look on her face, he thought she'd guessed. Shifting his weight nervously, he glanced in the direction of the elevators, but he couldn't see them from here. Charlie might think he wasn't going to show up. God, he hoped she didn't go back to the lounge looking for him.

Then he heard voices coming from the office.

A man laughed. "I still say you oughta charge him for those," he said.

Then the clerk said something he couldn't quite hear, except for the words *Presidential Suite*.

"Even more reason," said the man.

The clerk, her face pink, returned with a small paper sack. "I think this is what you were looking for." She handed him the sack.

He peeked inside and, sure enough, three little foil packets lay there. He glanced up at the clerk, certain that his own cheeks were red. "Listen, I don't know where you got these, but I'll be glad to pay for—"

"Never mind." She smiled again. "Consider it my contribution to safe sex."

"Thanks." And now at least two members of the staff knew what was going on in the Presidential Suite tonight, he thought as he hurried toward the elevators. But that was okay. Just so Sam didn't know. At least not yet.

Once Sam realized they were both gone he'd figure out what they'd done, of course. Mark would have to face the music in the morning.

And he knew Sam wouldn't be happy. But when Mark explained that he had to do this to keep Charlie from falling off a cliff, Sam would understand. Besides, considering the way Sam had been holding onto Ashley the last time Mark had checked, Sam might be very mellow by tomorrow morning.

AS SHE STOOD by the elevator waiting for Mark, Charlie opened her tiny red purse and took out her lipstick. The brass elevator doors made a reasonable mirror, but her hands were shaking so much she had a tough time getting the lipstick on straight.

Well, she'd done it. She'd convinced him to throw caution to the winds and make love. And now she was scared silly.

So much depended on this encounter. After all, both of them had been quite open in their letters about wanting to find a mate. And no matter how attracted they were to each other, if the sex turned out to be a disaster, they might decide to end the relationship tonight.

Now that the moment was at hand, she was afraid she'd misrepresented herself to him and he'd be disappointed. She'd billed herself as a sexually adventurous woman because she'd wanted to attract a sexually adventurous man.

Mark had sounded that way in his letters, too, but he'd turned out to be a bit more conservative in person, considering his hesitation in the beginning. Was he expecting her to be the aggressor once they were alone?

While writing to him in the privacy of her apartment, she'd been so sure that she could be that kind of woman. She sought out adventure in her work, why not in her sexual relationships? Now she wasn't so confident. She tucked her lipstick back in her purse, right next to the two condoms she'd brought along, just in case. Well, just in case was about to happen, exactly as she'd fantasized.

She was about to discover whether she had the nerve to turn fantasy into reality. Fluffing her short hair with her fingers, she gazed at her reflection. She certainly looked the part. It was quite a dress. No wonder Ashley had been worried.

A couple approached the elevators. Although they pretended not to notice her, Charlie knew better. While they waited for the elevator they kept glancing in the polished brass doors to check her out.

It didn't take much imagination to guess what they were thinking. Any woman loitering by the elevator at this hour, in this outfit, had to be waiting for the man of the evening to get a room for the two of them. Not many other explanations came to mind. After what seemed like eons, the elevator arrived and whisked the couple away.

More eons seemed to pass as she paced the area pretending to study the potted philodendron, the blinking lights above the elevator, and the hotel's insignia stamped into the sand of the ashtray.

"Charlie. Here I am. I'm so sorry to keep you waiting."

She turned, her heart racing, to find Mark coming toward her. Well, this was it. Warmth flooded through her. He *was* a very yummy-looking guy. Maybe she could be more aggressive than she'd thought.

He'd hooked his jacket over his shoulder and he held a key folder in his free hand. He smiled at her, looking far more confident than she felt. "I thought I'd be faster."

"It's okay." She was impressed that he'd remembered to grab his jacket from the back of his chair. "Sam and Ashley didn't see you?"

"Nope. They were very involved." He tucked the key folder in his jacket pocket and looped the jacket over one arm before stepping over to the elevator and punching the button. His finger trembled the slightest little bit. Maybe he wasn't totally cool about this, either.

"I'm glad it seems to be working out for them," she said.

"Me, too. For several reasons." He cleared his throat and glanced at her. For the first time since he'd approached the elevator he looked unsure of himself. "By the way, I don't want you to worry about…well, anything. That is, I have…"

"Oh." She blushed. "I have some, too."

"Yeah?"

His look of surprise made her feel the need to explain. "It's probably my backpacking experience. When you're heading into the wilderness, you try to anticipate every—"

He stepped toward her and cupped her warm cheek in his hand. "I think it's wonderful that you brought condoms," he murmured, gazing into her eyes. "I'm flattered that you brought them, to tell the truth. I should have, but I'd really decided this wasn't going to happen."

When he stood this close to her she had trouble breathing. But she wanted to say something important, so she drew in a quick breath and used it all in one rushed little speech. "In our letters, we talked a lot about how great sex would be between us, but what if it's not?"

There. She'd put her worst fear out where they could see it. She gasped for air and searched his gaze as she waited for his response.

He rubbed his thumb over her cheek in a lazy caress and his confident manner returned. "That's never crossed my mind."

"It hasn't?" She peered at him in astonishment. "Why not?"

He looked genuinely puzzled. "Why would it?"

"Well, because we've never been together, and

everybody has different reactions to…I mean, not everyone has the same…" She stared at him as he continued to look bewildered. "You've never had bad sex?" she asked finally.

"No. No, I haven't." He sounded surprised that she'd even ask. "Why, have you?"

"Of *course*. I thought everyone had."

"Not me. I don't understand how you could. I mean, everything about it is so wonderful. It doesn't matter if you're cramped, or the temperature's not right, or you don't have a lot of time. It's still…" His eyes glowed as he gazed into hers. "Making love is great," he finished softly. "And this will be the best."

She was totally astounded. Everyone she'd ever known who was willing to talk about it had been able to come up with at least one horror story.

"The elevator's here." He stroked her cheek one last time and moved his hand to the small of her back. "Let's go," he murmured.

She stepped into the mirror and wood-paneled cubicle ahead of him. "You really never have had a bad time of it?" she asked again as she turned to face him.

"No, I really never have," he said with a patient smile. "Women are designed for such pleasure, how could you end up with anything else?"

"Now I'm really intimidated. I could be your first catastrophe."

"Not possible." He punched the button for their floor.

"Of course it's possible."

"Nope. And I'll show you why." He handed her his coat. "Would you hold this a minute?"

"Okay." She wasn't sure what was going on, but she took the coat.

"This is why." He cradled her face in both hands and covered her mouth with his.

And there it was again—Fourth of July going on inside her body. Oh, that mouth, that tongue…. Her thighs began to tremble and her heartbeat pounded in her ears. She'd never been this pumped up, not even when she was about to run Class Five rapids.

He lifted his mouth a fraction from hers. "That's why," he whispered. "I've had good sex with every woman I've made love to, and none of their kisses felt as exciting as yours, so how can we go wrong?"

She couldn't talk. She could only moan a little. Apparently she'd stumbled onto a man who was an artist when it came to making love, and tonight he planned to create a masterpiece. Who was she to argue with that?

CHAPTER SIX

IF MARK HAD BEEN having second thoughts about the wisdom of making love to Charlie tonight, those second thoughts disintegrated the moment he kissed her again. As he'd thought the first time, she tasted and felt like his forever girl. Everything about her was right, from the spicy scent of her perfume to the shape of her mouth, from the color of her eyes to the way her body fit against his.

He'd always loved sex in general, and that had been part of his problem. He'd taken such pleasure in good sex that he hadn't considered even greater sex awaited him with the right woman, the perfect woman: Charlie.

Apparently she'd had some bad experiences with lovemaking. He shouldn't have been surprised. Come to think of it, all the women he'd made love to had told him of bad experiences. That had been another one of his problems, wanting to make it up to them for the crummy lovers they'd been with before. Obviously he'd been successful, too, because each of his fiancées had raved about the good times they'd had in bed with him.

But difficult as it was for him to admit, sex wasn't everything. At some point you had to climb out of bed and live together. He and his fiancées hadn't had enough in common to do that. But he and Charlie did. They'd discussed it all in their letters.

For three months they'd been building toward what was about to happen between them tonight. Their communication had created a tsunami wave of urges, and it was about to crash onto the shore. Sensible behavior was a joke in a situation like this. To deny the power of their attraction, to put it off until another time, was going against the laws of nature.

He had no intention of running from his destiny.

The elevator slid open on the top floor. No one had interrupted their elevator ride, and he took that as a good sign. "We're here," he said, looking into her passion-glazed eyes.

Her voice was husky with desire. "Good."

"Come on." Wrapping an arm around her waist, he guided her out of the elevator and turned to the right, as the clerk had directed him. At the end of the hall was a set of double doors. The number on the brass plate beside the door matched the number on his key folder. He'd never stayed in the Presidential

Suite of any hotel before, but no time could be more fitting than this.

As they walked toward the double doors, Charlie drew in a quick breath. "Mark, this looks pretty fancy. What kind of room did you get?"

"The right kind."

"But we didn't really need—"

"Yes, we did. Remember how we talked about letting go for a big splurge, even when your day-to-day living is more conservative?"

"Well, yes, but I still think—"

"Charlie, let yourself enjoy this. Let yourself pretend for one night that we're jet-setters. Maybe next weekend we'll go camping and rough it. But we can have fun with both, right?"

She gazed up at him. "You do know me."

"I think I do." He gave her a quick squeeze. "I need my jacket back. The keys are in the pocket." So were the three condoms the desk clerk had given him. He'd ditched the paper sack. He'd appreciated her delicacy in disguising what she was handing to him, but no way was he riding up the elevator to the Presidential Suite holding condoms in a paper sack. Jet-setters didn't do that.

Charlie handed him his coat. He didn't want to let go of her for even a minute, but he needed two hands to get the key out of the key folder in his pocket. Even so he fumbled once before he finally stuck the key in the lock and opened the door into a foyer.

Charlie gasped again. "Oh, Mark. This is… amazing."

"I think it's about right." He guided her into the entryway and his feet sank into thick carpet. A huge vase of flowers sat on a table in front of a large oval mirror, and soft music played somewhere in the interior of the suite.

"Look at these flowers," she said.

"I'm looking at you." His breathing quickened and he wanted her so much he felt dizzy. If he reached for her now, they'd make love right here on the floor.

But he thought they should absorb the ambiance of the place first. Tonight would be a very significant memory for both of them, and now that they were alone, he didn't want to rush it.

He smiled at her. "Go on in and look around. I'll lock up."

"All right," she said with an answering smile.

Closing the door and flipping the dead bolt, he took the time to transfer the condoms to his pants pocket before following Charlie down the short hallway.

In the doorway to the main part of the suite, she glanced over her shoulder at him. "I'll bet this is the best room in the entire hotel, isn't it?"

"Yep." He grinned, congratulating himself on making this choice. "I'm glad it was available."

"Well, so am I, because it's gorgeous. But you don't need to go making this a habit. I like simple things, too." She walked into the main room.

"I know." He leaned in the doorway and felt very proud of himself as he watched her. "I was listening, Charlie. For three months I've been listening. I know your favorite flowers are daisies. If I'd had more notice that we'd be here, I'd have filled the rooms with daisies."

She turned to gaze at him. "Don't even think of apologizing. I've never stayed in a place like this before. Not that I'm exactly *staying* here, of course."

"Yes, you are. You're staying here with me." He sure liked the sound of that.

"This is really stupendous." She spun in a slow circle. "You could have a party for fifty people in here."

"Let's not," he said as he surveyed the setting he'd chosen for his Charlie.

The lighting was subdued and elegant, the color scheme ivory and gold. The furniture looked antique, except perhaps for the longest sofa he'd ever seen in his life. He couldn't help thinking about what might be done with a sofa that big and luxurious.

Another huge vase of flowers sat on the coffee table, and a full-size dining table and eight chairs stood over by the floor-to-ceiling windows. The lights of the city shone through the sheer drapes covering the windows.

"No, let's not invite anyone but us," she agreed softly. "Two is the perfect number."

"I'm partial to that number, myself." He loved the sound of her voice. He'd begun to yearn for her even more after the first time he heard it on the telephone about three weeks ago. But hearing her voice on the phone didn't compare to listening in person and watching her lips move as she formed each word. He was mesmerized by her lips. He wanted to feel them over every inch of his body.

"Mark, I can't believe you rented this fabulous suite for our first night together. You make me feel so special."

He gazed at her standing in the middle of the ivory-and-gold room in her red, sexy dress, her color high, her eyes sparkling. "You *are* special," he said. "And the suite is nothing. But looking at you, knowing that we're finally alone—now that's about as special as it gets."

Her cheeks turned even pinker as she gestured to the doorway of the bedroom. "Shall we…see what the rest is like?"

"Absolutely." The rest was what interested him most. And when she started walking toward the bedroom, he knew exactly how he wanted this to start out. "Wait."

She turned back, a question in her eyes.

"I want to carry you through that doorway."

From the brilliance of her answering smile, he knew his instincts were right on. Tossing his coat on the long ivory sofa, he crossed the room and lifted her into his arms. Damn, but she felt good there.

She wrapped her arms around his neck and looked deep into his eyes. "It's as if you've set out to make all my dreams come true."

"I hope I can, because you're my dream come true." Heart pounding with anticipation, he carried her over the threshold.

Oh, yes, this room was the right choice. What a contrast with the one he was renting for him and Sam, with its typical quilted bedspreads covering a bed connected to a built-in headboard. Standard fare.

Not here. The dark antique furniture gleamed and gave a sense of permanence and tradition to the room. Mark wanted to create traditions with Charlie. They both loved holidays, and dogs, and lazy Sunday mornings. He laid her gently on a canopied bed covered in yards of white lace.

Her voice trembled. "Oh, Mark."

He leaned closer. "I'm here. Right here." He closed his eyes, almost tasting the kiss that would soon be his.

The bedside phone jangled.

He opened his eyes and looked into hers as the

phone rang again. They both turned their heads and looked at it. In keeping with the decor, the phone was a tasteful white-and-gold reproduction of an antique. That didn't make the noise it was giving out any more appealing to Mark.

"You know who it is," Charlie said.

"Yep."

"Maybe you should answer it, so they know we're okay."

He continued to stare at the ringing telephone, willing it to shut up. "Are you sure?"

"Yes."

With a sigh he reached over and picked up the delicate receiver. "Hello, Sam."

"Where the hell are you?" Sam's voice was tight with fury.

"I'm afraid I can't tell you that, but all is well."

"The hell it is. Damn it, Mark. I thought we had an agreement."

"And I'd planned to stick by it, but that was before I kissed Charlie." He glanced over at her and smiled. "That changed everything."

"You're hopeless, you know that? Totally hopeless!" Sam sounded terminally disgusted with him. "You're gonna make love to that woman, aren't you?"

Mark continued to gaze into Charlie's eyes. "Looks like it."

Sam let out a heavy sigh of frustration. "I shoulda

known you'd end up like this the minute I saw that red dress."

Charlie snuggled closer to Mark. "Ask him if he'd please take Ashley home, okay?"

Mark nodded. "Listen, Sam, Charlie wants to know if you'd take Ashley home."

"What if I refuse to do that unless you get your sorry ass down here?"

"I'm not coming down, and you're too much of a gentleman to leave Ashley in the lurch."

Sam blew out another breath. "I can't *believe* you did this. Well, yes, I can, but I don't want to. I want to wring your neck, but it seems I can't find out where you are without knocking on every damned door in the hotel, and I'd probably be arrested before I found the right one."

"Just give it up, Sam."

But Sam had more to say on the subject. "I hope you know you confused the hell out of the poor desk clerk. But, of course, like most women, she's fallen prey to your charms. I tried to bribe her to give me your room number, but she wouldn't."

"That has nothing to do with my charms. She'd lose her job if she gave out the room number."

Charlie smoothed her finger over his lower lip and smiled. "No, it's your charm."

"It's your charm," Sam echoed. "I told her I was a doctor and you were my brother and that it was up to me to give you your medication. All she'd let me do is call you on the house phone."

Mark chuckled. "Listen, I gotta go. Thanks for taking care of Ashley, buddy."

"Don't you *buddy* me. I just have one thing to say to you. If it's not too late already, don't you dare propose to her!"

Mark ignored that as he looked at Charlie. "Do you have any other messages for Sam?"

"Just ask him to tell Ashley that I'm fine, and I'll see her in the morning."

As Mark relayed the request he realized Charlie was unbuttoning his shirt.

"She won't be fine if you propose to her and then back out!" Sam bellowed. "If I can't stop you from doing the deed, at least don't propose to her!"

Charlie was pretty good at this button business. Soon she'd unfastened enough that she could pull apart his shirt and press her lips against his chest. He began to wonder what he was doing holding a telephone receiver to his ear when he could be doing much more interesting things.

"I think we've covered everything, Sam," he said. "I'll see you in the coffee shop tomorrow morning around ten, okay?"

"Don't *propose!*" Sam shouted.

"Good night, Sam."

As Charlie began to lick his nipples, he groaned

and tried to put the receiver back in its cradle. It took three tries, and all the while he could hear Sam shouting at him.

"What's he saying?" Charlie murmured, her breath warm against his skin as she nibbled and licked his bare chest.

"I have absolutely no idea." Mark let go of the receiver and abandoned himself to the joy of her moist kisses.

BREATHING IN THE SCENT of Mark's skin, Charlie felt like a kitten with her first taste of cream. The more she used her tongue to explore and excite him, the more she wanted to use it. He was delicious. Talk about a chemistry lesson. She'd never had this kind of basic hunger for a man's body in her life. She couldn't get his clothes off fast enough.

And then he interfered with her progress by grasping both hands right when she'd nearly unfastened his slacks. "Wait," he murmured.

"I want—"

"And I want you to." He rolled her onto her back, pressing her against the lace and satin coverlet as he kissed both her hands. "Soon. Not yet."

The coverlet under her bare back felt like a giant wedding ring pillow. She thought about that, and then Mark slipped his hand inside her dress and she couldn't think anymore.

Gazing into her eyes, he slowly stroked her breast. "Remember telling me how sensitive you are here?"

She trembled under the practiced touch of his hand. "Yes," she whispered. But she had never been this sensitive. And no man had ever caressed her this way, looking deep into her eyes while he touched her with infinite gentleness, infinite care. For the first time in her life she felt cherished by a lover.

"When you put on this dress, did you imagine me doing this?"

She nodded. But her imagination had failed her. She'd imagined him pulling the dress away in a frenzy of lust. This slow seduction, this building of anticipation for what was to come, was so much more exciting that she was shaking.

With a smooth movement of his hand, he stroked upward and pushed the dress off her shoulder. Still he held her gaze, postponing the moment when he would look at her. Heat shimmered in his eyes. "Did you imagine me undressing you?"

"Yes." She swallowed. "But I thought it would be fast."

"Did you?" He eased the dress off her other shoulder. "Even after you told me in a letter that you would like it to be slow and easy, to draw out the anticipation?"

"I thought…" She had trouble breathing. "I

thought…that would happen later. I thought that the first time you wouldn't be able to go slow."

"When it comes to loving you, I can do anything." He feathered a kiss over her lips. "Anything at all." Then he kissed her in earnest, making her mind spin and her body moisten while he slowly, carefully drew the top of her dress down to her waist.

He lifted his mouth a fraction. "Now lie still," he murmured. "Now that I can finally see your breasts, I want to take my time looking." There was a smile in his voice. "This is to satisfy the voyeur in me, and the tiny bit of exhibitionist in you."

"I'm not an—"

"Yes, you are. A tiny bit. Or you'd never have worn that dress. And I love that you wanted to show off for me. I hope you'll do it again. But I want my reward for being teased in the restaurant and on the dance floor. So don't rush me, Charlie."

She shivered with pleasure. He really had seen into the depths of her soul. She'd tested herself in other areas of her life, but never this way, and he knew she longed to push the envelope here, too. No wonder he'd never had a bad experience in bed with a woman. He paid attention, and he had perfect instincts.

Slowly he pushed himself to a sitting position and his gaze moved from her face to her breasts. He exhaled a deep breath. "Oh, Charlie. You were worth waiting for."

Her nipples tingled and tightened as he continued to look.

"You're so perfect," he said softly. "I love that tiny freckle beside your nipple."

She'd never been studied with such care, as if he were memorizing her and stroking her with his glance. A warm flush of arousal spread over her skin.

"You like me to look at you like this," he said, "don't you?"

"Can...can you tell?"

"Yes. By the way your nipples have darkened. They're so taut and ready. And your breasts are so rosy."

She moaned. "Oh, please. Please...kiss me there."

He leaned over her, the hair on his chest tickling her throbbing nipples. "I will." He nibbled at her mouth, her chin, her earlobes. "I will kiss you everywhere, Charlie. Even the places you think you're too shy for."

Her heart raced. So he remembered that, too. She'd confided that, although she was sexually adventurous, it might have to be coaxed out of her. He'd promised to make her feel uninhibited. The letters they'd written in those last few days had nearly scorched her hands as she'd read them.

"I had no appetite for dinner." His tongue found the hollow of her throat. "But I'm dying of hunger for you."

"Love me, Mark. I've waited so long." *All her life.* She tunneled her fingers in his hair, cupping his head as he trailed kisses along her collarbone and down the slope of her breast. When his mouth finally closed over her nipple, she cried out with pleasure.

Yet that was only the beginning. All God's creatures had a special talent, and she was learning Mark's. Somehow he knew…everything—when to move fast, when to slow down. When to lick and when to nibble. And where. Lord, did he know where.

She'd never known the underside of her breasts was an erogenous zone, or the spot right below her ribs, or her navel. By the time he'd dipped his tongue into that small hollow, she was a churning mass of needs, a shameless wanton who was so eager that, when he slipped both hands under her, she lifted away from the mattress so he could pull down the zipper of her dress.

"Ah, Charlie. I'll bet you want to show off those black panties for me."

"I do," she said breathlessly. But as he peeled her dress down, she realized she was still wearing her red high-heeled sandals. "My shoes—"

"Are staying on." His voice was gruff with passion. "That's for the slightly kinky streak we both have." He worked the dress over her feet, and his breath caught. "Oh, yeah. Black lace and red heels."

She quivered as he lifted her foot to run his tongue along her arch. Then he kissed the inside of her ankle and licked his way with maddening slowness up her quivering calf, all the while coaxing her legs farther apart.

"Feeling brave?" he murmured. Without waiting for an answer, he bent her leg and pressed his mouth against the back of her knee. Once he'd firmly established that she loved being kissed there by making her moan and writhe on the bed, he began a lazy journey up her inner thigh.

She clutched the coverlet and struggled for breath. "The lights," she said as an attack of modesty struck. "I wish you'd turn off—"

"Nope."

"But—"

His warm breath reminded her exactly where he was, hovering over the elastic of her panties. Tiny kisses punctuated his words. "You told me you might need to be pushed a little."

"I don't remember." But she did. She'd been so daring on paper.

"I do. And I'm pushing." His tongue traced the ridge of elastic circling her thigh. "Let me love you, Charlie, with the lights on."

Her heart had never beat so fast in her life, not even when she'd hung over a hundred-foot chasm on the end of a rope. "I'm sort of…scared."

He nipped the elastic with his teeth. "And sort of excited?"

Her throat felt tight. "Yes."

"Be patient, Charlie." His lingering kisses moved up the side seam of her panties and across the bikini-line top. "In a few seconds you won't be scared at all."

She lay there trembling uncontrollably. Her view of the white canopy over her head blurred as he moved lower, his lips brushing the lace, his tongue tracing its pattern. At last he pressed his mouth against the wet material covering his ultimate destination. The heat of his mouth and the firm pressure shot straight through to her womb and she gasped.

He breathed in. "Mmm. So sweet." He nuzzled her through the thin layer of satin.

Oh, that was good. Oh, that was *very* good. Her limbs grew heavy as a warm, syrupy feeling slipped through her body. And a wonderful tingling, tightening sensation swirled right *there*. Oh, yes. More of that. More…

And then, with casual ease, he pulled the material aside, leaving nothing between her and his hot, seeking tongue. No defenses. No fear. No restraint. Free-fall. Soft cries spilled from her lips as he coaxed her toward surrender.

And when her climax arrived, her response tumbled around them. Wild with the joy of it, she arched into his liquid caress and called his name, over and over, until she collapsed back upon the coverlet, eyes closed, breath coming in ragged spurts.

Gently he drew her panties off, and she could barely summon the strength to help him.

"You've…turned me into a rag doll," she murmured, so warm and contented as she watched him leave the bed and begin removing the rest of his clothes.

His glance swept over her. "A rag doll in red shoes. I couldn't ask for more."

"But I won't…be any fun."

"Sure you will," he said softly as he tossed his shirt across a nearby wing chair. "Give yourself a little time to recover, and you'll be dynamite." He kicked off his shoes and made short work of his socks.

"I may never recover." She gazed at him while he took off his slacks. Then he shoved down his briefs. "Then again…."

His smile was slow and easy, the smile of a man who knew what to do with the generous gift he'd been given. "You're recovering already." He levered himself onto the mattress.

She couldn't believe how the sight of his erect penis affected her. He'd just given her a shattering orgasm, and yet she was beginning to ache all over again. "Now look who's beautiful," she murmured, sliding her hand down the velvet length of his shaft.

"And holding on by a thread," he said in a thick voice.

"But I want to touch you." She wrapped her fingers around that tempting toy. "I want to—"

"Don't I wish," he said, gasping as he carefully re-moved her hand. He turned toward the bedside table and picked up a foil-wrapped condom. "I thought maybe we could fool around a little, but not this time. My control's shot."

She wasn't about to argue with him. The hollow-ness within her begged for what he had to give. She grew moist and ready just watching him roll the con-dom on.

He finished putting it on and glanced at her. "Maybe it's the shoes. I'm going crazy wanting to make love to you, knowing you're still wearing those sexy shoes."

She felt a quick stab of fear. The shoes were noth-ing like she usually wore. Tonight she'd gone for the glamour look, but she'd never be able to keep up that image on a regular basis. She smiled, to make her comment sound like a joke. "So you'd lose interest if I happened to be barefoot?"

He laughed and pulled her into his arms. "Not a chance."

"Usually I wear running shoes."

He nuzzled her neck. "While you're making love?"

"No." She was losing her train of thought. He was so good, so very good at this. "I mean... I'm not the high-heel type. I'm the running-shoes type."

He eased her to her back and his voice was soft as

he moved between her thighs. "Please don't run away from me, Charlie."

She looked up into his brown eyes, so filled with desire for her. *Oh, please let this be real.* "I'm not running."

"Neither am I." He probed gently, then slid deep with a satisfied groan. "Oh, Charlie." His voice caught. "I belong here."

"Yes." She held on tight, afraid to move. A feeling this perfect didn't come along every day. Being completely united with Mark was like having every good moment in her life distilled into one pure drop of happiness. He was an ice cream cone on a hot day, a campfire on a chilly night, wildflowers in the spring and pumpkins in October.

Staying perfectly still and locked tight within her, he searched her gaze with his. "Maybe it was only letters." He combed his fingers tenderly through her hair. "But my heart was in those letters."

She swallowed. "Mine, too."

"But still I signed them *Cheers,* or *Take Care.*"

She had, too, been careful. So careful.

"I wanted to write *Love, Mark.*"

Her heart swelled with an almost painful happiness. "You did?"

He nodded, and his voice grew husky. "I love you, Charlie. Even before tonight, I've loved you. I knew you'd be like this, so warm and beautiful and *right.*"

Her throat tightened with emotion as she trembled on the brink of tears. If he could dare such a statement, so could she. After all, it was the truth. She'd fallen more in love with him with each letter, even though she'd never been bold enough to sign hers that way, either, even though she'd been afraid of getting hurt.

She gazed into his eyes. "I love you, too."

He closed his eyes. "Thank God." When he opened them again, his eyes were luminous. "Then you don't think I'm crazy."

"No. Not unless we both are."

"Then be crazy with me." He began to move within her. "Be crazy in love with me."

All her doubts evaporated in the heat of his loving. They moved together as if they'd been born to bring each other pleasure. But soon even the word *pleasure* was too tame for the forces building within her.

Wild and unrestrained, her response dwarfed that first spike of temporary excitement he'd given her at first. Wonderful though it had been, it seemed minor now—an amusement park water slide compared to a plunge through raging currents as they headed for a thundering waterfall. With each powerful thrust he brought them closer to the edge.

"Be with me," he whispered urgently.

"*Yes.*" The waterfall pounded in her ears. Her body rose and fell with the turbulence of their mating.

"Be with me always."

"Oh, yes. *Yes.*" Her cries blended with his as she tumbled over with him, both of them hurtling toward a cataclysmic release. And through it all she held onto him for dear life. For life.

Afterward they lay sprawled together on the coverlet, both of them gasping for breath.

Finally Mark dragged himself up on one elbow and gazed down at her. "So it's settled, then. We're getting married."

She smiled at him through tears of happiness. "Of course we are."

CHAPTER SEVEN

SAM SPEWED HIS COFFEE halfway across the table. "You did *what?*"

"Take it easy, okay?" Mark glanced around at the other customers in the hotel coffee shop. "People are staring."

"That's because they've probably never seen a bigger idiot in their lives! Make that two. I'm an even bigger one than you for imagining for a minute that this might not happen. Of course it was going to happen, because you are doomed to—"

"Sam, she's the one. This is it."

Sam began mopping up the table. "Now there's an original line. Let me see. Have I ever heard that one before? Oh, come to think of it, I have. Only about *five times.* Dear Lord in heaven."

Mark had expected this reaction. He'd called wolf too many times. But Sam had to understand this time was for real. He leaned closer. "I swear to you, it's true. I'll swear on anything you want. My Astros

season tickets. If I screw this up, you can have mine
and give them to whoever you want sitting next to
you this season."

"If you screw this up, you won't dare appear in
public, so you might as well hand over those tickets,
and the Oilers tickets, while you're at it."

"Sam, I'll put anything you want on the line. My
car, my DVD player, my CD collection, my pool cue."

"Your pool cue?" Sam glanced up from his mopping. "Now that would make things interesting. I've
always coveted that pool cue. But don't be giving me
your Billy Bass. I don't want a singing fish."

"You're trying to make a joke out of this, but I'm not
kidding. What can I do to convince you I'm sincere?"

"Oh, I believe you're sincere." Sam tossed his
soggy napkin on the plate and grabbed a fresh one to
blot the coffee from his mustache.

"Then what's the problem?"

Sam looked extremely weary. "Just because you
believe all this now doesn't mean you'll believe it
later. You're sincere as hell until you figure out that
good sex doesn't make up for a tendency to nag, or
to gossip endlessly on the cell phone, or to run up the
credit cards buying expensive clothes, or to hate hiking and camping, or to be a terminally boring con-
versationalist. Have I covered all the fatal flaws that
have dynamited your impending nuptials?"

"That's just it." Mark grew desperate to convince

Sam that this time was different. "Charlie doesn't have any of those flaws. We've been through it all in the letters. We really are compatible, Sam. The whole *Texas Men* magazine idea of yours worked like a charm."

"Letters aren't enough." Sam pushed away his plate and leaned back in the booth. "As I've said about a million times, you have to spend time with her, and time spent doing the hootchie-coo doesn't count. You never notice a woman's flaws during those moments, because you're so in love with the whole concept of sex. One of *your* biggest flaws is that you're too damned good in bed. It's a real failing."

Mark laughed. Despite the seriousness of the moment, he couldn't help it. Nobody had ever accused him of being too good in bed. "Failing?"

"Yes, failing! Women sense your inborn talent and flock to you as a result. You naturally accommodate them, and you do it so well that neither one of you is left with a brain cell working. You're every woman's fantasy in the beginning, but before the sad story plays out, you're every woman's nightmare."

"Not Charlie's. I won't be Charlie's nightmare. We're perfect for each other."

He sighed. "I suppose that's always possible, but I want you two to have a long, long courtship before I even think about renting a tuxedo."

"We're planning to get married in two weeks."

Sam's eyes widened. "You're kidding."

"Nope. The sooner the better. It'll be a small ceremony, so—"

"It'll be a nonexistent ceremony. We're going to
fix this." He glanced at his watch. "You say she left
for home about an hour ago, so she's had time to
change clothes and relax a little. We'll drive over
there right now and tell her you were a bit premature.
Hug, hug, kiss, kiss, cancel, cancel. Come on."

"No."

Sam gave him a warning look. "Then I guess you
really want Jack to be your best man."

The thought made Mark's stomach churn. "No, I
want you to be my best man. But if you don't feel
you can stand up with me in two weeks, then I'll ask
Jack. Because I am marrying Charlie the Saturday
after next."

Sam's steely gaze wavered. "You'd really ask
Jack?"

"If I have to."

"And I suppose Ashley will be the maid of honor."

"That's who Charlie's planning to ask." He sensed
a weak spot in Sam's armor. Judging from Sam's earlier comments, he and Ashley had gotten along great.
They hadn't made as much progress as he and Charlie, but they'd become very friendly before Sam had
kissed Ashley good-night at her door in the wee hours
of the morning.

Mark cleared his throat. "I'm sure Jack and Ashley will enjoy each other's company," he said casually.

Sam's jaw clenched. "Oh, I wouldn't doubt that. I know Jack."

"We're planning something very simple. Just a best man for me and a maid of honor for Charlie. No other attendants. Just Charlie, me, Ashley, and… Jack, I guess. A late afternoon ceremony, followed by an intimate little dinner with family and friends, probably at the same restaurant where we ate last night, because that's where Charlie and I first met face-to-face."

"Do you hear yourself?" Sam grumbled. "You met her *last night*. And now you're planning the wedding."

"When we actually met isn't the point. We're in sync, Charlie and me. I suggested Jamaica for the honeymoon and she can hardly wait. We'll leave that next morning." He paused. "I suppose Jack will stay in Austin on Saturday night, maybe even do some sightseeing with Ashley the next day."

Sam gazed into his coffee mug. "You are such a damned pain in the ass. You know perfectly well I don't want Jack hanging around Austin."

"Then be my best man, okay? This is it—the very last time I'll ever ask you."

"Okay." Sam glanced up at him. "But I swear to God, if you back out this time, I'm going to join the DOA Support Group. I'll be a T-shirt-wearing, card-carrying member, maybe even president, and your life won't be worth living."

"I understand. It isn't going to happen." Mark remembered all the morning-after sessions with Sam when he'd announced his five other proposals. In all those other sessions he'd never felt so elated, so sure, so completely happy as he did at this moment. "Trust me."

Sam sighed and pushed his plate away. "I have no choice. I can't have you standing up there with Jack, and I especially can't have Jack standing up there with Ashley. He's not even remotely good enough for her. Now come on, let's get out of this joint."

"Fine with me." Mark was too excited to eat, anyway. "I have a bunch of things to do. Charlie and I are going camping next weekend, so that leaves me less time to take care of the details."

Sam stood. "At least you're taking her camping. That's a good sign." He sighed. "Maybe this will work out. But I'm afraid to hope. The setup is too sickeningly familiar for me to have hope."

"It will work out." Mark paid the bill and they both walked out carrying their garment bags over their shoulders.

In no time they were on the freeway bound for Houston, with Mark singing along to the radio. He felt great.

"I assume you told her about your other engagements, at least," Sam said.

"Uh, not exactly."

"Not *exactly?*" Sam reached over and switched off the radio. "What the hell does that mean?"

"I couldn't tell her right then, Sam. She was so happy, and I was so happy."

"And Mr. Happy was so happy. Lord Almighty, you are a piece of work. And when are you planning to break the news?"

"Next weekend will be perfect." He switched the radio back on, determined to maintain the good mood he was in. "We'll have plenty of time and we'll be out in the woods, enjoying nature. That's a much better time to tell her."

Sam turned the radio off again. "I'm not so sure. You'll be all alone out there. Nowhere to run if she gets homicidal."

"She won't. You really do worry too much."

"And you don't worry enough!"

"She'll be fine with it. You'll see." Mark punched the button for the radio, although his mood wasn't quite as jolly as it had been. Sam had found his only source of doubt, which was just like Sam—always looking at the horse poop instead of the pony.

But in this case, the horse poop might make a difference. Revealing his past was the only thing that scared him about this engagement. Each of the other women had known way ahead of time. They'd taken it as a challenge to try and break the curse.

He wasn't sure if Charlie would take that attitude. Therefore he wanted the setting and the mood to be just right before he told her about his miserable record with weddings. It was a touchy subject, no question.

Sam threw up his hands. "Well, maybe I won't have to worry about you running out on her. Maybe when you finally confess your sins next weekend, she'll push you over a cliff or drown you in the river. End of story."

THREE DAYS LATER, Charlie entered her apartment feeling very grubby from leading city slickers on a three— day hike through the hill country. The message light was blinking on her answering machine, and she knew some of those flashing signals were from Mark. Her darling Mark. How she missed him.

She wanted to call him back immediately, but she also hoped to spend at least an hour on the phone with him when she did. Before that she needed to stop by Glam Girl and discuss a few details of the wedding with Ashley.

Then, once she was in for the night, she could call Mark. Maybe she'd run herself a nice deep bubble bath and call him while she was in the tub. That could be fun.

After dumping off her gear, she hopped back in her dusty Miata and drove toward Ashley's shop. It was nearly five. Her timing was perfect. Maybe she and Ashley could go out for a bite to eat, since Charlie didn't think she had a thing in the house worth cooking.

Once she was married, Mark would handle the kitchen chores, and she was looking forward to that. He'd said he loved to cook, and with his sensuous nature she figured he was probably really good at it. Oh, he was sensuous, all right. They'd gotten very little sleep the rest of the night she'd spent in the suite with him. This weekend would be more of the same, except they'd be inside a tent.

Or maybe they'd try a change of scene. She fantasized making love to him in the middle of a little glen, where the wild grass grew thick enough to make a spongy carpet. Just thinking of that made her hot. She'd better direct her mind elsewhere if she expected to have a coherent conversation with Ashley.

Ashley hadn't been overjoyed with the news at first, but she'd come around. Once she'd realized Charlie was totally in love, Ashley had started believing the wedding might be a good thing. Both sisters would miss living in the same town, but Houston wasn't so far away. As an added perk, Ashley would have an excuse to spend more time with Sam.

Charlie was relieved once her sister came on

board. Besides appreciating her moral support, she needed her for some practical matters. Ashley had more of a flair for wedding-related details than Charlie, and her contacts in retail would help them come up with two dresses on short notice. Fortunately, Ashley was willing to do any necessary alterations herself.

Their parents had been another tough sell, but at last they'd given their blessing and had promised to fly down for the ceremony. This weekend Mark planned to call them before he drove back to Houston, so he could start getting acquainted, at least by telephone.

She'd suggested calling his mother, too, but Mark seemed to think his mother would respond better if they told her after they were married. That was the only aspect of the wedding that bothered Charlie. She couldn't imagine any mother preferring to hear about her son's wedding after the fact. But Mark had said he'd explain all about his mother next weekend on the camping trip, when they had more time to talk.

Then he'd kissed her again, and before long she hadn't had the slightest interest in discussing his mother. But she'd thought about the situation several times since then, and she was curious. His mother lived right in Houston. Since Mark's airline pilot father had been killed in a crash ten years ago, his mother Selena was his closest family member. Not inviting her bothered Charlie more than she wanted to admit, and she hoped to change Mark's mind.

She parked diagonally in front of Glam Girl next to a minivan. As she walked toward the shop she noticed that Ashley had several customers inside. She was happy for Ashley, who could always use the business, but she'd hoped Ashley would be finished for the day so they could talk about the wedding.

When she opened the door, her first impression was that all the women in the shop belonged to some kind of team. They wore identical T-shirts in deep purple with a logo on the front.

Ashley glanced toward the door as Charlie walked in. "Charlie, these women are here to see you. When you didn't answer your phone, they came here to find out if I knew when you'd be back."

"That's right," said a tall brunette. "We—"

"I'll give you what information I can," Charlie said, "but you'll need to make your actual reservation through the company." So they weren't Ashley's customers, but potential customers for Charlie. So much the better. With all the changes coming in her life, she could use the money.

"It's not an outdoor adventure they're after, Charlie." Ashley walked over and put an arm around her shoulders.

Charlie looked at her expression and flashed back fifteen years. Ashley had worn this expression and had used the same arm-around-the-shoulder routine when she'd had to break the news that the family dog had disappeared.

Panic set in, tightening her chest. "Is Mark okay?"

"Mark's fine," Ashley said.

"Then what's the problem?"

All the women faced her now, each regarding her with pity. Something was definitely wrong, but instinct told her she didn't want to know what it was or even who these people were. Their logo was a donkey kicking some poor guy clear into next week, and DOA was spelled out in large white letters above the picture. Kind of gruesome all the way around, she thought.

"There might not be a problem," Ashley said. She kept her arm snugly around Charlie. "But you owe it to yourself to hear what they have to say."

The tall brunette with striking gray eyes stepped forward. She had an air of polish and authority about her. "Charlie, I'm Deb Creighton," she said. "I guess you could call me the ringleader." Then she turned to the other four and introduced each one.

Still totally confused, Charlie listened as Deb introduced Carrie, the redhead on the end with the wire-framed glasses. She looked like the intellectual of the group. Next to her was Jenna, who wore her long blond hair loose around her shoulders and

looked as if she'd be happiest spending time on the
Gulf, catching rays. Then came Phyllis, a slender
woman with shiny black hair, and Hannah, an ath-
letic-looking type whose taffy-colored hair was
nearly as short as Charlie's.

Looking closer, Charlie saw that each one of the
women had her name embroidered on her shirt, along
with a date. Aside from wearing these team shirts, the
women had one other thing in common—they were all
very attractive. Extremely attractive. Charlie wondered
if they'd been in the same beauty pageant which they'd
won in the year stitched onto the purple material.

After making the introductions, Deb cleared her
throat. "So here's the deal. On Monday I found out that
Mark O'Grady proposed to you over the weekend."

Ashley's fingers tightened on her shoulder and
Charlie's stomach pitched. "That's true," she said.

Deb looked her straight in the eye. "We're here
to try and talk you out of it. You see, we—"

"Talk me out of it? Why on earth would—"

"Listen to their story," Ashley said. "Then you'll
know."

"In the past seven years," Deb continued, "Mark
has made and then canceled wedding plans with each
of us. I'm the latest victim."

Charlie gasped. This couldn't be happening. She
was having a horrible nightmare and any minute
she'd wake up.

"In my case," Deb went on relentlessly, "he called it off ten minutes before the ceremony."

Charlie clutched her stomach. "Ten minutes?"

"I got two days' notice," said Jenna with a flip of her blond hair.

"I got one," said Phyllis.

Carrie adjusted her glasses and held up her hand, fingers outstretched. "Five hours."

"I was the luckiest," Hannah said. "I had four whole days advance notice."

Charlie wanted to run, but she felt weighed down, as if she might be dreaming this. She prayed that she was.

"I know this is a shock," Deb said, her gaze filled with compassion. "But, believe me, every single one of us would have given anything to know in advance, so that we could have avoided the heartbreak and humiliation."

Everyone nodded in agreement.

"But we've all been where you are." Phyllis tucked her dark hair behind her ears. "And we know that breaking off with him will be tough. Let's face it, he's fantastic in bed."

Charlie blushed. If this was a dream, that part was true enough.

"That's the hell of it," said Deb. "He's *wonderful* in bed. The best any of us has ever had. It's hard to totally despise the guy when he's…well, so talented in that area. Unfortunately, he has this bad habit of proposing after your first night together and then, when you're down to the wire, he cancels the wedding. Apparently he loves to get engaged, hates to get married."

Charlie's head began to hurt.

"He's a serial fiancé," said Jenna.

Charlie put her fingers to her pounding temples. "I can't...I can't believe this. I can't believe that what he said to me...was all a lie."

"Oh, it wasn't all a lie," said Deb. "He believes every word when he says it. But then he changes his mind. After I quit crying, I decided to track down his other fiancées, who all still lived in the Houston area, and we formed this support group."

"It's been wonderful for all of us," said Hannah. "We meet once a month, rotating among our apartments. We talk, drink wine, eat take-out, play Uno, trash Mark."

"Driving down to Austin to warn you is our first official project," said Carrie, earnestly peering at her through her glasses. "We're here to support you, to help you be strong, to make you see what has to be done. We can't let him claim another one of our own."

Charlie stared at them, feeling numb. "I can't believe it. I just can't believe it. He loves me!"

Deb nodded, her eyes full of sympathy. "I'm sure

he does. For now. Until he decides that something about you just won't do. Then it's *adios, muchacha.*"

"No." Charlie shook her head. "He wouldn't do that. We've been writing to each other for three months. We've discussed *everything.*"

"Did you discuss his mother?" Deb asked quietly.

A chill went through her. "I know…I know he wants to tell her after we're married instead of inviting her." She realized how damning that information was, now.

"I was number three," Carrie said gently. "After he jilted me, his mother refused the invitation for the next two. She told him to let her know after the marriage license had been signed, and she'd welcome her new daughter-in-law. She was tired of getting emotionally involved with us and then having to cut us loose again."

Charlie wished it didn't all make sense. But it did. Sometime during their wonderful night together, she'd told herself that Mark was too good to be true. Apparently he was. She gazed dully at their-T-shirts. She was afraid to ask, but she had to know. "What do those letters stand for?"

Deb's gaze was unflinching. "Damn O'Grady's Ass."

CHAPTER EIGHT

AFTER CHARLIE FINALLY convinced the DOAs to go back to Houston by promising them she'd stay in touch, she collapsed into the Queen Anne chair Ashley kept beside the three-way mirror. She'd never felt this tired, not even after her rim-to-rim hike through the Grand Canyon. But underneath her exhaustion boiled red-hot fury.

Ashley knelt in front of her and clasped both her hands. "Go ahead and cry, sweetie."

"I don't feel like crying." Her voice was tight and hard. "I feel like sending him over Niagara Falls in a barrel. And I will, once my muscles start working again."

"If that's what you want, I'll help you."

Charlie gazed at her sister and wondered what was strange about Ashley's reaction. Then she realized that Ashley didn't sound angry. Given the circumstances, she would have expected Ashley to be rounding up a posse and heading for Houston to avenge her little sister's honor.

What was it Ashley had said before the women dropped their bombshell? *There might not be a problem.* Yet when she'd said that, she'd known all about Mark's five broken engagements.

Ashley squeezed her hands. "I can tell you're still in shock. Let's go down the street and order up a couple of *margaritas grande.* That should help."

"Okay. But how come you're so calm?" Charlie stared at her in bewilderment. "Why aren't you foaming at the mouth? Or saying *I told you so?* Could anything be much worse than this?"

Ashley took a deep breath. "Not on the surface of it, no. But those women had been here close to an hour before you showed up. In that time I had a chance to scope them out, and none of them are like you."

Charlie's laugh was bitter. "They're all gorgeous, if that's what you mean. I feel pretty damned insecure knowing Mark was engaged to that bunch."

"You're gorgeous, too," Ashley said. "But putting that aside for now, keep in mind that he didn't marry any of them. Maybe you're his type and none of them are. I don't think you should be too hasty, here."

Charlie's jaw dropped. Then she began making the points she'd expected Ashley to be ticking off. "Look, we don't know for an absolute certainty that I'm his type, and his record is five canceled weddings."

"I know, but—"

"Worse than that, he's been writing to me for three

months, and in all that time he failed to mention this. Then he made love to me, *and* proposed, right on schedule. Obviously that's his M.O. I can reasonably expect him to cancel this wedding, too. Why wouldn't he?"

"Because Sam had a hand in the matchmaking this time."

"I know that. Mark told me the magazine ad was Sam's idea. So what? That only means Sam's an accomplice to the crime." She peered at Ashley with growing suspicion. "Did Sam tell you about all these engagements? Because if he did, and you didn't tell me, I'll—"

"No, he didn't tell me," Ashley said quickly. "But he did mention that Mark had been having a little trouble finding someone he could be ready to make a lifetime commitment to."

"A *little* trouble? That's like saying Alaska has a little trouble growing coconuts!" Charlie's energy returned. "Forget the margaritas. Let's drive up to Houston right now. I'm ready to do some serious damage to a certain stockbroker, and I have phone numbers for several women who will help me."

"We can if you want." Ashley stood and started pacing. "But before we head off, stop and think. Why do you think Mark put that ad in the magazine? He obviously can get dates without advertising."

In the past half hour, Charlie had become quite

cynical. "We don't know that, either. I'll bet the word is out on him in Houston. He probably can't get a date there anymore, so he needed the magazine to find new victims."

"I don't think so. I think Sam helped him analyze the problem, and the magazine was the answer. From what Sam said, the two of them took it very seriously, combing through the letters until they came up with you, someone who seemed perfectly matched to him. I think it's possible that they concocted this whole project to make sure there were no more broken engagements."

"Then why didn't he tell me that?"

"I'm guessing he was afraid to," Ashley said. "What would you have done if he'd confessed everything in his letters? Would you have been as excited about getting to know him?"

Charlie had to admit that she likely would have been turned off by the information. Before she'd met him, knowing such a thing might have made her much more wary. They certainly wouldn't have spent the night together on the first date.

Thinking about that night made her even madder. She'd been a lamb to the slaughter, dazzled by the luxury of the room, the luxury of an excellent lover. The Presidential Suite, indeed. "He should have told me before he proposed."

Ashley nodded. "I agree. And I don't want to keep

making excuses for him. Still, it would be a difficult subject to bring up." She sighed. "Maybe I shouldn't even be saying all these things. If you're ready to break it off with him, then do it. I wouldn't blame you. Nobody would."

"Some people would throw me a party." She gave Ashley a world-weary smile. "The DOAs are dying to have Mark be on the receiving end of a canceled wedding. Did you hear Deb ask if I'd consider going along with the wedding until five minutes before the ceremony?"

"Yes, and it's not your job to be the vehicle of their revenge. I can understand their feelings, but this is your life."

Charlie would love to accept all of Ashley's arguments, but she was so afraid she'd end up wearing a purple T-shirt. "You said none of them were like me. How were they different?" she asked finally.

"Well, Deb has a serious cell phone habit which drove me nuts, so I can imagine it would bother Mark. Jenna, the one with the long blond hair and the nice tan, is a shopaholic. She bought several hundred dollars' worth of stuff in no time and stashed it in the van. I think she would have bought more except her credit card was maxed out at that point."

A dim ray of hope began to penetrate Charlie's despair. "Mark and I discussed cell phones and excessive shopping in our letters."

Ashley gazed at her. "See? He's trying not to make another mistake."

"But what about Hannah, the one with the short hair? She looked athletic, like she could be an outdoor person, a hiker and camper."

"Well, she's not." Ashley leaned against the counter. "I wondered about her, too, so I asked. She prefers gyms. I also heard her scolding Jenna about buying so much, sort of like she was her mother or something. Some guys don't mind that kind of overprotective attitude, but Mark might."

"He does. He told me he hates being nagged."

Ashley nodded. "There you go. I think the guy is trying to work this out, Charlie."

"Maybe." Charlie sighed. "Of course I'd love to believe that, but I don't know, sis." She massaged her temples. "Tell me about the other two."

"Carrie, the one with the glasses, is very sweet, but she needs to find someone who's as excited about ancient languages as she is. It's all she talks about. As for Phyllis, the sleek, dark-haired one, she hates camping even more than the rest, but not a single one likes it."

Charlie turned all the information over in her mind. She couldn't deny that Mark had discussed these very things in his letters, although he'd never mentioned former girlfriends, and certainly not exfiancées. But then she hadn't named names when she'd brought up a few of her pet peeves. That hadn't seemed necessary.

"I don't mean to imply they're not all terrific women," Ashley said. "But Deb needs somebody who's into cell phone communication, and Jenna had better find either a millionaire or somebody who can put her on a budget. Some guys like to be mothered, and Hannah would be perfect for someone like that. Carrie ought to date only college professors in her field, and Phyllis should stick with urban types."

Charlie stood and walked over to the glass door of the shop to stare out at the traffic going by. She wondered if everyone else had this much trouble finding Mr. or Ms. Right. "I still wish he'd told me about all this before he proposed," she said.

"I do, too." Ashley came over and put her arm around her. "Maybe he's planning to confess everything this weekend when you go camping."

"Maybe he is, but that doesn't change the fact that he's canceled five weddings right before the ceremony. Maybe there's something about me that will turn him off and he'll cancel this one, too."

"You could postpone."

Charlie's gut tightened. "That doesn't feel like the solution. I'd only be dragging out the suspense."

"Then stop seeing him."

Her head told her to do that. Her heart rebelled.

"I probably should, but I...damn it, I don't want to. Not if there's a chance this could be for real."

"Then I have a suggestion," Ashley said. "This weekend you could be a pain in the butt."

Charlie glanced at her. "Excuse me?"

Ashley turned, a conspiratorial light in her eyes. "Whether his intentions are good or bad, he deserves to catch some grief for not telling you the whole truth."

"He sure does," Charlie said with feeling.

"Then go camping with him, but don't be the perfect companion. You could pretend to be sick, refuse to have sex with him and put him through a miserable weekend of playing nursemaid."

Charlie's heart began to lift a little. Torturing Mark sounded much better than cutting off all contact. "I could forget the wine and burn the food. I could make sure there were rocks under his side of the tent."

"You could slather mosquito repellent on yourself and then forget where you put the bottle."

"I could accidentally dump water on his sleeping bag."

Ashley grinned. "You're getting the idea. And all the time you're waiting to see if he confesses, you can test the heck out of his commitment."

"In other words, I'll make his life a living hell for two days and see if he cracks."

"That's right."

Charlie began to smile, too. "I could get into that."

CAMPING WITH the woman of his dreams was going to be heaven, Mark thought as they neared the turn-off to the campground. At the perfect moment, maybe as they were lying naked in the tent after making love, he'd give her the engagement ring he'd bought this week.

He'd agonized over the stone and setting, but he thought he had it right. A ring box would have been too awkward to tuck in his jeans pocket, so he'd asked for a small velvet pouch, instead.

He could hardly wait for the moment he would slip the ring on her finger. He'd left work early so they could score a campsite before dark. Fortunately the weather was unseasonably cool and the wild-flowers hadn't started blooming yet.

Although he would have loved to spend their first outing surrounded by bluebonnets and Indian paint brush, they'd have been surrounded by hundreds of other campers, as well.

Better to have some privacy. In fact, he was hoping for lots of privacy. As he pulled the Lexus into the sparsely populated campground, pleasure surged through him at the prospect of spending nearly two full days with Charlie.

She hadn't been very chatty on the drive out here, but he wasn't the kind of guy who liked constant con-versation. Carrie's nonstop monologues used to make him desperate for silence.

Besides, he imagined Charlie might be a little tired after spending the week backpacking with two different groups. Before they'd left he'd offered her the option of checking into a luxury hotel instead. He'd been so eager to have a camper for a fiancée that he hadn't considered that this could be a busman's holiday for her.

But his Charlie was a real trouper. She'd insisted they go camping as planned, and had guided him to one of her favorite spots in the hill country. The rolling, tree-studded landscape fed his soul after spending five days in the city. He felt privileged to be here with her.

Sam hadn't been so lucky this weekend. He'd hoped to spend time with Ashley, but he'd been called out of town on business. They'd have to wait until the wedding to resume their relationship.

Charlie surveyed the sites as Mark drove slowly through the campground. "Let's take that one over there." She pointed to a vacant spot near a shallow creek.

"Looks perfect." He pulled into the adjacent parking area and wondered how quickly they could set up the tent. Six days without holding Charlie had made him very eager. He'd discovered that even when Charlie dressed in jeans and a flannel shirt, she made his mouth water. He shut off the engine and reached for the door handle.

"No, wait. Maybe that one over there would be better." She pointed to one farther down the road.

"Okay." He didn't much care. He just wanted to get the tent up. Starting the engine, he backed out and drove a few hundred yards down to the next site. He didn't think it was quite as picturesque, but he didn't plan to spend much time admiring the scenery.

Once again he killed the engine and opened the door to get out. God, but it smelled great—a combination of wood smoke, dried leaves and the evergreen scent of cypress down by the creek. And Charlie liked being here. He was so lucky to have found her.

"I was wrong," Charlie said. "The other site is better."

"Good. I think so, too." So she was being a little indecisive today. Everyone was entitled to that once in a while. In no time at all they'd have set up camp, and then...then he could start making love to this wonderful woman. After that, he'd slip the ring on her finger.

He backed out and drove to her original choice.

"You know, maybe this is too close to the creek," she said. "It might be colder and damper than the other one."

He chuckled. Yeah, he knew what this was all about. She wanted their first camping experience to be perfect, and neither one of these spots was perfect, because no site would be.

Turning off the engine, he gave her a tender smile. "Either of these sites will be like Shangri-La if you're here with me. Next to the creek, or not so close to the creek, it makes no difference. So you can stop worrying about it, okay?"

"Okay."

He'd expected her to smile back, but she didn't. "Charlie, is something wrong? Because if you don't like either of these sites, we can go looking some more. I just thought—"

"I was thinking the creek might make too much noise."

"Too much noise? Didn't you tell me you loved the sound of gurgling water?"

"As long as I don't have a headache."

"And you have a headache?"

"Uh-huh."

"Well, damn." He reached over and stroked her cheek. "Have you taken anything for it?"

"Not yet. It just came on a little while ago."

His hopes for a quick setup and immediate gratification began to dwindle. Not only that, he wasn't about to give her a ring when she wasn't feeling well. "Did you bring anything for a headache?" He knew he hadn't. Camping always took away his headaches, so he never had the need.

"I'm pretty sure I have something in my backpack."

"Then let's get it." He popped the trunk and was

out of the car in no time. For some reason he hadn't figured a headache into his plans. But people got headaches, after all. And maybe in an hour or so hers would be gone. He'd waited six days. He could wait another hour.

Opening the ice chest stowed in the trunk, he took out a bottle of water and carried it, along with her backpack, up to the passenger side of the car. She hadn't opened the door yet, so he did it.

Then he crouched down next to her seat. "Tell me where to look, and I'll get the pills out for you."

She opened her eyes and turned her head toward him.

His breath caught. She was so beautiful, and her lips so full and sweet. They'd shared one brief kiss when he'd picked her up. It hadn't been near enough. "I've heard that having a good orgasm can cure a headache," he said softly.

A response stirred in her eyes. But then she sat up and took the backpack from him. "Thanks, but I think I'll go with ibuprofen this time." She zipped open a compartment in the backpack and sifted through the contents.

He tried not to feel rejected. He'd had headaches before, and they could really make you cranky. When she came up with a small container of capsules, he took the cap off the water and handed her the bottle. "Here you go."

"Thanks." She tossed a couple of pills in her mouth and swallowed some of the water.

He'd had such hopes for this weekend. Waking up this morning and looking forward to their trip, he'd felt like a kid on Christmas morning. But there would be other camping trips. He could live with a change of plans.

"Listen," he said. "If you're not feeling up to par, maybe we should go back."

"That's okay. I'm sure I'll be fine in a little while."

He laid his palm over her forehead. "At least you don't seem to have a fever." He allowed his hand to linger there, just for the excuse of touching her. "Tell you what. You sit here and relax, and I'll get the tent up and the sleeping bags inside. Then you can go in and lie down while I look for wood."

He liked that scenario. Maybe by the time he came back with firewood, she'd have recovered. And the tent would be ready and waiting....

"No, I want to help you with the tent. Since it's mine, I know how it goes up." She unsnapped her seat belt.

So did he. His small dome tent was the same kind as hers, but he decided not to argue with her. Headaches could really make a person irrational if they were bad enough.

They'd set up the tent together, and then he'd see that she was tucked inside shortly thereafter. He had a feeling if he could once get her into the tent and on top of a camping mattress and a fluffy sleeping bag, everything would start to work out.

In a few minutes they'd unrolled the tent on the ground in what looked like a reasonable spot to him. Once again he took a deep breath of the sweet-smelling air. Waking up in this place, with Charlie tucked in beside him, would be beyond his wildest dreams.

"I think we should put it over there," she said.

Boy, she was being *really* indecisive today. He decided to blame it on the headache, which was probably a result of tension. After all, they were getting married next week. Maybe she was freaking out about that. But some good lovemaking would loosen her up in no time.

He'd promised himself he'd tell her about his five broken engagements this weekend, but he couldn't tell her until she felt better. When he finally spread his messy background out for her to see, he wanted her to be in a wonderful mood and wearing his ring, not nursing a headache.

Until then he'd do what he could to make her happy. So he helped her drag the tent to a new spot. A rockier spot, from his quick inspection. "Charlie, I think the other place was flatter and softer."

She put her hands on her hips and glanced from the previous tent site to this one.

He took that moment to admire the way her posture emphasized her slim hips and full breasts. He wished she'd unfasten a button or two of her flannel shirt, but he could wait for her to turn into his little temptress again.

She would, once her headache was gone. The fading sunlight stroked her cap of blond curls, making her look as if she wore a halo. She was his angel. He was convinced of that.

"Nope," she said. "This is the best place."

He didn't agree, and it could become a problem if the rocks interfered with their fun and games later on. But if they did, it wouldn't be that hard to pull up stakes and move the tent. He'd done it a few times himself when he'd misjudged the location.

As he'd figured, the tent went up exactly like his, with two arched poles that crossed in the middle. But he let Charlie direct the action because she seemed to want to do that. Soon they had a nylon igloo-shaped structure that looked so inviting he wondered how he'd keep from trying to seduce her.

"Time for the mattresses and sleeping bags." She sounded totally matter-of-fact about it, as if she had no interest in what they might do once they covered the floor of the small tent with a soft layer of bedding.

"How's your head feel?" he asked as they walked back to the car for the rest of the gear.

"I'm afraid it's worse."

"Oh." Well, that could explain why she wasn't acting interested in sex. But headaches went away.

He could wait this one out. He could even wait until morning, if absolutely necessary.

Or maybe not. He paused as Charlie leaned over to pull a sleeping bag out of the back seat. The sight of those snug jeans and the memory of what was inside them left him shaking.

Now he was even more glad they'd chosen the site near the stream, because if her headache didn't disappear very soon, he might have to go sit in it and cool his crotch.

CHAPTER NINE

As an outdoor adventure guide Charlie had endured her share of hardships. She'd capsized while white-water rafting on the Arkansas River, banged her head against a rock and suffered a mild concussion. She'd fallen on a mountain-climbing expedition in the Grand Tetons, broken her ankle, and had hobbled to civilization using a tree branch as a crutch. She'd been bitten by a rattlesnake in the bottom of the Grand Canyon while out hiking alone, which meant she'd had to treat her own bite, an extremely unpleasant experience.

Yet she'd never suffered as much with any of those disasters as she was suffering now. Having Mark this close and not allowing herself to make love to him took more guts and discipline than anything she'd ever attempted in her life.

She'd counted on being angrier on this trip. But no matter how many times she reminded herself that he'd proposed without revealing his disreputable past, she still couldn't maintain enough righteous indignation to neutralize the effect of those deep brown eyes.

When he'd shown up at her door wearing a long-sleeved denim shirt, jeans and hiking boots, she'd nearly swooned with pleasure. He'd looked yummy all dressed up when they'd met at the restaurant, but she'd already decided she preferred this rugged image.

Of course he'd tried to engage her in a long, passionate kiss. Breaking away from that dizzying embrace had almost killed her, but she'd done it, telling him that they had to get moving if they expected to set up before dark.

They'd planned an easy car-camping experience for this first time, but even so they'd had to drive a ways before reaching the campground. She'd spent most of that drive staring out the window, because whenever she looked at Mark she wanted to grab him and kiss him until they were both breathless.

Now here they were, in a fairly deserted park, and the sexual tension was wearing her down quickly. For one thing, camping had always appealed to her. Maybe it was a holdover from her childhood when she'd made tents in the backyard, but the idea of setting up a temporary shelter in the woods seemed so incredibly cozy.

Lying cocooned inside a nylon dome listening to the wind in the trees, the babble of the water in the creek and the hoot of an owl had always given her tremendous pleasure. Add to that having the man she adored ready to crawl into the tent with her, and the pleasure potential increased almost beyond bearing.

She'd nearly given up the fight and thrown herself in his arms about ten times. Now she found herself walking toward that little tent clutching a sleeping bag and a self-inflating camping mattress so she could create a bed.

They couldn't work together on this. Putting up the tent had been torture enough, with accidental brushing of bodies and touching of hands. Laying down mattresses and sleeping bags would involve way too much close contact, not to mention the urges she'd have once the floor of the tent became a cushy mattress. When he'd suggested that a good orgasm might get rid of her supposed headache, she'd nearly abandoned the whole program.

"It's getting dark and you'll have trouble finding firewood if you don't go now," she said over her shoulder. "You should probably leave the sleeping bag and mattress setup to me."

"I can help. It won't take long."

She would just bet he'd help—help dissolve all her resistance until she was naked and willing. But no matter how much that appealed to her, she had a job to do this weekend. She was testing him, and falling into his arms wouldn't provide much of a test.

"I'm cold, Mark," she said. What a big fat lie that was. "I'd really like you to get a fire going as soon as possible."

"Oh." He set down his sleeping bag and mattress

on the campsite's concrete picnic table. "All right. But why not sit and relax while I get firewood? I can finish the setup when I get back."

"I'd like to get it done." She crouched down and put her rolled sleeping bag and mattress inside the tent.

He came to stand beside her and cupped the back of her head gently. "Don't forget to zip them together," he said softly.

How she longed to lean into his light caress and respond with the loving words he wanted to hear. In their letters they'd compared notes on sleeping bags to make sure theirs were compatible and actually would zip together.

But she was planning to sabotage all that. "I forgot to tell you," she said, "my other sleeping bag got trashed. I don't think this one's zipper is the same size as yours. We'll each have to be in our own bag."

He was silent for a moment. Then he crouched down next to her. "Charlie, what's the problem?" he asked gently.

Her pulse rate shot up. When he used that tone of voice with her, she had trouble thinking straight. All she wanted was to be in his arms. "Nothing's the problem." She pulled off the cinch around her rolled mattress and unfurled it on the tent floor.

"I think there is. You're acting…different. If something's wrong, then we need to talk about it. "

"Nothing to talk about." She didn't dare turn her

head to look at him, so she kept working, unfastening the straps on her sleeping bag and unrolling it on top of her mattress.

"I can understand that you might have the jitters about next weekend. It's a big step. But I think we're ready for it."

She was ready for something now. His tenderness reminded her of his soft murmurs when he was deep inside her. Where was her anger when she needed it?

She stood and left him crouched there while she walked over to get his mattress from the picnic table. "I have a headache, and my sleeping bag got wrecked. No big deal."

He sighed and rose to his feet. "Okay. I'll go get firewood."

No matter how she lectured herself, the confusion and sadness in his voice tore at her heart. For weeks they'd looked forward to spending time together in this setting, and she was deliberately spoiling it.

She took a deep breath. Okay. He'd already jilted five women. She didn't want to be number six. Unrolling his mattress, she positioned it over the bed of rocks under his side of the tent floor. The mattress wasn't nearly thick enough to cushion him from those rocks.

She unrolled his sleeping bag on top of the mattress before going in search of her water bottle. Then she climbed into the tent, nudged off her shoes, and zipped the flap closed as a subtle Do Not Disturb sign. After positioning the water bottle so it would gradually leak into his sleeping bag, she crawled fully clothed into her own, all the while feeling extremely underhanded. But he'd been underhanded, too. She had to remember that.

Not long after she'd settled into the sleeping bag, she heard the steady thwack, thwack of an ax biting into dead branches. Pretending to have a sick headache meant she couldn't watch Mark as he played Paul Bunyan. Damn. The sight of a gorgeous man chopping firewood got her juices flowing. Some women might fall for a bouquet of roses, but Charlie was a sucker for a stack of expertly chopped wood.

She could handle the chore herself, of course, usually better than the guys that she'd taken camping. Many times after watching them bungle through the job, she'd taken over. And she'd tried not to judge their manliness on that specific skill. She really had tried. Yet she could tell from the rhythm of Mark's strokes that he knew what he was doing in this area, too. Her delight had a definite sexual tinge to it.

Soon she identified the familiar crackle of a fire and smelled wood smoke. She adored the smell of wood smoke. Sitting beside a campfire with someone you liked ranked high on her list. Sitting beside it with someone you desperately wanted to make love to would be spectacular.

She hoped that someday they'd have a wonderful camping trip. But first she needed to find out what Mark O'Grady was made of. Surely this weekend he'd tell her about his ex-fiancées.

The muted clatter of pans indicated that he'd decided to leave her alone for a while and start dinner. His attempts to be quiet while he worked touched her. He really seemed to care. She'd grabbed a quick snack before he'd arrived to pick her up so that she could pretend not to be hungry. But as a delicious aroma drifted into the tent, she wondered if her mouth would water and give her away.

Moments later the zipper on the front flap slid open. "Charlie?" he called softly. "Would you like a cup of cocoa?"

She stifled a moan of disappointment, knowing she couldn't respond to the incredibly sweet gesture. He'd obviously remembered her saying how much she loved the stuff, and he was hoping a cup would make her feel better.

"Charlie?" he murmured again.

"Thanks for the thought, but I guess not," she said.

"How's your head?"

"Not great."

Silence followed her answer. Then he spoke with more determination. "Look, let's pack up and go back. This could be the start of something worse. I don't want to take chances with your health just because we planned this camping trip."

"I'll be fine," she said. "All I need is some sleep. I'll probably be much better in the morning. Go ahead and fix yourself some dinner."

"I don't think we should stay." There was no impatience in his voice, only concern.

"I do. Please, Mark, let's just wait it out tonight. If I'm worse in the morning, we can go back."

"Okay. We'll wait and see." He paused. "I love you," he said.

The words zinged through her, shaking her determination. She swallowed the sudden lump in her throat. "I love you, too," she said.

"That's all that matters," he murmured. "Sleep well." He put down the mug of cocoa and zipped the flap closed again.

As she lay there listening to his dinner preparations, she wondered if he'd consider spending the night in the car. For all he knew she had something contagious, and sleeping with her in the tent might be hazardous to his own health. She'd known men who were finicky about that, and it wasn't something she and Mark had ever talked about in their letters, maybe because they were both pretty healthy.

How to deal with sickness might be the only thing they hadn't covered in those letters. They'd hashed out the issue of children and thought two would be a good number. As for child care, they believed in keeping their respective jobs and cutting back equally when babies arrived. Other hot topics had also been dissected—spiritual beliefs, financial attitudes, politics.

She'd thought they'd probed into everything two people needed to know before they made a commitment. She'd thought her knowledge of this man eclipsed her understanding of anyone else she'd ever dated. Yet Mark hadn't told her that he'd come within a hair's breadth of being married—five times. There was no getting around it. That omission was huge.

And so she forced herself to be strong as she lay in the tent listening to Mark washing up the dishes. Later on, when she pictured him sitting by himself while he stared into the fire and longed for her, she clenched her jaw and vowed not to leave the tent and join him.

When at last the zipper on the tent flap slid open again, she pretended to be asleep. She kept her eyes closed and her breathing shallow as he rustled around getting ready for bed. Now she'd learned something else about him. He wasn't afraid of whatever germs she was carrying. Maybe that wasn't wise, but she appreciated his nobility in staying with her even when she could be contagious.

Of course he might be staying with her because

he hoped she'd miraculously wake up cured and they could engage in their favorite activity. But that wasn't going to happen. Ashley's final instructions were *don't have sex.* Considering how sex impaired Mark's judgment, it was excellent advice. Difficult advice, but excellent.

She judged from all the rustling around that he was taking off most of his clothes. *Or all of his clothes.* Her breath hitched at that thought.

"Charlie?" he whispered. "Are you awake?"

She didn't answer. But her body certainly did. His scent filled the tent, arousing her with potent memories of the last time they'd shared a bed. Her skin tingled, her nipples tightened and a sweet ache settled between her thighs.

No one had ever given her the kind of loving Mark had. She could understand why his other fiancées had held on to the relationship, even when incompatibility reared its ugly head. Any woman lucky enough to be in bed with Mark would be tempted to rationalize away any problems they might have out of bed.

When he slipped into his sleeping bag and drew in a quick breath, she knew he'd made contact with the soggy lining. He fumbled around until he encountered the water bottle. A tiny bit of water sloshed as he set it somewhere else. Most of the bottle had drained onto the flannel interior of his sleeping bag.

Maybe now he'd sleep in the car. His sleeping bag

was wet and no doubt by now he could feel the rocks under his side of the tent. She'd chosen this location on purpose because she'd been able to direct the tent setup so that her side was smooth and his rocky.

But he stayed. Soggy sleeping bag, rocks and potential germs notwithstanding, he stayed. When he rested his hand lightly on her shoulder, she somehow managed to control the quiver of awareness. His touch was heaven and hell, all rolled into one.

She wondered if he'd go further with the gentle caress. If only he would. She'd rebuff him, of course, but she was supposed to be asleep, so her rebuff could take awhile.

He didn't go further. Apparently all he wanted was that connection, because he lay there perfectly still, his breathing steady, as if all he needed was to be by her side. She fought the urge to wiggle out of her sleeping bag and snuggle against him, or better yet, invite him into hers where it was dry.

She did neither. Instead, she lay listening to the forest and the creek. In her agitated state, the whisper of the trees and the murmur of the water sounded like lovers in the dark. Eventually she fell into a troubled sleep.

MARK AWOKE wrapped around Charlie, who was still covered from nose to toes in her sleeping bag. During the night he'd given up on the clammy interior of his and had decided to sleep on top of it. Then he'd instinctively snuggled close to Charlie for warmth.

It was like trying to hug a full laundry bag. And yet he knew a loving, sensuous woman lurked inside all that goose down, flannel and canvas. The top of her head was inches from his chin, and her short blond curls were tumbled as if she'd been in a wind tunnel.

Of course he had another erection this morning. Or maybe it was the same one he'd had when he'd finally drifted off to sleep. One erection just blended in with another so far this trip. He'd left his briefs and T-shirt on because he'd felt silly going to bed naked when his lover was fully clothed and swaddled in her sleeping bag.

His jeans, with the ring still in the pocket, lay folded at his feet along with his shirt. He hadn't planned for his clothes to be in a neat pile. He'd thought they'd be strewn everywhere, wrenched off in a frenzy of passion. The weekend was turning out very differently from what he'd expected.

But it was a new day. Pale light filtered through the tent seams and the birds had started tuning up outside. Charlie had said she expected her headache to be gone in the morning. It was morning. The sun was out, which meant he could put his sleeping bag outside and dry the place where Charlie's water bottle had leaked.

Sometime today they'd also move this tent to another spot. He felt as if he'd been sleeping on a torture board all night. But if Charlie woke up and wanted to make love, then he'd worry about moving the tent later. If opportunity knocked, he planned to be standing right by the door ready to fling it open.

She stirred. When she began to move, he relaxed his grip so that she could turn toward him. She was so buried in the sleeping bag that when she rolled over to face him, only her eyes peeked out. She looked like a blue-eyed bandit.

"Good morning." He couldn't help grinning at the picture she made. "You look like Oscar the Grouch peering out of his garbage can."

Her eyes twinkled with laughter.

Oh, thank God. She's over her headache. "Actually, you look a whole lot better than that." He reached for the flap of the sleeping bag. As he drew it down below her chin, he brought her full, tempting lips out of hiding. His body began to hum eagerly in anticipation.

Without lipstick her mouth was the tender rose hue of the horizon at dawn. He decided that dawn was the perfect time to make love and give her the ring. "I never had the urge to kiss Oscar," he said.

The sparkle left her eyes. "You'd better not kiss me, either," she said. "My tummy doesn't feel so good. I might have the flu."

He gazed at her with longing while he fought his growing frustration. But it wasn't her fault if she was sick, and what she needed was understanding from him, not impatience. He tried to ignore the throbbing demands of his penis. "Does your head still hurt?" he asked.

"Not so much."

"Let's see if you have a fever." He laid his hand over her forehead and it was cool to the touch. Not wanting to lose even this little bit of physical contact, he moved from testing her forehead to combing his fingers through her hair. "No fever," he said.

"That's good."

He gave her scalp a gentle massage while he was at it. "Know what I think? I think it's an attack of matrimonial nerves."

"Well, I don't. I'm looking forward to this wedding."

"So am I. But I don't have much to do to get ready. You do. I can understand why you'd be stressing about it."

"Not really," she said. "Ashley's been a huge help with our dresses and the flowers. And once I'd reserved the church and the restaurant for the reception, there wasn't a lot more to do. If we were having a big wedding, that would be something else, but we're not. Once you and I apply for the license on Monday morning, I think we're all set."

He loved hearing the wedding details. He also loved watching the movement of her mouth. He wouldn't mind *feeling* the movement of her mouth, either, but for some reason she was keeping him at arm's length. It had to be the stress.

"Maybe we're all set for the wedding, but you might be thinking about the upheaval when we get back from our honeymoon," he said. "You have to move to Houston. We've talked about looking for a house. All that could give anybody a headache and a bad tummy."

"Do you have stress?"

"About the wedding? No. I've never felt so convinced of something in my life as I am that we should get married." He was pretty stressed right now, lying with her in the tent without being able to strip her naked and lose himself in her warmth. But that was temporary stress. Her attack of nerves would go away eventually.

He did have a problem, however. If Charlie was nervous about the wedding, he couldn't imagine how to tell her about his five previous engagements this weekend. She'd back out for sure after hearing that.

The best thing to do was tell her after they were married, after he'd proven that this time was different. They only had a week to go. A week from today they'd pledge their eternal love and then head off for Jamaica. He'd tell her during the honeymoon, after she felt truly and completely married to him. Yes, that was the answer.

In the meantime, he'd just thought of a brilliant idea. "Let me give you a massage," he said. "A massage will boost your immune system, in case you have the flu. But if it's a case of wedding jitters, it'll help relax you."

If his previous experience with giving women massages was anything to go by, soon they'd both be extremely relaxed—not to mention sexually satisfied. Then he'd give her the ring, and all would be well.

"I'd rather not," she said. "In fact, I'm getting up." In no time she'd scrambled out of her sleeping bag, unzipped the tent flap and crawled out into the morning light.

Flopping back on his uncomfortable bed, he swore softly. He couldn't figure out how Charlie had gone from being one of the most cooperative women in the world to being one of the most frustratingly perverse.

She didn't seem really sick, so he must be right that her headache and stomach problems were related to wedding jitters. He might be responsible for her panic because he'd asked her to get married so quickly, but he had several stress-busters up his sleeve. She wasn't letting him use any of them, and that was raising his own stress level considerably.

He might as well get dressed now, though. She'd left the tent as if her tail was on fire, so he didn't think there was much chance she'd be crawling back in and asking him to give her that massage. Damn shame, too. He'd found that a good full-body massage was a natural segue into great sex.

Once he'd pulled on his clothes he crawled out of the tent and discovered Charlie was building a fire. "I'll do that," he said.

"I know, but I'd like to." She added more kindling and struck a match. "I've felt so useless this trip. I'm going to cook you breakfast."

"That doesn't make sense if you have an upset stomach."

"Cooking will take my mind off it." The fire crackled to life. "And I'm tired of lying in that tent."

He wasn't surprised to hear that. He'd never intended their time in that tent to be so boring. But one thing was for sure. The woman knew her way around a campfire. Despite his frustration at their lack of sexual interaction, he was gratified to finally be with a woman who had outdoor skills. He hadn't realized until now how important that was to him.

Maybe the activity of cooking breakfast would help her work off her case of nerves. He sure hoped so, because every time she leaned over that fire, she touched off a blaze that threatened to drive him crazy.

CHAPTER TEN

CHARLIE WASN'T A GREAT COOK, but she enjoyed the challenge of turning out a meal using a campfire. She'd mastered bacon and eggs long ago because she happened to love eating them outdoors on a fresh, nippy morning like today. Add to that a cup of strong coffee, and she was in camper heaven.

But her purpose this weekend was to treat Mark to camper hell. Stage one involved screwing up the coffee by making it strong enough to eat through metal. She'd even pretend to enjoy it, and if he was a typical male, he wouldn't be able to admit that the coffee was too strong for him. She'd be totally wired for the rest of the day, but it was a small price to pay.

Carrying out her strategy took some concentration, which was good because Mark looked even more appealing this morning than he had the night before. She'd never seen him with such a manly growth of beard.

Apparently he'd shaved before their restaurant date this past weekend, so even though they'd spent the entire night together, his beard hadn't had time to grow out much by the next morning. But this morning was a different story. Every time she glanced in his direction he looked even more rugged and sexy than he had a moment ago. Her pulse was in permanent overdrive and her juices were flowing.

And then, oh, Lordy, he decided to chop more wood for the fire. Rolling back his sleeves, he took a large dead branch he'd hauled in the night before, propped it on a nearby stump, braced it with one foot, and began to reduce it to kindling-sized pieces.

As he worked rhythmically and efficiently, the muscles in his forearms bunched and his jeans pulled taut over his butt. Charlie stared at him, forgetting what she was doing until a hot cinder popped out of the fire and landed on her shirt.

She brushed it off and realized she'd lost count of the number of scoops she'd put in the coffee basket. She added some more for good measure and put the pot on the cooking grate.

Damn, but she wanted to make love to that guy. Watching him move around the campsite, she could hardly believe that they were engaged. A hunk who made her quiver with anticipation had said that he wanted to spend the rest of his life with her. But she had to remind herself that it might not come true.

She must not forget what she'd learned this week. Saying and doing might be two different things. Maybe he'd get cold feet the way he had five times before. Maybe something about her would turn him off and he'd call the whole thing off. It wasn't as if he wasn't capable of that.

So no matter how gorgeous he looked this morning, she had to put him through his paces. For starters, she could suggest he go find his razor. If he shaved off his beard so he didn't resemble a dashing pirate, then she might be able to resist grabbing him and pulling him into the tent with her.

The motor oil coffee was perking and she'd started her program of burning the bacon when he came over with an armload of wood. She turned to him with a smile. "I have this under control, if you want to go shave."

"Uh, sure." He set the wood down next to the fire pit. "Sure, I could do that," he said more eagerly. His eyes lit with excitement. "I'd be happy to shave."

She felt a little sorry for him. He probably thought he was shaving because she intended to make love to him after breakfast. But he might not feel so amorous after eating the breakfast she'd be serving.

As the scent of burning bacon filled the clearing, she wondered if he'd comment on it. When he didn't, she peeked over toward the picnic table where he'd set up his shaving gear. Uh-oh. Asking him to shave had clearly been a mistake. Now her love god was shirtless.

She gulped as memories of last weekend came

flooding back. Her mouth remembered the taste and texture of his skin, the tickle of his chest hair, the shape of his nipples. The smell of charred bacon was strong, but not strong enough to block out the sweet aroma of his shaving cream, an aroma that brought back the moist pleasure of their first kiss. And their second kiss. And all the kisses thereafter.

The bacon had shriveled until it resembled rusty barbed wire by the time she wrenched her attention away from the sight of Mark stroking his razor over his deliciously square jaw. All the while he never gave any indication that he'd noticed the smell of burning meat. His nostrils had twitched a couple of times, but he'd continued to shave as if the bacon was no concern of his.

She'd begun to wonder who was torturing whom by the time she removed the stiff pieces of bacon and cracked the eggs into the pan. She broke the yokes and saturated the whole mess with salt. When the eggs were crisp as a scouring pad on the bottom, she flipped them over and fried the hell out of the other side. Mark would need to fetch his ax to make any headway with this grub.

Personally she was so hungry she might eat it if he didn't. Secretly, of course. When she'd been chortling over her plans with Ashley she'd failed to recognize that she'd have to suffer right along with Mark.

She used a spatula to dish the unappetizing concoction onto a tin plate, which she set down on the picnic table. "It might be a little overdone," she said.

"No problem." Mark finished buttoning his shirt and sat down.

"I'll get some coffee." She returned to the fire and used a potholder to pick up the blue spatter-ware pot. As she poured two matching mugs full to the brim, the sludge that came out of the pot looked exactly like the stuff the garage had drained from her crankcase a month ago.

She put the mug next to Mark's plate and took a seat across the table from him, both to keep her distance and to observe his reaction.

"Thanks for fixing all this," he said as he picked up his coffee mug. "You're sure you don't want any?"

"I'll stick with coffee for now." She held her breath.

He took a swallow from his mug. His eyes widened, but he somehow managed to turn a grimace into a smile. "Wow, that's robust."

"I like it strong."

"Yeah, me too." He took another gulp of the coffee.

If she hadn't been watching closely, she'd have missed his shudder when he swallowed it. She decided to see how bad it was and raised the mug to her lips. Although she'd braced herself for the taste, her mouth wasn't ready. She nearly gagged.

He was out of his seat and patting her back in no time. "Easy. It's pretty strong stuff."

"I think…I put in too much coffee," she rasped.

"That can happen." He crouched next to her as he continued to rub her back. "Are you okay?"

She nodded. "Uh-huh. Thanks." She had to make him stop rubbing her back before she begged him to rub her all over. He had the most magical touch of any man she'd ever known. "Now go ahead and eat your breakfast before it gets cold." *Or petrifies.*

"All right." He seemed reluctant as he went back to his seat, either because he'd hoped the back-rub might turn into something else, or because he wasn't looking forward to this meal.

She'd guess both.

But to his credit, he sat down, picked up a shrunken strip of bacon and bit off the end. His attempts to chew the bacon sounded like a rock tumbler in motion. Then he swallowed and smiled at her again. "Crisp."

She stared at him. Apparently he was going to eat the whole meal and not complain. "It's not just crisp. It's burned beyond recognition," she said.

"Guess so."

"You don't have to eat it."

"Sure I do. You made it for me." He bit off another section with a sharp crunch.

She watched in amazement as he polished off one strip of bacon and started in on his first egg. He had to use a steak knife to cut it. But cut it he did, and popped a bite into his mouth.

After some pretty fierce chewing, he swallowed the mouthful of egg. "Nice and firm," he said. "I hate it when they're too gooey." He picked up his knife and began sawing off another section.

"Wait." Consumed with guilt, she reached over and grabbed his wrist before he put any more of that breakfast atrocity in his mouth. "I can't stand this. Don't eat another bite."

He gazed at her, his brown eyes warm. "What if I want to?"

"Well, I *don't* want you to." She took a deep breath. "I made it terrible on purpose."

He shrugged. "I know."

Her jaw dropped. "You *know?*"

"Sure." He grinned at her. "Nobody with your camping experience could be that bad at cooking over an open fire. You laid it on too heavily to be convincing."

"I could *so* have been that bad!"

"Nope. If you'd barely burned the bacon, I would have believed it was an accident. If the eggs were a little brown around the edges, I would have figured you misjudged the heat. But the coffee was a tipoff. I know you like coffee. You go camping all the time, sometimes alone. There's no way you wouldn't have learned how to make a good pot of campfire coffee at the very least."

Her face grew hot. "Why didn't you say something?"

He continued to smile at her. "I figured if I ate it without complaining, you might give in and tell me you did it on purpose, which you just did."

Her face flaming with embarrassment, she stood and walked over to the fire pit. "I'll start over." She grabbed a potholder and picked up the frying pan. "I think we still have enough coals to—" She caught her breath as he circled her waist with one arm and took the frying pan with his free hand.

He set it back down on the edge of the fire pit and wrapped his arm around her ribs, just under her breasts. His hold was gentle, but firm. There wasn't a trace of anger in his voice. "First I want to know why you did it."

Enclosed by his arms, with his breath warm on her neck, she felt her resistance ebbing way. A girl could only be so strong.

He leaned down and nuzzled the side of her neck. "And while you're at it, you can tell me why you've been deliberately avoiding having sex with me."

Oh, his lips felt so good against her skin. She closed her eyes and struggled to remember her game plan. "I haven't been—"

"Yes, you have." His tongue tickled the spot behind her earlobe. "At first I thought you were feeling under the weather because of wedding jitters. But after this breakfast stunt, I think you've been making up the sick part, too. How come, Charlie?"

She didn't know what to say, couldn't decide what to think, especially when he was playing havoc with her senses. The facts. What were the facts? He'd had dinner alone without complaint, slept on a bed of rocks in a soggy sleeping bag without protest, and had planned to eat her lousy breakfast.

After all that, she couldn't doubt his love and commitment. Not many men would have put up with her shenanigans, especially after they'd figured out her behavior was intentional. But he had, and now he didn't even sound upset—only concerned. And he was so warm. And she needed him so much.

She decided on a partial truth. "Maybe I don't quite believe that this is real. Maybe I needed to test you."

"I thought it might be something like that." He urged her closer, letting her feel his erection as he nibbled her earlobe. "Did I pass?"

Sort of, she thought. Mmm. His hand felt so nice sliding between her thighs, rubbing her gently through the denim.

Still, he really should have told her about his broken engagements. But as he cupped her breast, she longed to rip her clothes off so he could do it right.

Maybe she should tell him she knew. Except now…now he'd unbuttoned her shirt and slipped his hand inside.

She shouldn't let him do this until he'd explained himself, because…because…oh, that felt so good….

"I still hear doubts whizzing around in your head," he murmured against her ear. "But I think the rest of you wants to give in and let me love you."

FOR YEARS HE'D KNOWN he had a gift for seduction. He'd never needed that gift more. He only knew one surefire way to erase Charlie's doubts about his commitment. When he was buried inside her, he was as committed as he'd ever been in his life, and he believed she knew it on some basic level. Then, when she'd been well and properly loved, he'd seal the bargain by giving her the ring in his pocket.

He'd enjoyed every minute of his sexual encounters with his ex-fiancées, but enjoyment was far too flimsy a word to describe what he felt when he sank into Charlie's warm, moist body. He hadn't realized that such a feeling existed, and he was still at a loss to describe it.

There was unity—and yet he was aware of her special individuality that meshed so well with his. There was surrender—and yet he gave up nothing and gained everything when he made love to her. There was peace—and yet energy surged through him at the moment of connection.

He needed all of those things now, and so did she. "Come to bed with me," he murmured.

And she did, tumbling with him through the tent flap, kissing him frantically, her mouth hot and needy as she wrestled him out of his clothes with as much urgency as he was using on hers. They started with the most essential things, tugging at the snaps and zippers of their jeans.

They shoved off their shoes along with the jeans and with breathless half words agreed to forget about taking off their shirts.

"I just want you inside me," she said.

"And I want to be there. God, do I want to."

"Condoms," she said, panting as she wiggled out of her panties. "Where did you put the condoms?"

He shucked off his briefs to reveal his rigid penis. His chest heaved as he tried to remember what he'd done with the blasted things. He'd remembered to keep tabs on the ring, but not the condoms. A guy could only keep track of so much, and the ring was a priority. "They might be in my backpack."

She groaned.

So much for a smooth seduction. If he put his clothes back on to go get a condom, he might give her a chance to cool down. She might decide to start playing games again to test him. But he had to have the condom.

Or did he?

He pushed her gently down onto the soft flannel of her open sleeping bag. "Let's forget the condom."

Her gaze locked with his for several seconds. Then she swallowed. "Forget it?"

"We're getting married in a week." Holding her gaze, he moved over her. "You said you can hardly wait to have kids. Neither can I. We'll have great kids." His heart beat faster as he realized that this might be the perfect way to convince her that for both of them, there was no turning back.

She searched his expression, her blue eyes serious. "Are you sure you know what you're doing?"

"Yeah." He gave her a slow smile. "I'm about to knock you up."

She put a hand on his chest, holding him back. "I come from a long line of fertile women." She drew in a ragged breath. "You'd better be absolutely sure."

"That I want kids? You know I do. Two girls, or two boys, or one of each—I don't care. Let's start making them."

"I mean, you'd better be sure that you want to marry me."

He looked into her eyes and saw the doubts swirling there. "I'm sure," he said. "Are you sure?"

She nodded.

He sighed with relief. Her doubts were all about him, and he would make them go away. He would banish them forever.

"I want to marry you," he said softly. He leaned down and kissed her slowly and gently, telling her with his kiss how he felt. Then he lifted his head and gazed down at her so that he could use the words. "I love you."

The doubts began to fade from her eyes.

But he wanted them gone without a trace. "I've never made love to a woman without using birth control," he murmured, "because no matter how much I cared about her, I wasn't sure, not deep down in my gut, that she was my mate."

Slowly a light began to grow in her eyes. "And now you are?"

"Yes." He eased forward, closing his eyes with pleasure as the tip of his penis slid between the dew-drenched petals of her vagina. "Oh, yes."

She drew in a quick breath and clutched his hips.

He paused, opening his eyes. Then he held her gaze as he kept his penetration shallow, sliding slowly back and forth at the entrance to salvation. He wooed her as he never had any other woman.

Instead of empty, poetic phrases, he gave her the promises that mattered. Even if she didn't know that, he certainly did. "We're going to make it, Charlie," he said. "We're going to see each other through teething babies, grape juice on the rug, puppies in the flower bed, dings in the new car."

Tears glistened in her eyes. "We are?"

"We are. I thought so when we were writing to each other, but I knew it the minute I saw you. Believe in me, Charlie. Believe in me, my love."

Her voice was thick with emotion. "Oh, Mark. I do. I really do."

"That's all we'll ever need." In one smooth motion he thrust deep, and there it was, the feeling that went beyond words, the feeling he required more than life itself.

With a cry she lifted to meet him. "I love you," she whispered hoarsely.

"Just keep loving me." His throat constricted, and he blinked back his own tears. He'd convinced her. Dear God, he'd done it. "Just keep it up," he said in a husky voice, "because we're so good together."

"I know."

"So good." Still looking into her eyes, he settled into a rhythm that was all their own. They'd found that rhythm during long, lazy hours together that first night, and his memory of their joining had haunted him with its beauty.

And yet, the subtle barrier of latex between them had veiled the beauty. He'd had no idea what he'd been missing…until now, when the veil was gone and the splendor of loving Charlie was dazzling him. He reveled in her liquid welcome. He treasured the inner caress she gave him each time he surged forward. With each thrust, she seemed to open even more deep inside, like some exotic tropical flower.

Her cheeks grew pink, her breathing quick and shallow. And oh, her eyes. He'd never seen them like this, luminescent and wide, as if she wanted him to see into her soul.

He wanted her to see into his. Then she would know how he cherished her. Right here, right now, he was dedicating his life to her in the only way he knew how. He was asking her to carry his child.

He felt her tighten around him, heard her breathing change. "Soon," he whispered.

Her response was breathless and urgent. "Yes, soon."

His pulse beat against his eardrums like heavy surf. "I'm going to come inside you, you fertile woman. And you're going to have our baby." He was dizzy with joy at the prospect.

"Yes." She arched upward. *"Yes."*

Her convulsions brought on his. Her name rose to his lips as he pushed deep. With a groan of primitive satisfaction, he bestowed the most important gift of all—the future.

CHAPTER ELEVEN

CHARLIE LAY TREMBLING beneath Mark as the power of their decision engulfed her. She could not doubt him now. They were joined forever.

"Ah, Charlie." He settled gently against her, the shirt he hadn't bothered to take off brushing her skin. He kept his weight on his forearms as he trailed lazy kisses over her eyes, her nose, her mouth. "My love," he murmured. "My life. Thank you for trusting me."

"I do trust you." And she wanted to be as close to him as she could get. Impatient with the barrier of clothes they'd been too frantic to remove, she slid a hand up his chest and began unbuttoning his shirt.

Mark lifted up so she could finish the job. When his shirt hung open, she snapped open the front clasp of her bra and pushed the lace cups aside.

He eased back down, nestling against her bare breasts. "Much better."

"Much." With a sigh she closed her eyes and allowed contentment to fill her. The visit from the DOAs had robbed her of that, but now she had it back.

Birds twittered outside the tent and the creek babbled happily not far away. All was right with her world.

Mark resumed decorating her face and neck with kisses, and then he began to chuckle.

She opened her eyes. "What?"

"You lined up the tent so the rocks would be on my side, didn't you?"

After their spectacular lovemaking, she felt really guilty for all she'd put him through. He loved her so much, and she'd tortured him. "Was it awful?"

"Horrible." He nipped her earlobe. "But not nearly as bad as the bottle of water you dumped inside my sleeping bag. You must have been a terror as a little kid."

"I wasn't! I'm really not the type to pull mean tricks on people. It's just that—"

"I know." He ran his tongue along her jaw. "We all do crazy things when we're scared."

"I guess." Her heart beat a little faster. It was the perfect line to lead into his broken engagement history. Those other fiancées didn't bother her a bit, now, but she still would like him to tell her about them.

He gazed into her eyes, a smile curving his mouth. "But we are going to move the tent," he said.

"Okay." She waited expectantly. She would be so supportive and understanding that he wouldn't have to feel the least bit uncomfortable about all those past mistakes. Maybe she'd suggest that he take each of those women to lunch and apologize for what he'd put them through.

Or maybe not. She wasn't exactly jealous of those five beautiful women, but after all, he had been engaged to them, so he'd found them sexually attractive at some point. Instead of a lunch date, he could write them all letters. He'd become quite a good letter writer in the past three months.

His gaze darkened. "But maybe we won't move the tent right this minute."

"Okay." She was still sure that he planned to confess everything and throw himself at her mercy. But then his kisses moved down below her collarbone, and she began to suspect he had other ideas. When he cradled her breast, she felt his penis stir and harden within her, and her body answered with a quiver of awareness.

"It's nice not to have to worry about condoms," he said in a husky voice as he rubbed his thumb over her breast. "I can stay inside you and start over whenever the urge takes us." He leaned down and kissed the tip of her breast. "I'll bet I can tease a few more climaxes out of you before we worry about moving the tent."

Her pulse raced in anticipation. "Maybe." Oh, well. Confessions could wait. They had more pressing matters. Six days ago he'd taught her how talented he was. He could almost talk her into an orgasm. Why deprive herself of his skillful attentions now?

"Did you know you're even sexier in a flannel shirt than in that red dress?" He caught her nipple between his teeth.

"No." The light pressure of his teeth sent a signal to her womb, coaxing her into that now-familiar spiral that would coil ever tighter until he touched the spring, sending her into ecstasy.

He released her nipple, leaving it damp. Then he blew softly over the super-sensitive tip. "You drove me crazy, all covered up in red plaid, your shirt tucked in so snug, your breasts pushing at the material, daring me to touch you."

"I...didn't mean to...drive you crazy." She was amazed how quickly he could make her breathless with desire.

"You did, anyway." He flicked his tongue back and forth, then blew gently once again. "And the buttons looked as if they would come unfastened so easily. I looked at you and my fingers shook because I wanted to undo those buttons so I could see these beautiful breasts. And you wouldn't let me."

She regretted every squandered moment.

"And I remembered how you tasted, Charlie." He stroked her breast, caressing her until she shivered. Then he eased her arms out of the sleeves of her shirt, so that she was finally naked. "I remembered how good it felt to take your nipple into my mouth, to roll it over my tongue, to suck on it until you were almost ready to come."

She moaned.

"Do you want me to do that again?"

"Yes, please, yes."

"Let's see if I can remember how you like it."

Oh, he remembered, all right. And he added a new dimension when he bunched the sleeping bag under her hips. With his mouth still at her breast, he began slowly thrusting, building the tension, propelling her beyond reason, beyond caring whether anyone could hear her cries of heavenly release.

This time he didn't follow her over the precipice. Releasing her breast, he shifted the angle of his thrust, taking it deeper to stimulate her in a whole new way. She quickly climaxed again, her body quaking with the impact.

While she was still gasping, he held her close and rolled to his back on his side of the tent.

"The rocks…" she said breathlessly.

"Ask me if I care."

"But—"

"Ride me, Charlie. Ride me and come again."

She was helpless to refuse him. She'd learned that once he coaxed her onto this roller-coaster, she became his willing slave. And so she braced her arms on his chest and moved her hips, gliding up and down, suffused with lusty enjoyment.

"I love watching your breasts jiggle when you move like that," he said in a hoarse, passion-filled voice.

She looked into his heavy-lidded eyes and a thrill of sensuality shot through her.

"I love watching that sweet bounce. And you feel so good. So very good." He clenched his jaw. "Slow down. Slo-o-ow down. That's it. Now hold still." He reached between her thighs and brushed his thumb against her pleasure point. "Come again," he whispered, his brown eyes dark with excitement.

She gulped for air and closed her eyes as his lazy caress brought her to the edge. Then he increased the pressure just enough to catapult her into another orgasm. She threw back her head and dug her fingers into his chest.

When her arms grew too weak to support her, he gathered her close and eased her over until they lay facing each other, still joined. She gazed at him in awe. No one had ever come close to pleasuring her as he could.

"I love you," he murmured. Then he cupped her bottom in both hands and looked deep into her eyes as he began a gentle rhythm. "I love you so much."

She could barely speak. "I...love you."

His strokes became faster and more powerful, the glow in his eyes more intense. "I'm a part of you, now. And you're a part of me."

"Yes." She gripped his shoulders and held on.

"*Forever.*" He thrust deep.

"Yes."

"Forever." He shuddered and closed his eyes.

She held him close and absorbed the pulsing rush of his climax, her heart overflowing with love. She'd been a fool to ever doubt him.

AT LAST the moment had arrived, and Mark discovered he was more nervous than he'd expected. Charlie lay totally naked and relaxed on the soft flannel of her sleeping bag. She only needed one thing to make the picture complete.

But now that the time was here, he was worried that she might not like the ring he'd picked out. It didn't look like other engagement rings in the jeweler's case, but the first time he'd seen it he'd thought of Charlie.

He wanted it on her finger, tangible evidence of their bond, but in order to accomplish that he had to get past the moment of presenting it, the moment when she might indicate by some fleeting expression that the ring wasn't exactly what she'd had in mind.

With his other fiancées he'd allowed them to help him pick out the ring, because when it came right down to it, he hadn't known them well enough to make the choice without them. That in itself had been telling, although he hadn't understood the significance until now.

This time he'd wanted to pick out the ring by himself, and in the jewelry store he'd been so sure he'd found the perfect one. He realized that he'd attached a lot of importance to her reaction. If she didn't love it as much as he'd hoped, he would be crushed. He hadn't often allowed himself to be this vulnerable. Come to think of it, he never had.

Maybe he should get used to the feeling. Charlie had his heart in her hands, and she could do so much damage. She might not even know how much.

Well, now or never. Summoning what courage he could, he sat up and reached for his discarded jeans.

"Are you getting dressed?" she asked.

"No." He shoved his hand into the front pocket and his fingers closed around the black velvet pouch. "I…I wanted to…that is, I think it's time for me to—"

"Mark, don't be scared," she said gently. "I understand this could be nerve-wracking."

He glanced at her as he pulled the velvet pouch out of his pocket. She obviously knew what he was about to give her. Logic would tell her that he'd buy a ring this week. "You have no idea. Maybe we should have discussed it beforehand."

"Maybe. But I'm sure you had your reasons for not doing that."

"I did. I wanted to surprise you."

She looked puzzled. "Surprise me?"

He took the ring from the pouch. "Okay, it's not

a big surprise. You've already figured it out." Holding the ring between his thumb and forefinger, he extended it toward her, his heart thundering with anxiety. He swallowed. "I hope you like it, Charlie. Because it comes with all my love."

Her eyes widened and she sat up. "A ring?"

He nodded. Maybe she was surprised, after all. He couldn't imagine what she'd been expecting, if not a ring. But he didn't have time to worry about that. He was too busy worrying about her reaction to his choice.

"A ring," she whispered, her gaze fixed on it as she took it carefully from him. "It's…oh, Mark." She glanced up, tears in her eyes. "It's two daisies twining together."

"Yeah." She either loved it or hated it, and he was in agony wondering which it was. "I saw it and thought—"

"That I loved daisies," she said softly, staring at the ring as she slid it on her finger. "How perfect."

The breath whooshed out of him in relief. "Then you like it."

"I don't like it—"

He panicked.

"I *love* it!" She launched herself at him and threw her arms around his neck as tears rolled down her cheeks. "I love, love, love it. And I love you for knowing that I would love it."

"I didn't know for sure. I hoped." He was about ready to bawl, himself, out of sheer happiness that he'd guessed right.

She sniffed. "I need a really big hug right now."

"Me, too." As he gathered her into his lap, she wound her legs around his hips so they fit as neatly as two sections of a hinge. He wrapped his arms around her and held on tight.

Her voice was muffled against his neck. "Where did you find it?"

"I went to about five places." At last he could share what he'd been through this week. "And I kept looking at the ones that had just one diamond, and that didn't seem right for us. They even call them a solitaire. Did you know that?"

She nodded, her cheek rubbing against his shoulder. "Yes, I knew that."

"There's going to be nothing solitary about us," he said fiercely.

"Nope." She sounded so very happy.

Her joy filled all sorts of places that he hadn't known were empty. He was damned proud of himself for finding a ring that would make her cry. "So then I saw this ring, with two diamonds, each one in the center of a sweet little daisy. I think they call it filigree, or something like that."

"I call it gorgeous. I've never seen anything like it."

"That's the way it should be." He kissed her bare

shoulder. "Because our love isn't like anybody else's, either."

"Nope." She sighed with obvious contentment as she rested her cheek against his shoulder.

Her curls felt like silk against his skin. He reached up and combed through them, loving the way they wound around his fingers. "When your hair starts turning gray, I don't think you should color it or anything."

She laughed. "Where did that come from?"

He continued to stroke her hair. "I don't know. I was just thinking about all the years ahead of us. We'll get gray, and maybe a little rickety, but—"

She leaned back to grin at him. "Rickety? Speak for yourself."

He basked in the happy light in her eyes as he grinned back. "Okay, so we won't get rickety. We'll be skipping over these hills when we're ninety-two. I only meant that I'm looking forward to all of it. I don't want to miss a thing, even the gray hair. It's all part of the deal."

Her eyes grew misty again. "Yeah, it is. We're going to have a great life, Mark."

"Show me how the ring looks."

Obediently she stuck her hand in front of his face, fingers spread.

He held it steady and surveyed the ring, now that it was on her finger. It looked even better than he'd imagined. "They have matching wedding bands that look like stems and leaves woven together. I have a picture in my backpack."

"I'm sure I'll love them, too."

"And it fits, right?"

"Perfectly." She turned her hand so she could admire the ring. "How did you do that?"

"Talked to Ashley."

"Really?" She gazed at him. "She sure did keep the secret well. I had no idea."

"I figured I could trust her not to tell." He'd enjoyed his conversation with Ashley on Monday. It had only confirmed what he believed—that she and Sam had something special going on. Sometime during the reception dinner he'd probably reveal the stories he'd made up about them. The good will of the wedding celebration and a couple of glasses of champagne would pave the way, and they'd be ready to laugh about the whole thing.

He'd been secretly relieved that Sam had been called out of town this weekend. If he'd stayed in Houston, he might have spent the weekend with Ashley and they'd have figured out the prank Mark had pulled. He wanted to confess before that happened. Less incriminating that way.

"So did you and Ashley talk about anything else?" Charlie asked.

He looked into her eyes. "You. She told me that

you have a tender heart, and if I ever so much as bruise it, she'll run me down with her car."

Charlie nodded. "That sounds like Ashley."

"I told her she didn't have anything to worry about."

She met his gaze. "No," she said softly. "She doesn't."

CHARLIE HAD BROUGHT along her camping shower, a contraption that included a plastic bag to hold water and a shower curtain. She was glad they found a private spot to hang it, because Mark insisted on showering together, and the curtain didn't begin to hide their antics. The entire process took about two hours.

By the time they finally fixed a meal it was closer to dinner time than lunch, and Charlie, who'd had nothing to eat since the afternoon before, gobbled everything in sight. Then they moved the tent to a softer spot, built up the fire, and sat in low sand chairs in front of the flames as dusk settled over the campsite. They moved their chairs so the wooden arms were touching and held hands.

They talked about the wedding. She told him about the minister, a young guy who liked to tell jokes. And she described the flowers and the music she'd chosen for the organist to play. They marveled at how similar their taste in music was. He said he'd have chosen exactly the same numbers.

She couldn't remember ever being this happy in her life. Her existence was nearly perfect. Ninety-nine percent perfect. All she needed to be absolutely, positively sure about this relationship was for Mark to tell her about his other fiancées.

Maybe now, while they sat gazing into the embers of the dying fire, he would open up. She decided to give him a boost. "Are you sure you don't want to invite your mother to the wedding?" she asked. "I don't feel right leaving her out."

"We can invite her if you want," Mark said, surprising her.

"Really?" Charlie felt better already. "That's good. I'd like that. What's she like, your mom?"

"Complicated."

"What does she do for a living?"

"Teaches college chemistry, graduate level."

"Wow. That's interesting." Charlie didn't miss the clipped way Mark was answering her questions or the tense set of his jaw.

"I suppose," he said.

"Aren't you proud of her?"

"I guess, but I feel as if I hardly know her."

Charlie couldn't imagine such a thing. "But she's your *mother.*"

"Yeah, but she was always kind of remote." He seemed to make a visible effort to relax and his voice gentled. "She's what you'd call an absentminded professor, Charlie. If she'd been born a man, nobody would think anything about her preoccupied state of mind and her devotion to her career, but because she's a woman and she happened to have a kid, everyone expected her to pay attention to the kid."

"Well, yeah."

He shrugged and gave her a lopsided smile. "I survived."

"You told me in your letters that your mom was divorced. She never remarried?"

"Nope. Never even came close." He stared into the fire and rubbed his thumb over hers. "I used to think her marriage to my dad was so awful that she didn't want to risk another one. So finally I worked up the courage to ask her, and she said it wasn't awful, just a waste of her time. I think she might be one of those people who never should have married in the first place. She loves having the house and her little basement lab all to herself. Even having me around was a bother."

She heard the pain in his voice and squeezed his hand. "I doubt that."

"Oh, I don't. But like I said, I survived. I spent a lot of time over at Sam's house."

"Bless Sam and his family."

"I do. All the time."

"Then we should invite them to the wedding."

He smiled at her. "The kids are all scattered except Sam, but I was going to ask you if we could invite Sam's parents. I know we're keeping it small, but they are like my family."

"I wouldn't have it any other way." Even though he'd confessed nothing about his five engagements, she was beginning to understand how they could have happened. He'd been desperate to find someone and establish the happy home he'd never had, the one he'd envied every time he went over to Sam's. And yet he knew what divorce could do to a kid, so each time he'd realized that his coming marriage might not be a happy one, he bailed rather than taking a chance on hurting a child of his the way he'd been hurt.

Thinking back on his letters, she remembered a wistful note running through some of them, usually the ones he'd written in response to her telling him something about her mother and father, or her sister. She'd thought that was natural coming from someone who had no siblings and had been raised by a single mom. But she hadn't understood the depths of his loneliness.

Oh, yes, the reason for his five engagements was becoming very clear. And so long as he didn't see the potential for divorce with her, then that string was about to come to an end.

He gripped her hand tighter. "Charlie."

She turned her head.

His gaze was filled with yearning. "Come to bed with me."

Warmth flooded through her as she realized how much he needed her, how much he would always need her. Everything was going to be fine.

CHAPTER TWELVE

THEIR NIGHT TOGETHER was so exciting that Charlie forgot to worry about Mark's past. All that mattered was the very sensuous present. Besides, they still had lots of time for a discussion before he went back to Houston.

He was spending Sunday night in her apartment so they could apply for the license first thing Monday morning. Then he planned to drive back to Houston immediately. They both had a full week ahead of them in order to clear the decks so they could relax on their honeymoon. Charlie had exchanged assignments with another tour guide and would take out a group Tuesday through Friday in order to have the next seven days free.

But they didn't have to go back to work quite yet, and Mark's excellent lovemaking had put her in an extremely mellow mood by the time they returned to her apartment late Sunday afternoon. Camping with him had been great, but she was looking forward to spending some time together on a comfy innerspring.

"When do you want to call your folks?" he asked

as they put her camping gear away in the locked storage cubicle assigned to her apartment.

After his description of his own family life, or lack of it, she had no trouble understanding his eagerness. "We can call them now, if you're ready."

"I'm ready." He followed her up the steps to her second-floor apartment. "A little nervous, but ready."

"They're going to love you, so relax." She believed they would, so long as they didn't hear about the broken engagements right off the bat. She'd already decided that even when Mark finally admitted the sad truth about his background, she would hold onto the information for a while and not tell her mom and dad until after the wedding. No point in making them worry when there was no reason. And they would worry.

In fact, they were probably worrying now, she thought as she unlocked the door to her apartment. No matter how good an impression Mark made on the phone this afternoon, they'd still prefer to meet him before the wedding day. Charlie wished that were possible. She'd never intended to spring a husband on them like this, but marrying Mark next Saturday seemed like the exact right thing to do.

Because she was aware of Mark's nervousness, she decided to place the call to her parents as quickly as possible. After she and Mark had each grabbed a bottle of water from the refrigerator, she picked up her cordless phone and speed-dialed her parents' number.

Her father answered. "Hi, Button," he said, using his pet name for her.

She heard a basketball game in the background and pictured him in the den where he probably was watching the Bulls on TV. He'd be wearing his favorite Sunday outfit, gray sweats with holes in the knees and a soft blue sweater that matched his eyes.

"How'd you know it was me?" she asked.

He chuckled. "Caller I.D. Just put it in this weekend. We weren't going to bother, but then every damned time we called your Uncle Jack and Aunt Mary, they'd answer with *Hi, Hank and Sharon!* Your mother couldn't stand it, them having one up on us, so now we have it, too."

Charlie laughed. Her mother and her Aunt Mary's fifty-year-old case of sibling rivalry had developed into a family joke. She felt a pang of nostalgia for the old neighborhood in Arlington Heights where she'd grown up surrounded by aunts, uncles and cousins. But she and Ashley had agreed it had been good for them to try their wings somewhere else. And now Texas was in Charlie's blood.

"So what's this I hear about some guy sweeping you off your feet?" her father said.

Charlie glanced at Mark, who was circling her living room studying her framed photos from her backpacking and rafting experiences. "He's pretty special, Dad."

Mark turned and gave her a heart-melting smile. Then he crossed the living room and sat beside her on her futon sofa.

"He'd better be special," her father said. "I'm not walking my Button down the aisle and handing her over to some schmuck."

Charlie had a sudden panicky image of her father walking her down the aisle and Mark bolting out a side door. But of course that wouldn't happen. It *couldn't* happen. Too much was at stake now.

Besides, Mark didn't act like a man who had any intention of running. At this very moment he was gazing at her with complete adoration and rubbing his hand along her thigh while he waited for his turn on the phone.

"Mark's terrific," she said. "As a matter of fact, he's right here. He'd like to talk to you."

Her father chuckled. "Oh, sure he would. He's probably as excited about talking to me as I was when I had to face your mother's old man for the first time. But the sooner he gets it over with, the better. Put him on."

"Now, Dad, you're not gonna treat him like you used to treat my dates in high school, are you?"

"Whadya mean? I was very nice to those boys."

"You scared the hell out of them! All that talk about your bayonet skills in the Marines. Honestly. They thought if they weren't careful you'd use those skills on them!"

"Instilling a little healthy respect for the older generation never hurts."

"Dad, now don't you—"

"Oh, I'll be a pussycat, Button," her father said with another chuckle. "Give him the damned phone before he passes out from anxiety."

"Okay. Love you, Dad."

"Love you, too, Button."

As Charlie started to give the phone to Mark, she noticed a suspicious sheen to his eyes. She put her hand over the mouthpiece. "You okay?"

"Yeah." He cleared his throat. "It's just...the easy way you talk with him. The...the...love is so real."

Her heart squeezed and she leaned over and kissed him on the cheek. "And I'm going to share every bit of it." She put the phone in his hand.

He cleared his throat again and put the phone to his ear. "Mr. McPherson?" He paused. "Oh, okay, then. Hank. You know, it's a little late to be asking permission to marry your daughter, but—" He listened for a few seconds, and then he laughed. "Is that right? The ladder up to her window and everything?" He glanced at Charlie. "No, she didn't tell me about that. Yes, I definitely feel better now."

Charlie realized her father was describing how he and her mother had eloped thirty years ago, much to the dismay of both sets of parents. Come to think of it, her folks had set a precedent for this kind of hasty marriage. Maybe it would become a family tradition.

Mark laughed again and started talking about his adventures looking for the right engagement ring. She could tell from the light in his eyes that he was soaking up the fatherly attention and advice. She decided to leave the room and give him some privacy.

With a friendly pat on his thigh, she stood and walked out of the living room. She'd had that fatherly attention for twenty-seven years. She could afford to let Mark have it all to himself for twenty minutes.

Besides, she felt grubby and, fortunately, her apartment had a roomy bathtub. She stripped off her clothes as she headed for the bathroom and tossed them in a hamper once she reached it. Then she closed the door and started running water in the tub. Last of all she dumped in some of her favorite scented bubble bath.

A full-length mirror was bolted to the back of the bathroom door, and she paused for a minute in front of it. That was when it hit her—the woman reflected in that mirror could be pregnant.

Her heart beat faster as she laid a hand over her stomach. The concept was mind-boggling. And yet she hadn't been kidding Mark about the fertile women in her family. Both her mother and aunt had conceived their first children on their wedding night.

Her uncle Jack, father of five kids, used to joke that all he had to do was hang his pants on the bedpost and Mary was pregnant.

Charlie was no expert on the subject of getting pregnant, but she was somewhere in the middle of her cycle, and she vaguely remembered that was a productive time of the month. If frequency of intercourse made any difference, then she and Mark had certainly covered that base.

Pregnant. The thought was a little scary, but mostly thrilling. Since the moment when Mark had suggested abandoning birth control, he hadn't back-pedaled once. Far from it. He'd seemed absolutely determined that before the weekend was over she'd be absolutely, positively carrying his baby.

A man could cancel a wedding. He could cancel a reception and a honeymoon. But he couldn't cancel something like this. She smiled and turned away from the mirror. The DOAs were wrong. Mark meant business this time.

MARK FELT LIKE he'd known Hank for years when his future father-in-law turned the phone over to his wife, Sharon.

"Hello, Mark," she said, her voice warm.

"Hello, Mrs. McPher—"

"Nope, that won't do. Mrs. McPherson was my mother-in-law, and she was a dear lady, but she

sucked her teeth while she sat and watched TV. You'd
better just call me Sharon."

"Okay." Mark grinned. He could hardly wait to
meet Charlie's parents. They sounded like a Mid-
western version of Sam's.

"Charlie tells me you can cook," Sharon said,
"which is a blessing, because she's not interested in
the process unless you put her next to a campfire, and
most modern kitchens aren't set up for that."

"I can cook." Mark continued to smile as he
thought of Charlie's attempts to sabotage him with
Saturday's breakfast.

"Well, I'm relieved." Sharon laughed. "The two
of you won't starve. Now what about gifts? The relatives are driving me crazy up here because you're
not registered anywhere. You'd better do something
about that or you're liable to get about twenty-five
very ugly cookie jars."

"I'm afraid we won't have time to register anywhere," Mark said. Then he had an inspiration. "Tell
you what. How about if you ask them all to hold off,
and we'll plan to come up there and visit over a long
weekend. We'll get more organized about what we
might need, and we can do the gift thing then."

"Oh, I would *love* that," Sharon said. "We can
have a big barbecue in the back yard, and invite all
the relatives…." She hesitated. "Unless you think a
more formal reception would—"

"No!" Mark had already begun to envision the happy scene, and it was exactly what he'd longed for his entire life. "A barbecue would be great. Perfect. Tell us when you want us there."

"Over Memorial Day?"

"We'll do it. I'll make sure Charlie hasn't booked a trip, but if not, count on us."

"I'll do that." Sharon's voice quivered with excitement. "What fun." She took a deep breath and lowered her voice. "I realize you're getting married quickly, but Hank and I got married quickly, too. We were young and stupid, but it worked out, because we were desperately, hopelessly in love. I'm hoping you are, too. That's really all I need to know."

"We are."

"I can hear it in your voice. I can hardly wait until I can see it in your eyes. Then I'll rest easy."

"I understand," Mark said. "Don't worry. Charlie's my whole world."

"That's good. Very good. Listen, could I talk to her a minute? I want to consult with her about what I'm wearing. What's your mother wearing?"

Mark gulped. "Well, I'm not sure—"

"Oh, never mind. I wouldn't really expect you to know. Boys don't generally pay attention to those things."

"I'll get Charlie," Mark said, desperate to avoid the topic of his mother. He wondered if there was any way he could convince her to come this time. Obviously it would make a huge difference to Charlie, and probably to Charlie's parents.

He'd heard water running in the bathtub, so he carried the phone through the bedroom to the door and tapped on it while he kept his hand over the mouthpiece. "Charlie? Your mom wants to talk to you."

"Okay," she called through the door. "You can bring the phone in here."

He opened the door to a sight that made his tongue hang out—a rosy blond nymph in a bubble bath that almost, but not quite, covered her up. Instantly he began to develop an erection, which didn't seem quite kosher while he still had her mother on the phone.

She glanced at the bulge in his pants and grinned.

He felt himself blushing and he pressed his hand tighter over the phone's mouthpiece. "Charlie, it's your *mother.*"

"I doubt if she'd be shocked."

"I know, but still."

"I won't splash, so she won't know where I was when you brought me the phone." She stuck out a damp hand. "Would you dry me off?"

"Uh, okay." First he wrapped the cordless phone in one thick towel. Then he got another towel and dropped to one knee beside her to dry her hand.

All the while, clumps of bubbles kept shifting on the surface of the water. It reminded him of the view from an airplane flying through intermittent clouds, except here the landscape under the clouds was way more interesting. Instead of nubby, tree-dotted hills or the regimented pattern of a city, he was treated to a nipple peeking out here, a knee revealed there, and a heartbreakingly short glimpse of a triangle of gold curls darkened to bronze by the water.

By the time he handed Charlie the phone, he was a desperate man. His jeans pinched at the crotch as he gingerly rose to his feet.

"Hi, Mom!" she said, holding very still in the water. She kept her gaze fastened on Mark's fly and her grin widened. "Yeah, things are developing nicely here. Soon I'll have everything in hand."

He rolled his eyes to the ceiling. He needed to get out of there before she made him laugh…or strip down and climb in with her. Now there was an idea. But he'd wait until she ended the phone call. He'd spend the time in her bedroom, out of temptation's way. Slowly he backed out the door.

She waved a soapy hand at him.

Standing in her bedroom with the memory of her in the tub wasn't any easier on him, especially when he looked at the inviting expanse of her bed. On impulse he walked over and folded the sheets back. Then he closed the curtains over the room's only window and turned on a bedside lamp.

Just doing that made him get even more excited.

The room wasn't as fancy as the Presidential Suite had been, but Charlie's touch was there, and that made it special. The comforter on the bed was hunter green, and over the bed she'd hung a print of a wolf peering through snow-covered branches.

The only other furniture in the room was a sturdy dresser that looked like an antique. The top was crowded with framed family pictures, but until he had Charlie to help him identify people, trying to figure out who everyone was made no sense.

Instead he started taking off his clothes as he listened to the murmur of Charlie's voice while she talked to her mother. Once again he became aware of the same easy affection she'd shown her father, and he experienced the same visceral reaction, the same deep yearning.

And then he had another insight. None of his other fiancées had been this close to their families. He hadn't thought that mattered, but maybe, on some level, it had mattered a great deal. Besides creating his own little family, he wanted to be part of an extended one, too.

God, he hoped Charlie was pregnant. He'd thought about it the whole time he was talking to her mother. Mentioning the possibility of grandchildren to her was a little premature. No, *very* premature. But he'd wanted to, anyway. He had a feeling that she'd be pretty damned excited about the prospect.

By Memorial Day they'd know if Charlie was pregnant. What a homecoming that could be for her. And for him. He couldn't pretend that he wouldn't think of it that way, as his homecoming, too. The visit might mean even more to him than it would to her.

Charlie's voice grew slightly louder. "Love you, too, Mom. See you soon. 'Bye."

Mark quickly finished undressing. With all the lovemaking they'd done so far, their chances that Charlie was pregnant were already good. But he wouldn't mind making them even better.

CHARLIE LAID THE PHONE beside the tub and was considering getting out when Mark walked through the door, naked and ready for action. The sight of his aroused body took her breath away. Knowing she'd caused him to become that way made her feel like a million bucks.

She gazed up at him and that lovely tension he inspired began coiling inside her again. "Maybe it's time I got out."

"Not necessarily." His gaze swept hungrily over her. "I was thinking of coming in."

"Really?" She tried to judge whether they'd both fit. It would be fun trying, at least. "Then I'll make room for you." She rose to her knees as he approached the tub.

As he stood next to her and started to get in, it struck her that she was missing a golden opportunity. She was in a perfect position to give him a thrill before he climbed in with her.

The woman she used to be wouldn't have been so bold as to suggest it. But because of the way she and Mark had started out, because he thought of her as bold and daring, she had become that person.

"Hold still a minute," she murmured.

"What—" He gasped as she curled her fingers around his penis.

She glanced up at him. "May I?"

His lips were parted, his eyes glazed over with passion. "Oh, babe, you never have to ask permission."

"I'll remember that." Her damp hands slid easily over his hot, smooth shaft. She wasn't experienced in this, but she was tuned in to him, and what she lacked in knowledge she planned to make up for in imagination.

"I'll remind you." He drew his breath in sharply as she dipped her hands in the water and stroked him again.

When she twisted her hands lightly in opposite directions, he moaned with pleasure. Good. She was doing something right. Teasing him even more with long, lazy swipes of her tongue, she gripped and twisted gently again.

"Oh, *Charlie*."

"Like that?" Still caressing him, she gazed upward.

His gaze was hot and intense, and he seemed transfixed by the sight of her loving him this way. He buried shaking fingers in her hair. "You know it."

"I thought so." Still keeping her gaze locked with his, she took his penis slowly into her mouth.

He groaned and started to shake.

Man, she was loving this. What a feeling of power. Looking up at him while she put him through such sweet torture made it all the better. His eyes darkened, then darkened even more. She continued using all her weapons—hands, mouth and tongue. The more aroused he became, the more she ached, but she was having too much fun to be concerned about her own satisfaction.

He began to pant, and his shaking grew worse. Finally he squeezed his eyes shut, gripped her scalp and eased away.

"But don't you want more?" she murmured. She knew he'd enjoyed every second of his little treat.

His laugh was a hoarse bark. Still cupping the back of her head, he opened his eyes and sank to his knees on the bath mat. His gaze was hot and his fingers tightened on her scalp. "Yes," he whispered fiercely. "More, more and still more." Then he kissed her, plunging his tongue into her mouth.

She wrapped wet arms around his shoulders and hung on for dear life as his kiss grew more frenzied.

Still devouring her mouth, he rose, drawing her up with him. Then he lifted her from the tub.

Instinctively she wound her legs around his hips and he carried her, dripping water and suds, to the bedroom. Her heart pounded in frantic rhythm with his. This was the kind of man she'd longed for, the kind who would lay her wet body on the bed without a thought about soaking the sheets, the kind who needed her so desperately that he couldn't wait for towels.

He had to be inside her, *now*. He thrust deep and kept thrusting until he rocketed them both into space.

CHAPTER THIRTEEN

DRIVING BACK to Charlie's apartment complex after taking care of the marriage license paperwork the next morning, Mark couldn't believe how much he was looking forward to saying the vows. He wished he could do it today. The idea of leaving Charlie and going back to Houston didn't seem right.

"Maybe I should just kidnap you and take you home with me," he said.

She sighed and squeezed his hand. "I'd be a willing captive, but it probably wouldn't be a good idea. I need to be here and you need to be there, at least until Saturday."

"That sucks." He brought her hand to his mouth and nibbled on her fingers. "By the way, do you have any bookings over Memorial Day weekend?"

"Not yet. I try to avoid it, because so many backpackers are out then that there can be gridlock on the trails. Why?"

"I sort of told your mom we'd come back there for a visit." He glanced her way to see if she minded.

Apparently not. She was grinning from ear to ear. "You did, huh?"

"She wanted to know what to do about the relatives buying presents, and I told her we'd had no time to register anywhere. I thought we could take care of that after the fact and then go up to Chicago for a party. Your mom seemed to like the idea."

"Oh, I'm sure she loved it." Charlie laughed. "I'll bet she's planning a barbecue in the back yard."

"She did mention something about that." Mark was thrilled that Charlie didn't have anything scheduled and they could plan the trip. When he got back to Houston he might start looking into the flights.

"I hope you're ready," Charlie said. "She'll invite every last one of the clan, and I have to warn you that some of them are crazy. They'll probably make you pitch horseshoes and play croquet until you drop. And the water-balloon fights usually get way out of hand."

Mark pictured the scene as he navigated the streets of Austin. She had no idea what such a prospect meant to him, but she would find out. "I'm gonna love it," he said softly.

"I hope so. And if you don't like Jell-O salad you're in trouble, because there will be at least six kinds."

"I'll eat every one." He stopped at a red light and looked at her. "By Memorial Day we should know."

"Know what?"

"If you're pregnant."

She flushed and looked almost shy. "Oh. I guess so." She looked at him from under her lashes. "If I'm not, it won't be for lack of trying."

"And I cherished every minute of it."

"Me, too."

As he accelerated away from the intersection, he gripped her hand tighter. "I want you to be pregnant. I want to be able to tell your folks, and your whole family, that we're having a baby."

"My mother will go nuts."

"I'll go nuts." He turned into her street and sighed. "I sure don't want to go back to Houston today. I want our life together to begin right now."

"I wish it could. But Saturday isn't so far away. We'll—hey, that's Ashley's car parked in front of the apartment."

Mark wouldn't have known the sleek little Mustang belonged to Ashley because he'd never seen her car before. But as they pulled into the covered parking adjacent to Charlie's apartment building he could see that Ashley was sitting inside the Mustang.

"Shouldn't she be down at her shop?" For some reason finding Ashley waiting for them made him nervous. It wasn't part of the plan, and right now he didn't want a single glitch in the plan.

"The shop's closed on Mondays. But I still wonder what she's doing here." Charlie opened the car door and hopped out as soon as he turned off the engine.

Ashley got out of her car, too, and started toward them.

"Hey, you," Charlie called. "What's up?"

"Oh, I just thought I'd come and talk to Mark
about something before he left for Houston," Ashley
said. "I take it you two went to see about the license."

"Yes," Charlie said.

Ashley's glance flicked over her. "I thought you
were getting sick on Friday."

"I—"

"She got over it." Mark came to stand beside
Charlie and hoped his apprehension didn't show.
"What did you want to talk to me about?"

Ashley took off her designer sunglasses and
glanced up at him without the trace of a smile.
"What's this I hear about a rash I'm supposed to
have?"

Oh, shit.

"Rash?" Charlie asked. "What rash?"

Mark gazed at Ashley as his mind raced. "I guess
you talked to Sam."

Ashley's cheeks grew pink, and for a second her
indignant manner slipped. "Uh, yes, I did."

"And you probably told him about the transvestite
thing." He couldn't believe the subject would come up
during a telephone call, which might mean that she'd
actually *seen* Sam this weekend, after all. That would
explain the blush. But he was still in deep doo-doo.

Her indignation returned. "Yes, I did. And he's ready to kick your butt, or so he said. He's not happy with you, Mark."

Mark winced. He was definitely in for it, now.

"What's going on?" Charlie glanced from Ashley to Mark. "What's this all about?"

"Look," Mark said. "I can explain everything. I—"

"It seems that Sam's trauma with the transvestite was bogus," Ashley said, still gazing intently at Mark. "Not only that, but he told Sam that I needed rehabilitating, too. Supposedly I broke out in a rash every time I was attracted to a guy."

"*What?*" Charlie cried, turning toward Mark. "You made all that up?"

"Yeah, I did." He focused on Charlie. He cared about what Ashley thought, but Charlie was the one who concerned him the most. Should he spill the beans about the broken engagements now? Or did Ashley already know?

He'd guess not. Sam wouldn't take the liberty of telling, even when he'd found out the trick Mark had pulled.

"Why did you?" Charlie asked.

Damn it. The doubts were back in her eyes. This was not the place to confess everything. She might cancel the wedding on the spot. If she did that, he would...well, he would have no more reason to live.

He took a deep breath. "Because Sam insisted on coming along. He thought I might move too fast, and he wanted to be there to slow me down. I felt sort of embarrassed that he insisted on being there for our first meeting, like I was some sort of sex maniac—"

"Are you?" Ashley asked.

"So I decided to work the whole thing into a double date," he finished, ignoring Ashley.

Charlie looked betrayed, and he hated that. He gripped her shoulders. "Dreaming up those stories was the only way I could think of to make Sam and Ashley go along with the date, because neither one of them needed a blind date, obviously."

"No, just a neurosis," Ashley said.

He continued to focus on Charlie. "I was going to tell them both at the reception, and I hoped we'd have a good laugh over it."

"Ha, ha." Ashley folded her arms over her chest.

"You should have at least told me this weekend," Charlie said.

"You're right. I should have. And I apologize for that. Charlie, I love you so damned much, and I'm petrified that something will come between us." He lowered his voice. "I beg you not to let this shake your confidence in me. It was a dumb thing for me to do, but at the time it seemed like the only way to make sure we had the best possible start."

She gazed into his eyes, and slowly her frown disappeared. "We did have a good start," she said.

"We sure did."

"A wing-ding of a start." A smile tugged at her mouth. "I guess I can't be too hard on you, considering the rocky bed and the soggy sleeping bag and the burned breakfast. Oh, and the headache."

"Yeah," Ashley said. "What happened with that headache? I thought it was supposed to develop into something debilitating."

Mark vaguely realized that Ashley must have been in on the scheme of Charlie's fake illness, which meant she was the pot calling the kettle black, but he didn't even feel like making a point of it. He smiled back at Charlie as relief flooded through him. "As I said, she got over her headache."

"Seems like," Ashley said.

"So you forgive me?" he asked Charlie.

"Uh-huh."

"I believe I'm the one you should be asking for forgiveness," Ashley said. "And Sam."

Feeling generous, Mark turned to her. "I do ask it, Ashley. And I'll talk with Sam the minute I get back to Houston. For some reason I didn't think he was getting back from San Francisco until sometime today."

There was that blush again. "The, uh, business didn't take as long as he thought it would, so he caught an earlier flight."

Charlie stood next to Mark. She stood very close. He could feel support radiating from her.

She studied her sister. "When did he get back?"

"Yesterday, around noon."

"And he called you yesterday?" Charlie asked. "How come you didn't come over to confront Mark last night? You knew we'd be home."

Ashley's gaze shifted. "Well, actually Sam didn't call. He drove to Austin from the airport."

Charlie began to smile. "Hmm. Sam arrived in Austin yesterday afternoon, but you're just now getting over here to lecture Mark. Why the long delay?"

"Well, we—"

"Never mind." Charlie walked over and hugged her sister. "I know why. I'm thrilled for you. I think Sam's terrific."

Ashley looked as if she might be having trouble keeping her anger stoked up. "He is terrific," she agreed, "but Mark shouldn't have made up those stories."

"Think about it, Ashley," Charlie said. "Don't you realize that if Mark hadn't cooked up that whole deal, then you'd have had no excuse to go on the date last weekend? You wouldn't have met Sam until the wedding, and you certainly wouldn't have spent the night with him just now. So there."

If Mark had been head-over-heels in love before, he was Charlie's devoted slave now. Not only had she forgiven him for his crazy stunt, she'd stood up for him when her sister would have continued to toss blame his way. He slipped an arm around her waist and gave her a subtle squeeze to let her know how much he appreciated what she'd done.

Ashley gazed at her sister for a long time. Then she glanced at Mark, and back at Charlie. "You do look good together," she said, almost to herself.

"That's because we belong together," Mark said. "I think it might turn out to be true for you and Sam, too."

Ashley's body language softened even more as the stiffness went out of her spine. "It's possible." Then she straightened and shook her finger at Mark. "But so help me, you'd better do right by this sister of mine. That threat to run you over with my car stands. And as you can see, I have a fast car, with a strong bumper and big tires."

"I'll do right by her," Mark said.

"Yes, he will." Charlie gave him an adoring glance. "And you'd better get on the road, Mr. Right. Didn't you have an appointment you didn't want to miss?"

He checked his watch. Sure enough, he was out of time. He'd taken all his stuff out of her apartment before they'd driven downtown so that he could leave immediately after dropping her back at the apartment. But leaving Charlie was like cutting off an arm.

He decided to make it quick so it wouldn't hurt so

much. "I'll see you on Saturday," he said. "I'll call tonight." Then he kissed her hard and climbed back in his car. All the way out of the parking area he kept looking in his rearview mirror to catch a glimpse of her standing there watching him leave. The next time he saw her, she would be wearing white.

CHARLIE WATCHED Mark's black Lexus until it disappeared around the corner. Saturday seemed like an eternity away. She didn't want to guide her group of backpackers tomorrow. She wanted to be with Mark. Going into her empty apartment would be dismal. Their breakfast dishes were still in the sink, and the towel he'd used would be hanging on the rack in the bathroom. It would be filled with his scent. She—

"So I'm guessing you had sex, after all."

She blinked and glanced over at Ashley. For a moment she'd forgotten Ashley was there. And what had she just asked? Oh, yes. She'd asked about sex.

"Yes," she said. *Unprotected sex.* She didn't plan to mention that to Ashley, who would go into orbit if she heard that.

"So I'm assuming he came clean about the broken engagements."

"Well, no, he didn't."

"He *didn't?* Oh, Charlie, that's not good."

"It doesn't matter," Charlie said. And it didn't. Not one bit. Mark had shown her in every way that counted that he expected to live the rest of his life with her.

"What do you mean, it doesn't matter?" Ashley jammed her sunglasses on top of her head, as if she needed both hands to make her point. "Of course it matters. His integrity is in question here. I just found out about that business with the rash and the transvestite. I was willing to let it go, considering how it all turned out, but you could be letting yourself in for a purple-T-shirt, girl!"

"No, I'm not."

"How can you be so sure?"

Because he wants me to have his baby. But that was a private decision between her and Mark, and besides, Ashley might put a different interpretation on it. She might think Mark was irresponsible.

"I'm just sure, that's all," she told her sister.

Ashley let out a long, exasperated breath. "Why did you go to bed with him if he didn't confess?"

Charlie opened her mouth to explain how Mark's endearing willingness to suffer had melted her heart.

"That's okay. It doesn't take much imagination to figure it out. When they coined the phrase *bedroom eyes,* they were referring to Mark." She gazed at her sister. "So the wedding's on?"

"The wedding's on."

"Then we'd better get cracking. We have lots of

details to tidy up if you're really and truly getting married on Saturday."

Charlie felt a jolt of excitement. For some reason it hadn't seemed completely real to her until this moment. She was getting married!

ON MONDAY NIGHT Mark drove down the tree-lined street where he'd grown up. He passed the Cavanaughs' place where cheerful lights were on in several rooms as usual, and he wished he were stopping there, instead. But he didn't need to make a personal visit to convince Sam's parents to attend the wedding. One phone call had been enough.

His phone call to Sam's folks this afternoon had gone a lot smoother than the late lunch he'd had with Sam today. Sam had been boiling on a couple of counts. One was the transvestite story. But Mark had taken his cue from Charlie and convinced Sam that without the wild stories, Sam wouldn't have met Ashley. Eventually Sam's lawyer logic had come into play, and he'd grudgingly admitted that discovering Ashley was worth whatever Mark had put him through.

But on the second point—that Mark had neglected to confess his past misdeeds to Charlie—Sam wouldn't budge. He was totally put out with Mark about that. He thought Mark should drive to Austin tonight and lay it all out for her.

Mark had refused, and he still wasn't sure why Sam was sticking with the wedding plans after that flat refusal. Maybe it had to do with Mark's decision to visit his mother tonight and plead with her to attend the ceremony. Come to think of it, Sam had lightened up considerably after Mark had told him about that. Sam was the only person in the world who had an inkling of the desolate landscape that had been Mark's childhood, and he'd offered to go along tonight as moral support. But Mark needed to do this by himself.

He parked in the drive of the two-story house. In contrast to the lights blazing from the Cavanaughs', the O'Grady house was dark, except for a faint light coming from the window wells in the basement where his mother had her lab. Even the front porch light was off.

Walking up to that darkened doorway, he once again became the lonely little kid who'd forced himself to leave the warmth of the Cavanaughs' home each night and return here, because he had some pride, after all. The Cavanaughs were good people who'd tried to console him by saying that his mother was brilliant, that she might even win a Nobel Prize someday.

He would have settled for lights glowing in the windows, a welcome hug, even company in front of the television set. He'd prayed for the day when he'd be old enough to go to college, and he'd chosen dorm life over an apartment, just so he could surround himself with noise, people and light. Lots of light.

As he used his key to let himself in, he wondered if he'd be able to get her attention tonight. His record wasn't very good on that score. When he'd lived here as a kid, he'd often ended up going to bed without ever having the discussion he'd wanted. Sometimes, when the matter was urgent, he'd written a note and stuck it under the coffeepot in the kitchen. But he wouldn't do that tonight.

Once inside the door he pushed the buzzer she'd installed that sounded down in the lab, a device she'd created so she'd know whenever he'd arrived. He used to wonder if she even heard it. Flicking on lights as he went, he started down the steps to the basement.

He knocked on the door before opening it. Sure enough, she was sitting on a swivel stool with her back to him, hunched over several petri dishes. Her half glasses were perched on her nose, her laptop computer was positioned to her right and the fingers of her right hand rested on the keys.

Selena O'Grady was slim and still very pretty, with only touches of gray in her dark brown hair. He knew she'd never color it. She wouldn't want to take the time. She rarely even got it cut, leaving it long enough to catch up in one of those big butterfly clips at the back of her head.

As usual, she had on sweats and an oversized T-shirt, her at-home uniform. On campus she wore slacks, blouses and blazers, which might or might not go together, depending on whether she was in the middle of a big project. She was usually in the middle of a big project.

As he gazed at her absorbed in her work, his heart gave a funny little lurch, and he realized that the resentment he usually felt when in the presence of his mother was gone. She'd been a mere twenty-two when she'd had him, certainly not old enough to understand that she shouldn't have a kid, given her need for this work of hers.

She'd only followed what society had preached to all young women in those days. He wondered if his forgiveness had to do with his love for Charlie, and he decided it probably had everything to do with that.

He cleared his throat. "Hi, Mom."

"Hi, Mark." Her voice sounded typically distracted, and she didn't turn around. "Just give me a minute here."

Once those words would have made him angry. She'd said them a million times, and then she'd left him hanging, sometimes for hours.

Tonight he smiled. "I can't give you a minute, Mom. I need all your attention, and I need it right now. It's a matter of life and death."

She spun around on the stool and pulled off her glasses. Her eyes were wide. "What did you say?"

Damn. He should have tried that line years ago. He walked toward her. "I'm getting married."

She rolled her eyes. "No, you're not, but I'm sorry to hear that another sweet young thing expects you to."

"No, this time I really *am* getting married, and I want—no, *we* want you to be there."

She fluttered her hand at him. "Like I said before, you can let me know after the fact—not that I really expect that to happen." She sighed. "I'm sure this is my fault, somehow. If you want to go into therapy, I'll pay for it."

He didn't contradict her. Some of his problems were her fault. But he couldn't blame her anymore, now that he realized that from the beginning she'd been doomed to fail at motherhood. If she'd known that beforehand, he wouldn't be here.

"I don't need therapy," he said. "But I do need you to come to this wedding. It's Saturday."

"Saturday? That's only—" She paused in confusion. "What day is this?"

"Monday." He couldn't help grinning. She was so flaky.

"Monday. Hmm. I thought it was Tuesday. Anyway, Saturday is only five days from now."

"Which is five too many for me. Mom, I want you

to be at this wedding. It's in Austin, and you can ride down with—"

"Austin? You're not even getting married in Houston? Well, then it's out of the question. I can't spare the time from this project, even if I thought you would go through with it, which I'm afraid you won't. I wish you would finally marry someone, because you need a family. I know that. Let me pay for some therapy."

"No therapy. I'm going through with this wedding. And I want you there."

"Oh, Mark, I just can't. Now, if you'll excuse me, I need to get back to work." She swiveled the seat of her stool around until she was facing her petri dishes again.

A week ago he would have let it go at that. He crossed to where she was sitting, gripped her shoulders and turned her to face him.

She stared at him in astonishment. "Mark?"

He crouched down so that he could look directly into her eyes. "Listen to me, Mom. For all those years when you were too busy with your work to pay attention to me, I never begged you to give up your work because of something I needed. Never. I never thought I was important enough, or that what I wanted was important enough. Now it is."

"But—"

"I'm marrying Charlie on Saturday, and we're going to have a family soon. Before you know it, you'll be a grandmother. And if I have anything to say about it, you'll be a damn good one, because I'm going to be a real pest, starting now. I want you to plan on that wedding. Sam and I will pick you up at ten for the drive to Austin. And I won't take no for an answer. I love you, Mom, and I want you there on my special day."

She stared at him in shock for several long seconds. Finally she took a shaky breath. "Well, if you put it that way…."

"That's the way I'm putting it." He smiled at her. "So it's settled. Ten on Saturday. I'll call you at eight and remind you."

She nodded, looking dazed. "That's a good idea."

He gave her a quick hug and kissed her on the cheek. "I'll let you get back to your project, now."

"Okay."

He turned and walked toward the door leading upstairs. On impulse he glanced back, fully expecting her to be engrossed in her work again.

Instead she was gazing after him, a tiny smile on her face. "I'm happy for you, Mark," she said.

"Thanks, Mom." He took the stairs two at a time, and when he exited the house, he left every light he'd turned on still burning.

CHAPTER FOURTEEN

"I'M SURE HE'LL BE HERE any minute, Button."

"I'm sure he will, too, Dad." As Charlie sat in the recreation hall of the church twenty minutes after the wedding should have started, she fought to stay calm. But if one more person told her Mark would be there any minute, she might scream. Although her poor father meant to reassure her, his comment didn't help.

Everyone had tried to reassure her, even the five women who didn't believe Mark would ever show up and had driven down from Houston today to be with her in her hour of need. She wished they hadn't come.

First of all, she'd had to explain their presence to her parents. Although her mom and dad had tried to stay positive after she'd insisted Mark would not make her victim number six, his lateness was damning him with each minute that passed. Secondly, the DOA group's presence reminded Charlie that each of them had once been as confident as she that they would become Mark's wife. And they'd each suffered a huge disappointment.

But Mark would be here, and he would say his vows this afternoon. She had to believe that or go crazy. He was late, but he would be here.

The original rendezvous point had been Ashley's apartment. Charlie's parents were staying there, and so Charlie had decided to get dressed there, too. Sam, Mark and his mother were to have arrived at Ashley's an hour before the wedding was scheduled to begin. Charlie was clinging to the knowledge that Mark had convinced his mother to attend the wedding. That had to be significant.

But they hadn't shown up thirty minutes past when they were due and there had been no answer at either Mark's or Sam's apartment when Charlie had called. Ashley had decided they should leave a note on the door and go to the church to meet the only other guests, Sam's parents. All the while Charlie had worked to stay calm.

The scheduled time for the wedding had come and gone while Charlie, Ashley and their mother and father had waited in a small room off the main sanctuary. Still no Mark. Then the DOAs arrived.

Finally they'd decided to abandon protocol when the minister suggested they all adjourn to the church's recreation hall. Charlie had given up on making a grand entrance in her dress and now sat, her veil thrown back and her shoes off while she tried to ignore the wall clock nearby. Everyone else struggled to keep a conversation going except Mark's ex-fiancée, Deborah, who made numerous calls on her cell phone trying to find someone who could locate Mark.

Watching her, Charlie wished Mark didn't hate cell phones so much. If he had one, he'd be able to call her from wherever he was. Or maybe he'd found a telephone and had left a message. She mentioned it to Ashley and they both ducked into the church secretary's office to call and check the messages on their answering machines. Nothing.

As they were leaving the small office, Charlie touched her sister's arm. "I hate saying this, don't even want to think it, but what if…what if there's been…an accident?"

Ashley's gaze was troubled. "I thought of that, too, but I didn't want to bring it up unless you did. The police wouldn't call either of us if that happened."

"They would call Sam's parents, though." Charlie put a hand to her churning stomach. "Maybe we should ask them to check their answering machine messages, too."

Ashley nodded. "Maybe we should."

So after that, three people trooped into the church secretary's office every few minutes.

Finally Charlie couldn't stand it any longer. She got up and faced the people sitting around on folding chairs. "I don't know what's happened," she said, "but this is getting more and more uncomfortable for me, and probably for everyone here. If it's all right with Ashley, I think we should all go back to her apartment and wait there. At least we can give people something to eat and drink." She glanced at Ashley. "Maybe something strong to drink."

Deb snapped her cell phone closed and stood. "The DOAs have that covered," she said. "We have plenty of booze stashed in the van in anticipation of this."

Her assumption that Mark would decide against the marriage filled Charlie with righteous anger. Feeding that anger was a growing fear that Deb might be right. She wasn't about to reveal that fear. "He *is* coming," she said. "I don't know what's happened, but he will be here."

Deb's gaze was filled with sympathy. "I hope so. I truly do."

"He will be here," Charlie repeated with as much conviction as she could muster. But the doubts had started to creep in.

DRESSED IN HIS tux shirt and slacks, Mark paced the shoulder of the road getting dust on his shiny black shoes as he muttered every foul word in his vocabulary. If his mother hadn't been within earshot, he would have belted those words out and directed them right at Sam.

Damn it to hell, he *knew* they should have brought

the Lexus. But Sam had been so all-fired hot to drive his baby over, arguing that he didn't much like Mark's Lexus and he'd have to drive it all the way back to Houston once he dropped Charlie and Mark off at the airport in the morning.

Sam finally got off his cell phone. "Road service should be here soon," he said. "They lost us on the system the first time I called, but now they promise to be here ASAP. In the meantime, we can sit here and admire the bluebonnets."

Mark had been happy about the bluebonnets two hours ago. He'd been thrilled that the wildflower show had begun in time for his wedding day. But at the moment he didn't care a damned bit about flowers. He gave the phone in Sam's hand a malevolent glance. "What kind of stupid cell phone only takes calls for road service, anyway?"

"It's the kind I like, okay? You don't even have one, period, so don't give me your crap. I don't want a regular cell phone for the same reason you don't. I don't want a leash. This one does exactly what a cell phone is supposed to. It works fine for road emergencies."

"Yeah, it works just dandy, except if someone loses us in the system, whatever the hell that means. And if we had my car, we wouldn't even *have* a road emergency," Mark added, glaring at his best man. "But no, we had to bring your pile of junk."

"Don't you talk that way about Betsy. If you

hadn't made me stop the car to locate the dang wedding rings, she'd have taken us all the way to Austin."

"Yeah, and *then* the battery would have died in front of Ashley's apartment." Mark was furious, furious and scared. Things weren't going according to plan. "Why in God's name didn't you replace the battery this week?"

"Who replaces a battery before it dies?"

"In a critical situation like this, I would have! And about those rings, how could you not have them right in your pocket? Why were they packed in your suitcase in the trunk, for crying out loud?"

Sam threw up both hands. "It seemed logical! So shoot me."

"I just might. I can't imagine what Charlie must be thinking. It's a damn good thing I didn't tell her about those five other times I called off the wedding, which is what *you* wanted me to do, remember? If she knew about those, and we ended up being this late, she'd think I was backing out."

"Well, you're not," Sam said. Then he peered at Mark. "Are you?"

"Of course I'm not! How dare you say that?"

"I'll give you five good reasons."

"Oh, yeah? I have half a mind to leave you here and hitch my way to Austin!"

Sam stepped up nose-to-nose with him. "Well, what's stopping you, buddy-boy?"

"I am." Selena O'Grady walked over to the men and put both hands between them, pushing them firmly apart. "Honestly, you boys sound like you're eight years old and fighting over your blessed baseball cards. Yelling at each other isn't going to get us there any sooner."

Mark stared at her in amazement. He didn't think she'd ever heard one of his childhood arguments with Sam. He'd always assumed she was too preoccupied with her work.

As he looked down at the exasperated, totally parental expression she wore, a goofy grin tugged at his mouth. "You know what? You sound just like a mom," he said, without thinking. Oops. He watched in horror as her eyes filled with tears. He'd never seen that happen in twenty-nine years.

Her voice quivered. "I am a m-mom. I know I haven't been a very g-good one, but I've loved you the best I could."

His throat tightened. "I know you have. I didn't mean—"

"You're grown up now." Her lower lip trembled. "But I thought about what you s-said, that you'll make sure I'll be a good grandma." She sniffed. "You don't have to worry about that. I w-will b-be." And she began to cry.

Mark was scared to death that he'd start crying, too, right here in front of God and Sam and everybody. "Of course you will," he mumbled, and gathered his sobbing mother into his arms.

"Don't." She tried to squirm away from him. "I put on m-mascara. I'll get it on your shirt."

"I don't care." He cradled her head against his chest and his vision was a little blurry as he looked over at Sam, to see how Sam was taking this.

Sam swallowed, like he was having trouble keeping it together, too.

That made Mark feel a little better. In fact, he felt a lot better. Now it seemed like having the car break down was almost worth it. But he was still worried sick about what Charlie was going through. She could be thinking all sorts of horrible things. But at least she didn't know about those five ex-fiancées.

"Here comes the tow truck," Sam announced.

"Thank God," Mark said. "Now maybe we can get in touch with Charlie and tell her we're okay."

BACK AT ASHLEY'S, Charlie considered getting out of her wedding dress, but that would be admitting in front of the DOAs that she'd lost hope. So she kept it on, which meant she took up way too much of the space in the apartment. Nobody complained.

The liquor began to flow and was offered to Charlie several times. She'd refused for several reasons. First of all, she'd have to go to the bathroom, and that was a major job with the yards of material surrounding her. Second of all, she had only the barest hold on her emotions. One glass of wine and she'd lose it and start blubbering. She didn't want to blubber. Last, and most important, she could be pregnant, and alcohol wouldn't be good for the baby.

So she sat on a small stool with her dress spread around her. She figured she looked like Wedding Barbie, but instead of her daisy bouquet, which was chilling in Ashley's refrigerator, she cradled Ashley's cordless telephone. Every once in a while pain in her fingers would remind her she was gripping the phone way too tight and she'd relax her hold.

When the phone did actually ring, she came up off the stool and nearly dropped it. It caught in the folds of her skirt and she grabbed it before it tumbled to the floor. Then she had the toughest time pushing the right button, because her hands were shaking so much.

When she finally pulled back her veil and put the phone to her ear, she realized the room was dead silent. "H-hello?"

"Charlie, it's Mark."

"*Mark.*" The room started to sway and she sat down hard on the stool. "Are you okay?"

"I'm fine. I'm so sorry. I—"

"No accident?" Her ears buzzed and she was giddy with relief.

"No accident. Listen, I—" The phone crackled with static.

"Mark! I can't hear you!" She pressed the phone so hard to her ear that her head began to ache. More static fizzed in her ear.

"I—" The phone cut out, then in again. "—can't—reschedule—"

Her heart hammered under the tight bodice of her dress. "I can't hear you! Mark, what are you saying?"

Static was her only answer. Then the line went dead.

She took the phone from her ear and pushed the disconnect button while she prayed that he'd call right back.

Ashley was by her side, her voice tense. "What did he say?"

"I'm...I'm not sure. The reception was bad." Charlie was trembling, but she was determined not to lose it in front of all these people. "I'm hoping he'll call back."

Her mother put her arm around Charlie's shoulders. "You must have heard something, honey. Is he coming?"

Charlie had heard something, and the longer she held a phone that wasn't ringing, the more those words echoed in her head. *I'm so sorry. I can't reschedule.*

"Is everybody all right?" Sam's mother asked.

Charlie glanced up and noticed the woman was pale with worry. "Everybody's all right," she said, sounding like an automated message. "There was no accident." *I'm so sorry. I can't reschedule.*

"Do you think they're on their way, Button?" her father asked.

Charlie glanced around at ten anxious-looking faces. She knew what the DOAs were thinking. Sam's parents had watched Mark do this five times, too, so they'd probably come to a similar conclusion. Her parents and Ashley were still clinging to stray bits of hope, but she could tell the hope was fading fast.

Once she told them all what Mark had said, the hope would be gone. She only knew one thing at this moment. She couldn't bear to sit here and have everyone shower her with pity. Fortunately she'd hung the keys to her Miata on the rack Ashley kept by the front door.

She stood and handed Ashley the phone. "He's not coming," she said.

Everyone started crowding around her and talking at once.

"And I need to be alone!" she shouted above the din. For some reason she wasn't crying. Apparently she was too numb to cry.

The hubbub died down as everyone gazed at her as they might look at the victim of some horrible crime. Well, she was a victim, and she needed to come to terms with that and move on. She could do that best where she could hear the whisper of the wind through the trees and the gurgle of water over smooth stones.

She took a deep breath. "I need to be by myself for a while," she said. "I know that won't make you all real comfortable, but I promise to drive carefully."

"You're not driving," her father said. "That's out."

She leveled a look at him. "Yes, I am driving, Dad. I know I've made a dumb mistake in thinking Mark would marry me, but I'm not going to let that dumb mistake ruin my life. I need you—" She paused and turned to include everyone.

As her pulse raced, she stopped to take another breath before continuing. "I need all of you to demonstrate your confidence in me by letting me go off and think about this alone. I learned this a long time ago in the outdoor adventure business. If you treat me like a smart person who made a dumb mistake, I'll get over this. If you treat me like a dumb person who needs to be coddled and protected, I might not make it."

Her mother touched her arm. "Charlie, we only—"

"Please, Mom. Let me do this my way."

"Let her go," Ashley said.

Charlie turned to give her sister a look of gratitude. "Thanks, sis."

"Be careful," Ashley said.

"I will." Gathering her skirts, she walked to Ashley's front door, took down her keys and went outside with a rustle of white lace. She'd have to shoe-horn herself into the Miata, but she welcomed the challenge.

She welcomed any activity that would keep her mind busy and her thoughts at bay. The bluebonnets were in bloom. That was good. There would be plenty of traffic between Austin and her favorite campground. She'd have to drive carefully. Very, very carefully. And she would not cry until her tears could fall into the rushing creek and be carried away.

"I HATE CELL PHONES," Mark said as they barreled down the highway moments later. "Did I mention how much I hate cell phones? I hate the damned things. Hate 'em with a passion. When you don't need them, they work great. When you do, they don't work at all."

"How much did you get to tell her before the static took over?" Sam checked in the rearview mirror for cops and nudged the speedometer up a few more notches.

"I'm not sure how much she heard. She knows we're okay. Then I tried to tell her I couldn't get there for at least another thirty minutes. I asked if we could reschedule with the minister. I don't know if she heard any of it."

"We'll be there before you know it," Sam said. "Help me watch out for the black and white."

"Right. We can't get a speeding ticket, Sam. Make sure you don't get a ticket."

From the back seat, his mother reached forward and patted his shoulder. "It's going to work out," she said.

"Thanks, Mom. I hope so." He appreciated her comforting gesture, especially considering they'd been so rare in his lifetime. But he had a really bad feeling about this. A really bad feeling.

When they pulled up in front of Ashley's apartment, he looked for Charlie's little red Miata and couldn't find it. The bad feeling grew. Then he spotted Carrie's van. He knew it was her van—nobody else had that many bumper stickers in Latin.

His stomach began to churn. "I think the DOAs are here."

"Oh, Lord," Sam said.

"The what?" his mother asked.

"I'll explain later." He got out of the car. It was a miracle he remembered to help his mother out. He glanced at Sam. "I think I need to—"

"Go on," said Sam. "We'll follow at a more civilized pace, right, Mrs. O'Grady?"

Not waiting to hear his mother's reply, Mark took off at a sprint for Ashley's front door. By the time he rang the bell, he was puffing and his shirt was coming untucked from his slacks.

The door opened. Ashley grabbed him by the arm and dragged him forcefully into the room. "What do you have to say for yourself?"

He quickly surveyed the room and noticed every

last person was standing and ready for action. If he'd ever wondered what a lynch mob looked like, he no longer had to. The Cavanaughs were there, and all his ex-fiancées, and he recognized Charlie's folks from the pictures he'd seen. But Charlie wasn't in the room. He prayed she was in another room. "Where is she?"

"We're not sure," Ashley said, her voice deadly calm.

His heart stumbled. "What do you mean?"

"When you called to say you weren't coming, she—"

"I didn't! I called to say we *were* coming, and to ask if we could reschedule the minister!" As panic set in, his gaze swept the room again, taking in all of his ex-fiancées. He knew the answer to the question, but he decided to make sure. "I take it she knows about the other times."

Deb nodded. "Yes, she knows."

He swallowed. "Okay, doesn't *anybody* know where she went? We have to find her."

Charlie's father stepped forward, his expression ferocious. "Son, are you saying you *do* want to marry my daughter?"

"More than anything in the world." He worked to concentrate, despite the rushing sound in his ears. "We have to find her. Somebody must know where she went. What did she say when she left?"

"She said she had to be alone to think," Charlie's mother said. "When she was a little girl, that usually meant she wanted to go off into the woods somewhere."

And suddenly Mark knew exactly where Charlie was. "She's gone to the campground we went to last weekend."

Ashley nodded. "That sounds like what she'd do. She—" The doorbell interrupted her and her expression brightened. "Or maybe that's her!"

"That's Sam and my mother," Mark said.

"Oh," Ashley said. "Right." She went to answer the door.

Mark turned to the rest of the people gathered in the room. "Look, I'm going out there."

"So are we," said Charlie's father.

"Us, too," said Sam's mother.

"I think we got us a convoy," Sam commented from the doorway. "Where are we headed?"

Mark turned to him. "I'm sure Charlie's at the campground where we spent last weekend. Now that she knows about my past history, she thinks I've done it again. I have to go after her."

Deb stepped forward. "I have a brilliant idea. The DOAs will go fetch the minister and haul him to the campground, too. If you're finally willing to get hitched, then we plan to make sure it happens."

Mark gazed at her as his dream of a pretty little church wedding dissolved to be replaced by the image of marrying Charlie at the campground where they'd truly begun their marriage, where they might have conceived their first child. It felt right.

"I would appreciate that," he said. "I would appreciate that very much. If somebody will give me a piece of paper, I'll draw Deb a map so she can find the campground. Everybody else can follow Sam, my mother and me."

CHAPTER FIFTEEN

CHARLIE HAD THOUGHT she was perfectly rational when she'd headed out to the campground. But obviously she hadn't been operating on all cylinders, because she'd forgotten that by Saturday night on the first wildflower weekend in April the place would be packed to the gills.

She'd wanted to be alone, but that wasn't going to be easy. Every campsite was taken, and all of them were filled with *very* curious people. She had to admit she'd be curious, too, if a woman in an bedraggled bridal gown climbed out of a tiny car and started trudging over to the creek. She'd pulled off the veil about halfway through her journey and stuffed it under the seat, but she had no choice about the dress. It had to stay on.

Now she wished she'd changed clothes back at Ashley's when she'd had the chance. The DOAs had been right, of course, and only her stupid pride had prevented her from getting into something more comfortable. If she'd swallowed her pride and done that early on, she wouldn't be making a spectacle of herself in front of dozens of campers.

Braving it out, she picked her way through the trees, pausing every now and then to jerk her dress away from a bush where it had become entangled. Several times she heard the material rip, which gave her a certain amount of satisfaction.

Her goal was to cross the creek on a series of stepping stones and find some privacy on the opposite bank. Hiding herself while wearing a wedding dress with a skirt as big as the Liberty Bell would be tricky, but the trees grew closer together across the creek.

As she neared the edge of the water, two women about her mother's age approached. One was plump, the other fairly thin. Both had kindly faces.

"We don't mean to intrude," said the plump one, "but we wanted to make sure you…that you were okay."

"We both have daughters," said the thin lady. "And we…well, we wondered if you needed…anything."

Charlie looked over at the campsite where she guessed these two had come from and saw a couple of middle-aged men watching the proceedings. One was bald; one wore glasses. Probably the husbands. They reminded her of her dad.

She could see the concern in the expressions of the women, could even detect it in the stance of the two men. They acted so much like her parents would have under similar circumstances that something broke loose in her frozen heart. Her tenuous control snapped, and she sank to the mossy bank and began to sob.

She was vaguely aware of arms around her, comforting words, even tissues offered. Taking the tissues, she continued to cry. When the tissues she'd been given were soaked, someone thrust a cotton handkerchief toward her. The handkerchief reminded her of her father, who always carried one, and she cried even harder.

All her life she'd dreamed of a marriage as wonderful as her parents had. She'd believed that she'd have that with Mark. She'd been so wrong. And so very, very stupid. She never wanted to see him again, and yet…she could be carrying his child. Thinking of that, she soaked the cotton handkerchief, too. She began to wonder if she'd cry for the rest of her life.

And then, at last, the gusher slowed to a trickle, and finally she blew her nose and glanced up to find herself surrounded by sympathetic faces. The four original folks had been augmented by several more campers.

As much as she appreciated their humanity, this was exactly what she'd wanted to avoid. Her only consolation was that they didn't know just how much she'd been humiliated, or how completely she'd been warned beforehand.

She cleared her throat, but her voice was still husky with emotion. "Thank you all for wanting to help me," she said.

"Why don't you come over to our campsite?" said the plump woman. "We have some nice hot stew on the fire. We can make you some tea. I'll bet some tea would work wonders."

The kind offer threatened to start her off again. "Thanks, but if you don't mind, I'd like to cross over to the other side of the creek and have a little private time."

"But it's getting dark," said the husband with the glasses.

"We were afraid you were going to fall in." The other husband rubbed a hand over his smooth head.

From the way he said it, Charlie knew he thought she was planning to throw herself in. Drowning in this shallow creek would take some doing, but they probably didn't credit her with much common sense at this point.

She looked at all these well-meaning folks and knew she had to forge a compromise or they were liable to follow her across the creek. "As you've probably figured out, the groom didn't show up for the wedding."

Indignant murmurs sounded from the small crowd gathered around her.

"So I really need to go sit on my favorite rock

across the creek and get myself together. I know I'll feel calmer if I can do that."

"Then take my flashlight," said the guy with glasses.

"That dress is the problem," said the thinner of the two women. "Let me give you something else to wear."

Charlie wasn't about to change clothes at this stage. But the woman was right—the dress was a problem. "Anyone have a knife on them?" she asked.

"For what?" The bald man stared at her suspiciously.

"I want to shorten this dress."

"Oh." He looked relieved and even loosened up enough to chuckle as he handed over his Swiss army knife. "Guess it's already ruined."

In more ways than one, she thought as she found the scissors attachment on the knife and started hacking about two feet off the hem of the dress. It was slow going, and finally the plump woman took over to do the back.

"There," Charlie said when it was finally done. She felt lighter already. Life still didn't look very rosy, but it wasn't as dark as when she'd arrived here. "If you'll throw that material away for me, I'll gladly take the loan of the flashlight, and I'll be back for a cup of tea in about an hour."

"Fair enough," said the husband with the glasses as he handed her the flashlight.

She ended up taking her shoes off and tossing them across the creek. Her good throwing arm guaranteed they made it to the other side. Then, using the flashlight to light up the stones that had become shrouded in darkness, she picked her way across the creek.

Despite being a little shaky, she made it with only one slip, and she recovered enough that she only got wet up to her ankles. When she stood on the far bank she waved the flashlight to let them know she was fine, and someone waved a flashlight from the other side.

Picking up her shoes and putting them on, she used the flashlight to find her favorite thinking rock, one she'd discovered the first year she'd moved to Austin. She settled on it with a deep sigh, closed her eyes and listened to the wind in the trees and the water lapping against the stones.

Yes, the sounds reminded her of Mark and the magical time they'd shared in this place. That was another reason for her to be here, sort of like climbing on a horse after you'd fallen off. She loved this little corner of the world, and she would not allow Mark to spoil it for her. She would not.

Hot tears pricked her eyelids and she blinked them back. Enough. She would waste no more tears on him. She gazed up through the trees and found a single star in the navy sky. And then she closed her eyes. For the first time in her life, she had no idea what to wish for.

As Sam drove them slowly through the campground, Mark spied Charlie's Miata. "Hot damn," His voice quivered with excitement. "She's here."

Sam pulled the Chevy up next to Charlie's car and turned off the engine. "She shouldn't be hard to spot."

"Nope. I shouldn't have a bit of trouble finding her." Mark hopped out of the car.

"I advise you to take this slow," Sam said.

"He's right," his mother added, climbing from the back seat. "You've given her a real shock. Don't rush this and expect her to fall into your arms."

"Right." But motherly advice aside, Mark wasn't going to take it slow. He knew his Charlie. She wanted drama. If he had a chance in hell of pulling this off, he had to literally sweep her off her feet. But first he had to find her.

He approached the campsite nearest to Charlie's car. Four middle-aged people were sitting around the campfire. They all stood when he walked up.

"So you're the groom who didn't show," said one of the men, firelight glinting off his glasses.

"You ought to be ashamed of yourself," scolded a plump woman standing next to him. "That poor girl!"

"I feel terrible about it," Mark said. "And I'm here to make things right. Where is she?"

"I don't know if we should tell you," said the thinner of the two women. "Just exactly what are your intentions?"

"He's going to marry her," said Selena, stepping into the firelight. "And I should know. I'm his mother."

"And I'm the best man," Sam added, coming forward.

"And we're her parents," chimed in Hank McPherson, guiding his wife into the area with an arm around her waist. "We came all the way from Chicago to see this wedding, and by golly, we want to see it."

"Chicago?" asked the plump woman. "What part?"

"Arlington Heights," said Charlie's mother.

"*We're* from Arlington Heights, originally," the woman said, looking pleased. "What a small world."

It might be a small world, but Mark didn't see Charlie anywhere in it, and he was all out of patience. "Where is she?" he asked, wondering if she was hiding in the tent.

"Well, I guess we can tell him," said the guy with the glasses. "I mean, this looks like a wedding party. But you'd better plan on putting a ring on her finger, young man."

"We have the ring, right, Sam?"

"In my pocket," Sam said. "Just where you wanted it."

"And a minister is on the way," added Mark. "So where is she?"

"You're going to have the ceremony here?" asked the slim woman. "How exciting!"

"That's the plan, but we can't have it if you don't tell me where she is," Mark said, getting a little testy.

"She's gone across the creek," said the plump woman. "She said she needed to be alone to think, so we loaned her a flashlight and helped her cut a bunch off the hem of her dress so she could navigate the stepping stones."

"Oh, dear," said Charlie's mother. "I guess she won't be putting that dress in an heirloom box."

By the time she'd finished her sentence, Mark was halfway to the creek.

"Mark," Sam called after him. "It's dark out there! Take a flashlight!"

"Don't need it," he called back. "Charlie! I'm coming to get you, girl!" He stepped into the cold water, shiny shoes and all. Moonlight flickered on the water, but the stepping stones were only vague shadows in the darkness.

He didn't care. If he managed to find them, great. If he got wet up to his knees, he couldn't care less. In fact, if he fell in, that was fine, too. Only one thing mattered, and that was getting to Charlie.

Splashing through the water, he barely noticed the cold or how many times he slipped. And all the while he called to her and watched the woods. At last he saw her, a white, ghostly presence among the trees.

"You sure are making a racket," she said.

"That's because I love you." He lost his footing and plunged up to his knee in ice-cold water. He gasped and kept going. "And we're going to get married."

"I'll bet you tell that to all the girls."

He finally reached the opposite bank and grabbed a couple of roots to pull himself up and over. "I know you're furious because I didn't tell you, but I thought if I told you about the others, you'd doubt me." He walked toward her. "Now be honest, Charlie. If you'd known about those broken engagements, would you have been so willing to get married today?"

"I've known about them for a week and a half!" She hurled the information at him.

He felt sick to his stomach. "You did?"

"I knew when we went camping!"

As loud as she was getting, he figured the entire campground was listening. Sound carried in a place like this.

"I knew when we made love!" she bellowed. "Remember that? When you said we should make love without con—"

He leaped the rest of the distance and clapped a hand over her mouth. Then he grabbed her and held on tight.

She bit him.

"Ow!" He shook his hand, wondering if it was bleeding.

"That's only the beginning," she said, breathing hard as she tried to get away from him. "I know how to fight, and I fight dirty."

"Don't fight me, Charlie." He struggled with her and was amazed at how much strength she had for a woman her size. All that backpacking had given her some muscles. "Marry me. Marry me now. The minister should be here any minute, and Sam has the rings, yours and mine. Come on, Charlie. Let's do it."

"I don't want to." She kept struggling. "I used to want to, but I don't anymore."

"Yes, you do."

"Nope."

"Okay. You leave me with no choice." He hoisted her, kicking and flailing, over his shoulder and started back toward the creek.

"Put me down or I'll scream!"

"You're already screaming." He winced as she landed some pretty decent blows on his back. "Now stop it, or we'll both go in the drink."

"It would serve you right!"

"Yeah, but you'll end up there right along with me." He started across, and he was none too steady with a hundred and ten pounds of furious female over his shoulder.

She kept on hollering. "I don't care!" she cried as she pummeled him some more.

"I do." He gasped for breath and wondered how

John Wayne had done this in the old Westerns and made it look easy. "The ceremony will be a hell of a lot colder for both of us if we're soaking wet."

"There's not going to *be* a ceremony." She landed another hard blow to his shoulder blade.

It was enough to throw him off balance, and he knew they were going down. He managed to pull her into his lap as he landed on his butt in the water.

"Oh!" She sat there in apparent shock as the water splashed over them.

He knew that he had to act while she was still dazed if he expected to win this one. Cradling her head with one hand, he kissed her for all he was worth. At first she wouldn't kiss him back.

But then—oh, thank God—then she did. And there they were, kissing like fools in the middle of the coldest water he'd ever had the misfortune to sit in. But he'd risk frostbite on his genitals if he could get the right answer out of her.

Between kisses he managed to ask the question, but his teeth were chattering. "Will you m-marry me?"

She lifted her lips from his for a moment, and her teeth were chattering, too. "Depends. Are you c-consumed with l-lust?"

"You b-bet."

"G-good. Then I'll m-marry you."

"But I also l-love you."

She kissed him quickly. "I know. I l-love you, too. Now let's g-get m-married before we freeze to d-death."

CHARLIE HAD ONCE attended a Jewish marriage ceremony in which the couple said their vows while wrapped together in a shawl. She and Mark weren't Jewish, but they were married wrapped in a blanket provided by one of the recently invited guests.

Their guest list had grown from a few people gathered in a picturesque church to a sizable group of campers crowded around the campfire in one of her favorite places in the world. Charlie decided it wasn't the wedding she'd dreamed of. It was better than that.

For purposes of warmth, the minister stood on one side of the fire pit while Charlie, Mark, Sam and Ashley huddled on the other side. At Deb's suggestion, the original members of the wedding—Mark's mother, along with Charlie's and Sam's parents and the DOAs—joined hands in a circle that enclosed the fire, the minister and the four participants. The host of campers, who had plenty of clothes to bundle up in, took their cue from Deb and formed another, bigger, circle beyond that.

Charlie was surrounded by love.

And as she looked into Mark's eyes and repeated the words of the age-old ceremony joining man and wife, she knew she always would be.

"You may kiss the bride," the minister said.

A whoop went up from the inner circle of guests.

"Hallelujah, sisters!" shouted Deb. "He finally did it!"

Mark smiled down at Charlie. "*We* did it," he murmured.

"I make you drool, right?"

"Absolutely." Then his lips claimed hers.

EPILOGUE

SPLAT! A water balloon broke in Mark's face. Sputtering and running, he hauled one out of his bucket and aimed it at Charlie's seventeen-year-old cousin, Zach. He missed.

"Guess they don't teach you to throw in Texas," Zach taunted.

"I'm softening you up for the kill," Mark called back.

"Naw, he's mine," said Suzanne, another cousin. She aimed a good one, but Zach dodged out of the way.

"I'm golden!" he said with a laugh.

"That's what you think." But just as Mark was ready to fire, Charlie started across the yard carrying a pitcher of lemonade.

Zach grabbed her and used her as a shield. "Hold your fire! I've got your girl."

Charlie grinned at Mark. "I'm nothing in the grand scheme of things. Waste him, Mark."

But he couldn't do it. Putting down his bucket, he

held up both hands as he went toward her, smiling. "I give."

"Sucker," Zach teased.

"I sure am." He walked up to Charlie and winked. "Let me carry that."

Zach rolled his eyes. "Oh, here we go. You two are going to get sickening again."

Suzanne smacked the back of Zach's head. "Leave them alone. I think it's sweet."

"So sweet you want to puke," Zach said, but there was a twinkle in his eyes.

Charlie wouldn't give up the lemonade, so Mark kept her company over to the trestle table set up in a corner of the yard. He leaned closer. "When are we gonna tell them?"

"Right after everybody sits down," she said.

About that time, Hank, clad in an apron and shrouded with smoke from the barbecue, announced that the hamburgers and hot dogs were ready and people began lining up with plates and buns.

Mark looked at Charlie. "Which one of us is going to say it?"

Her face glowed with love. "You are."

He wanted to be the one, but he wasn't sure that was right. "It's your family."

"No, it's *our* family. And as its newest member, you should do the honors. It'll really put you in good with the relatives."

"Oh. Well, in that case, I'll tell them." Mark was so eager that he was guilty of rushing people through the line. And finally, after what seemed forever, the family, all twenty-six of them, were gathered around the long table.

When grace was over and Sharon started to pass the potato salad around, Mark stood and clinked his spoon against his lemonade glass. "Before we start, Charlie and I have an announcement to make."

She gazed up at him, her blue eyes sparkling.

He took a deep breath. "We've bought a house!"

Everybody clapped and cheered.

"Smart move, son," Hank said with an approving nod. "Interest rates are good right now."

Mark grinned. After all, it was his business to predict such things. "Yep. I know." Then he cleared his throat. "The house has a nursery in it," he added.

Eyes widened around the table, and then Sharon leaped to her feet and looked at her daughter. "Charlie?"

Mark squeezed Charlie's hand. "We're pregnant," he said. And in the ensuing round of congratulations, back-slapping and happy tears, he knew he'd come home at last.

The Future Widow's Club

by Rhonda Nelson

Dear Reader,

Jolie Marshall made a mistake that many women make—she married the wrong man. She was swept off her feet by a man after her mother's money and the only way she can get it back is to stay married to the thief until she can manage to steal it back. When other members of their small hometown recognise the hell she's going through, they decide to help her and invite her into a secret society of women—*The Future Widows' Club*—who have been treated like trash by their horrible husbands and prefer waiting for widowhood over divorce. But things turn sticky when Chris does end up dead and Jolie's alibi for the time of the murder is a FWC meeting. Then things get even more complicated when her old flame Jake Malone is named lead detective on the case.

I hope you enjoy Jake and Jolie's story and would love to hear from my readers. Be sure and drop by my website—www.booksbyRhondaNelson.com— and sign my guestbook.

Happy reading!

Rhonda Nelson

Despite the premise of this story, this book is lovingly dedicated to my husband, Darrell, whom I'm very blessed and thankful to have grow old with me.

PROLOGUE

"IF EVER a woman needed to be a widow, it's that one," Sophia Morgan said from the side of her mouth with a significant look across the crowded dining room.

Bitsy Highfield and Meredith Ingram leaned slightly back in their chairs and followed her line of vision. Looking sleek and polished as always, her short dark hair coifed in a flattering bob, Meredith instantly recognized the woman in question and her mouth curved knowingly. She shot Sophia a shrewd look.

Bitsy, as usual, wore her typical vacantly bewildered expression. "What woman?" Her penciled eyebrows formed a wrinkled line above her purple cat-eye glasses. "I don't see a woman."

"Jolie Marshall," Meredith hissed. "There." She gestured with a willowy bracelet-clad arm. "See her?"

Bitsy adjusted her bifocals, peered across the room. "Ah, yes. I see her. But if you ask me, her husband looks near enough to death as it is." Her wrinkled brow folded into an exaggerated frown. "Rather pasty-looking fellow, isn't he?"

Sophia swallowed a long-suffering sigh. "Not her, you idiot. *Her.* The young woman with the long auburn hair, wearing the cream suit. And that guy's not pasty looking, for heaven's sake," she snapped. "That's a statue of Poseidon."

And a poor one at that, but it was in keeping with the owner's taste. George Brown fancied himself an expert on all things Greek. His restaurant, *Zeus'*, was crammed with Greek statuaries and pictures of mythological gods, murals of Prometheus, Athena, Persephone and Zeus.

Which might have been appropriate were it not a steak house.

Sophia sighed, resisted the urge to roll her eyes. But it was the best Moon Valley, Mississippi, had to offer, so she ignored the tacky décor and carved off another bite of her filet.

Meredith snickered as Bitsy's blank look turned to one of dawning comprehension.

"Oh," she murmured. Then, "*Oh.* Why she's just a child!"

"Not a child, but a young woman," Sophia clarified. She harrumphed under her breath. "Too young to be shackled to that bastard of a husband of hers, that's for sure."

Meredith quirked a regal brow. "That's Fran Caplan's girl, right?"

"Oh, I've heard that story," Bitsy piped in, her voice dripping with gossipy innuendo. She was notoriously scatterbrained and clumsy, was blind as a bat—but her memory and hearing were sharp, both of which made her a valuable asset to the Club. "I heard Sadie talking about it a couple of weeks ago down at The Spa while I was getting my hair set."

That was hardly surprising, Sophia thought with a droll smile. Sadie Webster owned The Spa and the trendy hair and nails boutique, like most small towns, was the main hub of Moon Valley's gossip wheel. In order to satisfy her addiction to gossip and aerosol fumes, Bitsy kept a standing appointment. Much to the shampoo girl's chagrin, no doubt, Sophia thought with a wry smile. Bitsy was notoriously cheap, so tight that she tipped in coupons instead of cash. She and Meredith had tried to break her of the tacky habit, but alas to no avail.

"She and that Jolie are friends," Bitsy continued with a not-so-covert look at the woman in question. "I only caught part of the conversation, mind you— I was under the dryer—but apparently, from what I was able to piece together, she met that rounder on a vacation, she fell hard for him and he convinced her that he could take the proceeds her mother had gotten from her Daddy's life insurance policy and triple it."

Bejeweled fingers sparkling against the candlelight, Meredith calmly sipped her sherry. "I take it he didn't."

"No," Bitsy said. "That's what makes it so interesting. From what I gathered, he *has*—they own that new software company down on the square, something to do with business systems, the Internet and all that," she said absently. "He just refuses to give the money back. Somehow, despite the fact that they're partners, he's stashed it in one of those offshore accounts."

"Still," Meredith hedged, the perpetual voice of reason, "I don't understand. If she's a partner, then why doesn't she do something about it?" She shrugged a slim shoulder. "If the company is so successful, why doesn't she just hire a good divorce attorney and take half?"

"What good would that do if he's hid the money from her?" Sophia pointed out. "If he can show that the company doesn't have it?"

Bitsy inclined her head. "I know that she's talked to Judge Turner about it. There's also a shady prenup, though I don't know the particulars."

"So what's she doing?" Meredith asked.

Bitsy smiled and a determined glint flashed in

her pale blue eyes. She leaned forward, as though sharing a juicy secret. "Now that's the real mystery. If the rumors about her temper are true, then she definitely wouldn't sit idly by, but no one seems to know what she's doing about it. All anyone knows is that she is doing *something*. She's got a degree in accounting, she's on the board and has signature authority. My bet is that she's working that angle."

Sophia shifted in her seat, vainly wishing that she hadn't eaten that last bite of her steak. She firmly believed the *last bite* of every meal was what had made her pack on twenty pounds over the past two years. "Meanwhile," Sophia sighed, "he's making her miserable. He's a cheat and a liar. He's not the least bit discreet about his affairs and seems to delight in embarrassing her." She lifted her shoulder in a negligent shrug. "He's a bastard," she said glibly. Her gaze drifted significantly between the two of them. "And we all know what it's like to live with one of those."

Bitsy and Meredith both frowned, evidence of the truth of that statement.

Meredith gave Sophia another probing look. "So she's the reason we're here?"

Sophia nodded. "Her mother talked to me about it, asked us to intervene. I think she's a good candidate and I want to issue The Invitation." As founding members of the Club, they all had to agree. "Do either of you oppose?"

Bitsy snorted indelicately, her spiky gray curls bobbing. "I certainly don't. She's young. She could use some widow training, and from the sounds of it, the poor girl is going to need all the help she can get."

Never one to make snap decisions, Meredith's gaze slid to where Jolie Marshall sat across the room, seemed to take her measure. After a prolonged moment, she nodded. "I agree."

Sophia let go a breath, pleased. She lifted her glass, waited for the other two to do the same before readying their standard toast. The three shared a conspiratorial look, a secret smile. "To The Future Widows' Club."

CHAPTER ONE

"WOULD YOU LIKE to go ahead and order, Mrs. Marshall?"

Jolie forced a smile at the waiter and shook her head. "No, thank you, Charlie. I'll give Chris a few more minutes."

Charlie nodded, gave her an uncomfortable look, then swiftly moved away. A sigh stuttered out of her mouth as she lifted her water glass, the glass she'd like nothing better than to hurl across the room. But being as she'd like to aim it at her husband's head—and he wasn't here—she resisted the urge.

Chris, damn him, should have been here twenty minutes ago. The fact that he was late was no surprise—he enjoyed making her wait, another power play that she'd grown accustomed to over the past two years.

Two years—to the date—of sheer hell.

Though she was tempted to scream, then dive into

a pool of self-recriminations, Jolie checked the impulse. Making a scene, calling herself every kind of idiot, wondering why she'd made the disastrous decisions she'd made, pondering the if-only's wouldn't change anything. It wouldn't make her feel any better and, more importantly, it wouldn't get her mother's money back, or the money of any of the other investors for that matter.

Every ounce of her energy, every thought, had to be directed to that end, and having a therapeutic temper fit, then mulling over the wreck her life had become wouldn't get her any closer to that goal. So no pity-party, dammit. She'd simply have to cope. She smiled at passersby, blew out a small breath to release some of her current pressure, and imagined blithely signing her divorce papers.

It was nobody's fault but her own that she'd royally screwed up and now she was left with the unhappy, nerve-wrecking, miserable task of fixing it.

Which, thankfully, was going better than she'd initially anticipated. So long as she stepped carefully—translate: didn't rock the boat with her son-of-a-bitch husband—she could recoup the rest of her mom's investment within the next three months, as well as that of the other investors. Then she'd swiftly, gleefully file for a divorce. She chuckled darkly. He'd live to regret that token appointment to the board, she thought with no small amount of satisfaction.

Her cell chirped, snagging her attention. It wouldn't be Chris, she knew. Though he was late, he'd never give her the courtesy of a phone call to let her know why. Things like courtesy, respect, fidelity and friendship had fallen instantly by the wayside the moment he'd realized that she knew he was a thief. She'd learned other things as well. She hadn't known him at all, she'd found out too late. Since then, he'd been a condescending, sarcastic control-freak who delighted in seeing how angry, how wretched, he could make her feel. Given present circumstances and her admittedly short fuse, she made it entirely too easy for him, a fact that she was desperately trying to rectify.

She'd started carrying a worry stone in her pocket, and though she'd been tempted to hurl it at him many times—not to mention the fact that she'd rubbed a blister on her thumb—she couldn't deny that she found it soothing.

She finally fished her cell out of her purse, then flipped it open. Her lips quirked. *Sadie.* "Hey," she answered.

"Don't bother ordering," Sadie told her by way of greeting. Her usually chipper voice throbbed with outraged anger.

Jolie rubbed an imaginary line from between her eyebrows, cast a subtle look around the restaurant, then let go of a sigh. "Do I want to know why?"

"No, but I'm going to show you. Take a look at this."

A picture of Chris's red BMW appeared on her cell screen. His vanity plate—*U WISH*—glowed in the dark, proof that it was definitely his car.

But it was what was hanging *out* of the car window that drew her attention—a pair of legs.

Feminine legs that definitely didn't belong to her husband. A dark shadow hovered just out of view— her husband heaving atop the woman who owned the legs, she imagined.

Jolie smirked, not the least bit surprised. Well, it *was* their anniversary. She should have known that he wouldn't miss an opportunity like this. It didn't hurt because she didn't care—she *hated* him. But she loathed being humiliated and he purposely chose whom he screwed around with to coincide with her maximum mortification.

"Jolie? Are you there?"

"Yeah, I'm here," she sighed. "Give me a minute. I want to send that to my e-mail account. It can go into The File."

Though Chris didn't know it, Jolie had amassed quite a bit of damning evidence for his take-down and her subsequent divorce. She'd need everything in order to invalidate the pre-nup she'd foolishly signed, the one he'd said was for *her* benefit. Another lie.

While Chris considered himself too smart to be double-crossed, his arrogance was actually working to her advantage. She'd been steadily documenting his shady business dealings as well as the infidelity, the worsening drug habit, and the mental abuse. She fully intended to ruin him, to make him pay for the way he'd treated her and her family. He'd picked the wrong pigeon this time and if it was the last thing she did, she'd make him live to regret it.

"That bastard," Sadie hissed angrily. "I swear, I don't think I've ever hated a man more than that son-of-a-bitch. Please tell me you're close to finishing up," she pleaded. "Please tell me that you can leave that bottom-feeder soon. Before I do something stupid, like kill him," she growled in frustration.

Jolie chuckled lightly, heartened by Sadie's outrage on her behalf. A vision of her friend's short brown curls bobbing with indignation flashed through her mind. Shirley Temple meets Katie Ka-boom, she thought fondly. "I will," she promised. "Another three months, tops."

Thank God. She didn't think her nerves could stand anything else beyond that. She wanted her life back, wanted to be able to look at her mother without feeling the knee-buckling weight of shame hanging around her neck. In the meantime, she was avoiding her. Cowardly, she knew, but... The fact that her marriage wasn't a happy one was common knowledge in Moon Valley, so she didn't hold any illusions that her mother had no idea what was going on, but confirming the rumors then having to expand upon them was out of the realm of her ability at the moment.

Sadie grunted. "Another three seconds is too long. Honestly, I don't see how you stand it."

Jolie found her stone, absently rubbed it and smiled. "That's because you married the right man, and I married the wrong one."

Sadie had married her high school sweetheart, Rob Webster. They had two kids, a mortgage and a minivan, and were the picture of marital bliss. Did they have the occasional problem? Of course. Marriage, under the best circumstances, was still work. But they loved each other and they were both committed to the relationship, to their family.

Sadie sighed. "So what are you going to do?"

"Eat dinner," she said, forcing a lighter note into her voice, hoping her faux enthusiasm would prevent her friend from worrying. "I'm hungry."

Naturally, Sadie saw through the ploy. Hell, they'd

been friends forever—since Kindergarten. Aside from one other person, Sadie probably knew her better than anyone else.

"Do you want me to come over?" she asked softly. "Because I can. I can order a pizza for Rob and the kids and I can be there in—"

"No," she Jolie interjected. "But thanks for offering. I appreciate it." And she really did.

"This sucks, Jolie," Sadie said heatedly, her ire renewed. *"This sucks."*

It certainly did, she thought as she palmed her worry stone, but she'd endured two years of it and was too close to being able to return the investor's money, most importantly her mother's. She could endure another three months. Then she'd turn her evidence in to the rest of the board, return the investors' money and she'd leave him. He should have paid more attention to the morality clause, Jolie thought with a small smile.

But she couldn't wait to leave him. Imagining that scenario was the only thing that made things bearable right now. She clung to it like a life line, dreamed about it, prayed for it.

"I, uh… I know it sucks, but I can't leave yet. You know the score," she said, unwilling to talk about it over her cell. The laundering technique she'd successfully implemented—her way of insuring that everyone got their money back—wasn't a topic of conversation one discussed over the airwaves.

Technically, it was embezzlement.

But Chris had started it first, and the difference between her and Chris was that she didn't plan to keep more than what she'd originally put in. She was giving the money back to its rightful owners, while Chris on the other hand was simply keeping it for himself. "I'm almost there, Sadie. I just need a little more time."

"I know." Sadie exhaled a resigned breath. "Call me if you need anything, would you?"

"You got it." Jolie disconnected, then snagged Charlie's attention once more. She ordered a house salad, the filet, and a bottle of expensive wine all without the slightest hesitation—she'd charge it to the company. The idea drew a half-hearted smile.

"I'll get that order in for you right away, Mrs. Marshall."

Charlie turned and walked away, and a woefully familiar profile, one that made her belly clench, loomed instantly into view. The brave smile she wore faded, and though the knowledge that her husband was currently boinking some whore on their anniversary didn't make her so much as flinch, seeing Jake Malone with another woman made her belly tip in a nauseated roll. Jolie's mouth went dry and her eyes stung. Her hands trembled and she had difficulty swallowing past the inexplicable lump that had formed in her dusty throat.

Oh, God. Not this. Anything but this.

Jake and Nicolette stood at the entrance to the dining room, presumably to wait for a table. Though she knew it was impossible, she thought she caught a whiff of fresh hay, the scent she'd forever associate with him. He loved horses, had an almost supernatural gift with them, one that had always fascinated her.

Rather than his usual T-shirt, jeans and boots, he wore a pair of khaki slacks and a white oxford cloth shirt open at the throat, cuffed at the wrists. Jolie imagined he'd ditched the tie as soon as his shift at the Sheriff's Department had ended. He'd worked his way up through the ranks, had finally earned his detective's badge, a feat she was certain he was proud of.

She couldn't know for sure, of course, because he wasn't speaking to her—he hadn't since she'd thumbed her nose at his request for "more time" and married Chris—but she knew him well enough to know that he'd be thrilled with the promotion.

His dark brown locks were mussed, a shade too long by his usual standards, and those soft gray eyes were presently drifting over his date. Jolie knew that look—that sinfully carnal caress—knew what it promised and she envied Nicolette in that moment so much that it hurt—and hated Chris Marshall more than she ever had.

Of all the mistakes she'd made, setting Jake aside for the bastard she'd married was probably the hardest to bear. One way or another, she'd get her mother's money back—even when she'd realized how terribly wrong things had gone, Jolie had never doubted that—but Jake... Jake, she knew, was lost forever.

Still, though she'd been at fault, she couldn't accept all the blame. Wouldn't, dammit. Though Jake had been there for her practically her entire life— hell, they'd been grade-school sweethearts, been voted Best Couple, Prom King and Queen, had always been together—the one time she'd *truly, desperately* needed him—when her father had died—Jake had done the one thing she'd never, ever anticipated.

He'd let her down.

Instead of being her worry stone, her best friend, confidante and lover, he'd cooled things off between them and focused on his career. He'd been more interested in being a detective than being hers and had basically put their relationship on the back burner. He'd abandoned her at a time when she'd needed him most.

They'd ultimately fought about it, which was why she'd taken that ill-fated vacation alone…and the rest had been history. She'd been ready to start a family. Jake hadn't been. Then Chris had come along, showered her with attention, expressed the same interests as her, and in her emotionally over-wrought state… Jolie sighed. A small town girl in the big bad world. In short, easy pickings. Furthermore, she'd never been able to do things half-way, had always been single-mindedly stubborn. And, for better or for worse, once she'd charted a course she never looked back, always saw it through. An admirable trait when she was right, but a bad one when she was wrong.

And choosing Chris had been wrong.

She'd later learned that he'd worked for the insurance company who'd insured her father. He'd apparently researched recent beneficiaries and decided to set his sights on her, and though she couldn't prove it yet, she firmly believed that he'd done this before to other unsuspecting women. Her lips twisted bitterly. He'd screwed her physically and financially and she'd made it easy for him.

Jolie would admit to many faults—she was impatient, hated to wait for anything and invariably squirmed through the three minutes she wasted at a traffic light. She had a horrible temper, one that had gotten her into trouble more times than she could conceivably count. But being *stupid* generally wasn't one of them, and it galled her to no end that she'd let that viper into their midst. That she'd brought him home into her insulated little world and created this mess.

The harried hostess finally arrived to show Jake and Nicolette to their table and it was with sinking horror that Jolie realized they were headed in her direction. A quick glance confirmed that the table directly in front of her was vacant. She suppressed a whimper, resisted the urge to squirm.

Oh, shit. Shit, shit, shit.

Jolie looked from the table to Jake and she swallowed tightly as her gaze connected with his. A hum of static raced up her spine and a flock of swallows took flight in her belly. The urge to flee nearly made her bolt from her seat, but she forced herself to stay still and determinedly lifted her chin. Showing fear of any sort wasn't in her nature and she had too much pride to let him know how much he still affected her.

"Will this table be all right?" the hostess asked.

Jake's probing gaze held hers and for a nanosecond she thought she read something other than mockery and indifference. She'd seen a glimpse of anger, of pity. But it must have been her imagination, because in the next moment, a sardonic mask replaced the sentiment and he smiled a lazy sort of grin rife with something akin to triumph. "It's perfect," he drawled, his lips curled into a smirk. "Absolutely perfect."

His gaze slid away, purposely discarding her, and he focused his attention back on his date.

Oh, no, Jolie thought as she drew in a shuddering breath. She took a much-needed sip of water. This was not going to work. There was no way in hell she would be able to sit here and enjoy her meal with Jake crooning to Nicolette at the next table. Purposely crooning, too. He planned to torture her. Not that she could blame him, really. Like any thwarted female, when she'd first come home with Chris, she'd enjoyed the fact that Jake had been sorry, that he'd realized he'd made a mistake and she'd stupidly flaunted her new relationship. Were the circumstances reversed, she knew she'd undoubtedly want to inflict a little revenge as well.

But she just wasn't up to it tonight. Wouldn't ever be up to it, not where he was concerned. It was just too damned hard.

Aiming for covert, but probably looking frantic, she snagged Charlie's attention as he walked by. Lowered her voice to a near whisper. "I've changed my mind. I'm, uh, not hungry after all." The truth, as she'd just lost her appetite.

Charlie frowned. "You want me to cancel your order?"

Jolie inwardly winced. Was it just her or was he speaking especially loud? "Not the whole order," she muttered quietly. "I still want the wine." In fact, now more than ever. Getting drunk sounded particularly appealing at the moment.

"The whole bottle?"

She nodded. "Yes, please. Now," she added meaningfully. She withdrew her credit card from her wallet and handed it to him.

Looking completely bewildered, Charlie vanished once more. Thankfully, he made the return trip in record time. She added a generous tip and then signed for the bottle, anxious to get the hell out of there. Though she didn't remember Nicolette having an exaggerated sense of humor in high school, Jake was laughing silkily at every word she uttered. Jolie refused to look at them—at him, specifically. She was used to being manipulated—she'd been married to a master for the past two years—and she wasn't about to let Jake do it as well.

She gathered her purse and the bottle and was just about to stand when a trio of older ladies stopped by her table. She recognized only one of them, Sophia Morgan. She was a rather petite lady, a little round, with pale blond hair cut in a trendy layered style and kind green eyes. She and her mother were friends and, like most women in Moon Valley, both belonged to the Garden Club.

Jolie caught a whiff of lilies and steak sauce as Sophia bent low and smiled down at her. "I'm going to give you a card," she murmured through a fixed grin. "And I want you to read it, then hand it back. Okay?"

Thoroughly bewildered, Jolie nodded. "Er… okay."

The other two women huddled closer—one tall and willowy wearing lots of high-end jewelry, the other short and plump with spiky gray curls—seemingly to block her from the view of other patrons. Sophia slid a small card across the table. Intrigued, Jolie shot her a curious look, then picked it up. The card was heavy stock, pale pink and embossed with formal silver lettering.

The Future Widows' Club…
where a woman
prepares for widowhood before her bastard dies.
You are cordially invited to join the FWC
to prepare
and fellowship with other widow-wannabes.

Jolie felt her eyes widen with shocked delight, a disbelieving laugh tickle the back of her throat and a smile slowly rolled around her lips. *The Future Widows' Club?* What on earth—

Before she could ponder it any further, Sophia deftly withdrew the card from her hand and replaced it with another. This one simply had an address, date and time. "Come join us, honey," Sophia told her. "Trust me," she said direly, her voice a lilting old south southern drawl. "You need our help."

Looking equally concerned, the other two women shot her commiserating glances. "You definitely do," the short one said.

And with those words ringing in Jolie's ears, the three shuffled off.

Though she hadn't meant to, her gaze once again found Jake's. He wore a curious expression, and those gunmetal gray eyes dropped to the card in her hand, then jumped back up and tangled with hers. He quirked a questioning brow.

Smiling, Jolie neatly pocketed it out sight. Let him wonder, she thought. Served him right for torturing her.

Though her stomach was still in knots, Jolie calmly stood, grabbed her bottle of wine and just as calmly made her way outside. She didn't spare Jake or Nicolette so much as the smallest glance. The impulse was there, of course—it always was when Jake was around—but thankfully pride prevailed.

Pride kept her head high and her back straight as she strolled to her car, and pride kept her from looking back to see if Jake had watched her leave. The moment she slid behind the wheel, though, pride abandoned her, and it was all Jolie could do not to cry. She wilted into the seat. Her belly quivered, her eyes stung, and she instinctively bit her bottom lip to prevent the sob that beckoned in the back of her tight throat. She gripped the steering wheel and lowered her head.

She would not cry, dammit.

If she could cry prettily, without anyone being the wiser, then yes, she might have given in to the impulse and sat in her car and squalled. It's what she wanted to do, what she needed to do. But unfortunately, she couldn't cry prettily. Her nose streamed, her mascara ran, ugly red blotches formed on her cheeks and beneath her eyes, and her upper lip swelled to twice its normal size. She invariably looked like she'd had some sort of allergic reaction, and Chris, she knew, would instantly recognize the implications and wrongfully assume that her tears had been for him.

Which would be intolerable.

She'd cried her last tear over Chris Marshall— over the mistakes she'd made—and she'd be damned before she'd give him any more satisfaction at her expense. The thought bolstered her resolve, then triggered another.

The card.

She pulled in a shaky breath, let it go, then pilfered through her purse until she found it. She reread the date—just the day after tomorrow, she discovered, oddly relieved—and the time and address. For reasons which escaped her, the innocuous little piece of paper felt like a life preserver, offered a ray of hope in her dim existence.

The Future Widows' Club, indeed, Jolie thought, with a soft chuckle. The idea was intriguing to say the least. She harrumphed. God knows she'd entertained the widow fantasy many times over the past two years. She'd never been much of joiner, tended to make few friends and keep her circle tight, but now this…

This sounded like the perfect club for her.

CHAPTER TWO

JAKE FELT every muscle go rigid with tension as Jolie grew nearer, then slowly leak out of him like air from a punctured tire as she walked past. He inwardly swore, resisting the urge to put his fist through the wall.

More than two years and it was always the same when he saw her.

Like a sucker punch to the gut immediately followed by the unhappy sensation of falling face-first off a cliff. Regret would ultimately follow, then before his heart could explode right out of his chest—or he could puke, a gallingly too-frequent occurrence after she and Marshall had first gotten together—good old righteous anger would bubble up from the almost-dry well of self-preservation, and he'd push his lips into a smirk and think about how he'd felt the day she'd married Marshall.

Eviscerated. Just two little words—*I do*—to someone else, and she'd gutted him.

He forced a thin smile at his date, pretended to peruse the menu. Rationally Jake knew that he couldn't place all the blame for their break-up at Jolie's feet. In fact, were he able to be completely honest with himself—and he couldn't yet because it still hurt too much—he couldn't place *any* of the blame with her. She'd acted completely within character. He'd been the one who'd stepped out of it.

After her dad had died, Jolie had looked to him to make good on all the promises and plans they'd made—marriage and a family—and, though he'd never doubted that they'd marry, for reasons he'd never been able to understand, he'd hesitated. Why? Hell, who knew? Some ignorant bachelor throwback mentality, he supposed.

He'd looked into those clear green eyes, seen his future—the one he'd always wanted with her looking back at him—and he'd unaccountably freaked. He'd thrown himself into making detective, told himself that he didn't want to commit himself any further to their relationship than what he already had. Not the real reason, of course, but in the end, though, when all was said and done, it hadn't mattered.

He'd hesitated—and in that one moment of groundless uncertainty, he'd lost her.

Initially the knowledge that her marriage wasn't a happy one had been a petty balm to his battered ego and even still, at times—like now—when he felt like the scab had been ripped off a wound that hadn't quite healed, he couldn't always rise above his wounded pride. If he was miserable, then it was only fitting that she be unhappy as well.

If she could have just waited, dammit. Given him just a little more time to get his head on straight.

Jake drew up short and inwardly swore. He'd traveled the road named Pointless many times—backtracking was futile. But as time wore on and the ache numbed, the idea of her being unhappy ate at him even more than the fact that she wasn't—could never be—his. His jaw hardened.

Because her husband was a bastard of the first order.

In the past couple of years Chris Marshall had been arrested for DUI, charged with possession—the usual stuff, marijuana, ecstasy—and had been the cause of more than one domestic disturbance in town. He didn't exercise the least bit of discretion when it came to dipping his wick. Married or unmarried, it was all the same to him.

He'd been jerked up a couple of times by angry husbands, but rather than having the good sense to be chastened, the bastard seemed to get off on the thrill of bagging another guy's wife, seemed to delight in provoking them. Jake grimaced. Hell, it was a miracle he hadn't ended up in the morgue sporting a toe tag to go with that trendy suit and pretty boy smirk he usually wore.

Furthermore, it was a miracle—not to mention a mystery—that Jolie hadn't left him yet. Jake had heard the rumors, of course. Despite the fact that Jake had cited his long-term friendship with Sadie's husband and the fact that he particularly liked the way she cut his hair—that he'd hate to have to find another stylist—Sadie nevertheless tended to let things *purposely* slip. Would she bring up Jolie to him? No. She knew better. But that didn't stop her from talking about Jolie to other people while she had him captive in the chair.

As a result, he had a vague understanding of the life-insurance money Marshall had conned out of her mother—scheming ass, Jake thought, disgusted—and an even vaguer understanding as to what Jolie was doing about it. The best he'd been able to discern, leaving Chris was a foregone conclusion, but apparently there was no way to recoup the investment in a divorce settlement, and getting the money back had to come first.

"I guess my sense of humor left when she walked out, didn't it?"

Jake blinked, and looked across the table. "I'm sorry?"

Nicolette sighed, pushing a hand through her short pale blond hair. "You were laughing at every word I said for the first five minutes we were here, which is flattering, by the way, considering that a sense of humor has never really been my strong suit." Her lips tilted into a knowing smile. "But the minute Jolie left, you zoned out on me and haven't so much as responded to anything I've said, much less laughed."

Jake passed a hand over his face to hide a wince. Shit. "Look, I—"

"Here's the thing," she said levelly as she bent to retrieve her purse. "I'm not interested in sex for the sake of sex, and I'm sure not interested in being a substitute."

"You're not a substitute," Jake told her, swallowing the futile bark of laughter that hit the back of this throat. Substitute? There was no substitute for Jolie. Hell, he'd looked, had tried to invest himself in other relationships. It hadn't worked. Instinctively he knew it would never work. There wasn't another soul on the planet who could make him forget to breathe simply by smiling, who could set his veins on fire with a mere touch of her hand. Jolie had been it…and he'd screwed up and let her go.

Nicolette paused and gave him a look that bordered closely enough on pity to make him want to howl. "You're still in love with her."

Jake summoned a laugh and shook his head, felt a sickening jolt of alarm hit his belly. "No, I'm not." He took a healthy pull on his beer. *Liar,* a little-heeded voice whispered.

Again, that sad provoking smile. "Fine," she said, clearly not believing him. "But whether you love her or not, there's still too much feeling there for my liking. Definitely too much for me to ante up more than what I already have." She stood. "Goodnight, Jake."

Jake smiled grimly as she walked away, trying to muster the irritation he knew he should feel, but in the end, he couldn't. Hell, she was right and he couldn't blame her. If she wanted anything more than a few hours of recreational sex, then she was barking up the wrong tree because he didn't have anything else to offer.

Just superficial feelings, superficial sex, superficial time.

The corner of his mouth hitched in another grim smile. It was all part and parcel of the new Jake, courtesy of his own stupidity.

JOLIE AWOKE from a sound sleep—one brought about by several glasses of wine and enough Krispy Kreme carbohydrates to drop an elephant—to the two words she hadn't been the least bit interested in hearing.

At least, not from Chris.

"Happy Anniversary, baby."

Despite the fact that she'd locked her door, Chris—even drunk and obviously high—had managed to let himself into her room, and had turned on her bedside light. His face was slick with perspiration, his eyes bloodshot and glassy. His pants were partially zipped, his shirt unbuttoned, and the beginnings of one helluva hickey was forming on his neck. He brought the stale scent of sex with him, making nausea curdle in her belly. A quick look at the bedside clock told her it was just after three. She grunted with disgust, then rolled over and attempted to ignore him.

It didn't work.

She felt the mattress shift as he dropped unsteadily onto the side of the bed. Then the sickening feeling of his hand sliding up over her hip, causing her flesh to creep. Repulsed, she instinctively jerked away from him. Jolie didn't know what the hell he was doing. She'd stopped sleeping with him the minute she'd learned the truth, absolutely refused to share anything beyond the house with him and looked forward to ending that arrangement as soon as possible.

Besides, she'd never liked this house. Located in a newer subdivision just outside the city limits it was cold and sterile, with designer grass and no trees. She had her eye on a little French Colonial fixer-upper on Lelia Street just off the square, one that would accommodate a cat, she thought, still miserably missing the long-time pet she firmly believed Chris had *made* disappear. Heartless bastard. After the divorce, she planned to put her accounting degree to better use, to take back her maiden name and hang a little shingle on the outside of the house.

Though many strip malls and shopping centers had cropped up on the main highway on the edge of town, the old town square was still the heart of Moon Valley. Fancy pavilions dripping with lacy fretwork and stocked with picnic tables anchored each corner and a beautiful fountain stood in the middle, paying tribute to a statue of Jebediah Moon, the town's founding father.

Every parade, be it Christmas, Homecoming, or Fourth of July, ended there, and the spot hosted their Annual Moon-Pie Festival each year. Between the Garden Club—Moon Valley citizens prided themselves on their ability to make things bloom—and the Civic Club, the quaint square was always dressed in her Sunday best. It epitomized Moon Valley life...one that her husband would never fit into.

"Get out, Chris," she said tiredly.

He slipped a finger down her arm. "I thought you might be feeling romantic."

Jolie barely resisted the urge to grunt in disgust. This just showed how completely out of touch with reality he could be. They weren't lovers, weren't in love. And whatever small amount of misplaced affection she'd thought she'd felt for him had gone by the wayside as soon as she'd realized what a scum-sucking, bottom-feeding thief he was.

She absolutely hated him—loathed him—with every fiber of her being.

And yet he thought she might be feeling romantic? If she weren't pretending to be half asleep, undoubtedly her eyes would pop out of her head.

He leaned over her and she felt his reeking breath hit her neck. She shrunk away from him. "Why don't we try and fix things, Jolie? They don't have to be this way."

Had he lost his mind? she wondered. In order to facilitate getting her mother's money back, Jolie had suggested to Chris that they keep up appearances for the business's sake. After all, she'd reasoned, Marshall, Inc. was still a relatively new business, one that despite his lack of character, his drug habit and his other vices, he'd managed to make flourish.

Unfortunately, word of his penchant for illegal substances and alcohol had begun to leak out and, though she'd managed to handle damage control, she grimly suspected that, despite their good-old-boy way of doing business, their local investors—the ones she'd unsuspectingly lured into Marshall, Inc.—were beginning to get a wee bit unsettled. Until she recouped all the money, that was a bad thing.

In one of his rare reasonable moments, Chris had agreed that keeping up the pretense of the happy couple was best. After all, anything that was better for his bottom line was better for him. Jolie had instructed him to seek his pleasure elsewhere—like he hadn't been doing that already, she thought with an inward snort—and had indicated that the marriage would continue in an in-name-only basis. So far he'd honored their system with irreverent, purposely cruel, efficiency.

She rolled over, putting as much distance between them as she could. "Yes, they do," she insisted through gritted teeth. *"Now get out."*

"No," he said, his voice belligerent yet eerily calm. He lurched clumsily to his feet, staggered, then started fumbling with his pants. "It's our anniversary, *darling,* and I'm going to do what every man does on his anniversary—I'm going to fuck my wife."

The first inkling of fear quickened her heartbeat,

prodding her out of the bed. The fact that he could make her afraid in addition to all the other things he'd managed to do to her lit her temper like nothing else could.

Jolie crossed her arms over her chest and summoned a sardonic smile. She cocked her head. "That's funny," she said, "because I have it on good authority that you've already fucked somebody else's wife tonight."

Sadie, bless her heart, had pulled sleuth-duty until she'd determined whose legs were jutting out of Chris's car. And she'd documented the proof with her handy picture phone. Jolie's lips quirked. The whore in question was one Emily Dean—*Sheriff* Dean's wife. Getting bolder and stupider by the minute, her unfortunate husband, Jolie thought with a wry twist of her lips. She just prayed he kept it together long enough for her to get everybody's money back.

Chris's sweaty mouth formed a sneer. "Jealous, are you?" He alternately stalked and stumbled toward her. "Don't worry. There's enough of me to go around."

"Then go spread it somewhere else," she threw back.

Though it nearly killed her, Jolie stood her ground. There was something about him tonight—a recklessness she'd never seen before—that absolutely chilled her blood. But she knew from experience that Chris fed off her emotions. If she showed him even the slightest hint of the fear currently chugging through her veins, he'd press his advantage...and she wouldn't care for the outcome.

His eyes were every bit as hard as his voice. "Now why would I do that when I have a tasty little piece like you at my disposal?" He twined a lock of her hair around his finger. "I mean, you aren't the best I've ever had...but you'll do in a pinch."

"Well, you won't, and I've developed higher standards." She jerked back, pulling her hair in the process and moved to go around him. He grabbed her by the upper arm, his fingers biting painfully into her flesh. She swallowed a gasp, fighting back fear.

"Just what the hell is that supposed to mean?" His red-rimmed eyes narrowed. "Have you been screwing around on me?" he demanded. He shifted his weight, seemingly having a hard time remaining upright. "Letting somebody else have what I'm not getting?"

Common sense told her taunting him in this state wasn't the brightest course of action, but the fury tightening every muscle of her body wasn't in the mood to entertain reasonable thoughts.

She blinked as though confused. "You're getting it," she said sweetly, "just not from me."

"Are you screwin' around on me?" he demanded, shaking her for emphasis.

Jolie snorted, rolling her eyes. "Now that's the pot calling the kettle black if I've ever heard it." She looked pointedly at his hand on her arm. "Let. Me. Go."

"When you've answered the question." His expression turned thoughtful, then shrewdly calculating. "I know you're not getting it from your old boy Jake. From what I've heard he's chasing every kitty *but* yours." He licked his lips, smiled. "But he leaves a fair amount of leftovers for the rest of us."

Jolie felt her stomach lurch. She'd shared her relationship with Jake with Chris when they'd first met—not everything, of course—but he'd managed to put the rest together once he'd moved to Moon Valley. It hadn't been hard. In a place where secrets were few and gossip frequent, Jake and Jolie's relationship had been almost legendary, their names linked since grade school, an extension of the other documented in yearbooks and newspaper clippings.

Chris had a way of ferreting out a person's weakness, then capitalizing on it. When he was feeling particularly spiteful, he'd invariably wield Jake like a knife, cutting little gashes into her already broken heart, occasionally parrying hard enough to puncture.

Like now.

She knew Jake had taken lovers—she'd heard and would never have expected him to remain celibate—but knowing it didn't prevent her from feeling like a rug had been jerked from beneath her feet when she thought about it. The idea of him touching another woman, of those big warm hands, that supremely carnal mouth doing the things they'd learned together to another woman…

Jolie tried to jerk free again and Chris smiled knowingly. He swayed on his feet. "That's what I thought. You're still my ever-faithful wife."

"I'm not your ever-faithful anything." Taking advantage of the various drugs—Viagra and ecstasy, she imagined—and alcohol wreaking havoc with his equilibrium, Jolie gave him a quick shove and wrenched her arm free. Chris wobbled, then his eyes flashed, and he did something he'd never done before, but something she'd recently feared was just a matter of time.

He back-handed her.

Clumsily, but the slap split her lip, made her ears ring and caused white spots to dance before her eyes. She reeled from the blow and her cheek blazed from the impact.

Seemingly spent, Chris fell back onto the bed, laid there and laughed. "Stupid bitch," he muttered. "I'll…teach you. I'll show you…who's boss." He flung an arm over his forehead, then passed out.

Though shocked and astounded, Jolie's first inclination was to *hurt* him. She wanted to slap him, claw him, beat him, pounce on him like a cat and not stop until every bit of the anger and frustration he'd dealt her had been given back three-fold.

When unconscious, he wouldn't feel a thing, and when conscious, he could hurt her far worse, so giving in to the fury would ultimately be futile, she knew. But she couldn't let it go completely. Couldn't let the incident pass without some form of retribution.

She decided on the passive aggressive approach, one she'd used many times over the past couple of years to make her feel better. Still breathing heavily, she marched into the bathroom, grabbed his toothbrush from the holder and, smiling grimly, scrubbed it around the toilet bowl. Then she put it back where it belonged.

Afterward, she calmly retrieved her overnight bag—the one she kept packed and ready for nights similar to this—and left. As always, her first inclination was to go home—home being her mother's small cottage on the other side of town—but like always she ruled out the option. Her mother had enough to handle without adding this newest development into the mix. Luckily Sadie had an empty apartment over the shop that had served as a refuge of sorts in the past, and it would certainly work again.

For the umpteenth time since this nightmare began, she felt the urge, the almost palpable need, to run to Jake, to lose the brave little soldier face and find solace in the safe-harbor of his arms. The thought made a whimper bubble up her throat and tears burn the backs of her lids, the ache of loss wrenching her insides until she thought she'd come apart. Unfortunately, Jolie thought as she sucked in a shaky breath, that wasn't a viable option.

Jake's arms were already full.

CHAPTER THREE

"THOSE WILL DO better if you plant them in the morning sun."

Feeling her hackles rise, Sophia gritted her teeth, straightened from the flower bed she'd been working in and turned to glare from beneath her straw hat at the infuriating man who'd issued the advice. Looking decidedly cooler than she, Edward Jennings leaned against her picket fence and regarded her with amusement.

Sophia made a grand gesture of alternately looking at the seven a.m. sun, her bedding plants, then him. She cocked a brow, silently questioning the validity of his eyesight, then twisted her lips into a superior smile. "Thanks, Edward, but I think I've been planting pansies long enough to know where they best thrive."

Honestly, she thought, exasperated. Just because he'd snatched the Garden Club presidency from her—a position she'd coveted since she'd planted her

first petunia, dammit—the man had become insufferable. One who lived two blocks over and who'd
developed the annoying habit of strolling by her
house.

Every morning.

Which was why she'd wrestled herself into a girdle this morning to go outside and work in her garden. Sophia pursed her lips.

Clearly, she'd lost her mind.

Edward inclined his snowy head and a wide smile
split his tanned face. "Ah, I see that now." His light
blue eye twinkled. "Your rump was in the way before."

A rebellious spurt of pleasure bloomed inside her
before she could squash it out. Damn the man. He
shouldn't be *looking* at her rump, much less letting
her *know* that he'd been looking at her rump.

Sophia dusted the dirt from her gloves and regarded him coolly, no small feat when she was quaking inside like a virgin on her wedding night. "Are
you suggesting, Edward, that my ass is so wide it
blocked out the morning sun?"

He dipped his head, chuckled, the sound at once
pleasing and masculine. Almost intimate. "Absolutely not. I was merely making conversation."

Sophia sidled forward, tugged her gloves off one
finger at a time. "A word of advice then, Edward,
since you don't seem to mind doling it out. If you'd

like to initiate a cordial conversation," she explained
patiently, "then you'd be better served to begin with
a simple, 'Good morning, Sophia.'" She smiled
sweetly. "Not offer criticism. People might get the
impression that you're an arrogant know-it-all with
an exalted opinion of your own wit."

He looked out over her garden, stroked his chin.
When his eyes found hers once more she detected
lingering humor and something else…something she
couldn't readily discern. Uncertainty, maybe? He let
go a small sigh. "Well, that would be most unfortunate," he said softly. "Thanks for the advice. I'll be
sure and keep it in mind." He inclined his head and,
whistling tunelessly, strolled away, leaving her standing at the fence.

Sophia felt her smile fade as she watched him go,
and something akin to disappointment welled in her
rebellious breast.

It most certainly *was not* disappointment, she told
herself. With slightly shaky hands, she crammed her
fingers back into her gloves, stomped back to the flat
of pansies she'd been planting before he'd interrupted her. Disappointment indicated that she cared
what he thought—about her and her rump, drat
him—and that was simply not acceptable.

She buried the spade in the ground, flipping dirt
aside with a little more vigor than was necessary. She

was sixty-two years old. Widowed, thank God, she added silently. Her children were grown and settled. She had four adorable grandchildren, a nice group of friends, and a multitude of enjoyable hobbies to fill her days. She sat back on her haunches, and glared down the street at his retreating figure.

The last thing she needed was some Paul Newman look-alike to take an interest in her ass, making her long for something futile and elusive...like passion and companionship. A golden romance to gild her later years.

Romance, Sophia thought, with a huff of disgust. Now there was a pipe dream. Or at least it had been for her. Memories unwound like a spool of thread through her mind and her gaze turned inward. She'd met and married Charles Morgan all within the space of a month. She'd been seventeen, just old enough to let those ripening teenage hormones over-ride what she liked to think was a fairly sound intellect, and that lone decision had shaped the course of her life as no other could have ever done. She'd thought she'd married a kind man with a good work ethic and a fine sense of family.

She'd thought wrong.

What she'd wound up with was a meaner-than-hell, lazy bastard who wasn't remotely interested in her or their children. By the time she'd realized that she couldn't change him, that no amount of prayer on his behalf was going to make him the husband she longed to have—the father her children needed—he'd had two blocked arteries and she'd already invested too much of her life in him to let him ruin her with a divorce. Everything they had, *she'd* worked for, and she'd decided she'd be damned before she'd give him half.

At the time, two friends, Bitsy and Meredith, had found themselves in similar situations, both of them married to men who made them wretched, and one night after one too many hands of rummy and one too many Bloody Mary's, the idea of the Future Widows' Club had been born.

Ultimately, it had saved her. Saved all of them. And now it offered hope to a new group of women trapped in loveless, miserable marriages. Women who needed a little vengeful humor to help them cope. Women like Jolie Marshall, Sophia thought, hoping that she'd come and join them. Women who, like them, preferred widowhood to divorce.

And why not? Sophia thought, particularly proud of her brain-child. Being widowed definitely had the advantage. Instead of half—half your friends and half your assets—a widow got to keep it all. People sympathized and brought food. Black was slimming. A widow was pitied, not scorned. She was deemed a survivor, not damaged goods. Then there was the life insurance, Sophia thought with a fond smile. She harrumphed. Charles had definitely been worth more to her dead than he ever had been alive. Aside from the birth of her children, planting that miserable SOB in Shady Memorial—in the hottest patch of earth she could find—had been the single-most bar-none *best* day of her life.

Which was what made the idea of entertaining any sort of feelings for Edward Jennings absolutely insane. It had taken her twenty-three years to get rid of the first man that had ever caught her fancy. What in God's name would possess her to want to try that again?

She knew why, though it nearly killed her to admit it—sex.

It used to be that practically no one her age was sexually active. Waning sex drives and impotency had all but obliterated sex from her social scene, but with the advent of enhancement drugs—Viagra, Cialis, Avlimil, etc.—sex had made a huge comeback with people her age. And with it, the needs she'd forgotten—or had deemed too trivial to waste her time on—had come raging back.

Her own sex drive had been below the radar, lying like a dormant volcano for years, but now— Sophia smothered a frustrated groan. Dirt flew as she attacked her planting with renewed vigor. Now, a couple of smiles from a blue-eyed gentleman and some raucous talk of multiple orgasms and erections at the bingo hall had left her so wretchedly horny that her yearly trip to the gynecologist was actually something she found herself looking forward to.

It was crazy. Insane. And yet she couldn't deny the ache in her breasts, the throb deep in her womb, the desire for a warm male body at her back.

Both Bitsy and Meredith had taken lovers over the years, but Sophia had always abstained. She'd deemed herself above such needs and had secretly pitied their continued dependence on men. After Charles, though many had tried, she hadn't been remotely interested in forming any sort of relationship with a man. One had been enough, thank you very much.

But something about Edward Jennings shook that stalwart reserve, made her watch those sexual enhancement commercials with the sort of puppy-dog longing that was downright pathetic, even made her yearn for something as simple as sharing coffee over the breakfast table.

Sophia fingered the delicate bloom of a purple pansy, then closed her eyes as she caught the faint tune of Edward's whistle. For the first time in her life, she was lonely.

CHAPTER FOUR

ACHING AND ANGRY for her friend, Sadie aimed her picture phone at the side of Jolie's bruised face and blinked back tears. Chris Marshall needed his ass kicked, she thought. Needed the absolute hell beat out of him for doing this to her. "Okay," Sadie said, releasing an unsteady breath. "I got that side. Now let me get a close-up of your lip."

Jolie nodded, tilted her mouth up, but didn't speak.

Sadie leaned in and took the shot, made sure that all the photos were good, then with a few keystrokes sent them to her e-mail account. She'd pull them up and print them so that Jolie could have them on hand when she went to the Sheriff's department to file the official complaint.

Seeing Jolie's car in the parking lot this morning when she'd arrived at The Spa hadn't come as a surprise. Her friend had used the apartment above her shop as a sanctuary many times over the past two

years, but seemed to be doing so with more frequency over the past few months.

But seeing the dark bruise—the imprint of Chris's
hand and knuckles—against the side of her face had
come as a complete shock. Up until this point, Chris
had never hit her, had preferred to inflict psychological—emotional—wounds. The fact that things had
escalated to this point convinced Sadie more than
ever that Jolie needed to be content with the portion
of money she'd managed to secure so far, give that
to her mother, and bail.

She wouldn't, of course, Sadie knew, equally irritated and exasperated. She was too damned stubborn, too determined that every person who'd
invested in Chris because of her home-town credibil-
ity got their money back. Noble? Yes. But not at this
price. It was too much. Too high.

Sadie swallowed, looked out over the square and
watched the early morning sun glint off the arching waters of the town fountain. A group of older men had already plopped down on one of the benches—the very
ones some of her patrons referred to as the Limp Dick
Benches, she thought with a small smile—and had
pulled out their pocket knives and wood. They'd whit-
tle for hours, spit tobacco, trade secrets and tell lies.

"Look, Jo," Sadie said softly, "I know you're tired
of hearing me say this, but give your Mom what

you've got, and let it go. *Leave.*" She gestured toward Jolie's battered face, her gaze softening. "This— This can only get worse. He was too drunk to do more this time, but what's to say that he won't be the next time? And there will be a next time," she told her. *"You know it."*

Jolie had moved to a mirror, was presently rummaging through her make-up bag, and refused to look up. Her long auburn hair with its distinctive natural flash of blond at the widow's peak was tucked behind her ears and her normally envious complexion was leached of color save the bruising on her cheek. Despite the fact that she was too curvy to be called thin, Jolie looked smaller, more fragile than Sadie had ever seen her, and there was a sadness that lurked in her pale green eyes that seemed to be slowly snuffing out her usual spark.

Once again the desire to hurt Chris Marshall surged through her, made her hands involuntarily curl into fists. Sadie could honestly say that the need to inflict pain upon another person had never been something she'd ever experienced, an idea she'd ever entertained. But were she a man, there was absolutely no question in her mind what she would do— she'd hurt him. And the scary part was she'd enjoy it.

Jolie winced as she carefully applied concealer to

her cheek. "Filing the report will make him think twice before doing it again any time soon," she said, seemingly unconcerned. "And it'll buy me the time that I need."

"That's what you said about the possession charge," Sadie argued, trying the keep the impatience out of her voice. God, it was so frustrating. She felt so powerless, so helpless. Watching this man do this to her friend... It was tearing Sadie up inside. Needing to do something proactive, she moved to the computer, logged on, pulled up the pictures and sent them to the printer.

"And it worked," Jolie replied. She slid a powder pad over her cheek, grimaced. "At least for a while, anyway."

"That's right," Sadie persisted. She leaned forward in her chair. "But only for a while, and not as long as you'd hoped. The fact that he's let his penchant for partying blind him to the bottom line ought to tell you something. He doesn't care anymore." She shook her head, gestured wearily. "There's no bargaining power left, Jo. No leverage. For the love of God, just leave," she implored.

Jolie turned, leaning against the faux marble counter. She chewed the unbroken side of her lip and, to Sadie's surprise, her eyes misted. "Sadie, I know you mean well, and I know that you don't understand why I have to do this. I know you're frustrated with me—" She looked away, shrugging helplessly "—but I *have* to do this. *I have to.*" She took a bolstering breath, sliding a knuckle beneath her eye. "Dad coughed up the money for that life insurance policy for over thirty years. Thirty years," she repeated significantly, her voice cracking with pain and determination. "When times were hard, he'd let the phone bill slide, or there might not be any meat on the table, but that life insurance was *always* paid. It was his guarantee for us, but mostly for her. It's *my* fault that Mom believed in Chris. *My* fault that he's here, that this is happening." She dragged in a bolstering breath, blinked back her moment of weakness. "I— I have to fix it. It's that simple."

No, it was that complicated, Sadie thought. Her shoulders sagged. Like her own family, Jolie had grown up one rung just above poverty level. Moon Valley had one main industry—steel—and the majority of its residents depended on it for their incomes. It was hard, particularly dangerous work, and every man who clocked in at Valley Steel was aware of the risks. Employees knew to invest in good work boots and sufficient insurance.

Sadie's father had worked alongside Jolie's— they'd been lifelong friends—and though, thankfully her dad had lived long enough to see retirement, sadly, in a cruel twist of fate, Jolie's father had suffered a massive heart attack just two weeks before he was supposed to punch out for the last time. Her family had been devastated. Jolie and her mom had always been close, had shared a special, frankly enviable, bond, but something about that tragedy had changed them.

Jolie had turned to Jake and, despite the fact that their relationship had been forged on the playground in the third grade—had been the stuff of fairytales, had never once wavered—for reasons Sadie had never understood, Jake had side-stepped like a spooked horse. He regretted it now, of course. She knew it. Could tell by the hollow look in his eyes, the harder edge regret had lent to his voice. But by the time he'd realized he'd made a mistake, Jolie had returned from Savannah with Chris in tow. Sadie sighed. And the rest, as they say, was history.

She shot Jolie a hopeful look. "Want me to have Rob kick his ass?"

Jolie chuckled softly, seemingly relieved by the subject change. "Thanks, but no." She rolled her eyes. "As gratifying as that would be—and God would it ever be," she said meaningfully, "there's no point in Rob going to jail." She pushed off from the counter and started tossing her makeup back into her purse. "I'm gonna go down and file the report before

I head to work and I'd like to beat Chris to the office this morning." Her lips quirked and a spark of droll humor lit her gaze, along with her usual determination. "Get a little *laundry* done before he comes in."

Sadie felt a grin tug at her lips. "Want me to signal you if he beats you there?" From her vantage point just across the square, Sadie could look out her storefront window and see if Chris was in the office. When Jolie and Chris had started the software company, he'd wanted one of the newer offices in a complex away from the square, but Jolie had insisted on being downtown. It had definitely ended up being for the best.

Jolie nodded. "Yeah, I'd appreciate it. I don't look for him to make it in before ten, but—" she pulled a shrug "—I could be wrong."

Sadie snagged the pictures from the printer tray, came around the desk and handed them to her. She felt a sad smile shape her mouth as she looked again at Jolie's bruised cheek, just visible beneath the makeup. Her heart ached. "Let me know if I can do anything."

"You do enough." Jolie smiled and jerked her head toward the ceiling. "Like letting me crash upstairs when I need to."

A thought struck, popping another bubble of dread. "How are you going to hide this from your mother?"

Jolie hesitated, backed toward the door and managed a grim laugh. "The good-old fashioned way—by avoiding her."

CHAPTER FIVE

JAKE SNAGGED yesterday's paperwork and his thermos from the cab of his truck, then made his way across the parking lot and into the Sheriff's Department. His second home, he thought with a half-hearted smile. The scent of bad coffee, stale body odor and antiseptic cleaner greeted him as he pushed his way through the scarred double doors. Housed in the newer part of the county courthouse, the Sheriff's department had been dressed in the cheapest possible government-issue décor. Metal desks, plastic chairs, beige walls, and serviceable tile. His lips quirked. Only the best for the good citizens of Moon Valley.

Looking as happy as a hooker on a front church pew, Faye Kellerton manned the dispatch desk with her typical unwavering surly expression. Be it Botox or simply a perpetual bad mood, Faye rarely smiled. In fact, Jake wasn't so sure you could even deem the slight incline of the corner of her mouth a true smile. It was more of a painful, gassy smirk.

He conjured a grin and gestured toward the discarded newspaper on her desk. "You finished with that, Faye?"

"Sure. Take it," she said, her voice a long-winded sigh that implied that he was wasting her time. "Aside from the classifieds, it's just bad news from cover to cover."

A regular little ray of sunshine, Jake thought as he absently scoured the headlines and headed toward his office. The mayor was still having trouble with skunks, he noted—apparently, several families of the stinky creatures had taken up residence under his house—and there was the controversy over who should pay for the renovation of the statue of Jebediah Moon. The Civic Club or the city? The Civic Club had donated the statue to the town, so the city argued that since the Civic Club had been the original purchasers, they should pick up the bill for restoration.

The Civic Club took offense and said that the statue had been a *gift,* and as such, they weren't responsible for the upkeep. In the words of one of their esteemed members, "I gave my mail carrier a set of socket wrenches for Christmas. Does that mean I'm supposed to repair them if they break?"

"Jake?"

Still smiling, Jake paused and looked up. Looking grave enough to raise concern, Mike Burke, a deputy and his long-time best friend, waved him over. "What's up?" Jake asked, every sense going on point.

Mike passed a hand over his face. "Look, I took a complaint early this morning and I, uh…" He grimaced. "I thought you'd want to know about it."

Jake nodded, somewhat surprised by Mike's awkward behavior. Hell, he hadn't seen him this jumpy since the night they'd "borrowed" the principal's car and parked it on the fifty yard line of the football field. "Okay," he said cautiously. "What was it?"

Mike shifted a few papers aside and tapped his finger on a stack of photographs. "This."

Jake frowned, then looked down at where Mike had indicated and felt his body go numb with angry shock. He picked up the stack, and though his guts were boiling with sickening fury, managed to flip through them with what he hoped passed for professional detachment.

The first was a head shot of Jolie, the side of her lush mouth split and an ugly bruise marring the right side of her face. His jaw tightened. It was quite evident that she'd been slapped.

Hard.

The second was a close-up of her battered cheek,

a large bruise, punctuated by three smaller more distinct discolorations—the bastard's knuckles, Jake decided. God knows he'd worked enough domestic dispute cases to recognize the pattern. The final photo was another close-up, this one of her mouth, and for whatever reason, this one managed to anger him more than the others, forcing him to swallow a curse.

God, she'd always had the sweetest mouth, Jake thought, tracing the familiar lines with his gaze. Full bottom lip, lush and suckable, and a slightly thinner upper lip with a distinct bow in the middle. Be it brimstone or a prayer, a smile or a kiss, he'd always had a thing for her mouth.

And Chris Marshall had broken it.

"What happened?" Jake asked, his voice low and throbbing with irrepressible anger.

Mike let go a breath. "Marshall came home around three this morning and broke into her room. He—"

Jake's gaze sharpened. "*Her* room?"

"Yeah, I'd wondered about that, too," Mike said, leaning a hip against his desk. "When I asked her about it, she said that they no longer shared a bedroom, that she'd moved into the guest bedroom over a year and a half ago." He paused. "Anyway, according to her he was drunk and high, said some ugly things to her," Mike said, being purposely vague, undoubtedly to keep Jake from getting angrier. "Then, when he wouldn't get out of her room, she tried to leave and he grabbed her. She jerked free, then he back-handed her, fell down onto the bed and passed out. Hell of an anniversary present, eh?" Mike added with a humorless laugh. "Sadie's given her a key to that apartment above her shop. Jolie went over there, spent the night, and from the impression I got, this wasn't the first time."

No, Jake knew it wasn't. Before he'd made detective, he'd worked the night shift patrol, and there'd been several times over the past couple of years when he'd seen her car parked in front of The Spa, the lights on in the upstairs apartment. Had he hit her then? Jake wondered as his guts twisted with angry dread. Or had she fled for another reason?

Seemingly following his thoughts, Mike shifted. "She says this is the first time that he's ever laid a hand on her." His mouth hitched into a half-grin. "And we both know she's not the type to put up with it."

Jake barely suppressed a snort. "No," he said, rubbing the back of his neck, a small smile tugging at his lips. "She's not." In fact, Jolie had a short fuse and, once it was lit, an even longer temper, one of the absolute worst he'd ever seen.

Unlike most people with a short fuse, however, Jolie didn't get angry over little things. She had to be thoroughly provoked, and it usually ended up being for someone else's benefit. Scrappy Doo, Jake remembered fondly. That's what he'd called her in grade-school. She'd been the number one champion for the underdog, always taking up for those too scared or too timid to take up for themselves.

Like in fourth grade when she'd pummeled the crap out of a boy twice her size for calling Jeremy Pickens "white trash." Or the year she spent walking three blocks out of her way to personally escort Lanni Wallace—a very small girl who had the unfortunate habit of wetting herself when she was frightened— to and from school to keep kids from purposely trying to scare her. Jake smiled, remembering. She was always the first to offer help, always a friend to the friendless. She was one of a kind.

Jake's gaze drifted over her picture once more, to the damaged side of her sweetly curved cheek, her busted lip and anger boiled to the surface once more.

There was nothing for it, Jake thought as he let go a tight breath. He'd have to hurt him.

"Mind if I ride with you to pick him up?" God, he hoped he resisted arrest. Then he could *legally* beat the shit out of him.

Mike grimaced, hesitated. "That's the thing. She

filed the report, but didn't want to press charges yet. Just asked for a copy of the report."

Jake swore hotly, feeling his blood-pressure rocket toward stroke level. Surely to God she wasn't going to be this stupid. She knew better, dammit. As many times as she'd heard him complain about domestic abuse cases—particularly those where a woman refused to have the abuser picked up...

He squeezed his eyes shut, summoning patience from a hidden source. "You encouraged her to press charges, right?"

Mike nodded. "Of course I did. But she wasn't interested. Said a copy of the report was all she needed to make him back off."

Jake swore. A copy of that report wouldn't be enough, he thought ominously, but Jake certainly knew how to persuade him.

Mike shifted uneasily. "I, uh... I realize that your first inclination would be to beat the hell out of him, Jake—I admit it was mine—but it would be a bad idea."

Didn't feel like a bad idea, Jake thought. Felt like a *fantastic* idea. The best he'd ever had. Nevertheless, he thought, with an inward sigh as reason prevailed, Mike was right. While he'd no doubt take great satisfaction in slapping the hell out of Chris Marshall—repeatedly—it was against the law. Good cops upheld the law, they didn't break it, and he'd be damned before he'd let a scumbag like Marshall provoke him into doing something he'd regret.

But that didn't mean that he wasn't going to do anything…it just meant he'd have to get creative.

He glanced at Mike. "Did you get the impression that she'd eventually press charges?" he asked, unable to believe that she wouldn't at some point in the foreseeable future do the right thing.

"Yeah, I did," he replied, his brow folded in thought. "But she's biding her time."

Then she had a plan, Jake thought, which was more in character. He handed the photos back to Mike and thanked him for letting him know. "There's a lot of water under the bridge there, but…" His throat tightened. "Anyway, I appreciate it," he finished awkwardly.

Mike shot him an uncomfortable look. "There's more."

More? Shit. "Okay," Jake replied, drawing the word out.

Mike shot a furtive look toward Sheriff Dean's office, then leaned in closer to him. "She showed me a couple of pictures that she didn't let me keep," he said. "They were of Marshall and—" He looked around again, lowering his voice "—Emily Dean."

Jake squinted, cocked his head. Surely to God he wasn't suggesting—

"Naked," Mike added significantly. "And otherwise engaged, if you get my drift."

Dumbfounded, Jake felt his eyes widen. "Are you saying that Marshall is fuc—"

"That's exactly what I'm saying," Mike interrupted with another furtive look toward Dean's office. "Got a brass set, doesn't he?"

Or a death wish, Jake thought, stunned. Dear God, if Dean ever found out, he'd kill him. He'd rip him limb from limb. Jake shook his head, attempting to absorb it. "Where'd she get the pictures?"

"She wouldn't say. But they were time-stamped from last night. Around eight," he added.

Around eight? But how was that— Jake frowned as the pieces clicked into place. His dinner reservation had been at eight and she'd been there, at the restaurant. Waiting for Marshall while he'd been shagging the Sheriff's wife. God, what a bastard, he thought again. He told Mike about seeing her at Zeus'. "So you know what that means?"

Mike nodded, shooting him a shrewd look. "It means she didn't take those pictures."

"Right. She couldn't have."

Mike arched a brow. "You think she's hired a private investigator?"

Jake shrugged, unsure. "It's possible." But knowing Jolie, he doubted it. He didn't see her putting that

much trust into someone she didn't know. If he had
to hazard a guess, he'd say Sadie—or maybe even
Rob—was helping her out.

Only one way to find out, Jake thought.

Mike regarded him with a shrewd smile. "Your
hair looks like shit, Jake."

Jake grinned. "You think so."

"Definitely. You could use a trim."

He agreed, nodded absently, and turned to leave.

"Keep me posted," Mike called.

"You got it."

AN HOUR LATER Jake walked out of Sadie's salon
with a neat cut and the information he'd been interested in. Even if Sadie wasn't Jolie's best friend, The
Spa was the first place to go to get the low-down on
what was happening around town. Information was
disseminated from within those walls with a fright-
ening efficiency that would no doubt rival some of
the FBI's best channels. Odd that the only woman
who was capable of keeping a secret owned the place,
Jake thought with a wry smile. Thankfully, in this instance Sadie wasn't interested in keeping one from
him. In fact, she'd been very eager to share.

Just as he'd suspected, Sadie had taken the pictures—the ones of Jolie and of Marshall. In addition,
she'd confided that she'd taken many more, that Jolie

was amassing quite a case for her divorce and her husband's subsequent take-down as a partner of Marshall Inc.

While she hadn't filled in every blank, she'd shared enough to let him know that things were considerably worse than what he'd ever suspected, and the genuine worry he'd heard in every word she'd uttered had compounded his own. The more he'd learned, the madder he'd become, and as such, he'd cruised around town until he'd managed to put Chris in his cross-hairs.

Chris hadn't been at home and, on a hunch, Jake had cruised by the Sheriff's house. Sure enough, Marshall had parked his flashy little-dick compensation three houses down.

Jake had waited for him to come out of the house, then fell in behind him. Marshall had stopped by the bank, by the post office, and had presently disappeared into a convenience store.

Jake parked in front of the door and smiled. He'd been waiting for just this sort of opportunity. He stayed in the truck until he saw Marshall move to the register, then calmly slid from behind the wheel. Just as Marshall reached for the door handle to leave, Jake pushed open the door—with a little more force than was technically needed—and it slammed into Marshall's face, knocking him backward off his feet.

Blood spurted from his nose and the coffee he'd been carrying had landed on his chest, scalding him. He rolled around on the floor, flopping like a fish out of water, howling with pain.

The clerk behind the counter squealed in belated alarm, grabbed a stack of napkins and hurried toward him.

Grimly satisfied, Jake stood over him. "Sorry," he said unrepentantly, his voice hard and menacing. "You should be more careful, Marshall. Accidents aren't fun and you don't appear to have a high tolerance for pain."

"Are you threatening me?" he asked, his voice an outraged nasal-like wail.

Jake cocked his head. "Merely stating the obvious. That looks like it might be broken. You should probably have it checked out." He picked up a package of M&M's, slipped a buck to the clerk, then smiling, made his way back to his truck. Not as satisfying as breaking the bastard's nose with his fist, Jake conceded as he pulled out of the parking lot, emptying M&M's down his throat, but it'd do.

CHAPTER SIX

ARMED WITH a marinated vegetable salad in a pretty cut-glass bowl—a good southern girl didn't show up for a party, meeting or any gathering of females for that matter, without having the consideration to bring food—Jolie stood on the front porch and, insides quivering, waited for someone to answer the door. The multitude of cars in the drive, not to mention the excited chatter coming from inside, told her that she had the right address. She'd successfully found the secret meeting place of the Future Widows' Club.

And after Chris's performance last night, the idea of being a widow had begun to sparkle with the shiny sheen of a brand new toy.

Evidently too hung over to work, he'd never made it into the office the day before—which had been a good thing because she'd managed to shuffle some things around and had netted another five grand for her cause—but he'd mustered the energy to go somewhere and had stumbled home at the relatively early hour of ten o'clock. His nose was broken, his eyes black, which had complimented both his mood and his soul, if you asked her, and he'd been fully prepared to finish what he'd started the night before—until she'd dangled the complaint she'd filed at the Sheriff's department in front of him.

For the time being, his desire to stay out of jail seemed to be greater than his desire to hit her, but in all honestly—like Sadie had pointed out—she didn't know how much longer that would hold true. He was becoming increasingly reckless, beyond caring. He'd been a hateful ass, so rather than laying into him the way she'd wanted to, she'd excused herself to the bathroom and gleefully used his toothbrush as a toilet bowl cleaner again. Petty revenge, but she happened to enjoy it.

The door finally opened, revealing the taller woman Jolie remembered from the trio at the restaurant. She wore lots of high-end jewelry and a stylish black hat over her short dark bob, one that would have looked nice with a sleek black dress, but hardly matched the trendy pink sportswear ensemble she had on.

"Ah, you made it," she said with a warm smile. Her gaze dropped to the bowl and her dark brown eyes gleamed with approval. "And you brought food. Come on in, dear," she told her, waving her inside, "and we'll get you settled. I'm Meredith by the way. Meredith Ingram."

Somewhat bemused, Jolie managed a smile and followed her into the foyer, where the chatter she'd barely heard outside rose to a delighted buzz. Meredith had stopped and was currently pilfering through a box, one filled with an assortment of little black hats. She decided on one, then swung around and, to Jolie's surprise, settled it over her head. "Oh," Jolie said. "Er…thank you."

Meredith studied her critically, made a face and shook her head. "Too round," she said as she whisked it off. "As you'll hear in a few minutes, finding the right hat is one of the first tasks on your list to prepare for widowhood—" she rummaged some more, pulled out another one and plopped it on her head "—but it can be a real pain in the butt, I tell ya, to find the perfect one." She inspected this one with the same thorough regard, then smiled. "But this one works nicely. It's a little big, and certainly not just anyone could pull it off, but with your hair and coloring it's trés chic. Prim and Proper down on the square carries it and it's a steal at under forty dollars," she confided, as though sharing a trade secret. "Let's put your dish on the serving table and I'll start introducing you to everyone."

Petering on bewildered, Jolie trailed behind her

deeper into the lovely antebellum house. To the left of the foyer was a long living room and, just beyond it, separated by French doors, was the dining room. A dozen or more women were in each room, all of them wearing casual clothes and black hats. They were huddled in circles, chatted and laughed amiably, and the sheer pleasure they garnered from each other's company pushed Jolie's lips up into a small smile.

"Here we go, dear," Meredith said as she moved a plate of canapés aside. "Just set your dish here and I'll get a spoon from the kitchen." She turned and was nearly knocked down by a small, plump woman racing by on a motorized scooter. The shorter woman from the restaurant, Jolie realized with a start.

Meredith staggered and put a hand against her heart. "Dammit, Bitsy, you nearly ran me over," she snapped. "Go park that thing before you kill somebody."

Bitsy eeked to a stop and, multiple chins quivering, beamed at her. "Sorry, Meri," she said with a chuckle. "I'm still trying to get the hang of it." Her eyes rounded with delight behind her small purple glasses as her gaze fell upon Jolie. "Oh, you came!" she cried happily. "I'm so glad." She leaned in and inspected Jolie's cheek, which still bore the bruise, and tsked softly under her breath. "Heard about that, the bastard. Well, not to worry," she said briskly.

"You're in the right place now. We'll get you trained up good until you can put that rounder out on his thieving philandering hide, or until he kicks it," she added grimly. "Whichever comes first." She gestured toward the table. "Go ahead and fix a plate, then come sit down. We're about to start." She tooted the horn and her head jerked backward as she shot off.

Smiling fondly, Meredith let go an exasperated breath. "The great fraud," she confided. "She doesn't need that thing. She's as healthy as a horse. She's just pissed because her kids wouldn't let her have a Harley. Now she's threatening to buy one of those mini-motorcycles." Meredith rolled her eyes. "As if that would be any better. She's blind as a bat."

Jolie chuckled, watching as Bitsy nearly upended an occasional table.

"Go ahead and load your plate, hon," Meredith told her with a glance at the table. "And be sure and try the petite fours before Bitsy spots them—she has a tendency to hide the whole plate, then take them home after the meeting. Sophia makes them and they're *divine*." Meredith hurried away, presumably to get a serving spoon for Jolie's salad.

Rather than risk insulting anyone, Jolie managed to put a small dab of each dish onto her plate, ladled up a glass of punch, then nervously made her way into the living room and found an empty chair against the wall. She'd just popped one of the petite fours Meredith had told her to try into her mouth when Sophia sat down beside her.

"I'm so glad to see that you've decided to join us," she said, her face wreathed in a welcoming smile. She pulled a small pale pink booklet with a black hat and gloves logo on the cover from a tote bag and handed it to her. "This is your handbook," Sophia said. "It has a to-do list for becoming a full-fledged member—things like getting your hat, your outfit, additional life insurance and whatnot—as well as our official rules and regulations. For obvious reasons, we're a secret society, but I know you're going to want to tell Sadie about us. Since she's capable of keeping a secret, that's fine, but it would be best if you didn't mention it to anyone else, okay?" With another warm, commiserating smile, Sophia laid a hand on her knee and gave her a pat. "Trust me, sweetie. Things are about to get better. We're here to help you."

For reasons which escaped her, in that instant the weight and toll of the past two years seemed to come crashing down on her—for the first time since this all began she let herself fully acknowledge how *terribly awful* things had been—and though she'd only met Sophia a handful of times, Jolie suddenly wanted to drop her head onto the woman's round shoulder and sob with relief.

Because she got it. She understood.

Not to belittle Sadie in any way—Jolie knew she genuinely worried about her—but there was simply no way she could understand how wretched Chris had made her feel. She couldn't because she had a husband who doted on her, who loved her fully, completely, and without the smallest bit of reservation.

Jolie bit her lip, blinked back tears and cast a glance around the room. But these woman…she had something in common with them, and she fully believed Sophia, believed that, with their help, things would get better.

Jolie swallowed. "Thank you," she said, her voice tight.

Sophia gave her knee a squeeze. "You're more than welcome." She smiled. "Now let's get this party started." Sophia stood and made her way to the front of the room.

"Good evening, ladies," she called above the still-chattering crowd. Smiling, she waited for them to completely quiet before continuing. "Welcome to another Future Widows' Club meeting. Before we begin Confessional, I'd like to take a moment to introduce a new member." Her gaze swung to Jolie. "This is Jolie Marshall. For those of you unaware of

Jolie's story, it's a sad but familiar one." Her lips curled with droll humor. "She married the wrong man. He's a thief, a liar, a cheater—" Her voice hardened "—and, as you can see by the bruise on her cheek, a bully as well." She lifted her shoulder in a negligent shrug. "He's a bastard."

The women all smiled knowingly, sending her encouraging smiles and woebegone glances.

"And, as such, she needs our help. We've all lived with one—and some of us still are—and we know what it's like. We know how to help her. Now let's take a moment to introduce ourselves, state our status, and offer condolences." She looked at the woman seated directly to her right. "Margaret, let's start with you and form a line."

To Jolie's continuing surprise, all the women stood up and began to form a line in front of her. The woman named Margaret smiled and offered her hand. "Margaret Bendall, Future, looking forward to your loss."

"Lynn Willis, Official, may the worms feast on his privates."

"Cherry Hawkins, Official, may the devil rot his evil soul."

"Gladys Kingsley, Future, may he burn in hell."

On and on it went. One after another the women moved through the line as though this were a true wake and she a true widow, sharing their own particular condolences for the premature death of her bastard husband. Jolie felt her smile growing wider as the line wrapped up, felt her heart growing lighter with each sincere shake of her hand. It was magnificent, wonderful, and more cathartic than she could have ever imagined.

"Of course, you know Meredith, Bitsy and I," Sophia said when they'd all taken their seats once more. "We're the founding members and have since planted our miserable husbands." She shot a look at Bitsy. "Or, in the case of Bitsy, had hers cremated."

Bitsy grinned. "Ashes to ashes," she said. Her twinkling gaze found Jolie's. "Made excellent cat litter."

A shocked chuckle bubbled up Jolie's throat.

"All of this is in the handbook, but we meet once a week, here at Meredith's house."

"The neighbors think we're playing bridge," Meredith interjected smoothly.

"Now, so you understand, our group doesn't in any way wish to offend poor widows who had good marriages and actually miss their husbands. But we're not like those women. Our men were—are— horrible. Looking forward to their deaths is what made—and makes—our lives bearable."

"Here, here," someone called.

"Doing the things in your handbook—fellowshipping with other widow-wannabe's—it's how we cope, how we survive. So like any proper funeral," Sophia continued, "we always bring a covered dish, we wear our hats—they're fetching morale boosters," she said with a fond pat of her own. "And the Future's always confess the progress they've made in bettering their future position as a widow. Be it finding the perfect pair of gloves to go with The Outfit, adding additional life insurance, updating a will, or investing in a pre-burial plan. Any proactive effort is recognized, so when you come back next week, we'll need a full report."

"Finding the outfit is a bitch," one of the ladies, Lynn, if memory served, piped up. A murmur of agreement moved through the room.

"And there's a list of insurance companies that'll offer the highest payout and insure without a physical in the back of your handbook," another added. "You'll still need a signature, of course, but that's easy enough to get with a little muscle relaxant added to his scotch." She inclined her head and lowered her voice. "See me when we're done, honey, and I'll hook you up."

"Do you have a will?" Bitsy asked.

"Er…yes," Jolie answered, trying to absorb it all. "We had to have them for the business."

"And you know where it's at?"

She did. It was in a safety deposit box in Moon Valley Savings and Loan. Jolie nodded.

Bitsy beamed at her. "Excellent."

"Okay, then," Sophia said briskly. "Let's begin Confessional. We'll start on this side." She gestured to her left.

Margaret sat back in her chair. "Well, as you all know, Ed's cholesterol is through the roof."

The woman next to her nodded sagely. "Nothing like a good massive heart attack to do the job."

Margaret's eyes danced with mischief. "Yeah, well. I've been dumping his egg substitute down the drain and adding a mixture of real eggs and whole milk to the carton."

A diabolical "oooh" of pleasure moved through the room.

"Very crafty, Margaret," Sophia told her. "Excellent. What about you, Gladys?"

Gladys cocked her head. "Oh, I haven't been able to do anything like that. Robert's healthy as a horse, meaner than hell." Her gaze turned a wee bit sly. "But I did finally talk him into buying a burial package. We've got an appointment next week to go down and pick out caskets, vaults, and plots."

Everybody in the room beamed at Gladys as

though this was an absolute coup. "Oh, wow," Meredith breathed happily. "Gladys, that's fantastic."

The woman seated next to her—Lois if Jolie remembered correctly—nudged her. "Those pre-burial plans are great," she confided. "Just think. You get to plan the funeral in advance, so that's just one less thing you have to do when he kicks it. Gets you one step closer to independence and it's a lot of fun," she added earnestly. She leaned in closer, smiled. "I've got Howard lined up. The minute he finally checks out, I'm ready, honey. I'm sitting on G, waitin' on O."

Jolie felt her eyes widen and another chuckle vibrate the back of her throat. She sat back and listened as the other club members matter-of-factly talked about the efforts they were making toward their widowhood, and was struck by the camaraderie among the group. There was a chemistry here, a bond that defied description, and though she'd only been a member for an hour, she already felt like she belonged. She couldn't wait to get home so that she could flip through her handbook and start doing some of the things the ladies had talked about. It was liberating, empowering, awesome even, this incredible sense of purpose she now felt.

Granted she might have to live with Chris for another three months, but rather than looking forward to a divorce as she'd been doing, something about looking forward to being a widow in the interim appealed to her even more. Did that mean she wished Chris would die? No, not really. At least not yet, at any rate. But she wouldn't mourn him if he did, that was for sure.

Sophia cleared her throat, garnering everyone's attention. "Okay, ladies. Time to call it a night. I'll see you all back here next week." She grinned, sent a meaningful look around the room, which everyone returned. "Until then… *Our un-dearly departed—*" she began.

"*—may he never rest in peace,*" they all finished in unison.

Jolie's smile widened and she quietly echoed the sentiment.

CHAPTER SEVEN

SOPHIA LET GO a sigh and sailed her hat across the room like a Frisbee, where it landed on the couch with a quiet thump. Per tradition after a meeting, she, Meredith and Bitsy had pulled chairs up around the serving table and were currently gorging on leftovers and homemade muscadine wine. She liked to dabble with various berries and had earned quite a reputation as an amateur wine-maker.

"Well?" Sophia said, plucking a pig-in-a-blanket from a nearby plate. "How do you think it went?"

The remaining petite fours in front of her, Bitsy licked a bit of fondant icing from her thumb and absently selected a second. "Like it always does—good."

"I think Jolie enjoyed herself," Meredith said. She dunked a wedge of honeydew melon into a tub of fruit-dip. "She really started to smile once we moved into Confessional, and I saw her flipping through her book several times."

Bitsy tilted her head thoughtfully. "I liked that hat she was wearing. Looked good on her, didn't it?"

Sophia nodded. "She's a very striking girl. Always has been with that bizarre flash of blond in her hair." She selected a brownie, vowing to walk an extra lap around the square for it as penance. "Her grandmother had it, too, you know."

"I noticed that again tonight," Meredith murmured thoughtfully. She adjusted another chair, leaned back and propped her feet up. "I've seen it with dark-haired people—usually men—but I've never seen it on a red-head."

"Where'd you get that hat, Meri?" Bitsy asked, still more interested in what was *covering* Jolie's hair.

Sophia and Meredith shared a smile. "Prim and Proper," they said together.

Having eaten the rest of her favorite treats, Bitsy popped a sausage ball into her mouth and chewed bemusedly.

Meredith glanced at Sophia. "Are you going to call Fran and let her know how it went?"

"The minute I get home," Sophia said, letting go a sigh. "This latest incident has really upset her." In fact, she didn't think she'd ever heard Fran so angry, hurt and frustrated.

Like most children, Jolie was laboring under the

incorrect assumption that, just because *she* didn't tell her mother something, that meant her mother didn't know.

Not so.

Though Sophia didn't know where Fran was getting her information—though she had her suspicions—her old friend was perfectly aware of everything that was going on. That's why Fran had contacted Sophia about inviting Jolie into the Club.

In a noble attempt to help protect her mother, Jolie was preventing her mother from directly helping her. Fran had been forced to do some behind-the-scenes maneuvering. If it had been her child, Sophia knew she would have undoubtedly done the same thing.

"Well, that's certainly understandable," Bitsy said. "If one of my son-in-laws ever raised a hand to one of my daughters, there'd be hell to pay." She nibbled on a cucumber sandwich, glowered at a plate of cheese straws. "There is absolutely nothing more despicable than a bully. Any man who hits a woman isn't a man at all—he's a coward. If I was Fran, I think I'd try to find someone to give Chris Marshall a good old-fashioned ass-kickin'. Did you see Jolie's lip?" she asked, outraged. "Poor thing."

"She filed a report, right?" Meredith asked.

Sophia nodded. "Filed the report, but is waiting to press charges. On what, nobody knows."

Bitsy grunted. "If she's smart she'll make sure *his* getting arrested coincides with *her* filing for divorce and finishing up with those sneaky dealings she's been using to get her mother's money back." She nodded succinctly. "That's how I'd do it if I were her."

Meredith and Sophia both blinked, startled at this abrupt pronouncement, then looked at each other. A bemused smile played on Meredith's lips and Sophia felt a grin tug at her mouth. Bless her heart, though there were times Bitsy could be as dim as a burned out bulb, occasionally a flash of brilliance emerged.

Like now.

Impressed, Sophia cast a glance at her friend. "Bitsy, that was inspired. I'd be willing to bet that's exactly what she's doing."

Bitsy shrugged, oblivious to the praise. "Just makes sense." She looked up as though another thought had struck and smiled. "Did either of you happen to see the paper this morning?" she asked, eyes twinkling.

Meredith chuckled. "I did."

Sophia shook her head. She'd been too busy fixing her hair and her face so that she could go out in the yard and plant petunias around her mailbox and wait for a certain blue-eyed know-it-all who made her old heart flutter like a doe-eyed virgin's. "What did I miss?"

"Oh, just another article about Mayor Greene's continuing skunk problem," Meredith chuckled. She bit her lip. "Apparently he decided to install a *small electric fence* around the perimeter of his house to keep them away."

Sophia felt her eyes widen and Bitsy positively chortled with glee. "I heard 'em talking about it at The Spa," Bitsy said. "Ginny Martin does the mayor's cleanin' and she was in there giving an eye witness account. Said the little suckers were hitting that fence and spraying like crazy." Bitsy did a comical impression—*jolt, freeze, jolt, freeze*—then slapped her knee and laughed harder.

"Needless to say," Meredith continued, "his plan didn't work."

Sophia chuckled quietly. No, she supposed not. For reasons unknown to Mayor Greene, the host of many professional exterminators he'd called in, and the entire town—with the exception of the three of them—couldn't understand why the crawlspace beneath the mayor's house had become Skunk Central. The pesky animals were digging holes in his lawn, making dens and alternately spraying, fighting and fornicating underneath his home and, as anyone could imagine, the odor was becoming quite…distinct.

But nothing less than what the old fart deserved, Sophia thought with a sanctimonious little nod.

For the past three years a city council member had been awarded the coveted Beautification Award. Her lips thinned. It was an appalling abuse of power, the height of political hypocrisy, and had been the scathing topic of more than one Dear Editor letter featured in the *Moon Valley Times*. Greene doled out the award to those who curried favor, and the rest of the town—who vehemently competed for the nomination—was left completely out the loop, their seasons of hard work ignored.

In Moon Valley that Beautification Award was the equivalent of a Nobel Prize. Gardening wasn't just a hobby in their little town—it was an Olympic sport. People guarded their tips and secrets with the sort of reverent regard worthy of the Holy Grail and having it handed over to unworthy candidates was blasphemous.

In fact, it stunk, so it was only fitting that the mayor should as well.

Sophia looked at the other two and quirked a brow. "Who has duty next?"

Bitsy, who admittedly had the best garden of the bunch, smiled determinedly. "I do."

"Throw out a few extra handfuls for our stinky friends, why don't you?" Sophia suggested slyly. "We want to make sure there's plenty for all of them."

CHAPTER EIGHT

"HEADED HOME, Malone?" Mike called as Jake unlocked his truck.

Jake turned. "Yeah," he said, dragging the word out. "I've got to feed, and I've got a mare I need to keep an eye on. She's due to foal soon." In the next couple of weeks if his calculations were right, Jake thought. He opened the door and tossed his case into the front seat, making a mental note to clean out his truck as the scent of stale fries and old coffee smacked him in the face.

Mike nodded, sucked in a breath and scanned the parking lot. "At some point we need to get together and talk about that information we received last week," he said, a significant implication hanging in his voice.

Jake grimaced. He knew Mike was right, but nonetheless found himself reluctant to get involved, and a week's perception hadn't given him any more insight than what he'd had when Mike had first mentioned the affair that Marshall was having with the Sheriff's wife.

Jake had made it a point to watch Marshall the past few days—one, he wanted to make sure that he hadn't hurt Jolie again—which was best for his continued good health, he thought ominously—and two, he'd wanted to see if Marshall was continuing to see Emily.

A couple of day-time drive-by's had concluded that he was.

Given the fact that the Sheriff had flexible hours and could arrive home at any time unannounced, Jake thought it was incredibly stupid for the man to risk getting his knob polished in the Sheriff's bed, but undoubtedly the risk held considerable appeal for the sadistic bastard.

Mike sidled over. "Any thoughts?" he asked.

Jake passed a hand over his face. "Should we tell him? Yeah, I think so." He winced, pulled a shrug. "But without the proof to back it up? I dunno, Mike. I'm not looking forward to telling him *with* the evidence," he told him. "Much less without it."

"I've been watching him, Jake," Mike said gravely. "The guy's going to *Dean's house*. He's banging his wife in his own bed."

"I know. I've been watching, too."

"If it was me, I'd want to know, and I'd be supremely pissed if a couple of my people knew it and didn't tell me." A muscle worked in his jaw. "He's a good man and they're making a fool of him."

Right again, Jake knew, but that still didn't silence the little voice that suggested he leave it be, that insisted it wasn't his business, much less his place. Technically, dammit, it was Jolie's. After all, it was her husband who was involved, her husband who couldn't keep his dick in his pants. Jake smirked. Of course, with that kind of thinking, she'd save a considerable amount of time and energy—if not ink— by simply running an ad in the paper and listing all of the women he'd had affairs with.

"Why don't you talk to Jolie and see if you can get her to give you a copy of the pictures?" Jake suggested.

Mike shot him an inscrutable look, then chuckled grimly. "You've got a better chance of getting them from her than I do. Why don't you ask her?"

While a part of him longed to jump at the chance for any reason to talk to her—to see her—Jake instinctively resisted. Just seeing her around town was hard enough. Talking to her, he knew, was beyond the scope of his abilities.

He hesitated, then gave his head a small shake. "She showed them to you. You took the report." Reasonable arguments, if not the complete truth. "If she'll give them to anyone, then it's you."

Mike nodded reluctantly. "All right," he sighed, rubbing the back of his neck. "I'll, uh... I'll give it a shot."

Jake shoved his hands in his pockets, leaned against the side panel of his truck and racked his brain for any sort of solution, preferably one that would spare Dean's pride and would prevent the Sheriff from spending the rest of his life in jail for murder.

Unable to find one, he shrugged. "I don't think we need to say anything without the proof to back it up."

Mike snorted. "As careless as that sonofabitch is, it wouldn't be too damned hard to get it ourselves."

He'd thought of that as well. With Marshall's reputation, a couple of pictures of him going in and out of the house would most likely suffice. That, or the next time Marshall paid Emily a visit, one of them could simply *forcefully suggest* that Dean go home. Though Dean was older than him and Mike, they'd nevertheless developed a friendship of sorts over the years, not to mention that Jake had a tremendous amount of respect for him. Keeping quiet felt wrong, but telling him didn't feel right either. It was just a bad situation all the way around.

"Last time I saw Marshall, I noticed he looked like he'd ran into a wall," Mike said slyly. "You wouldn't know anything about that, would you?"

Jake chewed the inside of his cheek, trying to suppress a grin. "It wasn't a wall. It was a door."

Mike chuckled under his breath, shot him a shrewd smile. "And you would know this because?"

"Because I was on the other side of the door. Clumsy bastard," Jake said amiably, pushing away from the truck. "He should really watch where he's going."

"Yeah," Mike agreed. "He could get hurt."

"Which is precisely what I told him." And precisely what he'd meant. If Marshall laid another hand on her, Jake wasn't so sure that a strong respect for the law would be enough to prevent him from hurting the louse.

Still laughing, Mike turned and walked away. "I'll let you know what happens with those pictures."

Good, Jake thought. Until then, he'd try to put it out of his mind.

CHAPTER NINE

"CAN YOU TALK?"

Jolie shouldered the cordless phone, walked down the hall and shot a look toward the bathroom. "Yeah. He's in the shower. What's up?"

"I saw Mike Burke come out of your office today," Sadie said. "Anything in particular that he wanted?"

Jolie grinned. Sadie didn't miss much and even if she did, she'd hear about it at The Spa. "Yeah," she said. "He wanted a copy of those pictures you took of Chris and Emily Dean."

"Did you give them to him?"

"I did," Jolie replied hesitantly. She'd shown Mike the pictures, hoping that he would let Dean in on what was going on, but Mike hadn't wanted to do that without the proof to back it up. Jolie understood, couldn't blame him really, and, though it was completely self-serving, she'd originally intended to keep the pictures in her own possession until she filed for divorce, strictly because she didn't want Chris aware of the fact that she was secretly documenting his behavior.

The less he knew the better.

But it was hardly fair to Sheriff Dean to hide the proof of the affair, and in good conscience, she simply couldn't tell Mike no. She'd made the copies and had felt better after she'd handed them over.

"Well," Sadie said. "For what it's worth, I think you made the right call. Dean's an innocent bystander in all of this as well."

"I know," she said heavily. They all were, except for her. She considered herself at fault for the original mistake in judgment. Jolie swallowed. "He, uh… He also shared something with me." Something that had made her heart alternately jump and squeeze, that had forced her to blink back tears long after Mike had left.

"Oh? What?"

Jolie let go a shuddering breath. "He told me who broke Chris's nose." She'd been curious about it, of course, but had refrained from asking because she knew Chris was just vain enough to draw the incorrect assumption that she cared. She'd just figured another pissed off husband had planted him a facer.

Sadie's voice positively vibrated with glee. "Oh, do tell? To whom do I owe my thanks? My gratitude? My firstborn?"

A broken laugh erupted from her throat. "Jake." Just saying his name aloud made something twist deep down inside her. Love and loss, regret and longing. His image rose readily in her mind, the slant of his cheek, that slightly full mouth, the very shape of his hands and the way his calloused palms felt against her own.

"Oh, Jolie," Sadie said, her voice tight with emotion.

She forced another laugh. "Last person I expected," she said. "I honestly didn't think he cared enough anymore to go to the trouble."

"I've told you all along that he did. He came in here the same day that you'd filed the report. Mike must have told him," she said, reaching the same conclusion that Jolie had.

"I, uh... I guess so," she replied haltingly, still having a hard time absorbing it, though he'd certainly come to her defense many times over the years.

One incident in particular stood out. Senior year, homecoming. They'd won. She'd been standing outside the locker room, waiting for Jake to come out when a couple of guys from the opposing team had walked by. One of them had mouthed off about her hair—she'd gotten that a lot over the years, particularly as a child. He'd called her a freak, then a witch. Jake had caught the tail end of the taunts and...

Jolie could still remember the way he'd looked that night. Dark hair wet from the shower, his face flushed from the heat and excitement of the game. He'd been muscled but rangy, a good-looking boy hovering on the edge of manhood. He hadn't uttered a single word, just walked up cool as you please, and slammed his fist into the guy's jaw. Then he'd dragged him up, hauled him over and shook him until he'd apologized to her. After it was over, he'd wrapped his arms around her. "Stupid idiot," he'd said. "Everybody knows that's the mark of an angel's kiss." Then he'd kissed her there as well.

Jolie released an unsteady breath. She could still remember the absolute bliss of that moment. He'd been her rock, her champion.

And she'd been too impatient. She'd given him up for Chris…and, though Jake might care enough to throw a punch on her behalf, she knew it was nothing more than what he'd do for anybody else. He hated a bully. Reading anything beyond regular human decency into it was an invitation for more heartache and, while she couldn't deny that she'd brought it upon herself, she'd had all she could stand of that for the time being.

She glanced at the clock and started. "Oh, crap. I've got to go. My meeting starts in fifteen minutes."

"You'd better hurry up then," Sadie told her, a

smile in her voice. "After all, you've got *a lot* to report this time."

Promising to call with a full report once the meeting was over, Jolie grabbed her purse and the spinach quiche she'd made, then headed for the door. She didn't bother telling Chris good-bye. He was still in the shower and, since courtesy wasn't something he valued, she'd just as soon not waste her time.

Jolie had shared her new status in the Future Widows' Club with Sadie the minute she'd left the meeting last week. She'd been too pumped, jazzed and excited to wait and had driven straight over to her house the minute she'd left Meredith's.

Predictably, Sadie had jumped on board with gleeful enthusiasm. They'd pored over the handbook together, laughing at the darkly humorous instructions laid out by the founding members.

Things like, *FINDING THE OUTFIT: The perfect ensemble for the funeral is simply a must. It puts you in the "widow" mind-set and gives you something to look forward to. The perfect veiled hat—to hide your tears of joy and small satisfied smirk—is particularly difficult to find. Start early!*

And *SHOW ME THE MONEY: Regardless of present insurance and assets, another half-mil is prudent. Contact your agent at once.*

X MARKS THE SPOT: Think of a treasure map,

and the will as your treasure. In this case, you don't want it to be a buried treasure that requires a long and possibly fruitless search. Make sure you're properly provided for—being sole beneficiary is best—and that the document is signed and stowed in a safe place.

PREPAY IS THE BEST WAY: Planning a funeral nowadays before one kicks the bucket is completely acceptable, even deemed considerate, thoughtful, and prudent. Take advantage of this perk, ladies! Have fun with it! Pick a plot, pick a casket, pick a service. Graveside or chapel? Efficiency now will make your special day run more smoothly. Your un-dearly departed…may he never rest in peace.

Jolie shook her head and laughed, remembering. But Sadie had been right—she *did* have a lot to report. She'd embraced the idea of being a widow with the sort of single-minded tenacity of a person clinging for dear life to the side of a cliff. The group had given her a purpose beyond getting her mother's money back. Being able to secretly thwart Chris made her feel empowered and alive—proactive. Better than she had in months.

Now, when he trickled acidic sarcasm over her, she merely smiled and thought about the additional life insurance she'd just purchased on him. She hadn't been able to get as much as the handbook suggested—that would have required a physical—but she'd added another hundred grand to what they'd already had. Getting the signature was simple enough. She'd slipped it in with other business which had required his careless scrawl and he'd signed the form without looking at it.

In addition to the life insurance, she'd found The Outfit. A black, fitted dress with sharp lines that accentuated her waist. A pair of long, sleek gloves and a pair of killer stiletto heels. The hat that Meredith had told her about at Prim and Proper.

And she hadn't stopped there.

She'd also bought a black merry widow corset, with a blood red bud nestled between the cups, matching lacy undies, and a pair of micro-fishnet thigh-highs. The fact that she'd never actually wear it hadn't kept her from dropping a small fortune on the outfit, nor had it kept her from trying it on. She'd felt like a femme fatale Mob widow…and she'd looked damned good, too.

Once she'd gotten the outfit, it had only seemed fitting to swing by the funeral home and pick up some literature on burial plans, and she had to confess that leafing through the little brochure had engendered satisfying visions of herself standing on a windswept hillside in her sexy widow gear, a mound of freshly dug earth at her feet.

The whole process had been wickedly fun, and

now instead of merely surviving her current hell, she could feel the cool breeze of freedom beginning to blow through her life. Even Chris had noted the difference.

"What the hell's wrong with you?" he'd sneered earlier this afternoon. "What are you smiling about?"

The comment had pointed out two things. One, she'd been stunned to realize that she *had* been smiling—for no apparent reason, it would seem. And two, the fact that she'd been so miserable for months that he'd noticed a smile meant that things were definitely taking a turn for the better.

Jolie slowed to a stop outside of Meredith's house and eagerly anticipated the time she'd spend with these women tonight. It was ridiculous she knew, but she'd found it intensely comforting that an invitation into the Club meant life-time membership regardless of a woman's marital status. She'd worried that when she finally kicked Chris's worthless ass to the curb that she'd have to give up her membership.

Meredith opened the door again and promptly handed over her hat. "Oh, good," she said darting a glance over Jolie's shoulder. "You beat Bitsy here— she's out test-driving one of those little mini-motor-cycles I told you about last week. Anyway, she took a real shine to your hat last week—even went down to Prim and Proper Wednesday to buy one for herself, but *someone* had just bought the last one." Her eyes twinkled knowingly. "My sources say that you've been busy this past week."

Jolie grinned. Sources, eh? she thought. This was Moon Valley. Nobody needed a source—all you had to do was make an appointment at Sadie's, walk around the square, or make a trip to the local garden center. "I've gotten a pretty good bit done," she finally confessed.

Meredith smiled at her as though she were a failing student who'd just aced an exam. "Excellent," she said warmly. Her gaze dropped to the dish in Jolie's arms and she sniffed appreciatively. "That smells wonderful. You know the drill, hon. Put it on the table, fix your plate and find a seat. We'll get started soon."

Jolie found an empty spot for her quiche next to a plate of mini-muffins, chatted amiably with Gladys, the woman who'd talked her husband into investing in the pre-burial plan. "It went smashingly well," Gladys said, positively aquiver. "You'll hear all about it soon enough. What about you, dear? Make any progress?"

Jolie nodded. "Quite a bit."

Gladys poured them each a glass of lemonade. "That's wonderful. Good therapy, isn't it? I remember when Sophia, Meredith and Bitsy first approached me about joining." Her gaze focused inward, presumably on the memory, then she blinked and looked at Jolie. "It saved me," she said simply. "Gave me something to do besides being miserable. I look forward to these meetings all week, have made some great friends. It's good to be with people who understand." She smiled. "I suspect that's what you think, too, isn't it?"

Touched by the insight, Jolie nodded. "Yes, it is," she murmured softly. She followed Gladys into the parlor where more and more of the women were slowly beginning to congregate.

Bitsy and Meredith were bickering over the scooter again—from what Jolie could gather, Bitsy had nearly run Meredith down again. Jolie stifled a smile. Bitsy had tricked out her little ride with a sewing basket and a couple of racing flags. She'd just noticed that Sophia was absent when she heard the front door open. A cake plate full of petite fours, tote and purse in hand, Sophia, looking harried but elegant as always, quickly made her way into the dining room to deposit her dish. Bitsy fell immediately in behind her and quickly loaded her plate down with Sophia's little cakes.

With an exasperated look at Bitsy, Sophia breezed back into the room. "Good evening, ladies," she called gaily. She wore a red pantsuit and had donned her hat. "It's lovely to see all of you again. I hope you all had a good week and that you have a lot to report." Her gaze drifted significantly over Jolie and a touch of humor curled her lips. "Unless there's any new business, we can start." She waited a beat, and when no one spoke, she let go a little breath. "Okay, then. Gladys, how about it? How did your meeting at the funeral home go?"

Gladys set her plate aside and smiled at the room at large. "Fantastic!" she chortled. "We took care of everything and get this," she confided, leaning almost off the edge of her seat. "I'd planned on suggesting that we economize based on being practical—when you're dead what's the difference between a three-thousand-dollar casket and a five-thousand-dollar casket, right? Well, I didn't have to say a word. Robert took one look at the price tag on those suckers and insisted that he be buried in the next best thing to a pine box. So not only did I get to plan his funeral, I saved several thousand dollars by letting him go with me."

A chorus of nods and praise for this accomplishment echoed around the room. "Just more for you, eh, Gladys?" Bitsy said. "Bank it for that cruise you're planning on taking."

"On the pretense of needing to 'get away', of course," Meredith chimed in with a sly smile.

"I *will* need to get away," Gladys said with a disgusted harrumph. She snorted. "God knows the old tight-wad has never let me go anywhere. When he's gone, I'm going to travel the world," she sighed dreamily. "I'm gonna go everywhere. See it all."

"I'm so glad that your trip to the funeral home exceeded your expectations, Gladys," Sophia told her. "I know you're thrilled."

Gladys sighed, patted her permed hair, then reached down and snagged a strawberry from her plate.

Sophia's twinkling gaze found Jolie's. "What about you, Jolie? I understand you've been very busy this week."

Jolie grinned. "I have been," she confirmed. "I've added one-hundred-thousand dollars worth of life insurance, found my outfit, and picked up one of those pre-burial plan packets from the funeral home."

The women all beamed at her, and Bitsy, Meredith and Sophia shared a proud look. "Oh, wonderful!" Sophia cried happily. "Wonderful, wonderful!" She laughed. "You certainly didn't waste any time."

Jolie poked her tongue in her cheek. "Yeah, well, I've wasted enough up until this point, haven't I?" she admitted.

"But you're making up for it now," Meredith replied. "And that's what's important."

"What are your plans for after your husband is gone, dear?" Bitsy wanted to know. "Anything you can share?"

Somewhat surprised by the question, Jolie tucked her hair behind her ear. "Er…yeah." She glanced nervously around the room. "I'm, uh… I'm looking at a little house on Lelia Street and I'd like to start my own accounting business." It's the first time she'd said it aloud; she hadn't even shared her plan with Sadie yet. Like a secret gift, she'd been keeping it to herself, but actually lending voice to her agenda made it all the more real, made something light and happy expand in her chest.

"Oh, are you talking about Maudy Hawkins's old place?" Lois asked fondly. "White siding, green shutters, big weeping willow tree in the front yard?"

"That's the one," Jolie said.

Meredith's face blushed with pleasure. "Oh, that's a lovely old home. I can see you being very happy there."

She could, too, Jolie thought with an inward sigh. She could see herself happy anywhere away from Chris.

Sophia moved the meeting forward, asked several other Futures what they'd been doing this week to further their widow cause. Margaret was still slipping real eggs and milk into her husband's egg substitute and Lois had reported picking up a prescription of Viagra for her husband. Initially Jolie hadn't understood the importance of this move, but Gladys had quickly explained that men with heart conditions were warned against taking the drug. Apparently, Lois's husband was just a few slices of bacon away from a good coronary and therefore didn't have any business taking the sexual enhancement aid.

"Dr. Gibson generally gives out the prescription regardless," Gladys told her. "The last time he refused to dole out a free sample, his tires were slashed."

Jolie felt her eyes widen and chuckled softly.

"Let me tell you, women around here take that stuff seriously. My daughter's a pharmacist and boy, has she told me some stories," she shared with a grim laugh. "Most of those women anchoring the front pew down at the Baptist church have acted like regular heathens when she's run out."

"Has anyone not shared?" Sophia called above the lively din.

On the far side of the room a thin woman with eyes the color of coffee gone cold raised her hand and blinked back tears. "I haven't."

Sophia's smile softened. "Sorry, Cora," she said. "I didn't mean to overlook you."

Cora shook her head, fished a mangled napkin

from her pocket and wiped her eyes. "It's all right, Sophia."

"Tell us what's wrong, dear," Meredith encouraged. The room had gone silent, their faces somber as they waited for Cora to share her story.

"Jed took the checkbook from me again," she said, her voice thick with unshed tears. "He goes with me everywhere now—to the market, the gas station. Doesn't let me have so much as a nickel of my own," she said bitterly. "Doles it out like I'm too incompetent to be trusted with his hard-earned money."

Sophia and Bitsy shared a look. "Cora, there's only one solution for this, one that we've told you before. You've got to get a job. Make your own money."

Cora's shoulders sagged. "What am I supposed to do, Sophia? I've got no skills. I've been a housewife for thirty years. Aside from cooking and cleaning, what am I qualified to do in today's society?"

"Well, I don't know, but there's got to be something," Bitsy pointed out. "You make the best cakes this side of the Mississippi. You've taken first place at the county fair for as long as I can remember. That's certainly a skill."

"That's right," another lady pointed out. "Your fondant icing brought tears to the judge's eyes last year. 'Seamless,' he called it. 'Absolutely perfect.'"

"Why not see if Dilly's Bakery needs some help?" Jolie suggested. "She was covered up the last time I was in there. I can't imagine that she wouldn't welcome an extra pair of hands, and she certainly does enough business to support another employee."

Cora frowned thoughtfully, seemingly mulling it over and when she looked up at Jolie there was a hint of hope in her melancholy eyes that hadn't been there before. A tentative smile shaped her thin mouth. "I do know how to bake," Cora confessed rather shyly.

"Well, of course, you do," Meredith told her. "If you think the fact that you're married to a tight-assed old bastard was the sole reason we invited you into the Club, then you'd better think again," she teased. "We wanted your baked goods."

Startled, Cora chuckled.

"You did bring a cake, didn't you, Cora?" Sophia asked, her keen gaze zeroing in on the dining room table.

"I did," Cora said with a wavery smile. "But it's all gone."

Sophia's shoulders fell and she let out a heavy, lamenting sigh. "Five minutes late and I missed it." She grinned warmly at Cora. "Now that's a marketable skill. Do as Jolie suggested and check with Mary Dilly." She nodded succinctly. "Dollars to donuts she puts you to work. Then you'll have your own money and you can tell that stingy husband of yours to shove it up his ass."

"Won't be easy, though," someone pointed out. "It's too damned tight."

The remark drew a hearty laugh from around the room and the pleasant sensation of being able to help another person settled warmly over Jolie's heart. Poor Cora. She couldn't imagine being that dependent on another person. Chris may have stolen money from her mother and their investors, but she still earned a salary at Marshall Inc. Still had her own money.

Sophia cleared her throat. "Well, ladies, we should probably wrap things up for tonight. We'll see you all again next week. Until then." Her lips twitched. *"Your un-dearly departed—"*

Jolie grinned. She was ready this time, lent her voice to the mantra.

"—may he never rest in peace."

CHAPTER TEN

SOPHIA WAITED until the last member walked out before turning to Meredith and Bitsy, and grinned. "She's coming along well, isn't she?"

Meredith nodded and her eyes twinkled with humor. "She certainly is. Jumped right in and started getting things done."

"Just showed how much she needed us," Bitsy said. She pulled a face. "I heard a little more about that husband of hers this week." They made their way into the dining room and took their seats around the table.

Arching a brow, Meredith dragged a cracker through a cheese ball. "Oh, really? Do tell."

Bitsy chewed the inside of her cheek, then shot them both a you're-not-going-to-believe-this look. "Suffice it to say that he's been seen coming in and out of the Sheriff's house."

Sophia and Meredith frowned.

"When the Sheriff's not at home," Bitsy said meaningfully, playing her trump card.

Sophia's mouth dropped open and Meredith gasped sharply. "He's sleeping with Sheriff Dean's wife?" she asked incredulously.

Bitsy nodded, pursing her lips. She selected a tea cake. "That's what I've heard."

"He must enjoy pain," Sophia said, struggling to comprehend that sort of stupidity, a wedge of cantaloupe virtually forgotten in her hand. "If Dean finds out, he'll tear him apart."

"Yeah, and Chris has already gotten his nose broken this week," Bitsy said. She waggled her brows. "I overheard a little talk down at The Spa. Jake Malone accidentally-on-purpose opened a door into his face."

Sophia nodded and smiled. She'd heard about it from Fran, who'd been eternally grateful to Jolie's old boyfriend for quietly coming to her daughter's defense.

"Jake Malone?" Meredith asked, evidently baffled. "Who's he? Somebody else's husband?"

Sophia shook her head. "No, he's Jolie's old boyfriend. He's a detective with the Sheriff's department. They were together for years—since third grade according to Fran—but things went bad after her dad died. Her mother's not altogether sure why—

Jolie's never really talked to her about it—but she's hoping that they'll eventually get back together."

"Well, they can't until that vermin she's married to is out of the picture," Meredith pointed out.

Bitsy popped a cherry tomato into her mouth. "Heard a little more about that, too. Three months."

Meredith's brow folded. "Three months until what?"

"Until she's got her mother's money back and files for divorce."

Impressed, Sophia cocked her head. "How *do* you find these things out?"

Bitsy just grinned. "I have my ways."

CHAPTER ELEVEN

WITH EVERY INCH that put her closer to home, Jolie felt the dread of her return sucking at her, dragging at her spirits and generally making her miserable but she'd put if off as long as she could. After leaving Meredith's, she'd gone to Sadie's. Rob had been pulling a double shift at the steel mill, so it had been just her friend and the girls at home. They'd had the television in the kitchen tuned into Emeril Lagasse, icing cupcakes and screaming "Bam!" at the top of their wee little lungs.

While other kids were interested in Cartoon Network, Nickelodeon and Disney, Sadie's girls—little curly-haired miniatures of their mother—were watching the Food Network, HGTV, and the Style Channel. Jolie felt a smile tug at her lips. They were undoubtedly going to be a force to be reckoned with when they grew up.

Jolie had hung around and pitched in, then helped clean up the kitchen, bathed the girls, and put them to bed. Tucking them in had been particularly bitter-sweet, their little round faces bathed in the glow from their angel night-lights. It had conjured back-burner dreams of having her own family, but she couldn't help but be eternally thankful that she hadn't brought a child into the mess she'd created with Chris. In addition to everything else, she didn't think that she could bear the guilt of making such a poor choice for her child.

After the girls had gone to bed, she and Sadie had talked about her meeting, her plans for after she left Chris—which had gotten Sadie's enthusiastic stamp of approval—and regular Moon Valley gossip.

Sadie had updated her on the continuing problem the mayor had been having with skunks. Reeking of skunk perfume and tomato juice, the mayor's wife had come into The Spa for her regular set and had bemoaned her lack of sleep due to the "screeching, howling and humping" going on beneath her house. Evidently the mayor had called in the County Agent, and after investigating, he couldn't find any particular reason why the odiferous animals had decided to burrow beneath the mayor's home, nor could he suggest any further technique of removing them that hadn't already been employed.

As for the continuing debate over the restoration of the statue in the town square, the city council and

Civic Club were engaged in the proverbial Mexican standoff, with neither party inclined to acquiesce. In the mean time Jebediah's stately bronze body was slowly oxidizing, turning black a result of the process. Jolie figured the Civic Club would blink first. A feeble smile caught the corner of her mouth. They'd been too proud of him to let him stand there and ruin.

Jolie wheeled her car onto her street and winced when she saw Chris's BMW in the drive. "Damn," she muttered, supremely disappointed. She'd hoped that he wouldn't be home—he usually wasn't—but, alas, it wasn't meant to be. What the hell, she thought, unwilling to let him wreck what had been a nice evening. She'd just do what she usually did—burrow in her room, curl up with a good book, a block of chocolate and try to avoid him. If he annoyed her too much, she'd pack her bag and spend the night in Sadie's apartment.

She didn't remember locking the door when she'd left earlier this evening, so evidently he'd been out and come back, she decided as she let herself into the house. With luck, he'd be passed out, sleeping off whatever he'd managed to get into tonight. A quick look in the living room confirmed that he wasn't holding down the couch—his preferred pit-stop after a night of drinking and whoring, she thought with an uncharitable smirk—and her first thought was that he'd probably gone on to bed. But then a curious sound reached her ears. Jolie stilled.

The shower.

Again? Jolie thought, her brow folding into a puzzled frown. Granted Chris was rather meticulous when it came to his daily grooming habits, but three showers in one day was a little excessive, even for him. Jolie didn't know why, couldn't account for it, but the oddest sense of foreboding shivered down her spine. Her gut hollowed, then filled with a combination of fear and dread. Oh, God, she thought. What had he done this time? She carefully set her purse on the couch and slowly made her way toward the back of the house to the master suite.

The first thing she noticed were the clothes he'd carelessly discarded before she'd left. They were left in an untidy heap at the foot of the bed. His wallet, too, didn't appear to have been moved from the dresser. Strange, because if he'd gone out, his things shouldn't be in the same place.

In the nanosecond it took to make this observation, her gaze darted to the bathroom door, from which no steam billowed out, and she noticed something that *did* look different. The bathroom door— which had been slightly ajar—was wide open…and from her vantage point she clearly saw something that made her stomach lurch with alarm.

Chris's leg was stuck at an unnatural angle out the shower stall door and a puddle of pink water had pooled on the floor.

Unable to stop herself, she gravitated toward the bathroom, moved though she suddenly couldn't feel her feet, could barely remember to breathe…and the rest of the scene came into view. The shower beat down on Chris's prone body. His eyes were open, unblinking, and a small hole cut through his chest. A silent shriek formed in the back of her throat. Then her voice caught up with the horror and she screamed.

SINCE BEING PROMOTED to detective, Jake had handled exactly three homicides, two of which had been crimes of passion, the other a drunken family dinner in which Frank Bolen had shot and killed his older brother Amos over a tub of butter. Amos hadn't passed it quick enough to suit Frank, so rather than merely waiting, Frank had reached for the snubnosed thirty-eight he kept handy in the back of his jeans. Frank had later claimed the shooting had been an accident, but according to other family members present, he'd calmly buttered his corn afterwards, then asked for the salt and pepper.

When tonight's call had come in, Jake had been finishing up in the barn, his preferred after-work hang out. He'd spent some time watching Marzipan, throwing a little extra feed into her bucket. This was her first foal and while Mother Nature usually didn't need any help, he'd still feel better if he could be there during the birth in the event there were any problems. She'd started bagging up, so foaling was imminent. It was merely a question of when. Less than a week, he felt confident.

Mike had taken the initial call, arrived on the scene, then per protocol, had contacted the detective on call—Jake. He'd been grim and direct. "Chris Marshall is dead. Poplar Street. You need to get over here."

Jake had walked past Jolie in the living room, her face a white mask of shock, and followed Mike back into the master bathroom. Various men's toiletries littered the counter and shower stall, and the metallic scent of blood hung in the air. Chris Marshall lay sprawled on the floor of the shower, his brown eyes open and blank, a single gun-shot wound to the chest, right through where his heart should have been if the bastard had had one. But that wasn't the most startling injury.

Jake blinked, certain his eyes had deceived him. "Where's his dick?"

Mike passed a hand over his face. "We, uh… We don't know. It's gone."

"Gone?" Jake repeated, unable to process the information. He looked at the neat cut where Marshall's penis used to be, then back at Mike for an explanation.

"This is how we found him," Mike said, equally baffled. He scratched his head. "All I did was turn off the water, call you and the coroner."

Okay, Jake thought, numbly shocked. So their killer had taken a trophy. And a sick one at that. "Have you had a chance to talk with Jolie yet?" he asked, unable to look away.

"Just briefly. She made the call. Said he'd been in the shower when she left. She came home and heard the water still running, then walked back here, found him, and called us."

"Any sign of forced entry?" Jake asked.

"Not that I noticed, but I haven't done a lot of poking around. Jolie said she hadn't locked the door when she left, but it was locked when she got back. She'd assumed that Marshall had been out."

Jake nodded, mentally running down everything that needed to be done. The Sheriff should be there any minute as well as the Evidence Tech, Nathan Todd. Jake imagined the only reason he'd beaten them there was because he'd all but flown to the scene.

Sporting pillow creases and mismatched socks, Leon Turner, the county coroner, shuffled into the crowded bathroom. "What have we got?" he croaked tiredly, evidently suffering from a head cold. "Tell me it's natural causes. I'm too sick to handle a homicide."

"Sorry, Leon," Jake said. "I hope you brought your vitamin C. We're in for a long night." In homicide cases, the coroner and law enforcement worked closely together as it facilitated preserving the evidence, which led to solving the crime. Of course, in this case, some vital evidence was missing.

"Shit." Leon passed a hand over his feverish cheeks. "Oh, well. I couldn't sleep anyway. Hard to sleep when you can't breathe. Gun-shot wound, eh?" He squatted down, inspected the body, then his ruddy face went slack. "What happened to his—"

"It's gone," Mike said again. "Gone when we got here."

Leon blinked, seemingly certain he'd misunderstood. "I… Hmmm." He frowned, looked closer at the body, at the hole in Marshall's chest, then gingerly tilted him to look underneath the body.

"Good one," Mike said amiably. "We didn't think to check up his ass."

Though he knew it was inappropriate—the man was dead, after all—Jake had to smother a laugh.

"I'm not looking— I—" Leon stammered, flustered. The top of his balding head turned pink. "I'm checking for lividity." He pointed to some purplish discoloration on Marshall's left butt cheek. "See this?" he said. "He's been dead for hours. Long enough for the blood to pool and mild *rigor mortis* to set in." His thick brows formed a line. "Seems like there'd be more blood loss," he remarked thoughtfully.

"The water was left on," Jake pointed out. "Most of it likely went down the drain. What's your best guess on time of death?"

Leon shrugged. "Leaving him in a cool shower's gonna throw his core body temperature off. Based on what I see here, four to six hours, but the M.E. will be able to tell you more." He grunted as he stood, arching a brow. "Who found him?"

"Jolie," Mike said. Jake listened to him repeat the story.

"Well, he was alive when she left and dead when she got home," Leon said. He glanced back at Marshall's prone form. "Based on my best guess, that's consistent with what I see here."

Jake and Mike shared a brief look. Leon's shrewd gaze bounced between them and then his watery blood-shot eyes widened. "You don't think she did it?" heaccused, his voice suggesting the very idea was blasphemous.

Did he think she did it? Jake thought. No. He couldn't imagine her ever being angry enough to kill someone. Knew instinctively that it wasn't in her nature. Hell, he'd seen her step over ant trails, nurture baby birds. As a girl, she'd taken in every stray, every unwanted animal—be it the two-legged or four-legged variety—and though he didn't know if she still did it or not, she used to volunteer at the local animal shelter. She hadn't killed him—couldn't have. She had too much respect for life, even Chris Marshall's, though he certainly hadn't earned it.

Nevertheless a good detective had to ask the hard questions, examine the evidence. And in most cases when a spouse was murdered, it was the husband or wife—whoever stood to benefit the most—who was responsible. And unfortunately, everybody in town knew that Chris had given Jolie a number of reasons to want to see him dead. Jake grimaced. Then again, that could be said of many people aside from Jolie.

He and Mike shared another look, one that Jake knew suggested they'd each reached a simultaneous deduction—Sheriff Dean.

Christ.

"We can't rule out anyone just yet, Leon," Jake told him, rubbing a hand over the back of his neck.

"Hell, you know that." He could already feel the tension creeping into his skull. This was going to get nasty.

Leon leveled a hard look at him and despite the fact that he bore an unfortunate resemblance to Boss Hogg, he looked quite impressive in that moment. "Just like you know she isn't capable of this."

"She said she'd been at a meeting," Mike interjected. "That sounds like an alibi."

He'd find out when he talked to her, which he wasn't going to be able to avoid much longer. The very idea made his stomach knot with anxiety. He hadn't actually spoken to her in almost two years, and these were... Hell, these were hardly ideal circumstances. *Your husband's dead and his dick's cut off— you wouldn't happen to know anything about that, would you, Jolie?* Jake swallowed a morbid laugh.

On the rare occasions he'd actually let himself imagine talking to her again, he'd never been quite sure what he'd say. But he knew the coming conversation wouldn't remotely resemble anything he could have envisioned.

Leon passed a hand over his face. "Keep me in the loop, okay?" he asked Jake. "Her father and I were friends."

Jake nodded. "I will. Why don't you see if you can round up some coffee? This is going to take a while."

"Wonder where Dean's at," Mike said bemusedly after Leon left.

Possibly destroying evidence, Jake thought, wincing as the unchecked notion popped into his head.

Mike hesitated. "You, uh… You don't think he might have… That he…" He couldn't bring himself to finish, but Jake didn't need to be clairvoyant to know what he was suggesting, and the thought had certainly crossed his mind as well.

"We hadn't told him yet," Jake said, shifting uncomfortably.

"But that doesn't mean he hadn't found out. The guy's dick's missing, Jake. That's pretty damned personal."

Yes, it was. And whether Dean knew it before or not, they were damned sure going to have to tell him now. Had planned on it anyway, but what they hadn't counted on was having to bring it up because of a murder investigation. One which, for the moment, their boss was considered a suspect.

"If you'll wait on Nathan, I'll go ahead and talk to Jolie."

Mike nodded. "Sure."

Jake felt every muscle in his body atrophy with stress, mentally braced himself for the coming conversation as he made his way back into the living room.

Jolie looked up and her pale green eyes tangled with his. That phantom sucker-punch hit him in the gut and for all intents and purposes the ground shifted beneath his feet. He cleared his throat and uttered the same words that had ended their relationship.

"We need to talk."

CHAPTER TWELVE

"I JUST HEARD on my scanner that Chris Marshall has been found dead," Meredith said, her usually cool modulated voice panicked.

The words had filtered through Sophia's sleep-muddled mind, and sat bolt upright in bed when their implication set in. "What?" she breathed into the phone.

"Shot," she said. "Leon estimated time of death four to six hours ago."

That ruled Jolie out, Sophia thought, because she'd been with them. Not that she'd truly suspected her, of course—if Jolie had wanted to kill her husband she could have done that a long time ago.

But she'd need an alibi, which was undoubtedly what had put Meredith into a tailspin.

"I haven't called Bitsy yet," Meredith said. "But I will."

"Yes, call her," Sophia agreed, climbing out of bed. "We'll need to get over there."

"Oh, Sophia, what are we going to do?" Meredith asked, her voice weak and wavery with worry. "I don't mind outing our Officials—they don't have anything to lose. But what about our Futures? It'll ruin them. Ruin the Club."

Sophia wedged the cordless phone between her shoulder and ear, then shimmied out of her gown and blindly groped in her closet for something to wear. "We'll stick to the same story we've told for years. We were playing bridge. They can't prove otherwise, can they?"

"No, no, you're right, of course," Meredith said. "Still, I just have a bad feeling about this, Sophia. A very bad feeling," she said ominously.

Be that as it may they couldn't afford to lose sight of the immediate problem, Sophia thought, and that problem was that Jolie didn't know what to say, which was why they needed to get over there ASAP before she inadvertently outed them to the entire community.

Meredith was right—it could be disastrous.

"Don't worry, Meri," Sophia soothed. "Everything's gonna be fine. Call Bitsy, and then come pick me up. We'll hash it out on the way over."

She just hoped they made it before it was too late.

CHAPTER THIRTEEN

WE NEED TO TALK.

Jolie looked up, her gaze tangled with Jake's and for the first time since she'd walked into that nightmare in the bedroom, she felt the hot rush of tears hit the back of her eyes. If her legs would have supported her, she would have launched herself into his arms. Someone had walked into her house—the place where she normally slept—and killed Chris. She kept seeing his face, his eyes, in particular, and though she'd honestly hated him, she couldn't—would never—wish death upon anyone. Any life, even his misbegotten one, was too precious.

Jolie cleared her throat. "Okay," she said.

His expression somewhat dark, Jake came around the sofa and sat down in front of her. "I need to ask you a few questions, and later, if you're up to it, we need to go down to the Sheriff's department and do an official report."

She swallowed, then nodded.

Jake's gaze darted over her shoulder and she heard the scuff of footfalls hit the hardwood floor. She followed his gaze and discovered Sheriff Dean and another man, one she vaguely recognized but couldn't name, standing in the room. Looking solemn, the Sheriff nodded at her, but didn't speak.

"Excuse me just a minute," Jake told her, pushing up from his seat. He walked over to where they stood, briefing them, she supposed. She heard phrases like gun-shot wound, time-of-death and odd trophy, the last of which she didn't understand, but couldn't make her numb mind process anything beyond breathing at the moment.

After a moment he returned and took the seat in front of her once more. He braced his elbows on his knees and let his hands dangle in the deep vee between them. His bleak expression didn't match the kind, concerned and somewhat helpless look in those silvery gray eyes. "Can I get you anything?" he asked. "Maybe some coffee? Water? A soda?"

Jolie shook her head. Her mouth was dry as dust, but her stomach would undoubtedly protest so much as a grain of salt at this point. "No, thanks."

He nodded. "All right. Mike gave me the abbreviated facts, but I need you to start at the beginning and tell me everything, okay?"

Jolie chewed her bottom lip and with difficulty, found her voice. "He was home when I left, in the shower."

"What time did you leave?"

"Er…a little before six. I was running late."

"Did you notice anything odd when you left? An unfamiliar car? Anybody walking a dog, or hanging around?"

She thought back, trying to picture the scene when she'd walked to her car, then shook her head. "No, nothing, but I… I didn't really look. I was in a hurry."

Jake shifted. "Mike said you didn't think you'd locked the door."

That was the thing that really bugged her, Jolie thought. She was almost certain that she hadn't. In fact, she rarely locked the doors. There'd never been a need. Moon Valley had always been a safe place, one virtually untouched by the ugly violence of bigger cities. "I can't say beyond a shadow of a doubt that I didn't lock the door, but I'm 99.9% sure that I didn't. I'm not in the habit of it."

He arched a brow. "But it was locked when you got home?"

"Yeah." She moistened her dry lips. "I thought he'd been out."

"And what time did you get home?"

"A little after eleven. After my meeting, I called

Sadie and dropped by her house to visit with her and the girls. Rob was pulling a double shift. She was lonely and…" Jolie hesitated, then she looked up, met his gaze and managed a ghost of a smile. "And I didn't want to come home," she admitted truthfully. "It's no secret that my marriage hasn't been a happy one."

Another flash of unreadable emotion lit his gaze, but he quickly blinked it away. "So you unlocked the door. Then what?"

Jolie thought back, replayed the memory, but had a hard time focusing on anything prior to finding Chris. That image—the absolute horror—was so stark it made everything else seem muted and unimportant in comparison. She closed her eyes tightly, hoping her lids would erase the vision.

Evidently sensing her train of thought, Jake cleared his throat. "You came in the living room," he coaxed softly. "Tell me what you saw, Jo. What you heard, what you noticed."

"I, uh…" Jolie scrubbed a hand over her face. "I noticed that Chris wasn't on the couch. He usually is, if he's home."

"Then what?"

"Then I heard the shower," she said woodenly, feeling the dread creep into her belly, infect her bones. "I thought it was odd because he'd been in the shower when I left. He showers in the morning as well, so I thought three showers? What's he gotten into this time? And I set my purse down and walked back to his bedroom."

"The master bedroom?"

"*His* bedroom," Jolie repeated. "We didn't share a room. Haven't since a few months into the marriage. Like I said," she repeated. "It's no secret we weren't happy."

Jake chewed the bottom corner of his lip and nodded, silently encouraging her to continue.

She cleared her throat, hugging her arms around her middle to stave off the chill residing there. She looked out the window, dimly noting the throng of cars parked in front of the house, hearing the ice-maker in the kitchen kick on, a wholly ordinary sound compared to the surreal, gruesome reality playing out around her. "The clothes he'd worn this afternoon were on the floor and his wallet was on the dresser. The bathroom door—" Jolie stopped short, resisting the image. She didn't want to see it again, *never* wanted to see it again.

"Was it open or closed?" Jake asked gently.

"Open."

"Had it been open?"

"No," she said, giving her head a small shake. "It had been partially closed. Just barely open. I'd glanced in there as I was leaving." She let go a shuddering breath. "There was no steam and… And it was cool." Nausea welled up the back of her aching throat. "Then I saw his leg. It was hanging out of the shower door and there was…there was b-bloody water on the floor."

Jake massaged the bridge of his nose. "Did you go into the bathroom, Jolie?"

She shook her head and forced herself to look at him, hoping that if she focused on his face she could push the other image away. She let go a stuttering breath. "Just to the door, close enough to realize that he was beyond help. Th-that he was dead. I saw the hole in his chest."

"What did you do next?"

She plowed a hand through her hair, tugging until it hurt to feel something besides the bizarre numbness that had invaded every nerve ending. "I got the cordless phone from the bedside table, then ran outside and called 911. I stayed on the porch until Mike got here. I didn't want— I couldn't be alone in here."

Jake nodded, seeming to mull over everything she'd said. He glanced up and caught her gaze. "You said you'd been to a meeting. What kind of meeting? Who were you with?"

Jolie let out a tired sigh. "I was at— I was with—" She blinked, stopped short and stared at him as a stark truth emerged through the fuzzy confines of her brain. She couldn't tell him where she'd been, she thought faintly. It was against the FWC rules.

Furthermore, even shell-shocked as she was, she had enough wits about her to realize that telling Jake she'd been to a *Future Widows' Club meeting,* of all places—when her husband lay dead in the next room—was going to sound…incriminating.

Her heart tripped and a new kind of fear, one borne of self-preservation, rocketed through her veins.

She'd undoubtedly be an initial suspect, Jolie thought weakly as more implications clawed their way through her foggy mind. She'd read enough suspense novels to know that, and had watched enough Law and Order to know how this would play out. She was closest to him, had the most to gain.

Oh, God. The life insurance. The outfit. The pre-burial plan.

She was going to puke. Or faint. Either way, she needed to be closer to the floor. She leaned forward.

Jake wore an odd frown and his gaze had sharpened. "Jolie, who were you with?"

"She was with us," Sophia said briskly as she hurried into the room. Looking harried and sympathetic, Meredith and Bitsy followed in her wake. "Jolie's part of our bridge club. We get together and play once a week."

Jolie wilted with relief. She'd never been more thankful in her life to see another person.

"We just heard, dear," Sophia said, coming around the sofa, shunting a startled Jake aside. She sat down next to her, draped an arm around her shoulder and squeezed. "We're so sorry," she soothed. "I hope you don't mind, but I called your mother. She should be here any minute."

Jolie nodded. The thought of her mom made the backs of her eyes burn. She'd missed her so much, but being around her after Chris had stolen her money had made Jolie feel so terrible, so unworthy, and so at fault she hadn't been able to stand the guilt. Until the debt was paid, it had been easier to avoid her. She knew her mom saw through the ploy, knew that she worried more about the money than her mom did, but that hadn't lessened the sizable weight of responsibility she'd felt.

"Is there anything we can do to help?" Bitsy asked. She tutted sympathetically. "Do you need a place to stay?"

"I hate to be rude," Jake interjected, "but you can help by leaving. You're not supposed to be here, ladies. This is a crime scene."

"But we just got here," Bitsy protested, shooting Jake a wide-eyed look.

"Nevertheless, I'm gonna have to ask you to leave."

Bitsy looked distinctly disgruntled, but Meredith merely nodded understandingly. "Of course. We just wanted to comfort Jolie."

Jolie thanked them, sending Sophia a significantly grateful look. "I'll go to Mom's," she told Bitsy. "But I appreciate the offer."

Smelling like cold cream and fabric softener, Sophia gave her another squeeze. "We'll be in touch tomorrow then, dear, okay? Don't worry. We'll help you get through this."

To the casual observer those words seemed innocuous, but Jolie knew they held a double meaning, one she desperately appreciated. She managed a grateful nod.

Sophia stood, and Bitsy and Meredith fell in next to her. "Sorry to be in your way, detective," Sophia told Jake with a sweet smile. "We just wanted to be here for our friend." The three trooped out as coolly as they'd trooped in and even Jolie recognized that it looked odd.

Jake shot her an inscrutable look, one that led her to believe that he wasn't completely buying her story. "You play bridge?" he asked.

"I'm learning," she hedged, making a mental note to brush up on the particulars. She'd be in big trouble if he asked her any questions regarding the rules of play. She'd never been much of a card player, a fact he was perfectly aware of, she knew.

Jake continued to study her, then after a prolonged moment in which she'd suddenly developed a keen interest in the pattern on the sofa, he finally nodded. "You were learning to play bridge at—" He looked up, waiting for her to fill in the blank.

"Meredith Ingram's," Jolie said, quietly relieved that they were moving on.

"What time did you get there?"

"At six."

"And about what time did you leave?"

Jolie squinted, trying to remember. "Around eight, I think."

Jake chewed his bottom lip, giving another thoughtful nod. "Then you went to Sadie's, right?"

"That's right. I called her from my cell and she invited me over."

"What time did you leave her house?"

"Around ten-thirty. The news was going off."

"And you came straight home?"

She nodded, sliding her nerveless palms against her thighs in a vain attempt to warm them up. "I did."

Jake leaned back and passed a hand over his face. "Are you up to doing a formal statement tonight?"

Initially she'd planned on getting it over with, knowing the chances of her being able to sleep were slim to none. Every time she closed her eyes she saw Chris's lifeless body behind her lids. It was awful. But now that she'd begun to overcome the shock, she thought it would be best if she had a little time to think about things first. She needed a plan. Her involvement in and recent actions with the FWC were going to make things very…difficult. Now that was an understatement, Jolie thought, suppressing the hysterical urge to laugh.

She shook her head, struggling to pull it together. "If it's all right, I'd rather just go with Mom when she gets here. Could I come by in the morning?"

Jake inclined his head. "In the morning will be all right, but we really can't leave it any longer. We're gonna need to search the house and surrounding area."

"That's fine," she said, thankful that her Club handbook and the pre-burial plans were safely stowed in her purse.

Jolie stood and gestured tiredly toward her bedroom. "If we're done for now, I'll, uh… I'll go ahead and pack a bag."

"Make sure you get whatever you're going to need for the next couple of days," Jake told her. "You'll need to stay out of the house until we're finished up here, okay?"

That was fine with her. Other than a few personal mementos, she wasn't interested in taking anything out of this house. Wouldn't care if she never came back. It had never been a home—more like a prison.

Jolie nodded, then made her way down the hall to her bedroom. She packed enough clothes and toiletries to last for a couple of days as he'd suggested, then made the return trip to the living room.

Looking pale and worried, her mother stood talking with Jake when she walked in. Jolie's heart squeezed, and the tears she'd been holding back finally welled up. Everything she'd been holding back came to a head, and in that moment she might as well have been five again with a scraped knee. She didn't want to feel guilty or responsible, didn't want to be brave or in charge or anything else for that matter.

She just wanted her mother.

Fran Caplan's lined face folded into a sympathetic frown when she saw Jolie. She abandoned Jake, hurried forward and wrapped her in a tight hug. "Oh, honey," she said softly as Jolie quietly sobbed into her shoulder. "Don't worry. Everything's gonna be fine, okay? Let's get outta here," she murmured softly. "You don't need to be here, Jo. Let me take you home."

Home, Jolie thought, envisioning lavender gingham and a canopied bed, worn hardwood and high ceilings.

Finally.

CHAPTER FOURTEEN

FEELING EQUALLY USELESS and helpless, Jake watched Fran do the one thing he'd wanted to do since the moment he'd walked back into the living room and sat down with Jolie—comfort her.

Every broken cry, every slight shake of her slim shoulders chipped away at the professional demeanor he'd tried to keep in tact. He had to do things correctly here, had to make sure that every *I* was dotted, every *T* crossed.

With his and Jolie's past history he knew Dean would try to pull him off the case and appoint another detective, but Jake firmly intended to fight for it. One, he'd taken the call, so technically it was *his* case, and two—his gaze inexplicably slid to Jolie and he swallowed—she needed him.

Particularly since something was off with her alibi.

Jake didn't know exactly what yet, but knew she was hiding something. Hell, even the most unsea-

soned detective would have picked up on the way
she'd mangled *that* particular question. Even if she
hadn't cut her answer off mid-sentence, the frozen
look of alarm that had captured her pale features had
been enough to cause major concern.

Furthermore, he *knew* Jolie, was familiar with
every nuance of her face—every expression—and the
one he'd seen when he'd asked for her alibi was equivalent to "Oh, shit." Jake felt a smile catch the edge of
his mouth. She'd worn the same look when she'd accidentally dropped his first badge off the side of the
fire tower, one of their favorite old haunts. Or the time
she'd backed his truck into the barn. She'd been "helping" him haul hay, had insisted that she could do it.

Fran caught his gaze as she absently patted Jolie's
back and mouthed a thank you to him. For what, he
didn't know. She gestured toward the door. "We're
going to go now. You can get in touch with her at the
house if you need to, Jake."

Jolie turned around. Her face was wet with tears
and red with embarrassment. She hated to cry, always
begrudging the presumed weakness. She used her
sleeves to wipe away some of the damage, then pulled
in a bolstering breath. "I'll, uh… If there's nothing else
I should do tonight, then I'll see you in the morning."

Jake nodded. "We're good," he assured. "Go with
your mom."

Fran took Jolie's bag and, murmuring soothing noises, ushered her outside. Jake watched her go, feeling the weight of impending disaster settle on his shoulders. At some point in the near future the other shoe was going to drop. He knew it. Could feel it.

"She's not doing the official tonight?" Mike asked.

After starting guiltily, Jake turned around. He hadn't heard him walk in. "Er…no. She wasn't in any shape," he said, releasing a pent-up breath. "She went with Fran tonight and will come down in the morning." He cocked his head toward the back of the house. "How's it going in there?"

"Todd's processing. Leon's getting worse. He needs to go home, but can't until the bathroom's done."

"What about Dean?"

Mike shot a quick glance over his shoulder, then looked back at Jake. "Oblivious," he said with a long whoosh of resigned air. "We've got to tell him."

A rectal exam would be more fun, Jake thought, grimacing, but Mike was right. It had to be done. "You've got the pictures?"

Mike nodded. "They're in my car, locked in the glove box."

"Get 'em," Jake told him. "Might as well get it over with."

Mike's mouth settled into a grim line as he strode past him and Jake silently echoed the sentiment. This sucked, but there was nothing for it. Dean had to be told, and the sooner the better given the current circumstances. If Marshall had been destined to have his dick cut off, it was probably better that it had happened post-mortem. Had Dean found out about the affair before the bastard had gotten himself killed, Marshall wouldn't have been so lucky.

Manila envelope in hand, Mike walked back into the house. "Where do we want to do this?" he asked, glancing around the open living room. "He might not appreciate us whipping these out in front of Leon and Todd."

Jake considered the kitchen, but deemed it unsuitable for their purposes. He looked down the hall. "How about one of the other bedrooms? That'll give us a little privacy."

Mike bobbed his head in assent. "You wanna go get him, then?"

Want to? Hell no. But he would. "Yeah, I'll do it," he said resignedly.

Jake made his way back to the master suite. Dean and Leon—who did look worse, Jake noted—were standing outside the bathroom door, both of them watching Todd do his job.

"Twenty years on the job," Leon was saying, "and I've never come across anything like it. What sort of killer emasculates a man, Dean?"

The Sheriff merely shook his head. "A severely pissed off one, I'd say," he sighed.

Jake cleared his throat. "Sheriff, a word please."

Dean looked up, excused himself and followed Jake down the hall. "Mike and I need to talk to you."

"Yeah, I need to talk to you as well," Dean replied. "Look, Jake. You know I can't leave you on this case. You're too close. It's too personal."

Jake felt every muscle clamp with dread. He'd been expecting it, of course. Still, he'd hoped that Dean would let it be. "Er…that's one of the things I wanted to talk to you about." He continued through the living room down the hall that led to the other end of the house.

"Where's Mike?" Dean asked.

"Back here. We, uh…" He looked back over his shoulder. "We wanted a little privacy."

Dean nodded, seemingly baffled, but followed him all the same. They found Mike in one of the spare rooms, Jolie's, Jake knew instinctively. The faint scent of vanilla hung in the air and the room was littered with small reminders of her. A jewelry box—one he'd made for her in shop in their junior year, Jake noted, mildly surprised—and various perfumes, lotions and creams lined the dresser. A couple of books, a candy dish of Hershey's kisses, a tube of chapstick and a ponytail holder lay scattered on the bedside table.

A pair of black pumps had been kicked carelessly off next to the door and her bathrobe had been slung over the end of the four-poster bed. It was the only part of the house that remotely resembled *her,* that suggested that she lived here as well as Marshall. The rest of the house had a modern feel—sleek chrome and glass, lots of white, gray and black, trendy art-work—but not this room. It was warm, had heart. An old quilt covered the bed, mismatched plates had been grouped together on one wall and framed pic-tures of family and friends covered the top of the chest of drawers.

"What's this about?" Dean asked, settling his siz-able hands at his waist.

Jake pulled his thoughts together, then glanced at Mike who wore a distinctly uncomfortable expres-sion—one that plainly said, "You tell him."

Jake looked away, pulled in a deep breath to sum-mon his nerve, then let it go and faced Dean. There was no easy way to say what had to be said. "Mike and I found out about something…and we thought you should know."

Dean nodded, acknowledging him.

Now or never Jake thought. "Emily's been seeing Marshall."

Dean's eyes narrowed. "What do you mean 'see-ing him?'" he asked suspiciously.

Mike handed over the pictures. *"Seeing him,"* he repeated, evidently reluctant to elaborate.

Several emotions streaked across Dean's face as he flipped through the damning photos—shock, disbelief, outrage, then anger. His face reddened and he sucked in a harsh breath, then let it go. "Where did you get these?"

Jake stared at the jewelry box to avoid looking at Dean. It seemed disrespectful somehow to intrude on such a private sort of pain. "Jolie brought them in last week when she filed the assault report against Marshall."

His head jerked up. "Last week?"

"Yeah. She showed them to Mike."

A white line emerged around his thinned mouth. "If you've known about this for a week, then why the hell am I just hearing about it now?" Dean demanded. "For God's sake, Jake. Mike." He threw his hands up in futile frustration, swearing hotly.

Mike shifted guiltily. "She showed me the pictures last week—she was keeping them until she filed for divorce—but she didn't give them to me until a couple of days ago. We didn't want to tell you without the proof. It's…" Mike kicked awkwardly at a silver candy wrapper on the floor. "It's not the sort of thing you tell a man about his wife without proof, Sheriff."

Jake shoved a hand through his hair. "Look, Dean, I'm sorry. It's ugly business and I—" He shook his head. "I know we should have told you sooner, but given present circumstances—" Jake jerked his head meaningfully down the hall "—it's probably better that we didn't."

It took Dean less than three seconds to absorb that reality. Granted he'd just learned that his wife had been balling the deceased, but he was still a cop and they all knew that if he'd had prior knowledge of the affair, he'd have been a suspect. At least a temporary one. He swallowed. "Who else knows about this?"

"Besides us? Jolie, of course, and Sadie Webster—she's the one who took the pictures. But she's got a good head on her shoulders. She's discreet." Jake hesitated. "And whoever your wife or Marshall might have told," he reluctantly pointed out.

Dean nodded curtly, then indicated the photos still clutched in his hand. "When did Sadie take these?"

Jake told him and Dean seemed to be mulling it over. After a moment, Jake blew out a breath. "As far as this investigation's concerned, it never happened, Dean. It's dead and buried."

Dean shot him a considering look. He knew what Jake wanted in exchange and was obviously debating the merit of letting him have it. He finally sighed. "I appreciate it. It's your case," he said. "Keep me informed." He nodded at them, then, pictures still in hand, turned and strode out of the room. "Call me if anything comes up," he called without turning around. "I've got to go have a talk with my wife."

Mike glanced at him, released a deep pent-up breath and shook his head. "Cheatin' wives, missing dicks," he said tiredly. "This has been a busy night in Moon Valley."

Yep, Jake thought. And it was only getting started.

CHAPTER FIFTEEN

SOPHIA ADDED a shot of whiskey to her coffee and joined Meredith and Bitsy at her kitchen table. "Got there in the nick of time, didn't we?" she remarked, letting go a profoundly relieved sigh.

"I'll say," Bitsy confirmed with a significant eye roll.

"Don't kid yourselves," Meredith snorted. "If you think for one minute that he didn't notice that something was off, then you'd better think again." She dumped a teaspoon of sugar into her coffee. "I was watching him. He's smart."

Bitsy tsked, snagging a lemon cookie from the plate Sophia had automatically put on the table. "Oh, Meri, why do you have to be such a prophet of doom? What's he going to do?"

"Dig around," she direly predicted. "Mark my words. This isn't over. He knows her, knows her friends." A humorless laugh erupted from her throat.

"Sadie, her very best friend in the whole world doesn't come to her rescue, but three old ladies who barely know her drag themselves out of bed and hurry to her side?" she asked skeptically.

"Sadie doesn't have a scanner," Bitsy argued, blithely unconcerned.

Nevertheless Sophia agreed with Meredith. This was by no means over. Tonight they'd avoided immediate disaster, but steps were going to have to be taken in order to preserve the Club. So long as everyone kept their mouth shut—and she fully believed that Jolie was capable of that—then everything should be fine.

Despite the reassuring thought, she couldn't seem to shake the odd sensation that their world was about to suffer a significant shift. All of Moon Valley's for that matter. The last person to be murdered in their little town was Amos Bolen, but there hadn't been any mystery attached to his death. Sophia rolled her eyes. His ignorant, hot-headed brother had shot him over a tub of butter.

But this? This had all the makings of a real drama. Stolen money, adultery, a hated victim and the town darling. If word leaked out about the FWC they'd undoubtedly wind up in a made for TV movie, portrayed by fat, aging actresses with fake Southern accents, bouffant hair, mobile homes and muumuus. Sophia inwardly shuddered.

"So what now?" Meredith asked. "Should we call an emergency meeting? Maybe avoid having meetings until this is resolved?"

Seemingly horrorstruck, Bitsy appeared oblivious to the cookie crumbs tumbling out of her gaping mouth.

"No," Sophia said. "But we need to make sure everyone sticks to the story." She turned to Bitsy.

"I'll handle it," she said with a succinct nod. "As it happens, I *know* how to play bridge."

Staring unblinkingly into the distance, Meredith cocked her head. "I should probably pick up a few card tables."

"Good thinking," Sophia told her. "A few decks of cards would probably be good, too."

With everything seemingly settled—or as settled as it could be for the moment—Bitsy carelessly bit into another cookie, then slid them both a sly glance and asked the one question that they'd all been wondering. "So, who do you think did it?"

Sophia leaned back in her chair, grimacing. "I dunno. Jake's got his work cut out for him, that's for sure. The man had *a lot* of enemies. Any one of them could have done it."

Meredith arched a brow. "Sheriff Dean could have snapped."

Deciding that chewing would improve her ability to sleuth, Sophia gave into temptation and filched a cookie from the plate, then munched thoughtfully. Meredith definitely had a point. Marshall had been sleeping with Dean's wife. That would certainly incite some men to murder.

"Emily Dean's just who he's been seeing recently," Bitsy said. "We can't rule out a jilted lover. Or a jilted lover's husband."

"Then there's always the money trail," Meredith chimed in. "He's certainly screwed a lot of people over in that regard."

Bitsy grunted darkly. "If Jolie were my daughter, I'd want to see him dead, I know that. Especially after what happened last week."

Sophia felt her eyes widen. "Fran?" she gasped. She immediately shook her head, resisting the idea. "No, she wouldn't do that."

"I wouldn't be so sure, Sophia," Meredith remarked, surprisingly concurring with Bitsy. She lifted a brow. "Mother's aren't above killing to protect their young."

Sophia knew that. Still... If Fran had wanted Chris Marshall dead, the last thing she would have done was suggest that Jolie join the FWC. It would have been too risky. Her actions over the past week—the life insurance, the pre-burial pamphlets, the outfit—

were going to be under intense scrutiny as it was without factoring in her secret membership in the FWC. Right now the only thing she had going for her was her "bridge" alibi and the fact that she truly was innocent. She related her thoughts to Bitsy and Meredith.

Bitsy who was able to be both fat and happy—unlike her, Sophia thought enviously—scarfed down another cookie. "I think you're worrying for nothing. She didn't do it. The truth will speak for itself."

"Ultimately, yes," Sophia admitted. "But in the mean time she'd better brace herself for sheer hell."

Meredith shrugged lightly. "She's been living in sheer hell for two years. She's trading one for another now, but without the primary source of her misery." She smiled shrewdly. "Which one do you think she's going to prefer?" She grunted as though it were a forgone conclusion. "I know which one I would."

And there was that, Sophia thought. She felt a smile flirt with her lips. "Spoken like a true Future Widows' Club member, Meredith."

"Don't forget that Jolie's one, too," Bitsy added knowingly. "Once *that* reality sets in, she'll be fine."

CHAPTER SIXTEEN

JOLIE'S HEAD JERKED UP as a knock rattled the glass. She leapt up from Chris's desk, moved to the window and peeked through the blinds onto the sidewalk. A sigh of relief leaked out of her mouth—*Sadie*. She hurried around to the front of the office and opened the door, quickly ushering her friend inside.

"You're here early," Sadie said, breezing into the room. She brought the faint scent of hairspray and strawberry jam with her. "You're not going to believe the crazy rumor I heard this morning. Bitsy Highfield called before I even left the house and said—" Her gaze caught Jolie's and stopped short. Her tentative smile fell. "Is it true?" she breathed disbelievingly. "My God, it's true, isn't it? He's dead."

"He is," Jolie told her.

Sadie's eyes widened. "Oh, my God," she said again.

"I, uh… I found him last night after I left your

house." She shuddered, still feeling a chill land in her midsection every time she recalled seeing his face. "It was too late to call you and I didn't want to wake up the girls."

Sadie sagged against the reception desk, then shot her a shaky look. "What happened?"

"Other than the fact that someone walked into the house and shot him, I don't know."

Sadie sat there for a minute, seemingly absorbing the fact that they now inhabited a world where Chris Marshall no longer existed. She blew out a deep breath, then lifted her shoulders in a small unrepentant shrug. "Wish I could say I was sorry, but I'm not," she said bluntly. "I didn't like him when he was alive, and I'm not going to pretend to like him now just because he's dead." She scowled. "I hate it when people do that. He was a mean-spirited bastard who made you miserable. Dying doesn't make him a saint. Far as I'm concerned, it's the first act of kindness he's ever shown you."

Jolie knew that she should at least pretend to be outraged over her friend's hard-hearted reaction to Chris's death…but in all truth she couldn't because after the initial shock of last night, she'd begun to feel the same way. Sadie was right. Dying didn't make him a saint. She wasn't going to pretend to mourn him—she didn't own the necessary attachment, the emotion needed to pull it off. He'd made her wretched. She'd hated him. Those were the unhappy facts. Did that mean she was *glad* that he was dead? No…but it certainly made things easier.

Last night after she'd gone home with her mother, she'd had a good bone-wringing cry. She'd whimpered, wailed and sobbed, and not necessarily in that order. She'd cried for her mistakes, for the things she'd lost, the pointless time she'd spent away from her mother. She'd had years of despair built up and being able to simply let it go and finally be with her mom had been very…cathartic.

When the storm of emotion had passed—leaving behind a raging headache, a splotchy face and a mountain of soggy Kleenex—she'd felt unbelievably better, like she'd been baptized by her tears, cleansed of her guilt.

It had been the oddest thing. She'd been sitting there at the kitchen table—the Southern equivalent of a shrink's couch, Jolie thought wryly—watching her mom scoop coffee from a generic can into the pot. Her mother had never spared any expense when it came to buying good coffee. It had always been her little extravagance, the *one* thing she wouldn't compromise on. Jolie had inwardly winced, thinking that her mother wouldn't have to buy generic coffee once she got her money back.

The fleeting thought had triggered an epiphany

and her brain, which had been numbed by the horror of finding Chris and by the lengthy crying jag, had suddenly been enervated with what needed—*had*—to be done.

Immediately.

She knew that Chris's assets would most likely be frozen—they usually were when a person was murdered—so she'd needed to act before that happened, which had only given her a narrow window of opportunity. She'd explained things as best she could to her mom, then left her standing in the doorway, wearing a frayed robe and worried frown. Armed with a sense of purpose and a thermos of generic coffee, she'd hurried down to the office.

She'd been here all night, going through files and folders, systematically scouring his office until she'd found the numbers and pass codes for the off-shore accounts—he'd cut a small hole in the leather beneath his executive chair and had tucked them there for safe keeping, where he could figuratively *sit* on the money—and she'd just accomplished the final wire transfer into her own account when she'd heard Sadie at the front door.

The minute Marge, their secretary, came in this morning, Jolie planned to instruct her to fill all open orders, issue checks to their creditors and pay their employees their last check along with a hefty severance bonus. She'd see to the investors, making sure that their original investment as well as their *correct* returns were given to them. Between what Chris had stashed in his private accounts and what she'd managed to slip aside, she'd have enough to do that as well as still have a nice little nest egg for herself.

It was finally over, Jolie thought, letting go a relieved sigh.

She relayed her plans to Sadie. "By five o'clock this afternoon, we'll close the doors and Marshall Inc. will be no more. I've got to go down to the Sheriff's office, file the official report, bury him, and that'll be it." Her shoulders sagged with relief and the first tentative bloom of hope blossomed in her chest.

Rather than looking impressed with her speedy efficiency, Sadie's brow folded into a small frown. "Jo, I hate to burst your bubble…but I don't think that's going to be *it*. He was murdered. There'll be an investigation."

Jolie nodded. "I know that. Jake's in charge. He, uh… He was there last night." And she'd never been more thankful to see another soul. He'd been amazingly kind, given the circumstances, and though she hadn't been completely herself, he'd seemed a little nervous talking to her. In retrospect, it was oddly endearing.

"That'll definitely work to your advantage, but

you realize that you're going to be a suspect. At least, initially."

"I know," she said, undeterred. "But I didn't do it, so I'm not going to waste my time worrying about it." She let go a heavy but determined breath and crossed her arms over her chest. Not altogether true—she would worry to some extent—hell, she'd be a fool not to—but she fully intended to move on. "I've wasted all the time I intend to waste, Sadie. I'm washing my hands of it—all of it." She gestured around the office. "I'm moving out of that house and I'm putting in an offer on that little place over on Lelia Street I told you about. I want to move on. I *need* to. I want my life back." Not an unreasonable request given what she'd been through, Jolie thought.

A worried line wrinkled Sadie's brow and she weighed her words carefully. "Jo, nobody knows more than I do how difficult things have been for you, but…you might want to rethink this. Being hasty could give the wrong impression." She bit her bottom lip. "A *guilty* impression."

Jolie squashed a frustrated wail. She knew that, dammit, but frankly she didn't care. She was innocent. Being in an unhappy marriage didn't make her a murderer. More like a survivor. Chris Marshall had dictated practically every aspect of her life for the past two years and she'd be damned before she'd let him do it from the grave. His days of yanking her chain were over. She was taking her life back.

Effective immediately. And though she was vaguely concerned about being investigated for a crime she didn't commit, she didn't intend to lose one more moment of her life because of Chris Marshall.

"Jake knows I didn't do it," Jolie told her. "He's damn good at his job. He'll find out who did it and when he does I'll be exonerated."

"I'm sure that you will, but it would be better for you to make his job easier rather than more difficult. Dean will be looking over Jake's shoulder." She grunted. "Given the personal history between the two of you, Jake may not end up being the one in charge of the investigation. Dean may pull him and assign another detective."

Jolie paused as a note of alarm hit her belly. *That* scenario had never occurred to her. She completely trusted Jake to find the truth. Not only was he good at what he did, he *knew* her. Knew that she wasn't capable of doing what had been done to Chris. But another detective might not be so discerning and she'd definitely make a convenient suspect. Still, she hadn't murdered Chris and furthermore, she had an alibi.

She told Sadie as much. "I'm innocent. Regardless of whether I move out or close this company or anything else, nothing changes that fact." She shrugged, trying to cast off the weight of worry dragging at her determination. "They can investigate me until the cows come home for all I care. They're not going to find anything."

JAKE LEANED BACK in his uncomfortable desk chair, passed a weary hand over his face and futilely wished he hadn't taken this call. "Look, Andy, I wish I could help you, but I don't know when or even if you'll get the body. Once the autopsy is completed, Jolie will have to make those arrangements. I'm just the detective in charge. I'm not making the funeral arrangements."

"I realize that," Andy explained with exaggerated patience, "but after calling around all morning, you were the person I was directed to." He paused. "Has Randy already called you?" he asked with irritated suspicion. "Is that why I'm getting the run around?"

Dubbed "Double Death" by the citizens of Moon Valley, Andy and Randy Holbrook were identical twins who'd gone into the funeral profession. Together, to start with, but three years into a prosperous career, they'd had a falling out and had since started individual businesses.

Moon Valley could comfortably support one fu-

neral home, but the population simply wasn't sufficient to support two, and as such, every time somebody died Andy and Randy fought over the body and
the bereaved like a couple of mongrels over a soup
bone. Dean had been called in to intervene countless
times, and the issue had even been raised at several
town hall meetings. People ought to be able to bury
their loved ones in peace, they'd argued, not be ha-
rassed and hounded until they wished they were dead
as well.

Jake swallowed a beleaguered groan. "No, I
haven't heard from Randy," he told him, hoping to
end the call.

"Good, because if he tells you that she's planning
on using Eternal Rest as opposed to Heavenly Har-
vest then he's lying. She was in here just last week
checking out pre-burial plans." He chuckled grimly.
"Bet she wishes she'd gone ahead and purchased one
then," Andy remarked somewhat gleefully. "Now it's
really gonna cost her. Dying isn't cheap, Jake." He
sighed sagely. "Not cheap at all."

Jake stilled as every sense went on point. "She
was in there last week?"

"Yep, so this fish is dangling on *my* hook. Randy
has no claim."

"Do you remember what day she came in, Andy?"

"I do. It was Thursday. I know because I always

do a follow-up a week after initial contact. I tried to call her yesterday, but she wasn't available."

Less than a week before the murder, Jake thought with an increasing feeling of dread. That wasn't good.

"She took some pamphlets home, said she wanted to show them to her husband."

"These plans, were they for her and him?"

"Nope. Just him. But that's not really uncommon, I'm afraid. Lots of people have a hard time coming to terms with their mortality—to their detriment," he tutted woefully. "You should really think about having a little look-see yourself, Jake. It's never too early to make arrangements. Death is certain, you know."

"I'll think about it," Jake told him distractedly. He uttered an abrupt goodbye, then sat back in his chair and rubbed his gritty eyes with the palms of his hands. What the hell had she done? he wondered, absolutely flabbergasted. Why in the hell had she been scoping out a pre-burial plan for her husband less than a week before he was murdered? She hadn't killed him—he knew it.

Last night while Todd had worked his magic and Leon had dozed on the couch, he and Mike had tossed some scenarios around and Mike had skeptically suggested that she might have hired someone to do it. That didn't fit either. Murder just wasn't in Jolie's character. Furthermore, a hired hit man wouldn't have cut off Marshall's dick. That was a personal attack, one that suggested the killer had some connection with the victim. If not an intimate connection, then at least one significant enough for the person to truly despise him.

And this case was going to be hard enough to crack without Jolie's bizarre behavior factored in. Leon had finally been able to take the body this morning around four. Last night, Jake and Mike had walked the perimeter of the house, looking for forced entry, discarded cigarette butts, footprints, anything that might indicate the presence of another person at the house.

They'd found nothing.

With the exception of the scene of the crime, their search inside had been equally futile. Jake had taken one end of the house, Mike the other. A glutton for punishment, he supposed, Jake had searched her room first. He'd found a box of sentimental mementoes stored deep in the back of her closet—a pressed posey necklace he'd made for her in grade-school, several cartoon Valentine cards signed in his untidy juvenile scrawl, pictures of them at various dances, an empty bottle of strawberry wine, the very one they'd shared the first time they'd made love. Jake swallowed. God, it had been so long ago, and yet the memory was still so vivid it could have been yesterday.

Graduation night. While other kids were hosting or attending parties, most of them getting hammered, he and Jolie had strolled hand-in-hand off the football field and headed straight for his truck. They'd been waiting for years, planning this particular night for almost as long. He'd gotten an older cousin to buy the wine, had stopped at a gas station and fed the condom machine a handful of change until it had spit out ten of the damned things.

Jake grinned, remembering. What the hell, he thought, tapping a pen against his desk. He'd been optimistic.

Then they'd headed up to their secret spot at the lake. He'd built a fire, spread a blanket and they'd talked about the future for hours. They'd shared that bottle, laughed and cut up, had simply enjoyed the night…then on an old quilt under a blanket of bright stars and the promise of a bright future, they'd enjoyed each other.

To this day, nothing could compare to the absolute perfection of that time. He'd been head over heels in love, half drunk and nervous as hell, no longer a boy, but not quite a man. She'd been sweetly shy, but eager and trusting, and she'd made him feel like the most important guy in the world.

Jake released a slow breath. What he'd give to go back and have a talk with that boy, to tell him the things he knew now so that kid could avoid making the mistakes he'd made. But he couldn't, and no amount of wishing would make it so.

At any rate, aside from the bathroom, they hadn't found anything incriminating anywhere in the house. The best Jake could figure, the killer had walked through the front door, followed the sound of the shower to the bathroom, then shot Marshall at point blank range. The assailant had turned off the water—Todd had found smudges consistent with gloved hands—had cut off his dick, with what, no one knew yet. Nothing in the house, they were relatively sure. A hand towel was missing from the rack behind the commode. Todd figured—and he hoped Jolie could confirm—that one had definitely been there, that the killer had used it to transport their odd trophy. Afterward, the culprit had turned the water back on, presumably to alert Jolie when she came home.

Jake hadn't found any evidence to support it yet, but he firmly believed that whoever had killed Marshall had been waiting for Jolie to leave. Waiting *where* was anyone's guess. Probably the street. Not in the yard, he didn't think. He'd looked last night for clues, but planned on going back over this morning as soon as he finished taking Jolie's official report.

He wanted to scour the house and surrounding area again today. Who knew? Maybe a few winks and the benefit of daylight would give him a fresh perspective.

Talking with Andy the funeral director this morning certainly had, Jake thought grimly. Those were not the sort of discoveries he was interested in, that was for damned sure.

Dean knocked a couple of times on the door frame, then walked into Jake's office. Lines of fatigue fanned out around his eyes and he had the pinched look that marked a night of too little or no sleep. "How's it coming?" he asked.

Jake relayed the pertinent facts, then told him about his conversation with Andy. He pulled a tired shrug. "My gut tells me it's a dead end, but it's still—"

"Odd," Dean finished. He arched a brow. "She's coming in this morning to file the official?"

Jake nodded.

"Are you keeping it under your hat, or are you going to ask her about it?"

"I'm gonna ask her about it," Jake told him. "I want to get a read on her." He rubbed his eyes. "Like I told you last night, she hated him—no question there—but Jolie's not a murderer. She's just not wired that way."

Dean hesitated. "You can't rule her out, Jake. You're gonna have to stick to her like glue. Given your history, can do you that? Better still, can you do it objectively?"

Jake nodded and felt his gut clench at the impending lie. Be objective where Jolie was concerned? Ha. "If I couldn't, I wouldn't have asked to stay on as lead."

"Keep me updated," he said. "And let me know when you find his dick," he added darkly. "I'd like to hold a separate sort of ceremony for it, if you get my drift."

Jake suddenly imagined Marshall's dick glued to the center of a bull's eye, a calmly furious Dean using it for target practice.

He cleared his throat. "Er…how did everything—"

"She's packing as we speak," Dean told him flatly. His lips twisted with bitter humor. "This wasn't the first time, Jake. It was just the last damned straw."

Surprised, Jake swallowed, then said the only thing he could think of. "Shit, Dean. I'm sorry."

"Ah, it's my own damned fault," he said wearily, leaning against the door frame. "I should have washed my hands of her the first time. She blamed the job, made me feel guilty. Said I wasn't paying enough attention to her." He pulled an offhand shrug. "I thought I owed it to the marriage to give it another go. So I did. At least this way I know I did everything I could to make it work." He shook his head. "Wasn't enough, but it wasn't my fault. She'll be the one to carry the weight of that mistake, and better her than me, eh?" He managed a half-hearted smile, then turned to go. "I'll expect daily reports and updates on all new developments."

Jake nodded. "You got it." He glanced at his watch, noting the time. He'd give Jolie another ten minutes and if she wasn't here, he'd run her to ground. If she'd checked into pre-burial plans, just what the hell else was she hiding? he wondered. What else had she checked into? Jake tensed as the obvious answer to that question dawned in his puzzled mind. He swore, pulled the phonebook from the desk drawer, flipped to the yellow pages—to the I section, specifically—until he found the listings he was interested in.

Insurance.

If she'd taken out any new policies on Marshall recently, things would take a nasty turn from bad to worse. Dread ballooned in his gut, anticipating what he feared he'd find.

Four calls later he found it. One-hundred-thousand. Added last Tuesday.

A stream of profanity spewed from his lips. He blew out a heavy breath, sagged back in his chair and felt the beginnings of one helluva headache claw through his skull. For someone he knew beyond a shadow of a doubt was innocent, she was certainly doing a damned bang-up job of looking guilty.

CHAPTER SEVENTEEN

SOPHIA POPPED a bite of maple link sausage into her mouth, shuffled over to her kitchen table and set the warmed blueberry syrup and stack of fresh, fluffy pancakes on the table. They joined a host of other breakfast favorites. Biscuits and gravy, grits, scrambled eggs, hot tea and orange juice. Stress tended to make her hungry and when that happened, she couldn't just settle for a mere muffin or a piece of toast—she had to eat buffet style.

This was particularly unfortunate as she was supposed to be dieting.

Sophia had battled her weight for years, diligently fighting every eager fat-storing cell in her body. The struggle would have been a whole lot easier if she didn't enjoy food—the sight, scent and taste of virtually any sweet, cake, pie, main dish or gooey casserole. Honestly, other than hominy—which she detested—she didn't cull much.

Furthermore, practically every occasion was celebrated with food. Holidays, birthdays, bad days and good days, deaths, etc.... Food played a prominent role in society and it was truly a pity—the height of injustice, dammit—that some metabolisms worked better than others.

Hers, for instance, seemed to be permanently stuck in neutral.

Sophia had always promised herself that when she turned fifty, she'd say to hell with it and eat whatever she wanted. She'd keep up her exercise—a good brisk walk was good for anybody—but once she hit the big five-oh, she'd trade her fat-free margarine for good old-fashioned butter, her low-fat frozen yogurt for rich, creamy pralines and cream ice cream. She'd take a sledge hammer to her scale, shatter it to bits before sweeping it into a dust-pan and gleefully throwing it away.

Two weeks beyond her fiftieth birthday however—a blissful two weeks in which she'd eaten everything that hadn't been nailed down and she'd gained seven pounds—she'd had a terrible nightmare. She'd dreamed that she'd had a heart attack and needed to go to the hospital, but she couldn't get out of the bed because she was too damned fat. The rescue squad had ended up taking a Sawzall to her bedroom wall and cutting a giant hole in the side of her house in order to accommodate her whopping girth. It had taken a wench and a back-hoe to get her out of the house, and they'd hauled her bloated, flabby hideous body away on a flat-bed truck, a melting king-sized candy bar clutched in her fist.

The next morning, Sophia had gloomily resumed her battle against the bulge.

She occasionally fell off the wagon—like now—but after last night, she felt like she deserved a little comfort food. She'd walk another lap around the block, two if need be.

Sophia started as a knock sounded at her back door. She rarely had visitors this early, she thought, wincing as she walked away from her warm breakfast. She opened the door, then horrorstruck, barely resisted the urge to slam it shut in her unexpected visitor's face.

"Good morning, Sophia," Edward said dutifully.

Sophia patted her uncombed hair, painfully aware of her unmade face and tattered chenille robe. She felt her mouth work up and down, struggling to dredge a syllable up her tight, mortified throat. "Good m-morning, Edward. What can I do for you?"

"I just noticed that you weren't outside this morning. You're not feeling under the weather, I hope."

Sophia's first thought was to blast him with an icy remark about unexpected house calls, but the kind concern in those compelling blue eyes, plus the warm knowledge that he'd actually missed her, prevented the impulse.

She tightened her robe around her middle—the one not poured into a bulge-smoothing girdle—and resisted the urge to whimper. "No, I'm not, but thank you," she said, somewhat stiffly. After all, she wasn't accustomed to being nice to him. It had always been easier—safer—to be surly.

He sniffed appreciatively and his keen gaze darted over her shoulder to the spread on her kitchen table. A grin slid across his surprisingly attractive mouth. "That certainly smells good," he commented lightly. "Are those blueberry pancakes?"

Sophia felt a smile flirt with her lips. "They are," she conceded.

His eyes narrowed, seemingly zooming in on the syrup. "And is that your homemade syrup?"

This time it was her eyes that narrowed. How did he know that she made homemade syrups? "It is," she replied slowly.

"Oh," he sighed, rocking back on his heels. "That's some count there, Sophia," he said with just enough sincerity and awe to make her want to preen despite the fact she looked like a bag lady. "I bid on a bottle at the Civic Club's silent auction last fall and won. Best stuff I ever put in my mouth."

He was clearly angling for an invitation, and even more clearly hoping to garner one through flattery. One that, despite her unkempt hair and ratty robe, he was going to get. Still, she had her pride, so she pretended to look put-out. "As you can see I have plenty," she said grudgingly. "Would you like to join me?"

He grinned. "I was hoping you'd ask."

Betting on it, more like, she thought with a silent snort, but she wasn't going to quibble because a ridiculous thrill had whipped through her, momentarily gluing her tongue to the roof of her mouth. For the first time in fifteen years a man—one that captivated every sense and made her feel like her skin was stretched too tight over her old bones—was going to put his feet under her table.

It was a start, Sophia thought, her insides quivering with anticipation. A beginning, she cautiously hoped, to an ultimate end.

CHAPTER EIGHTEEN

JOLIE GLANCED at her watch and swore as she hurried down the hall toward Jake's office. She'd promised him that she'd be here first thing this morning, but she hadn't counted on having to awkwardly console a crying Marge when she'd learned of Chris's death. Chris had always treated Marge abominably, had criticized, shouted, and cursed her for the smallest of infractions, so she was the last person Jolie had expected to shed any tears over her late, unlamented husband. Jolie had heard herself muttering things like, "Oh, yes, it's terrible," and "Yes, it's such a loss," but the words felt weird and distasteful coming out of her mouth.

Probably because they were lies.

Playing the grieving widow was *not* a role that would come easily to her, which was just as well, because despite Sadie's dire warnings, she'd decided against it, and once she made up her mind, it was set. She'd been living a lie for two years. She was finished, a fact she planned to share with Jake this morning.

While she couldn't tell him about the FWC, she nevertheless intended to make her position perfectly clear. She hadn't killed Chris, but she wasn't exactly *sad* that he was dead. Relieved, quite honestly, was more accurate. He could deal with those facts however he chose and if he decided to judge her for them, then so be it.

She drew in a bolstering breath as she neared his office and felt her stomach do an odd little flutter, a physical reaction to the knowledge that she was about to see him. Under normal circumstances her reaction would undoubtedly be considered inappropriate—particularly since her husband's body was barely cold, Jolie thought with a wry smile—but these were hardly normal circumstances.

Jake had been the love of her life—the one she'd let pride keep her from reclaiming—and Chris had been the bane of her existence for the past twenty-four months.

There was no comparison.

Jake's door was open and, given the one-sided conversation she heard as she neared his office, she guessed that he was on the phone, a hunch that was confirmed when she peered into the room. He glanced up and motioned for her to come in and take the only other chair in the room.

His office was small with a functional metal desk, a single beat-up filing cabinet crammed in the corner and covered with magnets, business cards and the odd sticky note. A couple of photographs had been adhered to the wall behind his desk with thumbtacks. The sight drew a smile. True to form, framing them had been too much trouble.

One was a family Christmas photo, his Mom, Dad, brother and sister. The other was a candid of Jake that she'd taken during her photography phase and admittedly, *he'd* been her favorite subject.

This photo was one that she'd been particularly proud of because it had captured him in such a true moment. He'd been standing close to Smoke, nuzzling the gray dappled horse's muzzle, and the respect and the love for the animal had been evident in every line of his face. The crinkles around those silvery eyes, the soft turn of his mouth. He'd been relaxed and unguarded…and sexy as hell.

Though genuine cowboys were scarce in Mississippi, Jake had always had that special spark, that easy grace and careless swagger brought about by hours spent in the saddle. While other men went to the gym or Roxy's Roadhouse after work, Jake had always spent his de-stressing time on the back of a horse, or at the very least, in the barn taking care of one. He had a keen understanding of the animals, a way with them that was frankly fascinating to watch.

His skills were somewhat legendary in their little part of the world and it hadn't been uncommon— even in his teenage years—for other owners to ask his opinion or seek his advice about a difficult animal.

Within months of her marriage to Chris, his grandfather had deeded twenty acres to him on the south end of the family property, a rolling landscape with hundred-year-old oaks dripping with Spanish moss, hearty maples and a clear swift-moving stream. In the spring hundreds of buttercups, wild poppies and Queen Anne's lace bloomed across the meadows, painting the hills and valleys with splashes of bright color.

He'd built the barn before the house, making sure that the animals would be taken care of first. Priorities, right? Jolie thought with a small grin. The house was a replica of his grandfather's old two-story farmhouse—the very one they'd always talked about having—but, according to Sadie and Rob who'd had the privilege of visiting, it had been updated with all the modern conveniences.

She'd occasionally torture herself by driving by, picturing him there before a crackling fire, book in hand. But as time had worn on, she'd stopped. Only a glutton for punishment would keep it up, and Chris had been punishment enough, thank you very much. Besides, it had just been too damned hard. It should have been her with him before that fire, her there sharing his bed. She'd never understand, never get over how terribly wrong things had gone.

Jolie took her seat, watched Jake scribble on a yellow legal pad, presumably taking notes.

"One-hundred-thousand, you say?" he said, shooting her a veiled look, one that had the dubious honor of simultaneously making her mouth dry and her stomach roll in a sickening pirouette.

Shit, she thought with ballooning dread. He knew already. Moon Valley was too small to accommodate discretion, so she hadn't harbored any illusions that Jake wouldn't find out about the life insurance and other things, but she damned sure hadn't counted on him ferreting out the truth so quickly.

"And she's the sole beneficiary, is that correct?" He hummed under his breath, tapped his pen against his notepad while she resisted the urge to squirm in her seat. "And this policy was taken out when?" Jake nodded, scribbled another note, then circled it. "All right, then. That's all I needed to know." He thanked whomever had been so bloody helpful then disconnected and shot her a considering look. "Have you slept?"

Code-speak for "You look like crap," Jolie thought, unreasonably perturbed. Evidently her concealer hadn't done the job.

"A little," she told him. "Have you?"

"I caught a cat nap this morning. I expected you earlier," he commented lightly. "Any particular reason why you're so late?"

"I ran by the office. I needed to let Marge know about Chris," she improvised, since it wasn't completely a lie. She could hardly tell him the truth. *I've been emptying Chris's accounts before you freeze them.*

He nodded, seemed to accept that excuse. After a moment, he blew out a prolonged breath, abruptly stood and shut the door. He leaned against it, crossed his arms over his chest and merely waited. For her to offer an excuse, she was sure, but she had no intention of obliging him. If he wanted answers, he'd have to ask the questions, otherwise he was outta luck. She certainly wasn't going to volunteer any more than she had to, at least not in the beginning. The more time she had to move the money, the better. With luck, she'd get everything done this afternoon. That was the plan, at any rate.

She felt the weight of that cool, calm regard for at least another sixty seconds before Jake finally muttered a hot oath and sat back down. He pulled a small black tape recorder from the desk drawer, spoke her name and date into the device, then turned it off and set it down between them.

He looked up and his gaze tangled with hers. "Before I turn this on, I need to ask you a question."

She knew he did—knew what he'd ask—and though a part of her resented it because he of all people should know better, undoubtedly the life insurance and her bizarre alibi had shaken his opinion. She couldn't blame him, but that didn't lessen the sting.

She returned that level stare, determinedly ignoring the flash of heat that hit her belly, and lifted her chin. "Sure. Go ahead."

"Did you have *anything* to do with this, Jo? Anything at all?" His voice was a mixture of exasperation and agony, indicating that he hated having to doubt her, which seemed only fitting because she hated it, too.

"No, Jake. I didn't. I hated Chris, which is common knowledge among my family and friends, but hating him and killing him are two completely different things. I could never have killed him."

A sigh of relief slipped past his lips. He sagged back into his seat, closed his eyes and rubbed the bridge of his nose. "Then please tell me why you were researching pre-burial plans last week?" he asked with weary irritation.

Jolie blinked. She'd been prepared to answer the insurance question, but she'd had no idea that he'd already heard about the pre-burial plan. How the hell—

"Andy called me this morning wanting to know when he could have the body," he explained, most likely as a result of her uncomfortable silence. His lips tilted. "He was afraid Randy would beat him to the punch and explained why he thought he had dibs. He mentioned the pre-burial plan—the one you investigated less than a week before your husband's murder," he added significantly. He leaned forward and shook his dark head. "I'm going to be honest, Jo. If it wasn't for your alibi—at least twenty of your bridge club members called this morning to verify your whereabouts last night, by the way—you'd be in deep shit. For someone who's innocent, you're doing a helluva job making yourself look guilty. Dammit, what gives? What have you been up to?"

Jolie cast around her semi-frozen brain and tried to think of any reason—aside from the truth, of course, which she couldn't share—why she'd been scoping out funeral arrangements last week for her perfectly healthy husband.

She forced an uncomfortable laugh. "There's nothing w-wrong with b-being prepared is there?" she asked, her voice a little too bright to be believable.

"Being prepared? No," he said. "It's the timing of your preparations that raises concern."

He did the waiting thing again, pinning her with that gray gaze until the silence practically screamed between them. Feeling like a kid who'd been called into the principal's office, Jolie barely resisted the urge to squirm, and to make matters worse, she could tell by the set of his jaw that Jake was disappointed that she wasn't going to confide in him. She hated that look, barely refrained from spilling her guts just to make it go away.

"Fine," he finally relented. "Don't tell me. I'm just trying to help you here." He blew out a breath. "What about the life insurance? Why did you add another hundred grand when you had enough to cover the business and your mortgage?"

"You can never have too much insurance," Jolie told him, quoting the agent who'd sold her the policy. "Furthermore, Chris owed debts that weren't on paper," she added darkly. Ones she firmly intended to take care of the minute she left here. Odd, though, she thought. When she'd been pouring through the accounts and tallying expenses early this morning, she hadn't factored in *any* of the life insurance. That would end up being a tidy little sum to add to her nest egg.

Jake quirked a dark brow. "By that are you referring to the life insurance money he swindled away from your mother?"

Surprised that he knew, Jolie glanced up. "Er…yeah, I am." She frowned uncertainly. "How did you—"

"Sadie," Jake interrupted, filling in the blank. "Don't be pissed. She only confirmed what I'd heard around town. After you came in and filed the report, I, uh… I went down and had a talk with her. She told me about the insurance money."

And everything else, most likely, Jolie thought, but curiously couldn't drum up any outrage that Sadie had confided in Jake, particularly after Chris had hit her. She'd never thanked him for that, Jolie thought suddenly. She bumbled her way through it. "I, uh— I appreciated what you did. With the door and all," she clarified.

A half-hearted smile caught the corner of his mouth and she felt that meager, woefully familiar grin in places that hadn't known a touch of emotion in years. "Wasn't as satisfying as using my fist," he said with a small lift of a muscled shoulder, "but I improvised." He paused, searching the side of her face for any lingering damage. "Bastard," he muttered.

"Yes, he was," she readily agreed. "Which is why I hope that you'll understand and not pass judgment when I move on. He made me miserable. Wretched. Am I sorry that someone murdered him? Yes. Am I sorry that he's out of my life? No. I know it seems harsh, but—" She drew up short, tried to find the words to frame the way she felt. She shrugged helplessly. "It's just the way it is."

Jake nodded. "Moving on is fine, Jolie. From what Sadie told me, you definitely need to." He hesitated. "That said, please keep in mind that everything you do, especially over the coming weeks, will be under intense scrutiny and—" he raised one eyebrow meaningfully "—it'll make my job a whole lot easier if you aren't doing things that make you look guilty."

"Like dancing on his grave?" she suggested innocently.

Surprise jimmied a chuckle loose in his throat and he shot her a startled look. "Yes. Dancing on his grave wouldn't be a good thing."

She made an exaggerated moue of disappointment. "There went that plan."

He passed a hand over his face, trying to wipe away his smile. "If there's anything you need to tell me, now would be a good time. I don't want anymore surprises."

Jolie felt a blanket of guilt settle over her shoulders as she shook her head. She hated lying to him, but she couldn't out the FWC. Too many members were still shackled to bastard husbands and the FWC was the only thing making their lives bearable. God knows the past two weeks she'd spent as a member had made her feel tremendously better. She couldn't tell him.

"Sadie seemed to think that Dean might pull you from this case," Jolie said, opting to change the subject. "Is that going to happen?"

To her vast relief, Jake shook his head. "No. He wanted to, but was, er, persuaded to let me remain as lead. I was given strict instructions to keep Dean up to date…and stick to you like glue," he added.

Jolie repressed a shudder as another inappropriate thought flitted through her head. Though she knew he'd meant to scare her—or warn her, most likely—her thoughts had instantly turned in another direction. She knew what it was like to have Jake stick to her like glue. In the past he'd been very adept at making her fall apart…then putting her back together. A bittersweet pang squeezed her chest. It was just one of the many things she missed about him.

She blinked, trying to pull her thoughts back together. When she looked up, Jake was watching her closely, an odd expression on his face. "Er…does Dean know about Emily?" Jolie asked, once again fishing for a subject change.

He leaned back once more. "He does. Mike and I told him last night."

"How did he take it?"

"She's moving out. They're finished."

Damn Chris's hide, Jolie thought, angry and disgusted. "I'm sorry," she said, wishing there was something she could do to make things right.

"For what?" Jake asked. "Wasn't your fault."

"Maybe not directly, but I'm the one who brought him here." She looked away, then picked at a loose thread. "You have no idea how much I regret it."

"It's still not your fault, Jolie," Jake insisted. "Emily's a big girl. She knew what she was doing and, according to Dean, this wasn't the first time. Don't beat yourself up about it."

"The sonofabitch never could keep it in his pants," she muttered, unable to let it go. Dean was a good man. He deserved better. And she didn't care what Jake said, while she might not be completely to blame, she was indirectly at fault. She'd brought him here and infected her town with his cancerous—

A bark of laughter erupted from Jake's throat. "And still can't. We still haven't found it."

Confused, Jolie glanced up. "Found what?"

Jake's eyes widened in belated regret, then he shifted and swore hotly. "Christ," he muttered. "I'm such an idiot."

"Found what?" she repeated. She had a sickening suspicion, but surely he didn't mean what she thought he meant.

"His penis," Jake finally told her. "His killer castrated him."

Jolie gaped, equally horrified and revolted.

"You, uh, must not have noticed."

She snorted. "No, I didn't. I lost interest in Chris's penis a long time ago. Other than documenting who he'd been sticking it to for my divorce file, that is." Jolie shook her head, unable to make it process and though she knew it was horrible, she had the almost overwhelming urge to laugh. There was something very satisfying about poetic justice.

"Do you have any idea who might have done this?" Jake asked her.

She snorted. "Anyone in particular? No. But I'll give you everything I've got in my file. I've been keeping up with everything—the shady business dealings and adultery—for the divorce. Dean's wife wasn't the only woman he was screwing around with. He wasn't particular, I can tell you that. Nor was he very smart." Jolie chewed the corner of her mouth and looked up. "I know he's your boss, but are you sure Dean didn't know about Emily before last night? I know Chris had been going to their house."

Jake shook his head. "He didn't. I'm sure of it."

Since it was that same assurance that told him she was innocent, Jolie didn't argue. Most likely Jake was right. Still, Chris's hijacked dick shed a whole new light on things. That was personal. Someone *really* hated him. Come to think of it, Jolie decided, lots of people really hated him and each one of them with good reason. Jake wouldn't find himself short on suspects, that was for sure. For her part, however, she just wanted it over with. And to that end, she needed to be able to bury him, her last official act as his wife.

"Er…any idea when I'll be able to arrange the funeral?" she asked him.

"The M.E. should be finished with the body in another day or so. Just get in touch with Andy and he'll handle that end of it."

Jolie nodded, relief melting her spine. A couple more days, and then that would be it. Her life would be her own again. Or at least as much her own as she could make it while she was a murder suspect, at any rate.

"Did Chris have any family?" Jake asked curiously.

"No," she deadpanned. "He sprung fully grown from the loins of Satan."

Jake's lips twitched and he shot her a look. "That's cold, Jo."

She smiled, then let go a small sigh. "I honestly don't know. He told me a tragic story about his parents being in a car accident. At the time I bought it, but now…" She shook her head. "He told so many lies. If he's got any family, they've never contacted him or vice versa."

Jake seemed to be mulling that over. Finally, he gestured toward the tape recorder. "We should probably get started."

"Okay."

"Mind if I come by later and pick up that file you told me about?"

"Not at all," she replied. "It's in the apartment above Sadie's shop. Keeping it at the office or in the house was too risky."

"Makes sense. Had you contacted an attorney about the divorce?"

"I had. Lanny James."

Jake whistled low and his gaze seemed to sharpen. "Pulling out a big gun, eh?"

Jolie smiled, shrugged. "I was in for a fight. I knew Lanny had a better shot than most to handle him." Lanny had been looking forward to it, too, Jolie thought. He was an old dog who didn't bark, just bit, which made him one helluva divorce attorney. He'd given her invaluable advice; he was the one who'd encouraged her to start the file. He didn't go into a courtroom without the ammunition to annihilate an opponent. Chris's death had robbed her of that satisfaction, but at least this way she was spared the mess and expense.

"I'll have to talk to him," Jake said, shooting her a level look.

Her lips slid into an unconcerned smile. "Talk to whomever you have to, Jake. I'm innocent. Nothing you're gonna find will change that."

That silver gaze caught and held hers, momentarily sucking the air from her lungs. "Am I gonna find anything else that will *challenge* it?"

Depended on where he looked, Jolie thought, chewing the inside of her cheek. "Let's hope not," she replied, forcing a smile.

His gaze narrowed, instantly seeing through her flimsy, evasive answer and he muttered an exasperated curse. "Can't you see that I'm on your side? That I'm trying to help you? Why are you making this harder than it has to be?"

"You're the detective, Jake. Figure it out."

He managed a weak grin. "Very cute, Jo. I'm just not sure you understand the gravity of the situation. If any other guy had this case, alibi or no, you'd make a *very* convenient suspect."

She crossed her legs and leaned back in her seat, doing her best to ignore the frightened shiver that tripped down her spine. "I do understand that, but being a convenient suspect doesn't make me guilty. The truth will speak for itself." She had to believe that.

He lifted a sardonic brow. "And I'm sure all the innocent people on death row had the same opinion."

He was trying to scare her, and to her discomfort, it was working. Still, she couldn't tell him about the FWC. She couldn't betray her fellow Future Widows. Furthermore, telling him about them wasn't going to help him, because it wouldn't do one damn thing for his investigation. Jolie lifted her chin, but refused to respond.

Looking extremely put out, Jake heaved a long-suffering sigh. "Fine. We'll do it the hard way. What time do you want to meet me at the apartment?"

"When ever works best for you," she said sweetly, willing to be partly accommodating.

He grunted. "Six, then."

"I'll see you there."

Jake blew out another breath, rubbed his eyes, then to her vast relief finally flipped on the recorder. "Okay," he said. "Let's start at the beginning…"

CHAPTER NINETEEN

ARMS CROSSED over his chest, Jake stood in Sadie's shop and peered out her storefront window across the square, watching Jolie tape a sign to the inside window of Marshall Inc., presumably one announcing Marshall's death. She wore a pair of khaki slacks and a form-fitting ribbed shirt that hugged her curves, the very ones he's spent too much time thinking about this morning while she'd been in his office, Jake thought, doing his damnedest to ignore the commingled flash of heat and affection that warmed both his heart and his groin.

She'd pulled that thick, striking hair back into a sleek ponytail and secured it with a stylish patterned scarf. Gold hoops dangled in her ears and despite the fact that she'd had very little sleep, she looked curiously refreshed. Her lips were curled in the faintest hint of a smile and the tension she'd seemed to have carried around for the past couple of years had lessoned, making her, if possible, even more beautiful than she'd already been.

Last night when Mike had called him, Jake had realized then what he was in for. He'd known that he'd have to talk to Jolie, be around her, particularly if the investigation played out the way he'd assumed. And for the most part, it had. He'd been simultaneously filled with anticipation and dread, with longing and regret. He'd braced himself, had literally felt every muscle clench in preparation, for what simply being in her presence would do to him.

He couldn't be around her without going into sensory and emotional overload. Her smooth vanilla scent, that silky laugh, the sweet curve of her familiar face. Between those things and the ever-present hum of awareness—the sheer need to simply feel her body against his, the brush of her hair beneath his chin—he'd been in a state of weary but pleasant agony for the better part of twenty-four hours.

This morning when she'd walked into this office, every cell in his body had reacted to her presence. He'd felt her in his blood, in his very bones. At first he'd avoided looking at her because he'd known the instant his eyes met hers, he'd lose his breath. An odd, not altogether pleasant feeling, that was for damned sure, Jake thought with a silent chuckle. Even knowing about the life insurance and pre-burial plan, even knowing that she'd gotten herself into a helluva mess and that she planned to hold out on him, hadn't lessened the impact.

Nevertheless, focusing on the job ahead and keeping her delectable little ass out of jail had to take top priority.

He'd spent the majority of the day at the house, going over the scene once more. He'd combed the house from end to end and had spent a lot of time walking the yard, making sure that he hadn't missed anything the night before. He was convinced that whoever had entered the house had done so by way of the front door. It would have taken too much time to heave the garage doors up and out of the way to go in via the carport, and the back gate had been padlocked.

Which meant the killer had to have entered from the front and, given that, one could reasonably assume that *someone* had seen *something,* whether they knew it or not.

To that end, Jake had spent a couple of hours canvassing the neighborhood. Unfortunately, while none of Marshall's neighbors were particularly concerned that he was dead—and more than one had seemed almost ghoulishly delighted—not a single one of them had noticed anything out of the ordinary.

From her vantage point in the kitchen, Mrs. Dotson across the street had noticed Jolie leave, but had said that one of her children had decided to give their pet hamster swimming lessons in the commode and she'd been forced to abandon the dinner dishes. It was after dark when she'd returned to the sink and by then she said she'd been so tired that she wouldn't have noticed Freddy Krueger lurking in the bushes.

Whoever had waltzed into that house hadn't looked out of place, had looked as if they belonged there, or at the very least had a legitimate excuse for being there. Taking that into consideration had left him with the unhappy task of checking out Jolie's close friends and family, namely Sadie and Fran. Did he think either one of them did it? Gut instinct told him no. But the sooner he ruled them out, the sooner he could move on with the investigation. Jolie was the epicenter—he had to work the circle closest to her, then fan out.

He'd purposely arrived at The Spa a little early to get a read on Sadie. Sadie loved Jolie, he knew. They'd been play-pen playmates—their parents had been friends—and had ended up having a sisterly bond as a result of that long-time acquaintance.

Sadie had been very emotional when she'd talked to him following the night Chris had hit her friend. She'd complained of Jolie's stubborn streak with ex-asperated affection—one he completely understood—and had called Chris a "mean-spirited snake." Jake had to agree with that assessment as well. It seemed wrong somehow to be questioning her for holding the same opinions he himself held, but her role as Jolie's most trusted friend entitled her to more knowledge of the situation than any other person, which gave her more of a motive to hate him than the rest of them.

Nose burning from the scent of hair color and perm solution, Jake waited for her last client to leave before posing the question he'd been waiting to ask. "What's she hiding, Sadie?"

Sadie, who'd been dropping coins into the cash register, stilled. "W-what do you mean?"

Pathetic stall tactic, but he'd caught her off guard and her reaction just confirmed what he knew—Jolie might not have killed Chris, but she'd definitely been doing something they didn't want him to find out about. Given the nature of his most recent discoveries, it was probably something incriminating.

He mentally swore.

"I know about the pre-burial plan and the life insurance she took out last week," Jake told her, a fact Jolie had probably already shared with her, but he felt compelled to impart as well. "But there's more." He braced a hand against the desk. "I know she's innocent, Sadie, and I want to help her, but I don't want anything coming up and biting me on the ass on this. I need to know *everything*."

She refused to look up. "I wish I could help you, Jake, but I can't. You know she didn't do it. That's all you need to know, right?"

Jake shook his head. "It doesn't work that way. I've got Dean looking over my shoulder and the D.A. isn't going to be too far behind. Come on, Sadie," he cajoled. "I know she's your friend, but are you sure you're being the best one you can be to her? I don't think she appreciates the gravity of the situation."

Sadie shut the drawer and looked up. Worry lined her forehead, but determination firmed her pert jaw. "I kept her mom in the loop, Jake. That was a risk, but I could justify it. I— I can't do anymore. I'm sorry. As for the gravity of the situation—" she shrugged helplessly "—you know how she is. Once she makes her mind up, that's it. There's no changing it."

He'd gotten no more than he'd expected, he supposed. Still, it had been worth a shot. "So she came to your house last night?"

"She did." Her brow folded into a thoughtful frown. "She got there around eight—the girls and I were cooking—and left about ten."

"Were you home all night?"

Sadie's lips quirked with a hint of droll humor and

crossing her arms over her chest, she leaned a hip against the desk. "I wondered how long it would take you to get around to it."

Jake shrugged, a sheepish grin tugging at his mouth. "I gotta ask, Sadie."

"I talked with Jolie last night right before she left to go to Meredith's—she mentioned that Chris was in the shower, by the way—then I left and went to Mom's for dinner. Rob was pulling a double, so the girls and I were on our own. We were there for about an hour...home by seven." She smiled and her eyes twinkled. "Does that cover everything? Does my alibi pass muster, Detective?"

"I'm sure it will once I've checked it out."

She shot him a look, then snorted indelicately. "You're barking up the wrong tree, Jake. I might have been tempted to cut his dick off, but I'd have never had the nerve to shoot him."

Jake winced. "She told you about that, eh?"

Sadie nodded. "She did. Only fitting, if you ask me. He'd never been anything but a dick, anyway."

Pretty much the consensus, Jake thought, unsurprised by the amusing observation. "What about you? Have you got any theories about who could have done it?"

Sadie paused to consider the question and her gaze turned speculative. "I don't know," she said thoughtfully. "He had a lot of enemies, but when you factor in the whole cutting-his-dick-off part, I'm thinking that you're most likely looking for a woman." She cocked her head and slid him a droll glance. "Can't see a man having the stomach for it no matter how much he might have hated him."

Jake had arrived at the same conclusion. Cutting off Marshall's dick had been the ultimate insult, the final salvo and the entire concept smacked of distinctly feminine revenge. He was most likely looking for a jilted lover, which meant that a trip to see Emily Dean would undoubtedly be on his agenda tomorrow. Now there was something to look forward to, Jake thought, as dread balled in his gut. If she was the one who'd murdered Marshall, she'd undoubtedly be entertaining similar thoughts about him and Mike for outing the affair which had ultimately ruined her marriage. A bulletproof vest and a cup probably wouldn't be out of order, he thought with a dark chuckle.

Sadie finished tidying up and slung her purse over her shoulder. "Jolie's on her way," she said. "Wanna follow me outside so I can lock up? Rob's got evening shift tonight and—" she glanced at her watch "—if I leave right now, we might actually have time to eat dinner together before he has to leave."

"Sure." Following her outside, he looked out

across the square and tried to avoid staring at Jolie as she made her way closer to them…but it wasn't easy. With every step that put her nearer to him, he could feel her—feel his belly hollowing, then clenching, then hollowing again.

The faint scent of petunias, pine mulch and fresh-cut grass wafted toward him on the late afternoon breeze and the sun played hide and seek with low, smeared clouds. Despite the fact that he'd lost his pretty bronze sheen, Jebediah stood proudly on his little patch of marble, seemingly enjoying the soft gurgle of the nearby fountain. On the other side of the square an elderly couple held hands, strolled un-hurriedly to some unknown destination.

Sadie jerked her thumb toward her car. "Hey, Jo, I'm heading out," she called out. "I want to catch din-ner with Rob before he leaves for work."

Jolie waved her on. "Go on," she told her. "I'll call you later."

"You'll be at your mom's?"

"Yeah."

Sadie nodded, then slid into her car. She waggled her fingers at them as she drove away. Thirty sec-onds later, Jolie arrived in front of him. Several strands of dark red hair had pulled loose from her ponytail and whispered around her face. One in particular had swept across that lush mouth and clung distractingly. "You got here early," she re-marked with a twinkling smile. "Checking out Sadie, were you?"

Jake's gaze slid away from her, and he felt a grin tease his mouth. She was too damned smart for her own good. God, how he'd missed that. "Just asking questions."

She headed toward the back of the building to the entrance to the apartment. "Well, Mom said whenever you get ready to *ask some questions* to be sure and call first. She'll put a blackberry cobbler in the oven."

A bark of laughter erupted from the back of Jake's throat as he followed her up the steep stairs. Black-berry cobbler was his absolute favorite dessert and Jolie's mother made the best he'd ever eaten. "What?" he joked. "You think you have my whole strategy figured out?"

She fished the key out of her purse, then threw him a look over her shoulder. "Not your whole strategy per se," she said drolly, "but we've read enough sus-pense novels to have a general idea of how things are going to go."

Jake felt a sigh slip through his smiling lips. "I'm just doing my job."

Jolie pushed open the door and made her way in-side. Tall windows painted rectangular wedges of golden light on the worn hardwood floors. "I know.

And if I haven't said it yet, I'm glad that it's you that's got this one."

Something warm moved into his chest. "Yeah, well, you might not be glad if I can't figure out who did this." He grimaced. "So far I've hit nothing but dead ends."

"But you're just getting started, right?"

Jake wandered into the living room part of the giant studio, noting the small touches which told him Jolie had definitely spent a lot of time here. A bottle of nail polish, a paperback book and a hair clip sat on an end table, and he could detect the faintest hint of vanilla in the somewhat musty air.

"I am," he told her. "Still, I'd like to have a little more evidence to work with. Other than a couple of smudges on the faucet, there's nothing." He shoved his hands in his pockets, shook his head. He told her about canvassing the yard, then speaking to the neighbors. "Naturally nobody saw anything."

"Chris hadn't exactly ingratiated himself with the neighbors." Jolie pulled a brown accordion file from one of the kitchen drawers, walked over and handed it to him. "But maybe this will help."

Jake accepted the folder, randomly flipped through it and felt his eyes widen. "The mayor's daughter?"

"Yep."

"Christ." What a friggin' nightmare. The sheriff's wife, the mayor's daughter. Was there any prominent citizen in Moon Valley that he hadn't screwed over?

"I'd like to get in the house tomorrow and get my things. Is that going to be all right?"

Still engrossed in the file, Jake nodded. "Yeah. We've gotten everything we're going to get out of there, I think, and everything else has been documented." He looked up. "You could actually move back in if you'd like."

She chewed the corner of her mouth and shook her head. "Nope. I just want to get what little is mine and move on, not move back," she added significantly.

"Technically it's all yours now."

"I don't want it. Everything that belonged to Chris can be sold with the house."

Jake nodded. Given what Marshall had put her through, he could easily see why she wouldn't want to live in the house anymore. Still, she should probably exercise a little discretion when it came to actually putting it on the market. He hesitated, then told her so. "I think that you should wait until this is resolved. Like I told you before, everything you do is going to be under intense scrutiny…and considering the fact that you took out an insurance policy last week and researched a pre-burial plan for him, you're being looked at pretty hard as it is."

"I'll think about it," she said evasively.

Jake felt his nostrils flare as he pulled in a slow breath. She obviously had absolutely no intention of following his advice. She had to be the most provokingly stubborn female he'd ever encountered in his life. "Think real hard, Jo."

"I will," she said, the tone of her voice adding a *not*. "Did you need anything else tonight?" she asked. She dropped a glance at her watch. "Because if not, Mom's cooking. You're, uh… You're welcome to join us if you'd like," she said, awkwardly issuing the invitation. There was something distinctly vulnerable about the tentative way she tendered it. "There'll be plenty."

Jake's first impulse was to accept, to latch on to any reason to be with her. And hell, as far as that went, he had a reason—Dean had told him to stick to her like glue. But somehow he didn't think enjoying dinner with her would qualify as true surveillance. After a moment, he shook his head. "Thanks, but I can't. I've got to feed the horses and, er… Marzipan is due to foal any day now."

Her expression brightened. "She is?"

Jake nodded. Marzipan had been "her" horse. She'd gone with him to the sale when he'd bought the sweet-tempered almond-colored mare. She'd even named her. After they'd broken up, Jake had been tempted to sell the horse, not wanting any unnecessary reminders of Jolie around, but he'd never been able to summon the nerve. It had just felt wrong somehow. "It's her first," he said, "so I want to be there."

And from the wistful expression on her face, she wanted to be there, too, Jake realized, feeling a tingly whoosh swoop through his midsection. The last damned thing he needed to do was even indirectly try to pick up where they left off, to spend more time with her than was absolutely necessary. Which made him the biggest fool in the world when he offered to call her when the foaling started. "If you'd like to be there, that is."

A big smile slowly dawned across her lips and she nodded. A bizarre charge passed between them, one that heralded if not a new beginning, then at the very least a truce. "I'd love to be there," she said, her voice somewhat strangled. "Thanks."

Jake nodded, unable to tear his gaze away from hers. Jesus, he'd missed her, still ached for her in places that he hadn't known could hurt. "Okay, then," he finally managed to say, and gestured toward the door. "We should probably get going."

Jolie nodded, seeming to come to her senses as well, and followed him downstairs. She locked up, then after a brief but awkward goodbye, Jake made his way back to his car. He slid behind the wheel and swore. Repeatedly. "Idiot," he muttered.

As if things weren't complicated enough.

Hell, her friggin' *husband* wasn't even in the ground yet and all he could think about was how much he wanted to feel the sweet curve of her cheek beneath his palm, the taste of her lush mouth against his lips. It was crazy, insane even. Jake pictured Dean's thunderous expression, could just hear him— *and you call this objective?*—and felt a burst of wry laughter well up in his throat.

He needed his head examined, Jake decided. He truly did. Just because Marshall was dead didn't mean they could just pick up where they'd left off. A lot of bitter water had flowed under the bridge— and he was responsible for most of it.

No matter how much he'd like to blame Jolie for jumping the gun with Marshall, for not giving him the time he'd asked for, he knew he'd been the one ultimately at fault. In the moment when she'd needed him most, he hadn't been there for her, had let her down. It had been his biggest fear and like a self-fulfilling prophecy, it had come true. Jake swallowed, still unable to account for the supreme ignorance of that hesitation. He lived with it, carried it around with him all the time. It was the height of idiocy to think that she'd ever truly forgive him for it, courting heartache to even hope that she might.

Furthermore—and he suspected he'd be reminding himself of this a lot over the next few weeks—he'd do better to spend his time thinking about how to clear her of possible murder charges. If he didn't, he could very well see himself trying to kiss her through a quarter-inch of Plexiglas.

CHAPTER TWENTY

"WELL?" MEREDITH ASKED with exaggerated patience. "What have you learned?"

Sophia pushed her half-eaten slice of pie away from her and mourned the loss of the rest of the delightful dessert. After that huge breakfast a couple of mornings ago, she couldn't justify eating the whole thing.

At just after two, they were sitting in Dilly's Bakery—supporting a beaming Cora who worked enthusiastically behind the counter—and going over the latest developments. Sophia would have preferred a three-way phone call—she'd needed to be pruning an out-of-control butterfly bush—but Bitsy didn't trust "the airwaves." Who knew who might be listening in? she'd argued, so they'd agreed to meet for tea at the bakery.

"I called Jolie last night," Sophia told them. "She went in yesterday and closed the business. She's repaid the investors—and Fran, of course—and is planning on meeting someone from Moon Valley Realty about selling her old house and buying that little bungalow on Lelia Street that she mentioned at last week's meeting."

Bitsy whistled low and beamed. "Why she's not wasting any time at all, is she?"

"It would seem not," Meredith said. But she didn't seem to share Bitsy's enthusiasm for Jolie's swift actions. A line of worry emerged between her brows. "Don't you think that she ought to be a little more careful, Sophia? You know…in light of her involvement with us?"

Sophia had thought that as well, but couldn't fault Jolie for moving as quickly as she had. She told Meredith and Bitsy about Jolie's concern over the possibility of frozen accounts. "If she'd waited on that, who knows when she'd have been able to give everyone their money back, most importantly her mother's."

Bitsy shoveled another bite of lemon-blueberry pound cake into her mouth and swallowed thickly. Her chins jiggled as she bobbed her head in a sanctimonious little nod. "Sounds to me like she's using her head."

Sophia resisted the urge to reclaim her plate and finish her pie. "She's just ready for it all to be over with."

"I know," Meredith sighed, propping her chin up with her hand. "I just wish she didn't have to be so…hasty. Makes her look guilty."

"Jake knows about the pre-burial plan and the life insurance," Sophia told them gravely.

Meredith gasped and her eyes widened. "Already?" she breathed, straightening in her seat. "But how?"

She gave them both a droll look. "Apparently Andy called wanting the body and mentioned the plans to Jake."

Bitsy's doughy face folded into a disgusted scowl. "I swear, if it weren't for having to go to another county to be laid to rest, I'd be damned before I'd let those morbid vultures have my business."

She could always pay them in coupons, Sophia thought.

"How did he find out about the life insurance?" Meredith asked.

Sophia shrugged. "Put two and two together, I suppose." She released a heavy sigh. "But he still doesn't know about the Club, and Jolie has assured me that she isn't going to tell him. He tried to pump Sadie for information yesterday afternoon, but thankfully she didn't tell him anything, either."

Bitsy snorted. "She better not. I save my best coupons for her. Those dollar-off's will dry up in a heartbeat if she opens her mouth, I can tell you that."

Sophia resisted the urge to roll her eyes, certain that Sadie fervently wished those coupons *would* dry up. Everybody who worked in any sort of service capacity within a fifty mile radius of Moon Valley certainly did.

"What will we do if he finds out?" Meredith asked, blithely ignoring Bitsy's dire coupon warning.

"We'll cross that bridge when we come to it," Sophia said. And pray they didn't come to it.

"I don't think we have anything to worry about," Bitsy interjected, seemingly unconcerned as usual. "She's not going to tell. If she doesn't tell, then he can't find out about us, right? I mean, we've been careful. We've had to be to keep it together for so long, right?" Her gaze bounced to Meredith. "Stop worrying, Meri. Everything's gonna be fine. Are you going to eat the rest of that cake?"

A faint grin tugged at Meredith's mouth as she slid Bitsy her leftover dessert. "You're right, I suppose," she relented. "Still, I can't help but be nervous."

Her thin face red with pleasant exertion and wreathed in a smile, Cora appeared at Sophia's elbow. "Can I get you anything else, ladies? Mary just pulled some hot apple fritters out a few minutes ago. They're divine."

Sophia's mouth watered, but she imagined having to buy all new support hose and woefully shook her head. "No, thanks, Cora. I'm good. How are things going here? You look happy."

Cora's smile glowed with delight and just the smallest hint of much-needed pride. "Oh, Sophia, I am. Mary's just a joy to work with, and I've always loved to bake." Her grin turned downright triumphant. "Then there's having my own money, of course. I bought a new cake pan last week. It's shaped like a rose and it's just lovely. I can't wait to—" She drew up short and ducked her head. "I know it's just a cake pan, but it was so nice to get something just because I wanted it."

Meredith offered Cora a warm smile. "We're proud of you, Cora. You always had it in you, you know."

"You don't know how much I appreciate being a part of our *bridge group*," she said earnestly, her fingers twisting into her apron hem. "Don't know what I'd do without it."

Sophia, Bitsy and Meredith all shared a significant look. "We're glad to have you, Cora," Bitsy told her.

Cora looked over her shoulder. "Well, I'd better get back to work. The mayor's coming in shortly to pick up his order and I haven't gotten it together yet." She wrinkled her nose. "He smells terrible," she whispered, leaning down where only they could hear her. "But what can you do? Poor man still hasn't gotten rid of those skunks." With a shake of her head, she turned and walked back behind the counter.

Meredith sniggered. "And he won't until one of us wins the Beautification Award," she muttered under her breath. "It's my turn, right?"

Bitsy nodded. "I've got it—" *it* being their secret skunk attractor "—in the trunk of my car. Don't let me forget to give it to you before we leave."

"Oh, don't worry," Meredith assured her. "I won't. I swear if he doesn't give you that Award next week, I'll figure out a way to get those stinky suckers *inside* his house. Or maybe I'll just plant the stuff all around his house—at the rate we're going through it, it would probably be cheaper."

"He could give the award to one of you two," Bitsy demurred, preening. "You both have lovely lawns as well."

Sophia snorted. "Not as nice as yours, but I appreciate the compliment."

Admittedly her yard was looking a lot better this spring—she'd certainly spent a great deal more time outside working it…but it hadn't been because she'd been angling for the Beautification Award.

More like she'd been angling for Edward.

Sophia still flushed like a school girl every time she thought about their delightful breakfast the other morning. Edward had been excellent company, complimenting her—even though she'd looked like a total hag, she thought, mentally writhing with re-

membered mortification—and had praised her cooking, then had even insisted on staying until they'd finished all of the dishes.

That had been refreshing, Sophia thought, grudgingly impressed. God knows her own lazy, shiftless
husband had never so much as put a coffee cup in the
sink, much less taken the trouble to wash it. Once everything had been done, every excuse to linger used,
Edward had thanked her and promised to reciprocate
the gesture. He could make a decent biscuit, he'd told
her, if she'd be willing to try one.

Sophia had been stunned—if she wasn't completely off her rocker, he'd essentially asked her for
a date—and had merely toyed nervously with her
hair and nodded. So far the invitation hadn't come
through, but she'd purposely stayed indoors the past
couple of mornings because she loathed the idea of
looking eager, or God forbid, needy.

Furthermore, though she hadn't determined precisely how just yet, Sophia wanted to make sure that
all of Edward's…parts were in working order. She
didn't want to get too attached to him—or the idea
of having sex with him—if he wasn't going to be
able to seal the deal. She hated to be callous or un-
feeling, but she wasn't buying a pig in a poke here.
Time was running out. If she was ever going to have
an honest-to-goodness bonafide orgasm again, she

had to act quickly. And if you asked her poor neg-lected—intensely rejuvenated—hormones, the sooner the better.

Bitsy fished a couple of coupons from her purse and laid them on the table. One was for fifty-cents off a roll of paper towels, the other for a Lean Cuisine.

Sophia heaved an exasperated sigh. "Honestly, Bitsy, can't you just put down some change? Cora's thin as a rail! What does she want with a low-calorie meal?"

Bitsy's eyes rounded. "Oh, you're right. Here," she said. She replaced it with a quarter off a half-gallon of ice cream. "She could use that a whole lot more, eh?"

Sophia looked to Meredith. "Can't you do something about her?"

"I was instrumental in talking her out of the motorcycle. You'll have to tackle the coupon issue."

Bitsy's gasped as though just remembering something important. Eyes gleaming behind her purple glasses, she rummaged around in her purse until she'd found a mangled newspaper clipping. "You only *think* you've talked me out of the motorcycle," she said, sliding the paper to Meredith. "The idea of getting a motorcycle license was the deciding factor against making that purchase. But this," she said, her voice ringing with satisfied excitement, "this is what I'm getting. It's on order. Acid green with purple racing stripes." She practically wriggled in her seat. "Isn't it wonderful? We should all have one. Then we could ride together. Get matching helmets and jackets. We could be the Moon Valley Marauders or something."

Meredith frowned, adjusted her reading glasses, then her mouth dropped open. "You can't be serious," she said faintly. With a disgusted huff, she handed the paper to Sophia.

"A pocket rocket?" Sophia asked her, inspecting the ad. "Isn't this a kid's toy?"

"Technically, yes," Bitsy admitted, not the least bit embarrassed or chagrined. "But it doesn't require a license, it's gas and electric, will go up to thirty-five miles an hour, and it'll hold up to two-hundred-and-fifty pounds."

Sophia quirked a brow.

Bitsy scowled at the quiet recrimination. "I'm dieting," she said, irritated.

"Bitsy, be that as it may, I don't think this is a good idea. You could get hurt."

She shrugged, unconcerned. "If it's safe for kids, then it's safe for me." She bobbed her head determinedly. "I want it. I'm gonna have it."

"Do as you please," Meredith said stiffly, "but don't say we didn't warn you." She removed her napkin from her lap, wadded it up and tossed it on the table. "You're blind as a bat. You don't have any business trying to ride something like that. You'll end up getting yourself killed."

Bitsy grinned and raised her palm. "Talk to the hand 'cause the head's not listening."

Meredith harrumphed. "You'll be listening when your kids try to have you committed."

"Nah," Bitsy said, blithely unconcerned. "They're too afraid I'll leave my money to my cat and my coupons to them."

Sophia suppressed a grin. Knowing Bitsy, her kids better realize that very scenario wasn't completely out of the realm of possibility.

"But I do appreciate your concern, Meri," Bitsy told her, leaning over to give her an air kiss. "It's nice to be loved. Now what say we do a little shopping, eh?" Her smile turned a wee bit sly. "We'll need a new outfit for the funeral, won't we?"

Oh, she hadn't even thought of that, Sophia realized with a pleased start. Per tradition, every member of the FWC attended the funeral in support and appreciation of the newly widowed. To the casual observer, they merely looked like concerned friends, paying their last respects, but in truth the event officially kicked off their celebration. Sophia smiled.

And if there was one thing the FWC knew how to do it was party.

CHAPTER TWENTY-ONE

JOLIE FINGERED the single long-stemmed rose loosely held between her gloved fingers and waited for Reverend Hollis to finish the final prayer said over Chris's casket. The warm afternoon sun beat down on her back and a slight breeze ruffled her veiled hat.

Flanked by her mom and Sadie—both of them wearing somber but relieved expressions—and the entire FWC at her back, Jolie finally felt the beginnings of true closure wrap around her, felt it clawing away at two years of misery and regret, and by the time Hollis muttered the final amen, she had to suppress a triumphant whoop of joy.

It was over.

Or as over as it was going to be until Chris's murderer was found, but at least this was an official beginning to the rest of her life.

"And that's it," Sadie whispered quietly as she

turned and wrapped Jolie in a warm hug. "You made it."

Sadie had no more than let her go when her mother gathered her up. "It's over, hon," her mom breathed. She could feel her soothing relief washing over both of them, could feel her mom trembling with it.

Jolie smiled, but didn't speak. She couldn't. She was too overcome. The past several days had been a flurry of activity for her. She'd closed the business, satisfied the investors—most especially her mom— and the profound sense of comfort that doing that brought her had made it worth every miserable moment of the past two years. Just knowing that she'd made things right, that she'd have made her father proud, and that her mother wouldn't have to worry, wouldn't have to scrimp or scrape to get by anymore, had lifted a tremendous weight off her shoulders.

In addition to all of that, she'd cleaned out her things from the house she'd shared with Chris and, despite Jake's dire warnings about being hasty, she'd listed it with a Realtor, the same one who'd negotiated the deal for her for the house on Lelia Street.

Her mom had told her that she was welcome to stay at home with her, of course, and, while Jolie appreciated the offer, she wanted *her* own space, something that was hers and hers alone. She couldn't wait to move in, set up her office and flex her neglected decorating muscle. Other than her bedroom, she'd never been able to arrange things to suit her own tastes. She liked rich colors and the combination of old and new, and she couldn't wait to pick out paint samples and furniture.

Sophia, Bitsy and Meredith, all of them looking polished and gorgeous in varying spring shades, moved toward her. "You look smashing, dear," Sophia told her with an approving nod. "Like a true widow."

Meredith leaned in. "Plan on staying a little longer this week. It's customary in our little group to celebrate a new official's status."

"That's right," Bitsy chimed in. She did a little hip-roll shimmy dance move. "We're gonna *party*."

Meredith frowned and looked to Sophia who whacked Bitsy on the upper arm. "Cut it out, fool," she admonished. "We're at a bloody funeral, for Pete's sake," she hissed, looking around to make sure no one was paying attention.

Bitsy blinked and straightened, properly chastised. "Oh, right. Sorry."

Jolie barely smothered a chuckle. The trio moved aside and slowly the rest of the FWC members came by and, their faces arranged in purposely somber expressions that in no way matched the delight in their eyes, wished her a softly spoken congratulations. Several mentioned the upcoming party and like Bitsy, seemed to want to dance. Thankfully, they refrained because from the corner of her eye—prompted by a not-so-gentle nudge from Sadie—Jolie caught sight of Jake. A tremble shook her belly, forcing a shuddering breath to escape her lungs.

He wore his trademark khaki pants and a cuffed white oxford cloth shirt. His dark brown hair was tousled and a pair of trendy shades covered his eyes. The prerequisite cell phone was clipped at his waist and she could tell by the flat shape of that usually carnal mouth that he was supremely displeased.

In fact, *pissed* was probably more accurate.

Jolie drew in a careful breath as a combination of fluttery air and dread wrestled in her belly. He'd obviously made a new discovery, possibly more, she thought warily, hoping that it didn't crush the bud of newfound neutral ground they seemed to have found.

Every time she thought about him offering to call her when Marzipan went to foal, a light hopeful feeling swelled in her chest and a tingle of tentative happiness sizzled through her blood.

Jolie knew better than to start entertaining the idea of a belated happily-ever-after with Jake. Even if he were willing, quite frankly she didn't know if she'd be able to pony up the emotional investment to pull it off. She'd given everything she'd had to him and the one time she'd really needed him he'd wavered. Which was what had ultimately sent her down the path she'd just gotten off of.

Did she love Jake? Jolie swallowed tightly as the truth readily rose in her heart. Yes, she did. Always had, always would. She ached for him, yearned for him, longed for that sense of closeness and familiarity—being his friend, and oh, God, being his lover. She wanted that back more than anything. But could they go back? Could *she* go back? Jolie frowned. She didn't know.

Granted she knew that Jake was sorry, that he regretted letting her go, then not having the nerve to try and reclaim her after she'd come back with Chris. He could have, too, Jolie thought. She'd been hurt and angry and miserable, but if he'd asked—just asked—she would have culled Chris in a heartbeat to have Jake back. He had to know it, Jolie thought. And he surely must have known it then…yet he hadn't so much as lifted a finger when he could have merely crooked it and she'd have come running.

Pride was a funny thing, she knew, because it had propelled her to bring Chris home in the first place. God, she'd been so stupid. It was amazing what two years of sheer hell could do to make one see things clearly.

Jake strolled toward her, stopped, then lazily looked her up and down. She felt that keen caressing gaze move up her legs, over her hips, linger over her breasts, then finally find her face.

"Nice dress," he said. "Bought that last week, didn't you?"

It had been in her closet, with the receipt stapled to the bag. He knew exactly when she'd bought it, and now he knew what she'd bought it for. Her breakfast rolled. "I did," she returned, albeit shakily.

Jake swore and looked away. "I need to talk to you when you have a moment."

Jolie shrugged, twirled her rose and refused to be intimidated. Dammit, she'd told him she was moving on. What exactly had he expected? "Now's good," she said, pretending to be unconcerned. "Mom will want to go on. Can you give me a ride home?"

"To which one?" Jake asked tightly. "The one I encouraged you not to sell—which you've put on the market anyway—or the one you just bought?"

Ah, so that was it. "Neither at the moment, unless you're interested in seeing my new house," she said. "It's on Lelia Street. Right off the—"

"I know where it's at," Jake interrupted, his voice

throbbing with pent-up anger. He told her mother that he'd see her home—in a considerably warmer tone than what he was using with her—then slid his hand around her upper arm and propelled her toward his car.

It was the first time in more than two years that he'd touched her and despite the fact that it wasn't the gentle caress she'd longed for, her body responded all the same. Her breath hitched in her throat, her mouth lost its moisture and a pulsing ache commenced in her nipples and between her thighs.

He opened the truck door for her, rounded the hood, then joined her inside. He waited for her to finish buckling her seat belt, then started the engine and bolted out of the cemetery.

"I came into work this morning and was immediately called into Dean's office. His sister works at the bank and she mentioned to him over the weekend that you'd cleaned out Marshall's accounts."

Jolie swallowed. "That's right."

His nostrils flared. *"The night he died."*

"It was after midnight, so technically it was the next day," Jolie clarified despite his thunderous expression.

"She also mentioned that you've closed all the business accounts." His tone was edged with disgust. "I saw you putting a sign up in the window last week. I just assumed that you'd put up a notice about

Chris's death." He chuckled darkly. "I assumed wrong. You didn't put up a death notice—you put up a damned out-of-business sign!" He wheeled around the square, then waited for a stream of pedestrians to make it across to the corner. "What the hell were you thinking? Do you have any idea how guilty you're making yourself look? Do you even care?" He glanced over at her, moodily inspected her outfit once more and seemed to get even angrier. "So help me God, if you've got on that black corset underneath that, I'm gonna have a friggin' stroke."

Jolie felt a flash of feminine pleasure hit the tops of her thighs and her lips rolled into a droll smile. "You went through my underwear drawer? Take your detective work seriously, don't you, Jake?"

Jake edged the car up to the curb in front of her new house, shifted into park, then cast her another glance and let go a seemingly tortured sigh. "Are you wearing it?"

She smiled. "It matches."

His gaze dropped to her breasts again and he swallowed. From the looks of things it was taking every ounce of patience he possessed to get through this encounter.

Strangely enough, she was finding it funny, a fact she knew she'd better keep to herself.

"Let me paint a picture for you," Jake said.

"We've got a dead husband with a wife who A.) has a credible yet curious alibi for the time of the murder, B.) researched pre-burial plans a week before his death, C.) took out one-hundred grand in additional life insurance the week before he died."

His expression blackened accordingly with his tone of voice as he continued to tick off her offenses.

"D.) bought the outfit she planned to wear to his funeral the week before he died, E.) cleaned out his accounts before the body had even been moved from the scene, F.) closed his business before the M.E. even finished the autopsy, G.) put the house up for sale, and H.) bought another one." Jake plucked his glasses off and slung them up on the dash. "If you were the detective on this case—or just any regular old citizen, for that matter," he added sarcastically, "what would you infer from this woman's actions?"

Yes, well, when you put it like that, she would admit that she looked a little guilty, Jolie decided. Nevertheless, she wasn't guilty and regardless of how bizarre her alibi looked, the fact remained that she had one. Furthermore, she was innocent.

"I'd infer that this wife had been married to a miserable SOB who'd delighted in making her wretched, and who'd stolen money from her mother and other hard-working citizens. I'd infer that the bastard had absolutely no redeeming qualities and that the wife—

who'd had her life on hold for the past twenty-four
months—was ready to move on as swiftly as possible, to wash the stench of her nasty, sorry-assed husband's life out of her own and endeavor to create a
new one as soon as possible." Her veil quivered as
she bobbed her head. "If I *knew* her," she said pointedly, "*that's* what I'd infer." She paused, punctuating the thought, then let herself out of the truck and,
head held high and stilettos clicking, made her way
up the sidewalk.

Gratifyingly, she felt his gaze on her backside as
she made her way to the door…and she liked what
she could *infer* from that.

JAKE SLAMMED his palm against the steering wheel,
then snagged the keys and met Jolie on the porch. He
did know her and, dammit, he did understand. He just
wished that she could use a little bit of discretion.
He'd walked into that meeting with Dean this morning and, for all intents and purposes, might as well
have had his pants down.

Not only had Dean informed him—*the damned
Detective,* by the way—that Jolie had cleaned out the
accounts, but he'd also known that she'd closed the
business, put the house up for sale and bought a new
one. Things weren't looking good, Dean had said.
Did Jake want to let this one go?

Not no, but hell no.

In light of everything that had been uncovered—and, dammit, he knew there was more—he couldn't afford to let it go. Guilty or not, she'd go to jail. There was too much circumstantial evidence floating around to prevent otherwise. It wouldn't matter that she had an alibi and the thick-headed, stubborn…Jake's gaze drifted over the backs of her legs—her fishnet hose, specifically—up over her gorgeous rump and slim back, and he felt another blast of heat detonate in his loins. He blinked. Aw, hell…what had he been thinking?

Oh, yeah.

"Jolie, I didn't say that I didn't understand it," he said with an exasperated sigh. "I'm just asking you to at least consider how it looks."

She inserted a key into the lock and, smiling, let herself inside. "That's just it. I don't care how it looks."

And therein lay the rub, he thought, exhaling a weary sigh. She'd made up her mind and that was that. Jake followed her into the living room, noting the worn heart-of-pine floors and custom built-ins. The spacious room had lots of nice molding, plenty of architectural detail. He caught her gaze and nodded. "It's nice."

She pulled that femme fatale hat off, ruffled her

hair and let it fall loose around her shoulders. "I thought so," she said with a satisfied sigh.

It was certainly homier than that sterile colonial she'd called home on Poplar Street, that was for damned sure. She gave him the guided tour, getting more and more excited as they moved from room to room. Other than her bedroom suite and office equipment, she had no furniture to speak of. She ticked off decorating ideas, and mentioned several improvements and upgrades she'd like to install.

"It needs a little TLC, but I can see myself here," she said, rubbing a hand over the mantle. "I can see myself calling it home."

A curiously unpleasant sensation twisted like barbed-wire in his chest and an awkward moment passed between them. There'd been a time when they'd both assumed that they'd make their home together, namely the one he'd built after she'd married Marshall.

Though Mike had called him a fool and his mother had asked him to stop torturing himself, when it had come time to build his farmhouse, he'd carried on with the plans that he and Jolie had put together. Granted, building it without her—not to mention living in it without her—had never been part of the plan, but Jake had genuinely liked what they'd put together and he couldn't see changing it simply to avoid thinking about her.

That, he knew, was never going to happen.

Furthermore, there was no point in being unsatisfied with a house just because every time he pulled into the driveway he'd think about her.

Hell, that had always been a foregone conclusion. They'd grown up together, had been through every first together. There wasn't a spot in this county that they hadn't explored, a place on the planet where he could escape from her. No matter where he lived, what he did, he couldn't outrun his memories. She'd had his heart since third grade and he didn't anticipate ever getting it back.

Jake finally swallowed. "I'm, uh… I'm sure you'll be happy here."

Jolie toyed with the netting on her hat, and glanced up at him. "I'm sorry I put you in a bad position with Dean," she said. "That was not my intention. I just knew I had to get the money out before the accounts were frozen. That's what I'd been working on, you know. Why I'd stuck it out. It was to return Mom's money, and the other investors, of course. If Dean's sister mentioned that I'd cleaned out the accounts, then she had to have mentioned what I'd done with it."

Jake nodded. He couldn't fault why she did it— noble intentions, he knew—but that didn't change the fact that he wished she'd just confide in him now.

Dammit, he hated being out of the loop. She needed to let him know what the hell was going on. How did she expect him to protect her otherwise?

"She did," he admitted. "But that doesn't change the fact that I looked like a fool. I can't afford those kinds of mistakes—and neither can you. Do you understand what I'm saying?"

He watched her chest flutter with an awkward breath. "Yes."

Jake pinned her with the full force of his gaze. "Then tell me what I need to know."

Jake waited, watched a host of emotion race across her face, her mouth work up and down. "I—"

His cell chirped at his waist. He swore and checked the read-out. It was Mike, so he had to take it. "What's up?" he asked, cursing the timing of this damned call.

"We've got a twenty on the penis," Mike said grimly.

Jake blinked. "Come again?"

"We've found Marshall's dick." Something that sounded suspiciously like a chuckle sounded into his ear. "You'll, uh… You'll have to see it to believe it."

CHAPTER TWENTY-TWO

TEN MINUTES LATER Jake, Jolie, Mike, Dean and Todd, as well as a crowd of morbidly curious on-lookers, stood at the base of the statue of Jebediah Moon and, dour faced, stared in abject fascination at the sight in front of them.

"Somehow I don't think this is w-what the City Council would c-consider an improvement," Mike commented, once again sounding perilously close to laughter.

Dean shot him a firm look and Mike flushed. "Sorry," he muttered.

Marshall's apparently semi-frozen penis had been glued—with what, Todd would have to determine, thank God—to Jebediah in a position that, if not anatomically correct, was at least in the general vicinity of where a penis should belong.

This case had just left Interstate Weird and exited onto Highway Bizarre.

"Who noticed it?" Jake asked, passing a hand over his face.

"Martin Mashburn," Mike told him. "He said he was just strolling by and noticed a part of Jeb that wasn't tarnished. Said he almost fell down when he realized what it was."

He supposed so, Jake thought, still shocked. He'd had advance knowledge and it was still pretty damned hard to believe. Who in the hell could have done such a thing? he wondered. And more importantly, why?

Though he dreaded it, he knew he had to ask. He shot Jolie an uncomfortable look. "Is this—" He cleared his throat. "Is this Marshall's—"

Thankfully, she didn't let him finish. "Limp and little," she said coolly. "That's definitely his."

The comment drew a shocked chuckle from them all, most especially Dean, who smothered his laugh with an unconvincing cough. "Well, Todd," said the Sheriff, "I don't envy your job on this one."

Looking distinctly unenthusiastic, Todd grimaced. "Yeah, me neither."

"What are you going to do with it?" Mike wanted to know. "They've already buried him."

Todd shifted uncomfortably, darting a hesitant look at Jolie. "I guess it needs to be given to Mrs. Marshall."

"It's Caplan," Jolie corrected, much to Jake's surprise. "I've taken back my maiden name. And I don't want it," she said. Her face had folded into a frown of disgusted distaste. "I don't care what you do with it."

Jake slid a veiled glance at Dean. He had a grim suspicion what fate awaited Marshall's severed penis. "Er…don't you need to process it first? Maybe see if you can figure out what was used to—"

"Yeah, I'll do that. Though frankly, I don't think I'm gonna find much."

"Yeah, that happens when you don't have much to work with, eh?" Mike jibed.

Dean's brows lowered again, prompting Mike to make another red-faced apology.

"Mike, you want to help me start questioning?" Jake asked, looking around the square. "I'll take one side, you take the other."

Surely to God, this time they'd find some sort of witness. No one could have possibly walked into the square and glued Marshall's dick to Jebediah completely unnoticed. Someone had to have seen something. The square was the hub of Moon Valley commerce. It was usually packed, Monday being especially busy.

Though looking at the slowly thawing grayish penis made his stomach roil, this could actually end up being the break in the case that he needed.

Mike nodded. "Sure. So long as I don't have to look at it anymore—or touch it—I'll do whatever you ask me to."

Jake turned to Jolie. "Do you need a ride to your Mom's?"

"I'll call her," Jolie told him.

"No need," Dean interrupted smoothly. "I'll give you a lift."

Though Jake didn't particularly like the idea, he couldn't very well object, and if Jolie was the least bit intimidated by riding with the Sheriff, she didn't betray so much as a blink of disquiet.

"I'll be in touch later," he told Jolie, a subtle warning that their interrupted conversation was by no means over.

She nodded and walked away with Dean. Jake looked back at Marshall's drooping dick and shuddered. Whoever did this was either really sick…or had one supremely twisted sense of humor.

For whatever reason, he suspected the latter.

JOLIE DIDN'T KNOW exactly what she'd expected Dean to say to her when they were alone in the car, but the apology she got on behalf of his estranged wife was definitely not it.

"I know there was no love lost between you and your husband, but as far as my wife's—soon to be ex-wife's," he corrected "—part in it, I'm really sorry."

Jolie blinked, somewhat stunned. "Well, I'm sorry for Chris's part in it as well." She stared at the radio, pretending to be interested in the other gadgets and gizmos she wasn't accustomed to seeing in her own car. For reasons that escaped her, something about his sincerity made her feel worse instead of better. Then she knew why. "I should have come to you as soon as I found out, but…" Somehow telling him that shoring up her grounds for divorce was more important to her than his right to know didn't seem very palatable.

"Jake explained," Dean told her, letting her off the hook. "Don't worry about it. It's done."

"Still… I'm really sorry."

"No hard feelings." He negotiated a turn and his dark brown gaze shifted to her. "I guess Jake told you she moved out."

"He did."

"Ah, well. It's for the best."

He was probably right, but agreeing felt like bad form, so she kept her mouth shut.

"He's still in love with you, you know," Dean said conversationally.

Jolie felt her heart trip, then race.

"It was against my better judgment to leave him

on this case, but he's convinced that you're innocent and any other detective may might not be so inclined to keep your best interests at heart."

"I *am* innocent," Jolie felt compelled to point out. "And I'm very thankful that he believes me."

Dean flicked her a glance. "A thankful person wouldn't let him get called on the carpet for things that he's too close to the investigation to see." He pulled into her mother's drive, shoved the gearshift into park, then turned to face her. "I don't think you killed Marshall, Jolie. Aside from your alibi, you were working too hard to get away from him legally without having to resort to murder." A weak smile caught the corner of his mouth. "Besides, you protested dissecting a dead frog in biology—I can't see you having the wherewithal to shoot Chris." He shifted. "That said, there are other issues that make you look damned guilty and if there's anything else that's likely to crop up, you ought to have enough respect for Jake to let him know. He's not the enemy. He's trying to help you." He lifted one shoulder in a negligent shrug and smiled. "Just think about it. End of sermon."

Slightly surprised by the unexpected lecture, Jolie nodded and moved to get out of the car. "I will. Thanks for the ride home."

"Anytime," Dean told her.

Her stomach knotted with tension, she straightened and watched him drive away. Good grief, what a damned mess, Jolie thought, wishing she had some idea as to how to fix it. She could either betray the FWC, or betray Jake.

Either way someone got hurt.

Aside from listening to him tell her not to do the things she'd wanted to do—like closing the accounts and business, putting the Poplar Street house up for sale and buying another—there was really no reason why she shouldn't have told him. Furthermore, after she'd shifted the money, there was really no reason—apart from catering to her own comfort—not to tell him that it had been done.

By keeping those things from him, she'd indirectly escalated the importance of the one thing she *had* to hide—the Future Widows' Club.

She could not—*would not*—out them, no matter how much Jake felt betrayed.

There was too much at risk for them, for past, present and future members. For women like Cora, Gladys and Margaret. The Officials—like her, Jolie realized with an odd start—didn't have as much to lose. Their lives were their own now, their miserable husbands dead and buried.

But what about the Futures? It's what made their lives bearable, what made them keep going from week to week. And the minute the group became public that would all be over with. Oh, there were some people who'd laugh it off, think that it was funny, even some she suspected who'd want to join.

But then there'd be a select few who had good decent husbands who wouldn't understand and it would be those few who would turn the FWC and all of its members into social outcasts or morally bankrupt second-class citizens. The anonymity was its only protection, what made it especially unique.

Jolie shook her head, firmed her resolve as she walked up the steps. She wouldn't be responsible for taking that away from them. Not to save her own skin and certainly not to spare Jake's feelings. She was sorry, but that was simply the way it had to be.

Her mother stood at the stove stirring a pot of marinara as Jolie walked into the kitchen. She'd been to see Sadie and a fresh new color had replaced the faded shade she'd had just the day before. A container of gourmet coffee sat proudly next to the pot, causing Jolie's lips to slip into a pleased smile.

"Looked like there was a big brouhaha down at the square when I came through," her mother said. "I tried to call Sadie and see what was going on, but no one answered the phone at The Spa."

Jolie sank down into a chair at the kitchen table. "I didn't see her, but she was probably there. Someone, presumably the killer, glued Chris's missing penis to the statue of Jebediah Moon." Though she knew it was inappropriate, Jolie felt her lips twitch and she forcibly quelled a laugh.

Her mother stilled, then slowly turned around. Marinara dripped from the wooden spoon in her hand unheeded onto the floor. For a moment she appeared as if she'd been cryogenically frozen.

Then she burst out laughing.

Jolie let the laughter she'd been holding back explode into a hysterical peal of guffaws that made her lose her breath.

"Oh, my God," her mother wheezed brokenly. "I know it's horrible, but I just think it's too funny. He was always so proud of that p-penis and…there's just something…poetic about him being buried w-without it." She wiped her streaming eyes, struggling to get herself under control, but like Jolie, didn't seem to be making much progress.

"Oh, Mom, it was horrible," she told her. She pulled in a deep breath in a vain attempt to stem the humor still lingering in the back of her throat. She swallowed, recalling the sight of his pitiful little dick stuck awkwardly to that statue. "It had been frozen."

"Shrinkage, then," her mom deadpanned. "What a tragedy."

Jolie shook with silent laughter until her sides

hurt. "Yes, well. That poor Nathan Todd was left to 'process' it, and Mike and Jake were charged with the duty of interrogating passersby to try and determine who'd glued the penis to the statue." She snickered again. "Should be interesting to hear how they tactfully broach that subject, huh?"

Her mother's smile turned thoughtful. "It was glued, you say?"

"Yep."

She hummed under her breath. "Wonder how they pulled that off. Must be *some* glue if it held a frozen penis in place."

Jolie rested her head against her palm. She hadn't thought of it that way. "I guess so."

"Probably used that Mega-glue, you know that kind they show on the commercials that can hold a three-ton truck by a broken chain."

Her mother turned back to the stove and tended to her sauce. "Has Jake gotten any more leads on who might have killed Chris? Is that what he wanted to talk to you about?"

"No. He'd gotten wind of some of my recent activities," Jolie said drolly, "and wanted to express his displeasure."

"Can't blame him, can you?" she asked. "He is trying to help you."

For the love of God, how many more times was

she going to hear that today? "I know," Jolie told her, trying to sound grateful rather than exasperated.

"I understand why you can't tell him about the FWC," she said lightly, "but there wouldn't have been any harm in sharing the other stuff with him."

Jolie felt her jaw drop.

Her mother turned around and smiled benignly. "Who do you think encouraged your invitation?" she asked. "You know Sophia and I are friends."

She did, Jolie thought, still shocked and dumb-founded, but she'd never put it together. Actually, come to think of it, she'd never really put any thought into why Sophia, Bitsy and Meredith had approached her. Nor had she thought anything about the entire FWC attending the funeral. Her mother hadn't batted an eye…and no wonder, Jolie thought, her gaze swinging to her mom.

She'd known.

Undoubtedly she'd known everything, all along, she suddenly realized. And Jolie had gone to so much trouble to avoid her, to hide the gruesome details that weren't common knowledge at The Spa, at the Garden Center. In the nanosecond it took to make that deduction, the truth dawned and she gasped.

Sadie.

"Don't be mad at her, dear," her intuitive mother said gently. "She was just being a good friend."

She knew, still… She and Sadie—who was ordinarily very trustworthy when it came to keeping a secret—were going to have to have a little talk about exercising discretion.

"Don't you say anything to her," her mother admonished, evidently reading her line of thought. "She knew I was worried about you, and you couldn't look me in the eye." Her mother tsked. "It was heartbreakingly dreadful."

Jolie swallowed. "It was too hard, Mom," she confessed. "I was so ashamed."

"And I understood that, which is why I never pushed it." Her expression softened. "But I can't tell you what a relief it is to put all of this behind us, and though I know it's awful of me to say this—which is why you'd better not ever repeat it—I hope they never find who killed Chris." She shrugged and turned back around. "Far as I'm concerned, that person did the world a favor, and most assuredly did you one. Whether you'd divorced him or not, he'd never have been completely out of your life. People like him—soul suckers—they just hang around forever, feeding off other people's misery."

She'd never spoken it aloud either, but her mother had just neatly described how she felt about Chris's killer as well. She hadn't wanted Chris to die, had certainly never wanted him to be murdered. But she was not sorry that he was out of her life, and she was definitely better off as a widow than she would have been as a divorcee. Her mother was right. Divorce wouldn't have been the end of it. He would have dropped back into her life, sprinkling the acid of his presence and infecting everything she ever touched. She knew it.

This way it was over. She'd buried him today and she could finally move on, an action she intended to embrace beginning right now. Jolie felt a slow grin move across her lips.

After all, if Jake kept her out of jail, she'd have a house to decorate.

CHAPTER TWENTY-THREE

HER INSIDES QUIVERING with pent-up anxiety, Sophia patted her hair and smoothed away a non-existent wrinkle from her trendy linen pantsuit as she made her way up Edward's carefully manicured walk. Bulbs, vines and delicate flowers and shrubs bloomed in perfect harmony around his garden and every blade of grass had been tended with razor-perfection.

A closer look at his flower beds showed not a single weed and from the looks of things, he'd made his own mulch because, unlike some of the cheaper bagged varieties, every piece was uniform in shape and size, giving each cultivated inch a more polished quality.

Sophia pursed her lips and reluctantly acknowledged the bit of grudging admiration trying to worm its way into her jealous heart. And he didn't just plant the no-brainers—pinks, petunias and impatiens—he'd chosen finicky plants which required a great deal of time and maintenance, ones that had to be nursed and coaxed.

Edward opened the front door and a welcoming smile spread across his lips and infected those Paul Newman blues. "Ah," he sighed. "I thought I saw a new flower out here. You look lovely, Sophia."

Again she found herself resisting the ridiculous urge to preen. She was in her early sixties. She had stretch marks, varicose veins, wrinkles and cellulite. At best she'd held up well, but she knew she was far from lovely. Nevertheless, she smiled and said thank you, and did her best to hold her ground and not bolt like the frightened coward she suddenly felt like. "I was just admiring your garden, Edward, and I must confess I have to take back every uncharitable thing I've ever said about your being undeserving of the Presidency of the Garden Club." She cast an approving eye around his lawn. "You've done a wonderful job here and from now on when you offer advice, I daresay I'll be listening a little more closely."

Those blue eyes twinkled with mischief and he gave his jaw a thoughtful stroke. "No longer 'insufferable with an exalted opinion of my own wit' then?"

Sophia flushed, but lifted her chin. "That's right. It would appear that you do know it all and I stand corrected."

"Well, I'd like it better if you'd stand inside. Come on in," he told her, opening the door. "My biscuits are going to burn."

"That would be a tragedy," she replied drolly.

He looked back at her over his shoulder and a smile that affected only one side of his mouth shaped his lips. "Tragedy is a bit dramatic, but it would definitely be unfortunate seeing as that's what I promised you for breakfast." His gaze caught and held hers. "Disappointing you would be the tragedy."

His low voice resonated with a combination of innuendo and sincerity and once again her body experienced another slow simmering burn. Sophia knew she had absolutely no business checking into Edward's private affairs, but that hadn't kept her from contacting a good friend who worked at the local doctor's office. She'd asked her to check Edward's charts and, while Sophia had waited with bated breath, the woman had come back on the line with a good report. Everything seemed to be in good working order and he'd never been prescribed any sexual enhancement aids.

She'd hung up the phone, let go a small shuddering breath, then raided her refrigerator until she'd soothed the nerves she'd wrecked by making the call in the first place.

Edward's kitchen was large and spacious with high ceilings, glass-fronted cabinets and antique reproduction appliances. A long trestle table served double duty as a work island and dozens of worn, gleaming pots and pans hung from an old door that had been fashioned with big hooks for easy storage.

The scent of buttery biscuits filled the room and the table had been loaded down with all of her favorite foods, the very ones she'd made for herself the morning he'd shown up and joined her for breakfast.

He saw her looking at the table and a flash of red color hit his cheeks. "I, uh… I just wanted to make sure that I had everything here that you liked."

Touched, Sophia struggled to find her voice. "Thanks, Edward. My mouth thanks you, but my hips are pissed."

He chuckled, the sound warm and intimate in the fragrant kitchen. "There's nothing wrong with your hips. They're perfect." He turned around and tended to a pan of scrambled eggs on the stove. "I should know. I've been admiring them for months."

Sophia blinked. "For months?"

He shot her another look over his shoulder. "I've been coming by your house for months, which is blocks out of the way from my own. What did you think I was doing?"

"Walking for your health."

He grunted. "If I wanted to walk for my health, then I damned sure wouldn't be strolling past your house. Seeing your rump sticking out of a flower bed does things to my old heart that could be downright dangerous at my age."

"Do you have a heart condition?" she asked, grateful for the sentiment but suddenly wary of possible…problems.

"Not in the literal sense, no," he told her cryptically. "I'm healthy as a horse."

Sophia released a relieved sigh. "That's good."

"Thank you. I wasn't aware that you were concerned." He turned around once more and emptied the pan onto an awaiting plate. "At least, I hadn't been until Janice Lowery told me that you'd asked about my general health. She's a friend of mine as well."

Sophia's tongue stuck to the roof of her mouth and every ounce of blood she possessed raced to her face. Her heart tripped and emptying her stomach became a genuine fear. She'd kill her, Sophia decided. The minute she left here, she fully intended to run Janice to ground and rip every salt-and-pepper hair out of her head.

He grinned. "Did I pass muster?"

"You did," Sophia told him tightly. "Right up until this moment." She snatched her purse from the counter and hurried from the room. God, she was so embarrassed. She wanted to crawl into the nearest hole and die.

"Sophia, wait!" Edward called, hurrying after her. "Please wait. I'm sorry. I shouldn't have said anything. I just— Aw, hell, I was flattered and I—"

Sophia felt mortified tears burn the backs of her eyes and, muttering a string of dire curses, darted through the dining room. She'd almost reached the door when Edward caught up with her. He snagged her arm and turned her around.

"Sophia, please," he said softly. "I'm sorry. I shouldn't have said anything. It's just you've given me *hell* all spring and I—" His voice turned into a tortured growl. "You make me crazy. Half the time I can't make up my mind if I want to kiss you or throttle you. You're prickly, but sweet, and you're unlike any woman I've ever known…and I've wanted you for…forever."

Startled by the confession, Sophia glanced up. Edward tenderly cupped her cheek and before she could form a protest—or even prepare herself for that matter—his gaze dropped to her lips, and his mouth followed suit and she suddenly found herself being kissed. Her knees all but buckled and the tears that had been borne of mortification suddenly turned to tears of joy. She tore her mouth away from his. "Your biscuits will burn," she warned breathlessly.

He kissed her lids, then her nose, then the corner of her mouth. "To hell with the biscuits."

Sophia sagged against him, smiled against his lips and with a slow, desperate groan of surrender, she wrapped her arms around his neck and simply gave herself up to the exquisite perfection of the moment.

After all these years of being alone—and being with the wrong man—she'd earned it.

CHAPTER TWENTY-FOUR

JAKE SHIFTED tiredly in his seat, continuing to watch Jolie roll dark gold paint onto her living room walls. The smooth tunes of Norah Jones wafted out her open windows, weaving around his senses.

Wearing a pair of frayed denim cut-offs and a white tank top, her hair pulled up into a messy ponytail, she looked like a poster girl for home-improvement. Watching her stretch and reach, seeing her belly-button play peek-a-boo every time she moved, had turned into a sadistic form of torture for him.

Hell, he should just go home, Jake thought, wearily rubbing a hand over his face. He'd left work this afternoon, had dropped by the barn long enough to feed and determine that tonight probably wasn't going to be the night for Marzipan, then remembering Dean's latest edict to "watch her every move," he'd driven back and parked across the street from her house.

She knew he was there, of course. She'd looked

out the window, seen him sitting there, then when she'd figured out that he'd put her under surveillance, she'd smiled and waggled her fingers at him.

Smart-ass, Jake thought, feeling a faint grin tug at his lips. The best he could tell, other than working on her house and doing away with all the extra office furniture and equipment she didn't need from Marshall Inc., she'd done exactly what she'd told him she planned to do—move on. If it wasn't for the lingering fear that haunted those pale green eyes, he'd buy into her whole unconcerned facade, but he knew better. She might be moving on...but that hadn't kept her from having a healthy fear of going to jail.

He'd checked back with the insurance companies that had covered Chris and so far she didn't seem to be in any hurry to meet with them and satisfy her claim. He'd followed her around town the past couple of days, watching her load her car down with various domestic goods. He'd tailed her to Moore's Furniture on the square, had pulled his truck up in front of the huge glass-paned windows and watched her select her furniture. At one point she'd held up a couple of pillows, pointed at each in turn and quirked a brow, soliciting his opinion.

Typical Jolie, Jake thought. She wasn't going to let him know that she was the least bit worried about who'd killed Chris or about being pinned with his murder. Pretending to be confident in her innocence, she was moving blithely along seemingly without a care in the world, completely oblivious to the fact that her sweet little ass was on the line and that becoming someone's bitch in prison could too easily become a reality if this case didn't break soon.

As he'd predicted, the D.A. had sought him out, wanting to know all of the particulars on the case. Jake had filled him in, making certain that he realized Jolie's alibi was tight, even if everything else had been shaky. But true to form, the D.A. had been skeptical. "If it walks like a duck, talks like a duck, it's a damned duck," he'd argued. Jake had held his ground and presented a host of other suspects—each of which Jake had culled as well, though he'd neglected to share that—and hoped that something significant happened soon. If it didn't, he didn't know what would happen.

The case was getting cold, and frankly, no one seemed particularly interested in seeing Marshall's killer brought to justice, himself included. Nevertheless, a crime had been committed and he was bound by the law to do everything in his power to see that the person responsible was punished to the fullest extent of that law.

Rather than risk Jolie's wrath, he'd covertly

scoped out Fran and ruled her out as a suspect. She'd been at the Methodist Church Bazaar the night of the murder and dozens of people had confirmed her whereabouts. Dean had vouched for Emily, and the mayor's daughter had been off with Tad Ralston, the county agent who'd been trying to solve the mayor's skunk problems. To no avail, Jake thought, grimacing as he remembered the stench. His eyes had watered while he'd waited at the door. Jesus, he didn't know how they stood it. It was awful.

As for working the money angle, Jolie had done such a good job of covering up for most of Chris's antics that the majority of the investors hadn't realized until she'd paid them back in full that Chris had been screwing them. That had derailed that potential train of thought.

Aside from a single green thread and a few fibers that were consistent with the other hand towel left in the bathroom, Marshall's dick had been a dead end as well. He and Mike had canvassed the square, talked to practically every resident in Moon Valley and none of them had seen a thing.

Either the person he was looking for was damned good, or Moon Valley residents were the most unobservant people on the planet. In fact, most people had been more interested in knowing what sort of adhesive had been used to glue the dick to the friggin' statue. Had to have been good glue, Otis Harper had remarked thoughtfully. He'd like to have some of—

Jake started as a knock sounded at his driver's side window. He looked up to see Jolie's smiling, paint-smeared face and swore. Feeling his cheeks flame with embarrassment, he lowered the window.

"You might want to take another course on stealth tactics, Detective," she remarked, her voice laden with droll humor.

"I was thinking."

"I noticed. It looked painful."

"It is painful," Jake told her, shifting uncomfortably. "My ass is numb."

Jolie held up a wet paint brush and cocked her head. "I have a cure. If you're going to have to watch me, the least you could do is help."

Jake smiled at her, shook his head. "Not dressed for it. I could ruin my shirt." As if that would be such a loss. Like he didn't have a dozen more white shirts. What the hell. It kept laundry simple.

To his slack-jawed astonishment, Jolie reached through the window and painted his sleeve. "Oh, darn," she deadpanned, eyes wide in mock innocence. "There goes that excuse."

A stunned chuckle bubbled up his throat. "You're evil, you know that?"

"I prefer resourceful." Eyes twinkling with devilish humor, she jerked her head toward the house. "Come in and help me, you big jerk," she admonished. "You've been sitting out here watching me for hours. What sort of man are you, anyway?"

Jake followed her, letting his gaze drop to her backside and felt an arrow of heat land in his groin. "The kind who hates to paint."

"Oh, you won't feel that way once you're high from the fumes."

Jake sighed. "So long as there's something to look forward to."

"You mean the pleasure of my company isn't enough?" she teased.

Just watching her had been enough, Jake thought, accepting a roller from her. "I'm still mad at you."

He heard a protracted sigh. "I'm sorry."

"Sorry that I'm mad or sorry that you're hiding something from me?"

"Both."

Jake methodically rolled paint onto the wall, admiring the color. "You could remedy that easily enough by telling me what I need to know."

"That's just it," she said, a hint of frustration entering that cool, lyrical voice. "You *don't* need to know. It won't help you, won't do anything for the investigation…but it could hurt a lot of innocent people and I—" She stopped short, dashed a stray strand of hair off her cheek. "I can't be responsible for that."

"Just because you don't think that it's relevant to the investigation doesn't mean that I wouldn't."

"Believe me, Jake. It's not."

He paused and let his gaze trace the familiar slope of her cheek, the delicate arch of her brow. A landslide of emotion and heat swept through him. "If you hadn't hidden everything else, Jo, I might."

She looked away, silently acknowledging the truth of that statement, then growled low in her throat. "I know that I should have told you about the accounts and whatnot, but I just didn't want to deal with the unpleasantness of it all."

His lips curled. "Translate: you didn't want to hear a lecture."

She turned around, darted a look at him and the corner of her mouth tucked into a grin. "That's probably an accurate assessment. But I was just tired of it, dammit. I told you from the get-go that I planned to move on, that I wasn't wasting another minute of my life. Is that so hard to understand?"

"I do understand," Jake told her. "I just wish you'd confided in me."

"We all make mistakes," she said, subtlety reminding him of his. She gestured toward a ladder. "Would you mind helping me move this?"

Jake nodded, grabbed one end and helped her position it where she wanted. For a while they worked without the noise of conversation, merely listened to Norah's smooth voice sing "Come Away With Me" and other poignant ballads, which undoubtedly made them both think about what they'd lost, what they'd missed. Jolie worked on cutting in the trim, occasionally asking for his assistance with the ladder.

When she'd finally finished the last corner, she paused and inspected her handiwork. "You think it's going to need a second coat?"

Without a doubt, Jake thought. He shook his head. "No."

She grinned and he felt that smile land in his heart, then settle behind his zipper. God, she was gorgeous. Simply breathtaking.

"Yes, it does," she said with wry exasperation. "But I'm willing to feed you first. How about I order a pizza?"

He wasn't hungry, but any reason to avoid painting appealed to him, so he nodded. "Pizza sounds good."

Her shrewd gaze narrowed and her smile widened. "You're not even hungry are you?"

"Oh, yes I am. I'm starving." He eagerly set his paint roller aside, affecting a frown. "In fact, I'm gonna faint from hunger. I don't think I can work anymore until I've had something to eat."

Jolie rolled her eyes, then set her brush length-wise over the bowl she'd been working from and started down the ladder. "You're so full of sh—"

She squealed as her foot slipped three rungs from the bottom. Lucky for her, he'd been admiring her ass, otherwise he might not have lunged in time to catch her.

She'd instinctively turned around to brace her fall and landed smack dab against his chest. The impact knocked the breath from his lungs in a startled whoosh, he lost his footing and toppled backward, landing painfully on his previously numb ass, Jolie right on top of him.

Her small body aligned perfectly against his and he barely had time to note the fit of her hips over his groin, the lush mounds of her breasts against his chest before she braced her hands on either side of his head and her eyes widened in shock-delayed humor. Laughter fizzed up her throat in a long infectious stream that made him chuckle, too, and soon they were both howling like a couple of psychotic hyenas. He settled his hands at her waist and absorbed the delectable feel of her shaking frame above his.

After a moment, her laughter petered out and she seemed to realize their position. Her light green gaze darkened to a mossy hue, then dropped to his mouth and she moistened her lips. He caught the faint fluttering of her pulse in her neck, carefully drawing in a vanilla scented breath and resisting the urge to kiss her, to align his mouth to hers and eat every breath she exhaled, to roll her over onto her back and make long, slow beautiful love to her.

The desire was there, of course, the pressing need to firmly root himself between her thighs, but with Jolie it was more than that. Always had been. There was something painfully sweet about being with her, where love met lust and turned the generic act of sex into a commingling of souls, a meeting of the minds, ritual instead of rote.

He wanted to taste her—needed to—more than his next breath, and yet he didn't. That move had to be hers. Given what she'd been through and how he'd indirectly contributed to it, Jake couldn't allow himself to take that decision out of her hands. He was hers for the taking, when and if she was ever ready.

And it wouldn't be tonight, he realized, squashing an immediate sense of disappointment as she ultimately rolled away. She covered the move with another laugh, tried to pretend the awkward moment away. "That was graceless, eh?"

"Not really," Jake told her, forcing a chuckle for her benefit. "You *swan-dived* into me."

"Are you hurt?"

"Yes," he said. He closed his eyes and massaged the bridge of his nose, barely resisted the urge to massage another part of his anatomy. "My painting arm is broken."

She snorted, leaned up on her elbow and glared at him accusingly. "Fraud. You just don't like painting."

He turned his head toward her and offered an unrepentant grin. "There is that."

"Fine," she said with a dramatic sigh. "You can watch me paint. Without my pizza. From your truck."

Jake laughed, lifted his right hand and wiggled it around. "Look at that," he told her, feigning delighted surprise. "I'm healed."

Her lips slid into a wry grin. "A miraculous recovery. I expected as much."

Jake gingerly got to his feet and offered her a hand up. "Must be nice," he told her. "With you, I never know what to expect."

She batted her lashes shamelessly at him. "It's part of my charm."

Indeed it was, Jake thought, hopelessly in love with her. He picked up his roller and set back to work while she called in the pizza.

Indeed it was…

CHAPTER TWENTY-FIVE

JOLIE WALKED outside, waved at Jake who'd been parked at her curb the majority of the day and, smiling, got into her car. Predictably, he dropped his shades in place and fell in behind her. He'd lessened his so-called surveillance over the past couple of days, had taken to driving by a couple of times a day, checking on Marzipan, then coming over after his shift.

Jolie felt a smile tug at her lips. For someone who didn't enjoy painting, he'd shown up each night this week in an old T-shirt and shorts, ready to get started. As a result of his help, they'd managed to get every room in the house painted except for the spare bedroom. He'd mentioned knocking that room out tonight and she'd very casually reminded him of her *bridge* meeting. Those carnal lips had slid into a knowing smile and he'd merely inclined his head. Maybe you could teach me, he'd said, a careless taunt that had made her heart skip an unsteady beat.

Jolie caught sight of him in her rearview mirror and felt a flutter of heat wing around her belly, then nestle between her legs. She let go a stuttering breath. Being with him every night, being able to covertly study the familiar cut of his jaw, those silvery gray eyes, and the way his muscles rippled beneath his shirt as he pushed his hands through those dark chocolate locks had been a feast for her senses. Every move he made was unhurried and sensual and reeked of familiarity. His presence warmed her in neglected places, making her shake like an addict in withdrawal.

The night she'd literally fallen into him had been the sweetest form of torture imaginable. Feeling that hard body beneath hers, that husky intimate laugh breezing across her neck and vibrating her nipples had all but made her come unglued. She'd been mentally praying—wishing—that he'd kiss her, and though she knew he'd wanted to, he'd held back.

As much as Jolie wished he'd have taken the decision out of her hands at the time, in retrospect she appreciated that he hadn't and the respect for her behind the decision. If things moved forward for them, it would be completely up to her. She knew him well enough to realize that he'd held back because he understood her desire to make her own decisions.

It hardly seemed real that Chris was gone and she was actually thinking about a tentative future with

Jake. Madness, she knew, but she couldn't seem to help herself. She'd wanted control of her life and in just under a week she'd managed to put the majority of what Chris had ruined over the course of two years back to rights. She'd sold his car yesterday and, while the house hadn't garnered an offer yet, she knew it was just a matter of time. Hell, whoever bought it was getting the damned thing practically furnished.

Since Jake had been so against her moving things along as swiftly as she had, Jolie had held off meeting with the life insurance agent. She'd been in a hurry to give everybody else's money back and therefore hadn't been too concerned with her own. Once that was done, there wouldn't be anything left to do.

When not working on her house, she'd managed to get her office up and running and fully anticipated officially opening for business in a couple of weeks. She'd already had a couple of potential clients drop by, the majority of them wondering why she hadn't simply converted Marshall Inc. into her headquarters, but as much as she liked the square atmosphere, she thought she'd enjoy the privacy of being one block removed from the hub of activity. She could reap the benefits without being in the middle of things.

Jolie pulled up in front of Meredith's house, snagged her purse and apple dumplings from the car and made her way up the walk. She turned to wave at Jake, who'd pulled in a couple of car lengths behind her, but paused as the thump of music reached her ears.

It didn't take long to recognize the tune and once she did, a bark of laughter erupted from her throat. Gloria Gaynor's "I Will Survive" vibrated through the walls, then practically knocked her down when Meredith opened the door. Decked out in black sweats, her black hat—which had been topped with a party hat—and a kazoo in her hand, Meredith smiled, darted a look over Jolie's shoulder, then spotting Jake, jerked Jolie inside.

"What's he doing?" she shouted above the din. "Why's he out there?"

"He's following me," Jolie explained. "I'm under surveillance." Which admittedly was nice, but a complete waste of his time if he planned on finding the real killer.

Meredith's perfectly lined brows folded into a faint scowl. "Oh, well. Let him sit there. We're going to party."

Jolie followed Meredith into the living room and when she walked in, every member of the FWC whooped with joy. Then they killed Gloria and started singing their own custom version of "Ding Dong the Witch Is Dead!"

"Ding dong the bastard's dead,
the mean old bastard's dead!
Who's old bastard? Jolie's old bastard!
Ding dong—and he was missing his dong—
Ha! Ha! Ha!
The mean old bastard's dead!"

They finished the end with a flourish, dragging "dead" out until Jolie was certain every pair of ears in a ten mile radius had heard them.

Which was particularly unsettling when she knew Jake was outside.

Before she could think about it anymore, however, someone turned the music back up, pressed a drink in her hand, and they formed a train, dancing around the living room.

Like Meredith everyone had donned black—except for her, Jolie thought wryly, who'd apparently missed the memo—and had placed a party hat on top of their regular widow hats. Looking even more lovely than usual—there was a certain glow about her—Sophia cha-cha-cha-ed up next to her, then pulled her out of the line.

"How's everything going, dear?"

"Great," Jolie called above the noise. She thought she'd better tell her about Jake, but Meredith had already beaten her to the punch.

"I've already been outside and taken him a drink and a couple of petite fours—had to practically wrestle the damned things away from Bitsy," she said, exasperated. "I told him that we were having an anniversary party for the Club."

Jolie grinned at her ingenuity. "He bought it?"

She snorted indelicately. "Of course, not," she scoffed. "He's a smart man...but he's got too much class to argue with an old woman."

Ah, yes, Jolie thought, inclining her head. That sounded about right.

"Anyway," Sophia told her, "tonight is your night, dear. This is your 'official' party."

She took Jolie's hand and tugged her toward the living room, leading her to a chair that had been moved to the middle of the room where Sophia typically stood, then urged her to sit down. Somewhat baffled, Jolie sat patiently while the rest of the members crowded into the room.

Sophia waited for someone to turn down the music, then snapped at Bitsy—who was doing a disjointed Egyptian Walk around the room while trying to eat a piece of coconut cake—to do it. *"For the love of God, Bitsy, would you turn that down?"*

Startled, Bitsy stopped and quickly moved to do as she asked. When the music was finally turned off, Sophia smoothed her hair, gathered her thoughts, and smiled. "Now then. As we all know, making the transition to Official status is an important milestone in a Future Widows' Club member's life. It's a rebirth of sorts, a new beginning. From here on out, Jolie will enjoy the privileges of her new status. She'll be revered, admired, even pitied by the unenlightened who don't realize that she's better off." Sophia shook her head at this presumed tragedy, then continued. "Tonight, we'll celebrate her newfound freedom by presenting her with this pin—" Sophia reached down and attached a small rhinestone hat and gloves pin— the same logo she'd noted on her handbook, Jolie realized—onto her collar "—and party!"

Bitsy cranked the music back up—the Dixie Chicks' "Goodbye Earl"—and, like her first meeting, everyone came by and paid their respects once again.

"May he rot in hell."

"May he never rest in peace."

"I envy your loss."

Bitsy started the train again, someone pressed another drink in Jolie's hand, and the entire congregation proceeded to get smashed, herself included. Meredith proved very adept at making Daiquiris, and Cora, of all people, ended up doing a table dance be-

fore the night was over. Most of the ladies had either
planned to spend the night or had arranged for someone to pick them up, but Jolie, unaware that she'd
need to do one or the other, ended up walking outside and asking Jake to take her home.

His eyes widened comically. *"You're drunk?"*

Jolie's lips were numb and the warm, languid
slide of the alcohol in her blood loosened her tongue.
"Yes," she said, climbing clumsily into the cab of his
truck. "I think I am."

Jake pulled away from the curb. "Some bridge
club," he muttered. "Tell me, Jo. Do you usually get
hammered at these meetings?"

Jolie let her head loll back against the seat. "Nope.
First time."

"Well, that's a relief."

"Poor Jake. You've been bored out here, haven't
you?" She glanced at him, then stared transfixed at
the way the dashlights illuminated the strangely
beautiful lines of his face. "You should be looking
for the real killer, not wasting your time with me."

He shot her an inscrutable, almost wistful look.
"Being with you—or even near you—isn't a waste
of time," he returned softly.

Her silly heart melted. That was too sweet not to
offer a small reward, so she leaned over and pressed
a kiss against his woefully familiar cheek. "I've

missed you," Jolie told him, then unable to make her neck support her head any longer, she let it drop against his shoulder and dozed off, the comforting scent of Jake and fresh hay in her nostrils.

The next morning when she awoke, she found herself in her bed, stripped down to her bra and undies and a note attached to her pillow.

I've missed you, too. Yours, Jake.

CHAPTER TWENTY-SIX

"HOW DO YOU THINK it's going?"

Jake dropped into one of the chairs flanking Dean's desk and tried to think of some way to tell his boss that he'd researched every angle and wasn't any closer to finding who'd killed Marshall than he'd been the night the man had been murdered.

He finally shrugged helplessly. "It's going…nowhere," he admitted, letting go a resigned whoosh of air. "I've followed every lead, checked every alibi, followed procedure and…nothing. Nobody saw anything, nobody knows anything. It's as if a ghost waltzed into that house and shot him."

Dean tapped his pen against his desk. "What about the penis?"

Yeah, what about it? Jake wanted to ask. All he knew was that Todd hadn't found anything significant. He'd refrained from asking what the evidence tech had ultimately done with it for fear he might not want to know.

Jake told him about the thread and the fibers Todd had found on Marshall's dick. "That's all I've got, Dean, and it's not from lack of trying." Jake ticked off everybody that he'd investigated, then shook his head. "I don't know what else to do."

"Sounds to me like you've done everything you can," Dean told him, his voice measured.

Jake knew he was supposed to infer something from that careful tone, but exactly what he didn't know. He arched a brow, silently asking his boss to spell it out for him.

"I'd say you don't have any other choice but to let this case go inactive, at least until new information surfaces."

"She didn't do it, Dean," Jake felt compelled to point out.

"I don't think she did."

So long as they were on the same page, Jake thought. Still, he couldn't help but feel like he hadn't done enough, that he should have looked harder. Quite frankly, he'd gotten so caught up in keeping Jolie under surveillance—translate: watching her for the sheer sport of it—that he hadn't devoted as much time to the case as he probably could have. Then again, he did think that he'd followed every possible lead. There simply wasn't enough evidence to continue.

Which meant that she was finally in the clear.

Jake took a deep breath, but when another thought surfaced the air stuck in his throat. If she was in the clear, then he didn't have to stick to her like glue anymore. He didn't have any legitimate reason to keep hanging around her, absorbing her presence, sharing her space.

Except for the reason that he was still head over heels in love with her.

Last night when she'd leaned over and kissed his cheek, Jake had felt the world shift back into brighter focus. The innocent unaffected gesture might have landed on the side of his face, but he'd felt it all the way down to the bottoms of his feet. His belly had filled with air, then flipped, and a shiver had worked its way up his spine.

And she'd barely touched him.

Christ.

He ran a shaky hand through his hair. "What about the D.A.?" Jake asked.

Dean leaned back in his chair. "I'll talk to him."

He didn't know what Dean could tell him that Jake hadn't already, but he supposed his boss's opinion carried more weight than his. At any rate, he didn't care because it was over. She was safe and that's all that mattered. He thanked Dean, then grabbed his portfolio and made the trek home. He'd planned on following the routine he'd started this week—change clothes, check on the horse, then head back to town, to her house specifically—but after watching Marzipan for a few minutes, Jake decided that going anywhere tonight was out of the question. He unclipped his cell from his belt and keyed in Jolie's number. "It's happening," he told her. "Do you still want to come out?"

JOLIE WHEELED her car down the narrow dirt drive that would deliver her to Jake's house and felt the strangest sense of anxiety and homecoming push into her throat. She knew this land and its owner as well as she knew herself and yet something about driving here now made her feel like her insides were too big for her body. She topped a little hill and, backlit by a beautiful setting sun, the house and barn rose in the distance.

The old farmhouse replica was white with green shutters, with full sweeping porches and tall multi-paned windows. Instead of going with modern asphalt shingles, Jake had opted for a green metal roof, one that would make beautiful music when it rained. A bittersweet pang squeezed her chest. From the looks of things, he'd built precisely what they'd planned. He could have modified things on the inside, Jolie knew, but if he'd kept the facade the same, then she thought it was relatively safe to assume that he'd left everything else as it was as well.

She pulled around back, close to the barn, then snagged the picnic basket she'd packed from the back seat. Evidently hearing her drive up, Jake stepped into the wide doorway of the barn.

"Hey," he called.

Jolie smiled, gestured toward the basket as she made her way toward him. "I thought we might get hungry."

Wearing a pair of faded jeans, beat-up boots and a navy blue T-shirt with a hole in the sleeve, he walked out and took the basket from her. "Thanks. Since it's her first, we could be in for a long night."

That's what she'd figured. As Jolie fell into step beside him, she felt the brush of his sleeve against her arm. A tingle hit her breasts, causing the air to thin in her lungs. "Er...how's she doing?"

Jake set the basket on a tack table, walked over to Marzipan's stall and put a boot up on the bottom rail of her door. "She can't get comfortable. Keeps circling, twitching her tail."

Jolie moved in beside him, put a hand over the top of the door and, throat tight with emotion, called the horse. Her ears pricked at the sound of Jolie's voice, then she walked over and nudged her muzzle beneath Jolie's palm.

Smiling, she rubbed the horse's velvety nose. "Look at you, Mama," Jolie told her softly. "Big, beautiful girl," she soothed. The horse sidled closer for more attention, nipped at Jolie's hair.

A deep masculine chuckle sounded beside her. "Looks like she's missed you."

Stroking her neck, Jolie darted a glance at Jake. "It's a feeling that's reciprocated." She paused, scoping out some of the other stalls. "So who's the proud papa?"

"Smoke."

Jolie turned her attention back to the horse. "Ah," she sighed. "Then we can expect a beautiful baby then, eh?"

Seemingly unable to stand still any longer, Marzipan resumed her pacing, absently nibbled at the feed in her bin.

Jake picked up the picnic basket and pilfered through what she'd brought.

"If you're expecting prime rib, then you're out of luck," she said. "I brought what I had on hand—peanut butter and banana sandwiches, chips and beer."

Jake looked up and a slow grin slid across those incredibly sexy lips. "Ah," he sighed. "A feast fit for a king."

Jolie rolled her eyes and helped him spread a horse blanket on the ground in front of Marzipan's stall. "Does that make you the king, then?"

He laughed. "That goes without saying."

"I suppose so," she agreed. "You've always been a royal pain the ass."

He opened a beer and handed it to her, then tutted under his breath. "Ah, now. That's a fine way to talk to the man who's saved yours."

Jolie bit into her sandwich and shot him a look. "What are you talking about?"

"I talked with Dean today."

"Oh?" she asked, intrigued by an indiscernible note in his voice.

"Yeah. He told me he thought that Marshall's case should go inactive until new leads or evidence surfaces."

Jolie frowned. "Inactive? What does that mean?"

"It means the case isn't closed, but we're no longer *actively* pursuing it." He smiled at her, but something about that half-hearted grin seemed…off. "In laymen's terms, it means you're in the clear." He took another bite of his sandwich.

"Oh," Jolie said, her eyes widening as the import sunk in. *Now* it was over. She felt her spine sag with relief. Her gaze slid to Jake's impassive profile and the reason he'd seemed off about the new status of the case surfaced belatedly in her sluggish mind.

If she was in the clear…then there was no reason for him to "stick to her like glue" anymore.

A sickening sensation swelled in her gut, pushing the bite of sandwich she'd just taken back up her throat.

No reason for him to come to her house every night.

No reason for him to be with her.

Jolie knew that she should say something, should pretend she was happy that she was no longer the prime suspect in a murder investigation, but she couldn't seem to muster the enthusiasm for the required response. The silence swelled between them, a grim reminder of the wedge that had been in place just a little over a week ago. She swallowed a whimper and tried to steady her suddenly shaking hands.

God, she didn't want to go back to that. She wanted to go back to him, for them to find their way back to each other.

Jake took a long draw from his beer, and then that silvery gaze drifted to her, causing her breath to hitch. "There's something that I want to say to you that's long overdue."

Jolie knew what he wanted to say, knew that it had to be said for them to move forward and, God, how she'd waited for it. She felt tears burn the backs of her lids and nodded at him.

"I'm sorry," he said simply. He didn't elaborate because he didn't have to. They both knew what had happened, both knew that he'd been primarily at fault. "I don't know what the hell I was thinking," he told her, his voice riddled with self-disgust, "and if it makes you feel any better, I've regretted asking for that time more than you can ever know." A bitter laugh spilled from his mouth, punctuating the truth of that statement. "So much more than you can ever know."

Every cell in her body warmed with delight and once again she was hit with the urge to simply rest her head on his shoulder, to feel those beautiful hands against her face. Jolie took a pull from her own beer. "Oh, I think I've got a pretty good idea. I've certainly regretted some choices I made, one in particular." She shot him a tentative look, then asked him the one thing that she'd always wondered. "Why'd you ask for it, Jake?" She moistened her lips. "Were you that unsure of me?"

She felt his soft gaze trace her face. "Oh, babe, I was never unsure of you. I was unsure of myself." He picked up a piece of hay and twirled it around his fingers. "After your dad died, I guess it all just sort of hit me, you know, how important I was in your life…and I wasn't sure I could live up to the expectation. I was afraid I'd fail you." He shrugged helplessly. "I got scared, and thought I'd better get my head on straight." He looked away and swore softly. "Stupid."

"You were stupid for thinking that you'd ever fail me."

"But I did," Jake said.

"Only because you walked away. If you'd stuck it out, I would have been happy no matter what." Jolie swallowed, then made a face. "Besides, you weren't the only one to blame. I should have had enough faith in you to wait it out. Instead, I got pissed off, then decided to get even." She grimaced. "And look what happened."

Seeming to mull it over, Jake took another drink. "And I regret that, too."

"We were both stupid," she said magnanimously.

He inclined his head.

She slid him a smile, relieved that they'd had this talk. "But you were more stupid."

He laughed. "Gotta have the last word, don't you?"

She shrugged unrepentantly. "Just tell it like it is."

A noise from the stall drew their attention and Jake's gaze sharpened, and then he bolted into action. He leapt up, then offered her a hand. "She's down," he said quietly. "Here we go."

An excited thrill whipped through her as she moved into place next to Jake. Marzipan had indeed lain down, fortunately in the center of the stall.

Jake lowered his head toward hers and she caught a whiff of his woodsy cologne. "That's a contraction," he whispered, inadvertently sending a chill down her spine.

Jolie watched, not realizing she was holding her breath until she was forced to let it go. Then something amazing happened. She grabbed Jake's arm. "I see hooves!"

He chuckled softly at her. "That's a good sign. Hooves first, then head, then the rest of the body."

She moved in closer, inadvertently—but oh so pleasantly—putting herself in front of him. Jake dropped his chin on top of her head, wrapped his arms around her waist and absorbed her weight against him. Jolie felt his breath leak slowly out of him, then her eyes fluttered shut, and she drank in the sensation of coming home. *This* was where she belonged, she thought.

Right here. With him.

Just as he'd predicted, the foal's head emerged next and though the baby was covered in placenta, it was easily recognizable as Marzipan's. "Oh, it's white," she said softly.

"I wouldn't be so sure," Jake hedged. "We'll have to wait until it's dry to really tell."

"Come on, Mama," Jolie softly crooned to the horse. "Almost there."

And then it was. The rest of the body emerged.

Marzipan made quick work of the placenta and the baby horse started to move around.

Absolutely awed and delighted, Jolie impulsively turned and hugged Jake. "Oh, my God," she breathed, bouncing on the balls of her feet. "That was…amazing."

Jake laughed, wrapping his arms even more firmly around her. His lips curling into an inherently sexy grin, he looked down and those twinkling silvery-gray eyes captured hers. And in that instant the mood changed. Her belly trembled, gooseflesh raced down her back, and the air leaked out of her lungs.

The hug might have been impulsive, but her kiss wouldn't be. She wanted him—wanted *them*—and wanted him to know it. Jolie reached up and tenderly framed his face with her hands, watching as his lids dropped at her touch, then ever so gently—reverently—pressed her lips to his.

The feeling was so exquisite, so perfect that for a moment she forgot to breathe.

The sky could have fallen, the earth could have opened up beneath her feet and she wouldn't have noticed.

Jake sighed into her mouth and she savored that breath, then slipped her tongue against his and silently asked for more.

With a low growl of almost desperate approval,

he pulled her closer, tunneled his fingers into her hair, then tilted her head to better align their mouths. He fed at her, sucked at her tongue, her bottom lip, then came back for more.

"God, I've missed you," he growled softly. "Missed you so damned much."

Jolie's heart melted…along with other parts of her. Her nipples tingled, her sex pulsed and every nerve seemed to vibrate. She couldn't feel enough of him, couldn't taste enough of him. It had been so long, so very, very long.

To her immense regret and frustration, Jake very tenderly ended the kiss, and breathing heavily, rested his forehead against hers. "Will you spend the night with me?" he asked softly. "Stay here and let me love you?"

Feeling a slow smile drift across her lips, Jolie nodded.

Jake kissed her again, seemingly unable to keep from tasting her. Then after checking on Marzipan and the foal, he threaded his fingers through hers and took his time leading her through the house.

As impatient as she was, she couldn't help but appreciate that he wanted to take things slowly, savor their reunion and honor it with the respect that it deserved. Her hand in his, he led her through the house, and just as she'd suspected, he'd stayed true to their plan, almost as if he'd prepared it for her return. Pressed copper tiles lined the ceiling in the kitchen and a small wood-burning fireplace sat in the corner of the room. The living room had been equipped with built-in bookshelves and big open windows that caught the late afternoon breeze.

It was beautiful, Jolie thought. Every bit as wonderful as she'd always imagined it would be. Despite the fact that she'd spent the past couple of weeks making her little house on Lelia Street a home, she suddenly didn't care if she ever went back there. This was where she belonged.

Right here, with him.

Jake tugged her toward the bedroom. "Do you have any idea how many times I've imagined you here?" he said, his gaze, hot with desire and warm with affection, slipping over her, feasting on her. Loving her. "How many times I've been driven from this room—this house—because being in it without you felt so wrong?"

Jolie felt tears mist her eyes. "Oh, Jake," she said unable to elaborate as her heart pushed into her aching throat. She knew what he meant because she'd felt it, too. She'd been like a ship without an anchor for years, drifting miserably through life without him, and the idea that she didn't have to anymore—that he was hers again—burrowed into her tripping heart and sent a warm tingle to her very fingertips.

He slipped the pad of his thumb over her cheek, guided her into the bathroom where he turned on the tap and adjusted the shower, then slowly set about undressing her. His fingers skimmed over her rib cage as he pulled off her shirt, sent gooseflesh racing up her back as he unbuttoned her shorts and pushed them down her hips. Soon she was naked, mesmerized by the sweet sensual brush of his hot hands slipping reverently over her body.

It had been so long and yet being with him was like stepping back into a long, slow beautiful dance. Easy, effortless…perfect.

Her breasts heavy, her sex wet and her heart racing, Jolie tugged his shirt from his waistband, drew it over the top of his head and cast it aside, then drank in the sight of him. Soft skin, hard perfectly sculpted muscle and bone. Crisp masculine hair, flat male nipples. Familiar. Loved. Hers.

She offered her mouth up for a kiss and savored the intoxicating taste of his tongue against hers, blinking back another hot rush of redeeming tears as he gently nudged her into the glassed-in shower. She let her hands drift over his back, feeling the muscle bunch beneath her fingertips. Then he bent and latched his greedy mouth onto her breast, pulling a startled gasp from deep in her throat.

Jolie closed her eyes and arched her back, purposely pushing her aching nipple farther into his mouth. His masculine growl vibrated against her, sending a cascade of hot fizzies through her blood, all of which raced to her heavy womb. She could feel his hot length prod her belly and purposely opened her legs and rocked her hips forward, pushing him through her drenched folds, then gasped when he bumped the most sensitive part of her.

Jake drew back, and his fevered gaze tangled with hers. "I've dreamed about this," he confessed, his voice a sweet rough whisper. "I wanted to go slowly, but I—"

"Don't," Jolie said, rocking against him once more. She didn't want to go slowly. She wanted to feel him deep inside her, desired that connection more than her next breath. She'd missed him so much and needed him even more. "We've got time, right?"

He knew what she was asking. What she wanted. Jake's gaze softened, drifted lovingly over her face, then he very carefully, very slowly lifted her up and pushed into her. Her lungs deflated as he slid into her and wrapping her arms around him, she clenched her feminine muscles, claiming him as her own. "All the time in the world, Jo," he said, wincing with pleasure as he filled her. "And you own every second."

Her eyes misted with emotion and he leaned forward and sipped up her tears. "I love you," he murmured. He bent and kissed her again. "Here," he said, his voice a soft husky whisper fraught with emotion. "Let me show you."

And as the water beat down upon them, washing away their mistakes, he did.

CHAPTER TWENTY-SEVEN

"Thank God," Sophia muttered irritably as the mayor's car finally pulled out of the drive. She, Bitsy and Meredith had made a point of learning his schedule and this was the only night of the week that both he and his wife were gone. They had a standing reservation at Zeus', which gave Sophia plenty of time to make sure that the coast was clear before she left her hiding place next to the garage and moved behind the heavy shrubbery around the foundation of the house. Yew, Sophia thought, battling her way inside. If she ever planted another hedge, she'd definitely plant yew.

Once in position, she lifted the scarf from around her neck and slipped it up over her nose. She didn't know why she bothered anymore. The stench of skunk was so horrible that she'd had to start throwing away her clothes after she came here. Honestly, she didn't know how they stood it. If it had been her house, she'd have moved out a long time ago.

Frankly, she'd hoped that Greene would come to his senses before it had come back around to her turn, but true to his ignorant, asinine form, the mayor had attended the Garden Club meeting this morning and bestowed another Beautification Award to yet another city council member, one whose idea of gardening extended to bought potted plants—*blasphemy!*—and plastic pink flamingoes.

It was outside of enough.

She, Bitsy—who'd ridden her new Pocket Rocket to the meeting—and Meredith, had gotten together after the meeting, and fuming, Meredith had given her their skunk attractant. If it wouldn't make too much noise, Sophia would fill her Shop-Vac and blow the stuff under the house so thick that every skunk in the state would congregate there, but alas it would make too much racket, so she stuck to the usual method. After duck walking around the house, she opened the foundation vents and starting tossing handfuls underneath. At least it was good exercise, she thought, deciding that she'd have another slice of cake when she got home.

Besides, over the past couple of days, she'd been getting a *different* kind of workout. Sophia's lips slid into a smile and she barely suppressed a giggle. She'd never been a giggler.

Or at least she hadn't until she'd started having sex again.

And not just any kind of sex. Wonderful, sweaty, down and dirty, sometimes tender sex. That first kiss from Edward had done something to her. Flipped an on switch that she hadn't known she possessed.

One minute he'd been pressing his lips to hers, and the next minute they were in his bed going at it like a couple of teenagers who were trying to get laid before anyone got home. It had been wild and wicked and later, when she'd begun to get embarrassed over her rash behavior, Edward had smiled at her, then kissed her again. "We're old," he'd said. "We don't have to play by the usual rules."

And he'd been right. She could be dead by the time they finished what would be considered a proper courtship. Furthermore, she'd waited long enough. She didn't want to wait anymore.

A flashlight blinked on right in front of her, blinding her, and with a startled yelp, she fell backward on her ass. What the hell?

"Good evening, Sophia."

Edward?

Horrified, Sophia scrambled up and goggled at him. "What— How—"

"I followed you." His gaze dropped to the bag in

her hand and he chuckled softly. "Catnip. Very crafty. I suspected as much."

Sophia had never been good with feminine wiles, so when she found herself in this horrible position, she didn't even bother. Instead, she threatened him. "Look, Edward. I don't know what you hope to gain by following me here, but if you've enjoyed our recent exercise—"

"Exercise?"

"You know what I mean," she snapped, blushing to the roots of her hair.

"It's sex, Sophia. We're having sex."

Though they were hidden behind eight feet of dense shrubbery, Sophia glanced around to make sure no one could see them. "Would you hush, please?" she begged, scandalized. "Sweet Jesus. What the hell are you doing here?"

He blinked at her. "I came to help."

Once again she found herself dumbfounded. "What?"

"Jimmy Pickens, the Beautification Award?" he scoffed, his usually amiable face dressed in a frown. "The man doesn't know his mulch from molasses. It's outrageous." He reached for the bag. "Give me some of that, would ya? I'll take the other side of the house."

True to his word, Edward moved around to the

other side and left a shocked but delighted Sophia squatted behind the mayor's shrubs.

That settles it, she thought as the smell of skunk all but choked her. She'd found her man.

After all, it wasn't just any guy who'd be willing to vandalize with her.

CHAPTER TWENTY-EIGHT

"AMAZING, ISN'T IT?" Jake asked. "Just a couple of weeks old and already the little guy is showing attitude."

Marzipan's colt, whom they'd named Ash because he'd ended up being a paler version of his father, galloped clumsily around the enclosure on tall, spindly legs.

Jolie chuckled, pressing her head against his upper arm, and the tender, unexpected warmth moved into his chest.

Contentment, Jake realized.

For the first time since they'd broken up, he was happy. Despite the two-year gap in their relationship, amazingly they'd picked up almost precisely where they'd left off, only at a better place because they both knew how precious their time together—their relationship, specifically—was.

Since the evening the colt was born, they hadn't

spent a night apart. For all the work that Jolie had done on her little house, she'd easily started calling his place home—which was only fitting because it should have been hers all along—and had quickly relegated the Lelia Street house as a full-fledged office.

Aside from the bed—which they'd left to accommodate nooners—everything else had been moved to the farm. Coming home to her was the highlight of his day. Be it in sweats or a negligee—and admittedly he had a thing for the black merry widow—when he walked through that door, she made him feel like she'd been waiting for him all day, whether she had been or not. Those slim arms would come around his waist, she'd lean up and kiss his chin, and regardless of what had happened during the course of the day, at that moment, everything became right in his world.

Because he was with her.

Jake curled his arm around her neck, propelling her reluctantly away from the paddock. "Come on. I've got a surprise for you."

Her hip bumped his as they walked along. "You do? What is it?"

"If I told you it wouldn't be a surprise."

He opened the truck door for her and waited for her to slide in. "Can't fault a girl for tryin', can you?"

Jake joined her in the truck, aimed it toward one of their favorite hang-outs and waited for her to realize where they were going. When it turned off on Rabbit Trail Lane, she figured it out and sent him a sidelong glance. "The fire tower?" she asked, surprised. "Wow," she breathed. "I haven't been out here in years."

Him either. He hadn't been able to go once they'd broken up. It had been too hard. He and Jolie had spent hours up in the loft, had plotted, planned, necked and loved up there and somehow making the trek up the stairs alone had never been something he could do.

He wheeled the truck off the main road and followed the rutted dirt lane until they were parked right next to it. Jolie didn't wait for him to open the door, but got out, shaded her eyes and looked up. "Yep. It's still tall."

Jake felt a chuckle bubble up his throat. "What? You think it's gonna shrink?"

She shot him a droll look. "Smart ass."

He put a hand over his heart, pretending to be wounded. "You go first," he said as they walked to the steps.

She turned, green eyes twinkling with warm affection. "So you can catch me if I fall?"

That was the plan, Jake thought, falling in behind

her. They'd always done it that way. She went up first, so that he could catch her, and he came down first for the very same reason. He wanted his body between her and possible danger.

Jolie hurried up ahead of him and mere minutes later they were at the top looking out over Moon Valley. It was gorgeous. The late afternoon sun gilded the trees and sparkled over the river, painting it bright orange.

Jolie braced her elbows against the rail and let go a soft sigh that hissed through his blood. Jake moved in behind and wrapped his arms around her.

"I'm not going to fall," she admonished softly.

"I know that," he told her. "I just want to hold you."

In fact, he wanted to hold her forever. He'd proposed to her in this very spot when they were sixteen, and somehow it seemed only fitting that they revisit it for the encore. Jake gripped her shoulders and slowly turned her around, then pulled in a shuddering breath and groped in his front pocket for the ring he'd placed there.

She gasped when she saw it and her hands flew to her mouth. "Oh, Jake," she said, her voice clogged with emotion.

He chuckled nervously, took her hand and slipped it on her finger. "You're gonna marry me."

She blinked, smiled. "Is that a proposal?"

He cocked his head. "More like an edict."

She pulled back and glared at him. *"Oh, really."*

"Someone told me to start as I meant to go on." He winced. "It's not gonna work, is it? The whole lord-of-the-manor, do-as-I-say-woman approach?"

She ducked her head and bit her lip to hide a smile. "No."

Jake heaved a dramatic sigh. "Fine. In that case, Jolie Michelle Caplan…will you marry me?"

Her misty eyes searched his. "Yes," she breathed, then tilted her chin up and offered him her lips. He didn't know how long they kissed, how long they stood there. Time, at least in this dimension of happiness, didn't exist.

When the sun finally slipped beneath the tree tops, Jake decided they'd better go down. He placed another lingering kiss on her mouth, then reluctantly made the trip back to the ground.

He was debating the merit of going out for dinner versus staying in and feasting on her, when he opened the car door and her purse fell to the ground, spilling all the contents.

Jake swore. "Sorry," he muttered and instantly dropped down and starting gathering up her things. He picked up a compact, a tube of lipstick, her wallet and…his gaze zeroed in on a little pink book with a hat and gloves on the cover, similar to the pin she'd taken to wearing since the night she'd gotten hammered at her so-called bridge meeting.

"Don't worry about…" Her voice trailed off as she looked up and saw what he held. She swallowed. "Jake, could I have that back, please?"

Jake looked away, summoning patience. This was the key to what she'd been hiding, he knew it. And yet despite the fact that she'd just agreed to marry him, she still wanted to keep secrets? "Jolie, you can trust me. Let me prove it," he implored.

Looking like she couldn't decide whether to puke or bolt, she chewed her bottom lip and whimpered.

"*Jolie.*"

She finally met his gaze. "Jake, if you look inside that little book, you have to swear to me that you'll never—and I repeat *never*—repeat a word of it to another living soul."

Geez, from the way she was carrying on you'd think she had the map to the Holy Grail in there. Jake nodded. "Okay."

She let go a breath. "Then you can look at it. But brace yourself," she added direly.

Jake flipped the little book open, read the title page and felt his eyes widen in shock. "*The Future Widows' Club?* What the hell is the Future Widows' Club?"

"Read on," she said miserably. "You'll figure it out."

Five minutes later, he closed the little book and though he knew what it was—and better still why she'd added the life insurance, checked out the burial plans and bought the outfit—he wasn't any closer to understanding it. "Let me get this straight," Jake said, trying to wrap his mind around the concept. "You're in a secret society of women who are *anxiously waiting* for their husband's to die?"

She nodded.

He frowned. "And this is where you were the night Chris was murdered? At one of these meetings?"

She nodded again.

"Christ." Jake looked away. "Jolie, for the love of God, why didn't you think this was relevant?"

"Because I didn't do it."

"I know that. Still…"

"I needed them," she said simply. "I was only a member for a couple of weeks before Chris died, but they were the best weeks of my life in the past two years." Seemingly exasperated, she looked away. "You're a guy. You're just not going to get it. I didn't want Chris to be dead, not really…but until I could file for divorce it was the best thing I had." She swallowed. "And it's all they've got. You can't take it away from them."

Knowing how miserable she'd been, Jake did understand. Did he agree with it? No. But, in all honesty, he didn't see the harm. He let go a breath. "I just have one question."

She looked up and quirked a cautious brow. "What?"

"Are you going to remain a member when *I'm* your husband?"

Her lips curled and she pulled a lazy shrug. "Lifetime membership," she said. "But I'll be mentoring to future widows rather than preparing to be one."

Jake cocked his head. "Fair enough, I suppose."

She gazed at him questioningly. "That's it? That's all you've got to say about it?"

"Was I supposed to say more? They're not hurting anybody, are they?"

"No."

"Then I don't see the problem."

A slow grin spread across her lips and those pale green eyes danced with affection. "I love you."

"I know," he said, placing a quick but tender kiss on her lips. "Which is the only reason you get to keep *playing bridge.*"

EPILOGUE

Six months later...

"I'LL BE HOME before nine."

Jolie's heart warmed as Jake kissed her cheek and then rubbed her belly. "You'd better be," he told her. "Mothers-to-be need their rest." He frowned. "And try not to get too upset, would you? Are you sure you don't want me to come with you? I could—"

Jolie blinked back tears and shook her head. "No. You can't. You know that." No one in the FWC was aware that Jake knew about them. They'd worry, and in light of recent events, they had all of that they could handle at the moment. Jolie swallowed tightly.

They'd buried Bitsy today.

"At least let me take you. You can call when you're ready and I'll come pick you up."

"I can drive, Jake," she said. "I'm only pregnant, not on medication."

"I know. I'd just feel better if—"

She gave him another peck and grabbed her purse. "I'll be fine. Don't worry."

Jolie slid behind the wheel and made her way to Meredith's on autopilot. She still couldn't believe it, couldn't believe that Bitsy was really gone. Granted Jolie had known her for a little over six months, but she'd grown very fond of the eccentric older woman. But the worst part was looking at Sophia and Meredith. They were shattered, particularly Meredith who'd warned Bitsy about getting the little motorcycle which had ultimately caused her death. Too vain to wear her glasses beneath the helmet, she'd crashed it through Dilly's Bakery. The impact hadn't killed her, but the heart attack which had immediately followed had.

Sophia had come up to Jolie at the funeral and told her that Bitsy's attorney had been to see her and that apparently Bitsy had left a box to be opened in the event of her death. Per Bitsy's written instructions, only Sophia, Meredith, Jolie and curiously, Sadie, were allowed to be present when the box was opened. Meredith had asked her to come early tonight. They were going to go through it before the rest of the FWC arrived. Jolie couldn't imagine what on earth could be in the box that could pertain to her, but wasn't about to ignore one of Bitsy's last wishes.

Eyes puffy and her face generally wracked with

grief, Meredith answered Jolie's knock. "Come in, dear," she said. "We're gonna open it in the back parlor."

Jolie nodded and somberly followed her to a room she'd never been in before. Windows lined the back wall, which overlooked a small enclosed garden with a big brick barbeque pit. "How are you feeling?" she asked, no doubt referring to the pregnancy.

Jolie managed a genuine smile. "Huge." Finding out that she was pregnant with Jake's baby had been a dream come true. She'd taken a broken road, but had finally ended up on the right one.

With him.

It seemed like a lifetime ago that she'd been involved with Chris, embroiled in a horrible nightmare of a marriage. As a result of that disaster, there wasn't a day that went by that she wasn't thankful for Jake, for his love and the relationship they shared.

He completed her.

There were times when she just looked at him and her heart would expand and she could barely catch her breath. Times when he dozed off, and she lay awake in their bed just so she could watch him sleep. Times when she woke him up because sleeping was the furthest thing from her mind. Be it merely holding hands or making love, he moved her in a way that defied reason and trumped logic. She could feel him in her bones, in her blood, and knowing that they'd created this little life inside her belly was a divine joy that often brought tears to her eyes.

Managing to look both strong and shattered, Sophia stood when they walked in. "Hello, dear."

Jolie's eyes misted and she crossed the room and hugged her. "I'm so sorry," she said, knowing it was inadequate. She couldn't even imagine a life without her best friend, couldn't think of going on in a world where Sadie didn't exist. As if on cue, Sadie made her way into the room.

"Thanks for coming, Sadie," Meredith told her.

Looking slightly bewildered, Sadie nodded, then sent Jolie a curiously nervous look.

Sophia pulled in a bolstering breath. "Well, the suspense has been killing me all day, so let's just go ahead and get it over with. Knowing Bitsy, it's her damned coupons," she said, her voice a poignant cross between a laugh and a sob.

Openly crying, Meredith giggled. "You open it, Sophia."

Sophia nodded, picked up a pair of scissors and cut into the box, then lifted the lid and pulled out a letter.

"Dear girls,
If you're reading this letter, then I'm dead.

(Well, that goes without saying, doesn't it?) Anyway, now that I'm gone there's no reason to keep hiding these things from you. In this box you will find some things that, at first, will appear odd—a couple of syringes, a crochet mallet, a gun, a pair of scissors and a bath towel."

Sophia looked up and frowned, then resumed reading.

"For the past decade or so I've kept a secret, one that I knew that I'd have to take to my grave. (Somebody see to it every once in a while, would you? I like daisies.) Sophia, Meredith, I know you think your husbands—and even mine—died of natural causes. Well, you thought wrong. I killed them. A healthy shot of vitamin K induced those random heart attacks mine and yours had, Sophia, and the crocket mallet sent your husband down that mountain, Meri. (He was drunk. The damned fool would have eventually done it to himself anyway, goin' on all those infernal nature hikes.)"

Meredith inhaled sharply, Sophia's face had gone chalk white and Jolie had had to find a place to sit.

She knew what was coming, but she simply couldn't believe it.

Sweet little scattered Bitsy? A cold-blooded killer?

Her gaze shot to Sadie, who seemed curiously reluctant to look at her.

"As for you, Jolie, I just felt so sorry for you that I had to do something. That SOB you were married to didn't deserve to live. Shooting him was planned. Cutting his penis off with my sewing shears and gluing it to the statue wasn't, but it was pure genius if you ask me. Sadie, you're here because I know you saw me altering dear old Jebediah and yet you never told."

Jolie inhaled sharply and her gaze swung to Sadie. "You knew?" she breathed.

Sadie shrugged helplessly. "I couldn't tell on her for having the courage to do what I couldn't," she explained. "It wasn't right."

Sophia and Meredith shared a look, then Sophia let go a small breath and continued reading.

"Sadie, you are truly the best secret keeper in the county and therefore deserve to be an honorary member of the Club. (Sophia, see to it, would you? This is my last nomination, after all.)

*"Finally, don't be mad at me, girls, and I
hope this doesn't change your opinion of me.
We were all married to bastards who needed
killin'—I was just the one to do it. I'll see you
in the hereafter. Until then...
Much love from your Bitsy*
*"P.S. I glued the dick to the bloody statue with
denture adhesive. Brilliant, eh? I've left a siz-
able fund that should take care of old Jeb, by the
way. In coupons, of course. Ha! Just kidding."*

Hands shaking, lips twitching, Sophia lowered
the letter and looked at both of them in turn. "Well."

"My God," Meredith breathed. "I never
dreamed— Never imagined."

Sophia shook her head, seemingly lost in her
thoughts. "Me neither." She looked heavenward and
blinked back tears, and Jolie listened as she said the
one thing that neither she nor Meredith had the courage to say. "Thank you, Bitsy," she whispered softly.

"What are we going to do with all this stuff?"
Meredith asked, typically moving on to practical
matters. "Everybody thinks our husbands died of
natural causes, but Jolie's is a different story."

Jolie knew that going to the police would probably be the right thing to do, but she couldn't bring
herself to suggest it. Bitsy was dead and buried—

they couldn't do anything to her. Furthermore, going to the police would involve outing the FWC, and Bitsy had worked too hard to protect it and to protect them, specifically. She gazed out the window, not really looking at anything, trying to think.

Then the barbeque pit seemed to swell before her eyes and she smiled and looked back at Sophia and Meredith. "How about a bonfire?" Jolie suggested. "It's a chilly night, after all."

Instantly taking the hint, Sophia and Meredith and Sadie shared a smile and five minutes later a big fire burned in the pit. Smiling, they each held a petite four in honor of Bitsy's favorite dessert, then lifted them up for a toast of sorts.

"Our un-dearly departed..." Sophia said softly.

"...may he never rest in peace."

Everything you love about romance...
and more!

Please turn the page for Signature Select™
Bonus Features.

Bonus Features:

BONUS FEATURES

the

Future
Widows'
Club

A conversation with
Rhonda Nelson

Tell us a bit about how you began your writing career.
Eek. I'm going to commit a cardinal sin among authors and admit that I read a bad book...and thought I could do a better job. Guess what? I was wrong. At least to begin with, anyway—and I still have the rejection letters to prove it. But I'd always been a reader, had taken a couple of creative writing courses in college, and things just sort of clicked from there. Writing is like breathing for me. I have to do it.

Do you have a writing routine?
I do. It's called get-out-of-bed-and-hit-the-ground-running. In all seriousness, I work better in the morning, when it's quiet and the house is empty. The problem is, I'm also a neat freak, so everything has to be done in the house before I can start. Beds are made, laundry's started,

dishes are done, etc...so that after I drop the kids off at school, I can come in, sit down and work without any distractions until it's time to pick them up from school. Ideally, I like to get my pages done for the day before they get home, but it doesn't always work out that way. When that happens, I barricade myself in my bedroom with Diet Mountain Dew and sugar-free cookies, and I don't come out until I've done as much as I can possibly do for that day.

When you're not writing, what do you love to do?
Oh, that's an easy one—read! While I'm working on a book, I always make these grandiose plans for what I'm going to do when I get finished. Top of the list is always to read. For instance, with this book, I'm telling myself that when I get done I can read all five Harry Potter books again, that I can read Janet Evanovich's Stephanie Plum series again, that I can watch all 110 episodes of *Northern Exposure*, and then the *Anne of Green Gables* movies again. Like I said, grandiose plans, but it's nice to dream.

What or who inspires you?
Ah, a hard one. I'm inspired by many things. When it comes to my writing or book ideas, anything can inspire me. Usually it's an article I read, or a throwaway comment, or an interesting story that begs the question *What if?* I'm inspired by the innocence of children, the clean smell of a

spring rain, roasting marshmallows over a campfire, good friends, good family, my husband's laugh and my faith in God.

Is there one book that you've read that changed your life somehow?
Well, er...the bad book mentioned in question one, and the Bible, of course.

What are your top five favorite books?
Oh, wow. Only five? Well, let's see. My absolute favorite book is *Lord of Scoundrels* by Loretta Chase. Loved, loved, loved that book. It's falling apart I've read it so many times. Others, in no particular order, would be *Solitary Soldier* by Debra Webb, *Son of the Morning* by Linda Howard, the Stephanie Plum series by Janet Evanovich and J. K. Rowling's Harry Potter series.

What matters most in life?
My faith and my family. Everything else is secondary.

If you weren't a writer what would you be doing?
More reading? Honestly, I don't know. I can't imagine doing anything else. Even when I'm on deadline and I'm tired and my arms are aching, it's still not work. It's writing, and there's nothing quite so perfect as finding the exact phrase to say what I want to say, to breathe a character to life on a page. Do I get tired? Of course. It can be exhausting, but it's a pleasant sort of exhaustion.

It's a solitary thing, and a host of insecurities come along with it—I invariably go through a this-is-complete-crap phase, one that thankfully a few words of praise from my wonderful, inspired editor can magically undo—but I wouldn't want to do anything else. Can't even wrap my mind around it.

Marsha Zinberg Executive Editor, Signature Select, spoke with Rhonda last winter.

TOP TEN
Reasons Widowhood Is Preferable
to Divorce

1 Instead of losing half—half your assets and half your friends—a widow keeps it all.

2 People offer sympathy.

3 Those same people usually bring food.

4 Black is slimming.

5 Less risk of humiliation—a dead husband can't remarry a twentysomething yoga coach barely out of braces with better breasts and a belly-button ring.

6 A widow is a martyr, whereas a divorcee is often unfairly deemed damaged goods or viewed with suspicion.

7 Life insurance.

8 More life insurance.

9 Death is permanent—no Jerry Springer-like meetings, courtroom brawls or bitter debates over who was right or wrong. (You were right, of course.)

10 The ultimate last word...and you have it.

TIPS & TRICKS

A page torn from the Future Widow's Club handbook.

Preparing for your future role as a widow requires a few prerequisites.

FINDING THE OUTFIT—The perfect ensemble for the funeral is simply a must. It puts you in the "widow" mind-set and gives you something to look forward to. The perfect veiled hat—to hide your tears of joy and small satisfied smirk—is particularly difficult to find. Start early!

SHOW ME THE MONEY—Regardless of present insurance and assets, another half mil is prudent. Contact your agent at once.

X MARKS THE SPOT—Think of a treasure map, and The Will as your treasure. In this case, you don't want it to be a buried treasure that requires a long and possibly fruitless search. Make sure you're properly provided for—being sole beneficiary is best—and that the document is signed and stowed in a safe place.

PREPAY IS THE BEST WAY—Planning a funeral nowadays before one kicks the bucket is completely acceptable, even deemed considerate, thoughtful and prudent. Take advantage of this perk, ladies! Have fun with it! Pick a plot, pick a casket, pick a service. Graveside or chapel? Efficiency now will make your special day run more smoothly. Your *un*-dearly departed...may he never rest in peace.

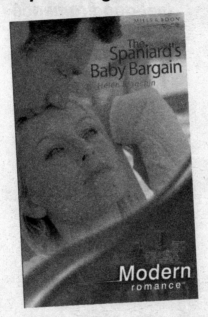

Through days of hard work and the determination to repair the torn fabric of their care-worn lives, three women will discover that what was lost can be found again...

ISBN 0-7783-0092-7

Tessa MacCrae has reluctantly agreed to spend the summer helping her mother and grandmother clean out the family home. The three women have never been close, but Tessa hopes that time away from her husband will help her avoid facing the tragedy of her young daughter's death and the toll it is exacting on her marriage.

With the passing weeks each of their lives begins to change. And for the first time, Tessa can look past the years of resentment and regret and see her mother and grandmother for the flawed but courageous women they are.

On sale 17th June 2005